Simon Scarrow is the bestselling author of twenty-two Eagles of the Empire novels, including *Rebellion*, *Death to the Emperor*, *The Honour of Rome* and *Day of the Caesars*. He is also author of the Criminal Inspector Schenke thrillers, including *Blackout* and *Dead of Night*. Simon shared his passion for history as a teacher for many years before becoming a full-time writer.

T. J. Andrews is the co-author with Simon Scarrow of three earlier bestselling novels, *Arena*, *Invader* and *Pirata*. He was born in Barking and grew up in Essex, not far from the Ancient Roman garrison at Colchester. After several years in publishing, he became a full-time writer. He lives in Surrey.

Find out more at: www.simonscarrow.co.uk and on
Facebook: /OfficialSimonScarrow
and
X: @SimonScarrow

Praise for Simon Scarrow's novels

'A good, uncomplicated, rip-roaring read'
Mail on Sunday

'An engrossing storyline, full of teeth-clenching battles, political machinations, treachery, honour, love and death . . . More please!'
Elizabeth Chadwick

'A new book in Simon Scarrow's long-running series about the Roman army is always a joy'
The Times

'Scarrow's rank with the best'
Independent

'Utterly authentic characters; a gripping plot. The perfect way to bring history alive'
Damien Lewis

SIMON SCARROW
AND T. J. ANDREWS

WARRIOR

HEADLINE

Copyright © 2023 Simon Scarrow

The right of Simon Scarrow to be identified as the Author of
the Work has been asserted by him in accordance with the
Copyright, Designs and Patents Act 1988.

First published in Great Britain in 2023
by HEADLINE PUBLISHING GROUP

First published in paperback in 2023
by HEADLINE PUBLISHING GROUP

1

Apart from any use permitted under UK copyright law, this publication may
only be reproduced, stored, or transmitted, in any form, or by any means,
with prior permission in writing of the publishers or, in the case of
reprographic production, in accordance with the terms of licences issued
by the Copyright Licensing Agency.

All characters – other than the obvious historical figures – in this publication are
fictitious and any resemblance to real persons, living or dead, is purely coincidental.

Cataloguing in Publication Data is available from the British Library

ISBN 978 1 4722 8750 2

Typeset in Bembo by Avon DataSet Ltd, Alcester, Warwickshire

Printed and bound in Great Britain by Clays Ltd, Elcograf S.p.A.

Map illustration by Tim Peters

Headline's policy is to use papers that are natural, renewable and recyclable
products and made from wood grown in well-managed forests and other
controlled sources. The logging and manufacturing processes are expected
to conform to the environmental regulations of the country of origin.

HEADLINE PUBLISHING GROUP
An Hachette UK Company
Carmelite House
50 Victoria Embankment
London EC4Y 0DZ

www.headline.co.uk
www.hachette.co.uk

BRITANNIA AD 18

BRIGANTES

PARISI

ORDOVICES

CORNOVII

CORIELTAUVI

ICENI

TRINOVANTES

DEMETAE

DOBUNNI

CATUVELLAUNI

Camulodunum

Merladion

SILURES

Abondun

Verlamion

Lhandain

Calleva

CANTIACI

ATREBATES

Durovernum

Lindinis

BELGAE

REGNI

DUMNONII

DUROTRIGES

Noviomagus

GAUL

LHANDAIN

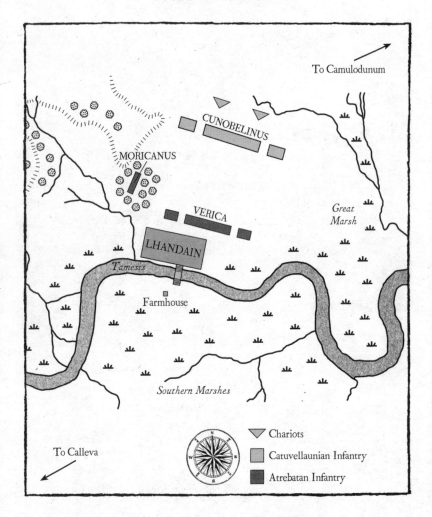

To Camulodunum

CUNOBELINUS

MORICANUS

VERICA

Great Marsh

LHANDAIN

Tamesis

Farmhouse

Southern Marshes

To Calleva

▼ Chariots

☐ Catuvellaunian Infantry

☐ Atrebatan Infantry

MERLADION

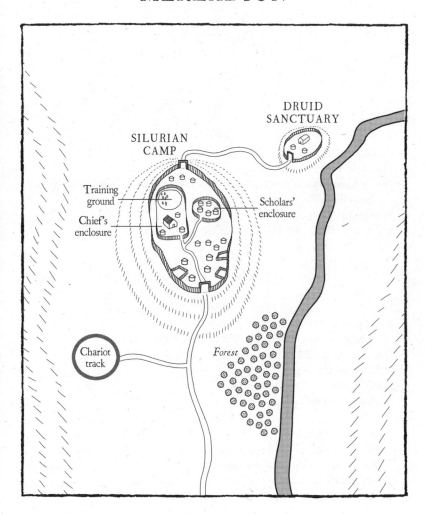

DRUID
SANCTUARY

SILURIAN
CAMP

Training
ground

Scholars'
enclosure

Chief's
enclosure

Chariot
track

Forest

CAST LIST

In Rome, AD 61
Caratacus: high king of the Catuvellaunians and warlord of Britannia
Caius Placonius Felicitus: historian
Nero Claudius Caesar Augustus Germanicus: last emperor of the Julio-Claudian dynasty
Mardicca: Caratacus's wife
Decius Spurinnus Tuscus: disgraced historian
Aelia: Felicitus's wife
Lugnus: tavern owner
Vulcatius Araricus: former senior centurion in the Twentieth Legion
Marcus Cominius Largus: a popular historian
Marcus Lucretius: son of Senator Marcus Lucretius Saper
Sextus Afranius Burrus: commander of the Praetorian Guard
Lucius: Aelia and Felicitus's infant son
Salidus: eldest son of Caratacus
Davos: doorman and servant of Caratacus
Spittara: retired gladiator

Britannia, AD 18–27
Catuvellaunians:
Cunobelinus: king of the Catuvellaunians
Adminius: Caratacus's older brother
Togodumnus: Caratacus's younger brother
Epaticcus: Caratacus's uncle and Cunobelinus's younger brother
Bellocatus: commander of one of the Catuvellaunian war-bands
Parvilius: commander of the royal bodyguard
Maridius: Caratacus's younger brother

Vodenius: Caratacus's youngest brother
Dubnocatus: a young warrior
Garmanus: a member of the royal bodyguard
Maglocunus: a veteran warrior
Baloras: tribal elder
Trenico: tribal elder

Atrebatans:
Verica: king of the Atrebates
Moricanus: prince and cousin of Trigomaris
Eppillus: Verica's older brother
Eboricus: a Druid scholar and the king's nephew

Silurians:
Vortagus: chief of Merladion
Mendax: commander of Vortagus's bodyguard

Dobunnians:
Antedius: king of the Dobunnians
Sediacus: the king's nephew
Lugovesus: a hard-drinking warrior

Trinovantians:
Vassedo: a skilled hunter and scout
Orenus: an elderly noble
Dubnovellaunus: deposed king of the Trinovantes

Others:
Bladocus: Caratacus's Druid mentor
Nemobnus: an exiled Regnian guide
Lugracus: High Druid at Merladion
Segorix: senior Druid at Merladion
Tejanus: retired gladiator, Adminius's bodyguard
Cadrus: a student at Merladion
Trigomaris: former ruler of Lhandain
Vegorix: a friend of Eboricus
Durrus: a friend of Eboricus
Bogiodubnus: king of the Durotriges
Tingetus: former king of the Regni

PART ONE

THE KING IN ROME

CHAPTER ONE

Rome, AD 61

They say history is made by great men and, when they are permitted, great women. Like much of what they say, that's complete rubbish. In truth, history is made by historians riding the toga tails of the great in the hope that some of the greatness rubs off on them. This history is no different.

It began on a warm summer evening at a banquet held to celebrate the news from Britannia. The native rebellion that had devastated three of the most important settlements in the province had been crushed. Tens of thousands of the enemy had been slain, along with their leader, some fiery harpy with a barbaric name. Banquets at the imperial palace were never as much fun as you'd think they'd be. Unless you were part of Nero's inner circle, the dining couches were not comfortable for any length of time. Although the dishes were served in a timely manner, none of the guests were permitted to start eating before the emperor did, by which time the food was cold, sauces had congealed and appetites had dulled. Then there was the din of hundreds of voices echoing off the high walls of the banqueting hall. In order to make conversation you were obliged to speak more loudly, which forced those around you to do the same and the overall volume increased steadily until your ears were straining to catch the words of the person reclining opposite, and your voice was threatening to give out as you shouted to be heard.

The only respite from the din was when the emperor's major-domo called for silence to announce the arrival of the next course, or the next entertainment. He had a fine voice, and so he should, being a former drill instructor of the Praetorian Guard. The man could project and I thought he was wasted here at the palace when he should be on the stage. The same could not be said for his master, whose thin, reedy voice barely carried beyond the first ten rows of seats, unless he shouted, in which case his lines were delivered in a shrill cry that set the audience's teeth on edge.

The only thing less tolerable than the noise was the enforced silence when the emperor's guests were subjected to one of his recent musical or poetical compositions. Some of the time he opted for what he considered to be comedy and the major-domo, standing behind his master, had to signify when the audience must laugh. Most of the time, however, Nero preferred tragedy and the tears of many in the audience were quite genuine, though not for the reason Nero assumed. Boredom mostly. Personally, I didn't cry, not wishing to encourage him. In short, the emperor's banquets might be considered as being the incomestible followed by the indigestible.

Then there was the question of the guests. A select few were personally invited by Nero to fill out the places closest to the gilded frame and purple cushion of the imperial couch on the dais at one end of the banquet hall. There were the usual cronies – the dapper and silver-tongued Seneca whose ludicrously fawning flattery was always taken at face value by Nero. Burrus, the commander of the Praetorian Guard who lacked Seneca's line in soothing platitudes but made up for it with dogged loyalty. Besides them there were the emperor's favourite actors of the moment, those senators currently in his favour and a handful of the capital's finest poets, musicians and even a few historians. It was always a good idea to have a few of the latter on your side if you didn't want posterity to drag your name through the sewer.

The rest of us guests were a mixed bunch. Summoned via curt invitations issued by scribes on the major-domo's staff, we were drawn from those deemed suitable to pad out the guest list. That included senators who were not part of the inner circle and spent most of the banquet staring daggers at those who were. Their wives, looking miserable in the knowledge that their arranged marriages had ended in them backing a losing horse. Sundry junior aristocrats and politicians on the make. Then there were the lesser representatives of artistic and intellectual circles: disdainful philosophers, moderately successful poets and playwrights aspiring to the lucrative rewards of

4

imperial patronage, painters and sculptors looking down their noses at the decor of the banquet hall, and sundry others. The last category included myself.

Caius Placonius Felicitus at your service. Historian.

I was at the banquet because I had recently completed the latest in a long line of hagiographic histories of Rome's noble families. It had been received well, not least by the senator who commissioned the history and was rich enough to ensure that copies of my work had been delivered to every single one of his peers in the Senate. Consequently, I expected to pick up a few more such commissions in the coming months. It was good work. It paid well and I could almost write such histories in my sleep. I'd invariably start with some spurious link to a legendary figure from Rome's past. If the commission was generous enough I might even discover a link to a mythological character – a minor deity in the family tree usually brought a smile to the faces of my clients. From there it was simply a question of going through the annals and inserting more or less obscure ancestors into accounts of key moments in Roman history. You'd be surprised at how many of my clients' forebears played a vital part in aiding Horatius's spirited defence of the Sublician bridge against Lars Porsena's Etruscan horde. Or those who led the charge in deposing Tarquinius the Proud. But then history tends to be written for those who can afford it.

I can't say that I was happy about the work, other than it earned me a comfortable living. Someday I wanted to write a real history. The story of a genuine hero that did not require constant embellishment of fictions, great and small, in order to make the story more acceptable. Naturally, there were very few figures from senatorial families in Rome willing to pay for a warts-and-all account of their lives, or those of their ancestors. Standing in the Senate House in the finery of their togas they talked of honour and integrity while being as venal as the leader of any of Rome's street gangs. There were few bribes they would not take to advocate a cause, no bribes they would not pay for political advancement for themselves, members of the family or their cronies. They'd happily stab each other in the back to achieve the same ends.

As I sat at the banquet and looked round at the faces of the aristocrats, I realised just how tired I was of telling their stories.

Then I noticed a late arrival being escorted to his place not far from me. A tall, large-framed man with long grey hair tied back by a simple leather strap. He looked to be in his mid-fifties or thereabouts. He had a full moustache that hung down either side of his chin and faded tattoos adorned his cheeks in swirls. There were more tattoos on his arms beneath the sleeves of a plain, belted tunic. A more Celtic-looking individual you could not imagine. Which meant that he stood out like a swinging dick at a eunuchs' festival. He took his place in the seating between the senators and the lesser guests like myself which implied he enjoyed a certain social status. I stared at him because I had never seen him before. Yet most of those around him exchanged a nod or acknowledged his arrival with a dismissive glance. So he was known in society circles and was not some freeloading gatecrasher who had somehow bluffed his way past the Praetorian guardsmen on duty at the palace. From the looks of some he was not universally welcomed here.

I leaned closer to my neighbour, a Stoic philosopher of minor celebrity who had just helped himself to a large goblet of Falernian as he chewed on a fancy pasty stuffed with minced veal.

'That man . . .' I gestured discreetly at the recent arrival. 'Do you know who he is?'

The Stoic turned to look and nodded. He chewed quickly and swallowed before he could speak. 'I know him. Rather, I know of him. He's from Britannia. Used to be the leader of the tribes who took up arms against our legions when we invaded the island during Claudius's reign. Caused us a bit of bother for the best part of a decade before he was run to ground and brought to Rome. He was supposed to be executed in the Forum, along with his family, but he turned out to be quite the eloquent speaker and flattered old Claudius into sparing them. They were given a house and a pension to see out their days in exile. They'll never be allowed to leave Rome.'

As he spoke, I recalled some of the details of his exploits. He did rather more than cause a bit of bother . . .

'I can't recall his name. Do you—?'

'Caratacus,' the Stoic cut in. 'At least that's what he's called here. I imagine it's something ghastly and unpronounceable in his native tongue.'

'Caratacus,' I mused, the first stirrings of curiosity welling up. He would surely have a decent story to tell as the man who had defied Rome for so long.

I watched him pick from the platters on the table in front of him. Two couches further along, in the direction of Nero, a muscular young aristocrat in a bright blue tunic was holding court over a small crowd of cronies of a similar age. They looked to be in their early twenties and were full of the boastful arrogance and confidence of their social class. They were loud too, and I caught a snatch of their boisterous banter as they ridiculed the appearance of the Celt reclining close by. Caratacus spared them a brief glance without betraying any feeling and turned back to his meal.

'You! Barbarian fellow!' the ringleader called out. 'Don't you know it's bad manners to arrive late to a banquet? Well?'

The Briton did not respond, nor even react, but chewed as he stared into the mid-distance.

'I'm talking to you!' The ringleader sat up and stabbed a finger at the Celt. 'Look at me when I'm speaking to you!'

His voice had risen enough for nearby guests to stop their conversation and turn towards the disturbance. Like a wave, the quiet rippled out to each end of the banquet hall. Aware that he now commanded the attention of all, the young man stood up on his couch and put his hands on his hips as he drew a deep breath.

'I call you out, barbarian. How dare you try to ignore me! Do you know who I am, damn you?'

Now the Celt glanced to his side and I swear I saw the faintest flicker of a smile on his lips before he replied in a clear voice with only the slightest of accents, 'Why, my friend? Have you forgotten?'

Perhaps it was the drink, or perhaps it was the innate stupidity of so many of his class. The young man puffed out his chest and stabbed his thumb at his breast. 'Marcus Lucretius! Son of Senator Marcus Lucretius Saper. And I am calling you out for showing a lack of respect for our emperor. You barbarian scum need to learn some manners.'

His cronies raised a cheer, but I saw the glint in the Briton's eyes as he stopped eating and calmly turned to face the young man. 'You would fight me?'

7

Lucretius laughed. 'Yes. I would fight you and crush you. If you had the balls to face me.'

'That,' said Caratacus, 'is a step too far, my Roman friend.'

Easing himself off the couch, he stood and drew himself up to his full height as he announced, 'I accept your challenge.'

At the end of the hall I could see the emperor and his major-domo regarding the confrontation and engaging in earnest conversation. Then the latter rapped the metal end of his staff on the marble floor.

'Hear me!' he bellowed. 'Hear me, all! His imperial majesty instructs Marcus Lucretius to teach a lesson to the exile. Clear the floor!'

The major-domo pointed to the space in front of the dais where some acrobats were just setting up for their act. At once they retreated to the sides, heads bowed. A Praetorian optio led a section of his men forward to mark out the combat area while Lucretius jumped down from his couch and strode towards the dais. I watched as Caratacus sighed and followed him. At once the other guests rose from their couches and made their way towards the dais for a better view. The senators, being closest, had the best view, but I was keen not to miss the action and so I climbed onto the table and used the side of my sandal to sweep some platters away to ensure safe footing while I watched the contest. A few others followed my example.

Lucretius shouldered his way through the senators and entered the open space, approaching the dais respectfully as he bowed his head to Nero. Caratacus eased a passage through the largely hostile throng, ignoring the hissed insults and even the elderly aristocrat who spat at him. Wiping the spittle away with the back of his hand, he moved through into the makeshift arena and stood alongside Lucretius before nodding his head in greeting. I saw Nero regard him with a smile as he rose to address the crowd.

'Romans! Friends! We have an unexpected addition to the entertainment programme this night.'

There were smiles and laughter, and Nero indulged them a moment before raising his hands for quiet and continuing. 'Young Lucretius has bravely stepped forward to defend Roman honour, impugned by the tardy arrival of this barbarian exile. It is time that we reminded this Briton of the value of civilised manners now that he has accepted Lucretius's challenge. I have decided that this fight shall be settled with bare fists, the winner to be determined by the submission of his opponent. To your places, gentleman and barbarian!'

There was an excitable hubbub as Lucretius stepped to the right of the emperor and flexed his shoulders, rolled his head and bunched his hands into fists. I could see now how powerful his physique was. One of those vain aristocrats who prize brawn over brains, I surmised. They fancy themselves as tough as gladiators, with the privilege of never having to face the dangers of entering the arena. His forearms were thick with muscle and his neck angled out from a line level with his jaw to his shoulders. By contrast, Caratacus was slender and sinewy and was twice the age of his opponent. I felt sorry for him. Having lost his kingdom and been captured and dragged to Rome to spend the rest of his days here, his misery would now be compounded by a beating. From the slight stoop of his demeanour and the world-weary expression on his face I feared that he had already resigned himself to defeat.

'Fifty sestertii on our Roman lad!' yelled the Stoic who had just climbed up beside me. 'Any takers?'

Although faces turned towards him no one accepted the wager, so certain were they of the outcome. In other circumstances I would have followed their example, but my purse was flush with silver thanks to the completion of my latest work and I had a feeling about this barbarian. There was something about Caratacus, something in the way he carried himself that indicated complete self-confidence, despite the difference in build and age. Besides, I felt a certain recklessness stir in my breast. 'I'll take the bet.'

We shook on it. The two men squared off on opposite sides of the open space while the Praetorians lowered their spears to the horizontal to mark out the notional line that spectators must not cross.

'Prepare to fight!' the major-domo bellowed and Lucretius lowered himself into a well-balanced half-crouch as he held his bunched fists out in front of him. Caratacus stood opposite with an almost insouciant air, arms by his sides.

'For the honour of Rome!' Nero cried out, winking at Lucretius.

That's when it struck me. This fight had been deliberately instigated from the moment Caratacus had arrived late. Lucretius must have been given word that Nero required the humiliation of the exile, and

9

here we were, waiting for the action to begin. Nero plucked up a napkin and held it up, waiting until he had the attention of both men. Then he flicked the cloth into the air and shrilled, 'Begin!'

'YAAARRRR!' Lucretius bellowed like a wild animal as he charged towards the Briton, fists raised as if he was about to throw them at his opponent. Caratacus's expression was coldly calculating, as he eased himself onto the balls of his feet and raised his hands to meet the onrushing aristocrat. He kept them open, palms raised, as Lucretius surged towards him. At the last moment, he stepped nimbly to one side, parried the nearest fist with his forearm and swung his right in as he pivoted on his leading foot to throw all his weight behind the blow. The punch struck the other man's ribs, close to the armpit. The impact drove Lucretius off to the side and he stumbled a few steps as he struggled to retain his balance. There were groans from the crowd and Caratacus backed off, keeping a close eye on the other fighter. The punch would have felled a different man but Lucretius was fit and strong and he spat on the ground as he approached again, more cautiously, fists and forearms held up to protect his head.

'That's better, son,' Caratacus addressed him like a teacher encouraging a young student. 'Keep your guard up, so. And watch for any sign of an attack.'

As he spoke, Caratacus lashed out with his leading boot. Lucretius looked down and made to dodge aside the feint, thereby providing Caratacus with a free chance to strike. He swung his left fist in a hook and as Lucretius moved to block it Caratacus pulled the punch and struck with his right, a straight blow to the jaw that sent the Roman reeling back in a daze.

'What did I say about keeping your guard up? And what about your footwork? You are behaving like a plodding tyro. Think before you move.'

He feinted again and Lucretius blocked the ruse attack and feinted back before launching a vicious undercut. Caratacus warded the blow off easily and backed off a couple of paces to give himself room. The audience was cheering their man on, some of them angrily now that his opponent had landed two blows with impunity. On the dais, I could see Nero begin to frown, his lips pressing together in a thin line.

'One last thing,' Caratacus smiled. 'Timing.'

He lunged forward and aimed a blow at Lucretius's face. Instinctively the latter thrust his forearms up and Caratacus dealt a flurry of blows to his midriff before Lucretius lowered his guard to block the attack. Whereupon, the Briton unleashed a powerful straight to his opponent's nose, snapping Lucretius's head back with an audible crunch. The Roman staggered back and swayed as Caratacus weaved nimbly from side to side in front of him.

'Are you ready to fight now, boy?'

Lucretius was burning with humiliation and rage and he pushed forward, swinging his fists wildly. This time a left glanced off Caratacus's shoulder and half spun him before he stepped back and recovered and then dealt with the barrage of blows from the other man, blocking and parrying. All the while Lucretius was using up his energy and becoming increasingly frustrated by the Briton's evasions. He pulled back and the two regarded each other warily as Caratacus cleared his throat. 'We've had our fun. Now it's time to put an end to the lesson.'

He came forward again, wheeling his fists in small arcs to distract Lucretius. Then, closing in, he ducked down and delivered a right hook to the Roman's knee. I saw the joint lurch to the side and the next moment Lucretius let out a howl of pain and he went down on his knees.

'Submit!' Caratacus called out loudly. 'Say it, say it loud!'

Instead Lucretius flailed and missed his target. 'Stand still and fight, damn you!'

'A fighter should know when he is defeated.' Caratacus stepped in and delivered two jabs with his left before unleashing his right so fast I could not follow the movement. Lucretius flopped back and collapsed on his back, arms outstretched and chest heaving as he struggled to breathe. Caratacus stood over him and I saw a marked difference in his expression: a wild-eyed look of feral triumph as he regarded his beaten foe. Then he recovered his poise and his features shifted into a look of cool disdain as he raised his fists and called out defiantly to the silent audience that surrounded him.

'I am Caratacus! King of the Catuvellaunian tribe and Warlord of Britannia! I claim my victory!'

His words echoed off the walls as the emperor and his guests stared back silently. I sensed the anger and embarrassment as clearly as if the room were filled with the stench of a tannery. Nero drew himself up and stabbed a pudgy finger at Caratacus.

'You are a prisoner of Rome. And here you will stay, exiled from your homeland until you die. That is all you are! Never forget, barbarian.'

With that, the emperor turned away and skulked off towards the door at the rear of the hall that led to his private quarters. As he disappeared I nudged the Stoic beside me. 'I'll have that fifty sestertii now.'

We climbed down off the table and once he had opened his purse and counted out my winnings I nodded my thanks and turned to go in search of the Briton. He had returned to his place and finished the remains of his meal and was putting on his cloak as I reached him. For an instant we sized each other up.

'I've never seen a fight like it,' I gushed admiringly. 'Where on earth did you learn to fight like that?'

Caratacus gave a bitter little smile. 'Here in Rome. In the gym at the bathhouse of Attilus on the Aventine, at the end of the street where my family and I are billeted. A wise man is always willing to learn from those who best him. Now, if you don't mind, I have outstayed my welcome here. I must go.'

Without waiting for a response he turned on his heel and strode away. I watched until he was lost from sight, my heart beating with excitement. At last I had found my real history. And I had found the hero whose story I must tell. But first, I had to persuade him to tell it to me so that I might commit it to writing and thereby prove myself as worthy of the title 'great historian' as Caratacus was worthy of the title 'Warlord of Britannia'.

'Tomorrow,' I muttered to myself, 'I must pay a visit to the bathhouse of Attilus.'

CHAPTER TWO

The following morning, after a light breakfast at my modest lodgings on the Esquiline, much of it spent listening to complaints from my wife, Aelia, about our neighbours, while our little boy, Lucius, wailed noisily about something or other, I made some enquiries and discovered that a retired gladiator called Spittara held sparring sessions at the bathhouse of Attilus at the eighth hour each day. I therefore went about my errands distractedly while I grappled with the thorny issue of how best to approach my prospective client. Caratacus, I sensed, was a difficult character. Presumably long experience had taught him not to trust Romans; he seemed to tolerate us at best, just as we tolerated the presence of a barbarian in our civilised midst. I doubted an appeal to the man's vanity would work, and I certainly couldn't offer him a fee in return for sharing his story with me. So how could I possibly convince the Briton to tell his tale to a citizen of Rome – the very same race that had beaten his armies and plundered his kingdom?

There was another question, of course. Who in this city would want to read about the life of an exiled British warlord, especially after the recent rebellion? But the more I considered the point, the more I realised the interest the project would arouse: Britannia, and its barbarian inhabitants, occupied a near-mythic place in the imagination of the humblest Roman. The image of the Celt as a brave and noble savage even held a certain exotic appeal among the quality who lived up on the Caelian Hill. The recent troubles in the province had done nothing to change that. Had I not seen the wife of a well-heeled aristocrat proudly displaying the golden torc around her neck to her fellow guests at a dinner party the other night?

And many of the best gladiators had lately taken to covering their arms in swirling Celtic tattoos; a few adventurous souls had even started painting their torsos with woad before each contest. No. Finding an audience would not be hard. The bigger problem was how to tease the tale out of the old king.

I had a few hours to spare, so I made the short trip down to the bookshops in the Argiletum in search of reading material on Britannia. Perhaps there I would find the answer to my question. I nodded a greeting at the wizened owner at my usual haunt and made straight for the history section. Browsing the pigeon-holes, I was struck by the paucity of material available on that distant island. Apart from the odd section in the general histories, the bulk of the Britannic material took the form of military memoirs written by officers involved in the late invasion. Most were self-serving accounts of glorious victory over the ignorant natives, including one ghastly volume penned by some minor governor of Africa called Vitellius. None of these works offered any real insight into the Britons themselves.

A cursory glance through the volumes concerning Gaul revealed much the same pattern. Almost every aspect of Gallic history was told from the Roman side. The Celts, like our other great enemies over the centuries, were only visible in the annals for as long as we waged war against them. Once they had fulfilled their dramatic purpose and submitted to Roman rule, they shuffled dutifully off the stage of history. Perhaps the same thing could happen to our empire one day, I mused. For if the Celts and their vast civilisation can vanish from history, what is to stop Rome from suffering the same fate? On the other hand, one might reasonably argue that, unlike Rome, the Celts had no literature of their own, no libraries, no written record to preserve their ancient knowledge.

And then, suddenly, it hit me: I had found my argument! The Celts had been driven back to the very fringes of our world. Most of their leaders had been killed or imprisoned, the sacred groves of their Druid cult had been destroyed, and their settlements had been thoroughly Romanised. Soon enough, their whole way of life would be lost to the mists of time. But as a guest of Rome, Caratacus was uniquely placed to add a Celtic voice to the historical record. This was his chance to tell things from the other side of the hill. By

14

committing his life to parchment, he would ensure that the story of his people would not be lost to future generations. Caratacus could preserve the world of the Britons in a small way, and perhaps even correct some of the grotesque clichés of his race that had taken hold in the collective imagination. I couldn't offer him a statue in the Forum, but I could give him a written monument to his brave struggle against Rome.

It was a convincing argument, I assured myself, almost certain to win Caratacus over to my way of thinking, and I set off for the Aventine a short while later with renewed purpose. The streets were choked with pedestrians, livestock and handcarts and I had to watch my step as I threaded my way through the crowds, avoiding the mounds of rubbish while sellers shouted the prices of their overpriced (and over-ripe) wares from behind their rickety timber stalls. Visitors to our city marvel at the wonder and majesty of Rome: really, the only wonder is how the whole chaotic edifice hasn't caught fire and burned to the ground yet.

The crowds thinned as I reached the streets higher up the Aventine. I have never much liked this part of town. Oh, I know the area is more fashionable these days, but it still carries the whiff of the slum. The houses are ugly, the inhabitants mostly boorish new men – merchants, warehouse owners and bankers grown fat off the profits from the trade on the nearby wharf. You know the type: hair cut in the fashion of our dear emperor, a seat near the front at the Marcellan theatre to watch the latest tragedy, tunics made from the finest silk and the gold rings to match. It is a dreary sort of place for a former king to live.

A queue had already formed by the time I reached the bathhouse of Attilus. I paid the admission fee to the pinch-faced slave and descended the marbled steps leading down to the inner courtyard. I breezed past the changing rooms and followed the younger bucks towards the exercise area in the centre of the courtyard. Nearby, a group of burly figures hefted up pairs of heavy stone weights with their huge hands. An attendant sat on a stool to the side of the yard, waiting to offer his services to the sweat-soaked competitors. He was an ugly, bald fellow with a towel draped over his shoulder and a strigil resting across his lap. He looked up at me with a disapproving expression as I approached. We both knew I did not belong in this place.

'I'm looking for Spittara,' I said. 'I understand he trains here.'

The slave nodded at a small crowd of men cheering on a couple of boxers. 'Over there,' he replied tonelessly. 'Spittara is the short-arsed one. Can't miss him. Great big scar on his face. But I wouldn't bother if I were you, Master.'

'Oh?'

'He doesn't train beginners.'

He looked away, his gaze returning to the weightlifters. I left the rude fellow and strode across the yard, stepping past the crowd to catch a better view of the sparring fighters. The short, wiry man, Spittara, stood to the side of the chalk ring, bellowing instructions at the younger of the two trainers. I recognised the older fighter at once from last night's banquet. Caratacus danced nimbly around his much younger opponent, delivering a flurry of quick jabs to the latter's midriff while the onlookers cheered him on.

'Move!' Spittara bellowed at the younger boxer. 'Don't stand still! You're not a statue, for fuck's sake!'

The man unleashed a ragged uppercut at Caratacus, but the Briton easily evaded it and then feinted with a blow to his opponent's face. The younger man jerked his head back, exposing his chest to attack. Caratacus duly struck the man with a solid punch to the breadbasket, drawing a cheer of approval from the spectators. The youth groaned as he staggered backwards, and Caratacus landed another sharp blow on his jaw before Spittara quickly stepped between the two men. He wagged a finger at the youth while Caratacus looked on.

'What did I tell you before, lad? You fight with your feet as much as your hands. How d'you think I survived all those contests in the arena, eh? It wasn't because of my height, was it?'

'No, sir,' the youth replied moodily as he nursed his jaw.

'Speed, lad, it's all about speed. You can be the hardest bastard in Rome, but you won't win a fight if you've got feet of clay.' Spittara looked round at the spectators. 'All right, let's have the next pair. Come on, ladies. Don't take all bloody day.'

Two other men stepped forward while Caratacus and the youth

walked over to a servant standing just outside the chalk ring. The servant worked quickly, removing the soft leather boxing straps fastened around their palms and forearms while the boisterous crowd swiftly turned their attention to the next pair of contestants. Now I saw my chance. I hurried forward, picking my way past the spectators as they roared on the two men trading punches in the ring.

As I drew closer, Caratacus and his youthful opponent looked up at me simultaneously. I glanced briefly at the youth. There was something curious about him, but I couldn't quite put my finger on it. I turned to face Caratacus.

'That was well fought. A splendid effort, sir. Almost as good as the show you put on at the banquet, I might add.'

A tiny groove formed above Caratacus's brow. 'And you are?'

I affected a slight bow. 'Caius Placonius Felicitus. Historian to the elite, at your humble service. We met briefly last night. I asked you where you'd learned to fight.'

'Yes, I remember.' The groove deepened. 'What are you doing here, Roman? Don't tell me you've come to learn the art of boxing.'

'Actually, I wondered if I might have a word with you.' I glanced again at the youth before returning my gaze to Caratacus. 'In private, if you wouldn't mind.'

The youth frowned then looked at Caratacus. 'What does this man want with you, Father?'

I glanced at him in surprise. Caratacus must have seen the expression on my face because he waved a hand at the younger man and said, 'This is Salidus. My eldest. The boy is a keen fighter, but he has a lot to learn . . . as he well knows.'

'A pleasure to meet you.'

Salidus regarded me with barely disguised hostility. 'What is your business with my father?'

'As I said, it is something I wish to discuss between us privately,' I replied.

Salidus cocked his chin defiantly. 'Nonsense. Whatever you have to say, you can say it to both of us.'

Caratacus glared at his son. 'Leave us, boy. Let us talk.'

'But Father—'

'Go and work on the punchbag.' Caratacus pointed across the yard at a leather sandbag hanging from a sturdy timber frame. 'Practise your combinations as we discussed. Go.'

Salidus spared me a final surly glance before he wheeled away and marched across the yard. Caratacus turned to me and made an apologetic gesture with his hands. 'Forgive him. My son doesn't trust Romans.'

'Really? Then he is no different from the rest of us.'

Caratacus smiled weakly. 'You mustn't blame him. Salidus has found it difficult here in Rome. My other children are too young to remember our old life in Britannia, but Salidus spent most of his childhood there. He is a proud Celt at heart.'

'He wishes to return home?'

'One day.' The Briton smiled. 'The boy has dreams. But I do not think any of us will ever see the land of our fathers again. We are prisoners of your emperor now.'

'You have a house on the Aventine,' I pointed out. 'A decent pension, a family. That is a strange idea of a prison. Many would kill to be in your position.'

'We live in a gilded cage,' Caratacus replied darkly. 'We are not confined to some forgotten cell in the Mamertine, of course, but the effect is much the same.'

'Still, there are worse fates,' I said.

'Are there?' He shook his head. 'I was a king, once. There is no dignity in living at the whim of another ruler. Perhaps I should have chosen death when your soldiers brought us here all those years ago, instead of begging that stuttering fool Claudius for mercy.'

'Then why did you do it?'

'A Roman officer, a prefect, came to visit me shortly before the triumphal parade. He convinced me it would be better to live out my days in peace than die for the satisfaction of the mob.' Caratacus gave a bitter laugh. 'I should have known better than to take advice from a Roman soldier.'

'A soldier, eh? What was his name?'

'Prefect Cato.' Caratacus waved a hand dismissively. 'Enough talk of the past. Well? Why did you want to see me?'

I paused as I considered how best to proceed. Caratacus would surely reject a direct approach, especially one made by a stranger. I would have to tread carefully around him, constructing my argument

18

in such a way that he could readily appreciate the merits of committing his story to the written word.

'I have a proposal,' I said delicately. 'One that I am sure will be of interest to you.'

'Proposal?' Caratacus repeated. 'What do you mean? Speak plainly.'

I did not answer the question directly, but instead stepped around it. 'The way you bested that imperial crony last night was impressive. You fought with tremendous skill and courage. It was, if I may, a display worthy of a great warlord.'

Caratacus shook his head, and there was a weariness to his voice as he spoke. 'I am lord of nothing now. My kingdom was trampled to dust long ago, under the boots of your accursed legions.'

'Then perhaps it is time to remind Rome of your greatness.'

'And how should I do that? By fighting more arrogant young upstarts?'

'By letting me write your story.'

Caratacus squished his eyebrows together. 'You? Write my memoirs?'

'Yes, why not?'

He gave a dry laugh. 'Your emperor thinks I'm a worthless barbarian. An opinion many of your citizens seem to share. I don't think you'd find much of an audience for your project, Roman.'

'You were a great king once,' I replied steadily, repeating the argument I had rehearsed on my way up the hill. 'The scourge of Rome. Soldiers and children alike trembled at the mention of your name. Your kingdom may have vanished, like many belonging to the Celts, but that does not mean it must be forgotten. It can live again, in the pages of history. Tell me your tale, and I can help preserve your name for all the ages. That is my proposal.'

'I am a Celt,' Caratacus said. 'Our histories are not written down. We do not reduce great deeds to mere words, like you Romans. They live in our hearts and die with us and they may become legends thereafter, or fade with memory.'

'But why take the risk of so much being forgotten?' I said. 'This is your chance to give your account of the long struggle against Rome.'

'What for? So your rich friends can amuse themselves at their literary salons reading about the uncivilised brute from the north?'

'This would be different,' I responded gently.

'How so?'

'You fought us for almost ten years and lived to tell the tale. That is unusual in itself. Most of our enemies have met rather more chilling ends.'

Caratacus grunted. 'It would have been better to die with pride, than live as an example of Roman magnanimity.'

'But you can use the situation to your advantage, don't you see? You have a unique view of history. No other Briton is in a position to tell their side of the story. If you work with me, we can tell the epic saga of a great Celtic hero. The first ever to be published.' I shrugged. 'At the very least, it would serve to correct all those vainglorious memoirs of Roman officers currently flooding the market. You could tell people how it really was.'

Caratacus studied me keenly with his grey eyes. 'And why would I share my tale with you?' he asked. 'A Roman screed, no less?'

I opened my mouth, poised to give my usual answer whenever the question of my credentials was raised by prospective clients. A few choice words about my long years of experience compiling the illustrious histories of Rome's noblest families, working to impossible deadlines and dealing with the endless requests from busy patriarchs and their demanding wives, followed by a brief (and suitably humble) summary of my talents, and a mention of the enthusiastic reviews my latest commission had received in the literary salons of Rome. References available on request.

But I sensed that this approach would not cut it with Caratacus. I could not hope to deceive him with flattery or abstract promises of an enhanced reputation amongst his peers in the Senate. I would have to try a different tactic.

'You are right, of course,' I said. 'I have no business writing the story of an exiled British king. Perhaps you could find some half-literate Gaul in our city willing to undertake the task instead. Someone with a firmer grasp of the Celt mindset. I can offer only one advantage over any other writer.'

Caratacus's eyes narrowed. 'And what is that?'

'Credibility,' I replied. 'I have spent my professional life embellishing the ancestries of the wealthiest, dreariest families in Rome.

My name therefore carries a certain amount of respect among our intellectual and artistic elite. Entrust your story to me, and it will be certain to gain the attention of every aristocrat from here to Pompeii.' I paused, saw a moment's hesitation on his face, and applied the killer blow. 'And what better way to demonstrate that you are the equal of our haughty elite, than by commissioning their favourite historian as your literary partner?'

'And who would pay you for this proposed work? If you're hoping for a generous commission from me, I'm afraid you're in for a disappointment.'

'I am not expecting a fee,' I reassured him. 'I propose to cover my expenses and labours with half of the proceeds from the book sales; the rest will go to you. If the book sells as well as I think it will, that will be a quite considerable sum of money. And I will be supplementing it by presenting lectures on the subject of the Celts and their culture, such as it is.'

'That is why you wish to tell my story? So you can make your fortune?'

'That is one reason. There are others.'

'Such as?' Caratacus laughed. 'Don't tell me you're interested in giving voice to an old Celt.'

I spread my hands. 'I have never written such a history before. It would be an honour, and a privilege, to relate the true story of a genuine hero for once.'

'The truth? There's not much appetite for that in your city.'

'It is better than peddling lies for the idle rich.'

I felt certain I had him then. I had employed every weapon at my disposal. 'Well?' I asked. 'What do you say?'

'It's an interesting proposition,' Caratacus said, stroking his chin.

'It's more than that,' I said. 'It's a chance to tell the history of the greatest warrior of our age.'

Caratacus smiled cynically. 'Save your flattery, Roman. If that was true I would not be the prisoner of your boy emperor. He would be my slave instead, or maybe a head adorning the centre post of my royal hall. Still, it's an interesting proposition. I don't know. I must think.' He pulled at the corner of his moustache for a moment, then made up his mind. 'Come to my place this evening. It is the house further up the street with a green door, next to the altar of Neptune.'

'When?'

'An hour before sunset,' Caratacus said. 'I will give you my answer then.'

A few hours later, in the fading light of the early evening, I made my way back up the Aventine. I had brought my writing utensils with me, more in hope than expectation that Caratacus might agree to share his story. The streets were less crowded at that hour as the quality retreated to their garish townhouses for dinner, and the wooden shutters were drawn across most of the shop fronts. I passed a couple of linkboys preparing torches to light the way through the streets for those wealthy enough to afford the service, and found the house I was looking for. The plaster on the perimeter wall was smeared with bird droppings, and the paintwork on the door was badly peeling. I rapped the knocker twice, then waited. After a short pause the door swung open and I found myself facing a thickset slave in a frayed tunic. He stood blocking the entrance while he regarded me with that mixture of suspicion and contempt universal to the doormen of our city.

'Yes?' he asked tonelessly.

'Caius Placonius Felicitus. I have a meeting with your master, Caratacus. He's expecting me.'

The slave nodded abruptly. 'This way, sir.'

I followed him across a narrow courtyard towards the main hallway. Weeds and grass protruded through the cracks in the ornamental paving. Most of the flowers had withered away, and I noticed that several of the terracotta roof tiles were damaged or missing. There was a faint odour of damp in the air. It did not strike me as the sort of residence appropriate for a king.

The doorman padded softly on his bare feet as he led me through the gloomy hallway. There was a mosaic on the floor of a gladiator slaying a two-headed serpent. From the other side of the house, I could hear the excited cries of children playing. We circled round the atrium and approached the study at the far end. The slave paused in front of the threshold and motioned for me to enter.

I stepped inside a sparsely furnished room, with a strongbox in one corner, a pair of padded stools and a threadbare curtain separating it from the rear of the house. Honeycomb shelving ran along the length of one of the walls, each compartment filled with papyrus scrolls.

Caratacus sat behind a walnut desk to my left, reading a book by the orange glow from several oil lamps. A pitcher and a pair of earthenware drinking cups rested on the desk beside him. At the sound of our footsteps, the Briton looked up and fixed his gaze on the slave.

'Thank you, Davos. You may leave us now.'

'Yes, master.'

He bowed and marched back towards the front of the house. Caratacus waited until he was out of earshot before he gestured to the stools.

'Please,' he said. 'Sit down.'

I sat on the nearest stool and placed my wax notebook and stylus on my lap while Caratacus reached for the pitcher. He began pouring a dark amber liquid into both cups.

'Beer,' he said by way of explanation. 'From Gaul. A friend in Lugdunum sends me an occasional supply. Not the same quality as the stuff we have back home, but it's acceptable. I hope you don't mind. I've never quite acquired the taste for wine.'

He handed me a cup. I stared hesitantly at the thick, foamy contents. A sickly sweet aroma filled my nostrils as I pressed the rim to my lips and took a sip of the malty liquid. It had a strong, bitter flavour that made me want to retch. How I managed to smile politely at my grinning host after that first gulp, I shall never know.

'Well? What do you think?' he asked.

'Delightful,' I said, ignoring the foul taste of ale in my mouth. 'Very . . . rich.'

'It's strong stuff. It'll put hairs on your chest.'

'It will?' I asked in alarm, as one does at the prospect of becoming as hairy as a barbarian.

Caratacus grinned. 'It's just a saying we have in Britannia.'

'I see.'

'You must forgive the dilapidated appearance of my dwelling,' he said unprompted. 'I have petitioned the palace to fix the various problems, but the imperial treasury is always finding new reasons to deny my request for funds.'

'Don't you have an income?' I asked.

'I draw a small pension, courtesy of the emperor, but it's not much and barely covers our day-to-day expenses.' Caratacus half smiled.

'Then how did you afford this house?'

'Oh, this?' Caratacus looked round the room, as if regarding its walls for the first time. 'It belonged to one of the late emperor's many enemies. A wealthy gladiator trainer with ideas above his station. As I understand it, he was part of a secret group of conspirators that attempted to assassinate Claudius.'

I searched my memory. 'The Liberators?'

He nodded. 'That's them. Anyway, the palace had the traitor knocked on the head, seized his property and sold off his troupe of gladiators and his country estate. My family was given the man's townhouse after the emperor spared my life. Something of a curse, as it turns out. The upkeep has proved challenging. This place drains money faster than a gambler with a set of crooked dice.'

'Perhaps I could have a polite word with some of my clients,' I suggested. 'They have influence. There might be a way to raise your pension.'

'That is kind of you, but I fear it would be a wasted effort. The emperor takes great pleasure in seeing me reduced to the status of a glorified beggar.'

'I'm sorry to hear that.'

'Are you? Most of your fellow citizens wouldn't agree. They see me as nothing more than a drain on the treasury. They frequently tell me to go back to my country. I would gladly do so, if only Rome would let me.'

'It must be hard here, for you and your family.'

'You can't imagine.'

'No,' I replied quietly. 'I suppose not.'

'It is not all bad. There are some pleasures that do not require much coin. I exercise daily, I play with the grandchildren. Mostly, I read.' Caratacus gestured to the book in front of him. 'Rome has taken much from me, but it has at least given me the chance to read and learn more about your culture and your history.'

'I didn't know Celts enjoyed reading.'

'And I didn't know that Roman historians took an interest in the affairs of exiled barbarians. So we may both allow ourselves to be surprised.'

I said nothing but felt a pang of sympathy for this melancholy figure. Despite the meanness of his circumstances and the petty humiliations heaped upon him by the palace, Caratacus retained a quiet dignity, in stark contrast to our spoiled emperor. I found myself developing a reluctant admiration for this hardened warrior. Perhaps the Britons were not the simple barbaric race I had imagined.

He took another swig of his ale and stared contemplatively at his cup. 'I've been considering your proposal,' he said at last.

Caratacus lifted his eyes to me. Here was the moment. I gripped my cup in my right hand and waited for him to go on.

'I will tell you my story, warts and all. But on two conditions.'

My heart was pounding with excitement. I nodded quickly. 'Yes, of course – anything.'

'One, I want this to be an unvarnished tale. It must be an honest account of my life and the invasion, however ugly it may be. I do not wish to sanitise the details to make it more palatable to the elite. To that end, I must insist on final approval of your script.'

'And you shall have it,' I answered readily, glad that I would be spared the painful exercise of glossing over history for a change. 'What is the second condition?'

Caratacus leaned forward, his elbows resting on the desk as he looked me directly in the eye. 'This history of mine shall not be published until after my death.'

I stared at him. For a moment I did not know what to say.

'Don't worry, Roman. I am an old man. You shall not have to wait very long before you can publish, if that is what you're worried about.'

'But I don't understand,' I said. 'Why delay?'

'I live at the mercy of your emperor. A memoir by one of his most notorious prisoners, so soon after Boudica's rebellion, is likely to draw his ire. At a stroke, he could reduce or withdraw my pension altogether.'

'Nero wouldn't dare do that,' I assured him. 'It would mean overturning the edict of the deified Claudius, not something that is done lightly.'

'Are you sure? I have heard it said that the emperor is quick to react to the slightest offence. Last night's fight will hardly have endeared me to him.'

'I suppose not,' I muttered. Caratacus had a point. From the little I knew about Nero, he did seem to have a rather thin skin.

'I've caused my wife and children enough grief,' Caratacus added. 'I have also read enough history to know that the truth is more acceptable when the protagonists are deceased. Swear that you will withhold the memoirs until I have made my journey with Lud to the Otherworld, and I will give you my story.' He shrugged. 'Who knows? Perhaps another man will be wearing the purple by then.'

I thought for a long moment. The prospect of exerting myself to write the life story of Caratacus, only to seal it in a strongbox for years to come, disheartened me. But on the other hand, I had chanced upon the story of a lifetime, and I was unlikely to find another subject as compelling as the British warlord. His tale had to be told, I knew. Even if I had to wait a long time before publishing it.

'Very well,' I said. 'You have my word.'

Caratacus's expression brightened. 'Good. Then let's begin.'

I sat up straight. 'Now?'

'Yes, why not? Unless you have something better to do?'

Without replying, I hurriedly snatched up my stylus and flipped open the wax notebook. Caratacus filled his cup to the brim with honeyed beer, took a sip and leaned back in his throne-like chair.

'Ready?' he asked. I nodded. 'Good. Then let us start at the beginning . . .'

CHAPTER THREE

You are taught that Rome cannot be defeated, that her enemies beyond the frontier can never hope for victory. You see before you a pitiful exile yearning for his homeland, and you marvel at how we resisted the might of the legions for so long. But all kingdoms can fall, and their kings with them. One day, even your emperor might become what I am now. You find that hard to believe, perhaps. Then hear my tale, and learn how I, Caratacus, once ruler of the Catuvellaunians and overlord of many tribes of Britannia, came to be in Rome today.

I was born in Verlamion, the largest settlement in the territory of our tribe. When I was two years old, my father, King Cunobelinus, received word at the royal court of the crushing defeat of General Varus and the Roman legions at the hands of the native tribes in Germania. My father was not a religious man, but when he heard this joyous news, he immediately ordered sacrifices to be made to the gods, and rich ceremonial offerings were cast into the River Ver. The Druids executed a pair of thieves, and their death throes foretold great victories for our people. Or so the tale goes. It would not surprise me if the truth was rather different. My father had a talent for bending facts to his political advantage. He would have made a fine Roman lawyer.

I was too young to remember, but I am told that it was a time of great hope for all those that opposed Rome. For long years the shame of our ancestors' surrender at the hands of Caesar had cast a shadow over our land. The tribes of Britannia had looked on with growing unease as Rome strengthened its grip over Gaul and Belgica, and they dreaded the day when the legions would cross the sea once more.

But the Varian disaster gave us fresh hope. For the first time, it seemed possible to defeat the legions. Moreover, freed from the anxiety of the prospect of invasion, my father was able to expand his influence beyond our tribal lands.

Shortly before my first birthday, our warriors marched on Camulodunum, the great capital in the land of the Trinovantes to the east. Their king, Dubnovellaunus, had vowed to resist any attempt to capture his stronghold, but his followers panicked at the sight of our approaching army, and after a brief struggle he took flight with his family and supporters and fled south across the Tamesis. My father promptly declared himself high king of both tribes, and for a brief while we knew peace in our land.

I was one of five brothers. Adminius, the first-born, was three years older than me. He had almost succumbed to a fever in his infancy, and our parents consequently doted over him, indulging him at every opportunity.

Soon after our family moved to Camulodunum, Togodumnus was born. From an early age he was a headstrong boy, stubborn but fearless, and I loved him dearly. Later on, our mother bore two more sons: Maridius and Vodenius. But in the winter after Vodenius was born she developed a sickly cough and a fever, and in the early spring she died. Father grieved deeply for many months after her death. Perhaps that is why he always favoured Adminius. He had inherited our mother's attractiveness and charm, and in many ways he reminded my father of her.

I spent my early childhood in Camulodunum. Our settlement looked nothing like your neatly gridded Roman towns. Back then it was little more than a sprawl of farmland, cattle byres and roundhouses, along with a few stone-built structures and a small quay on the river fronting the settlement. Goods would occasionally trickle in from Gaul on small merchant ships, bound for the aristocracy of our tribe and those worthies in the surrounding territories willing to pay a premium for wine and samianware. A series of earthworks topped with a stout palisade guarded the town against enemy attack. You would no doubt regard it as a filthy, barbaric place, compared to your own grand city. But it was ours.

Our household lived in the royal enclosure in the heart of

Camulodunum. I often played with Adminius and Togodumnus in the surrounding woodland and streams beyond the settlement. We hunted and fished and fought with each other, as boys will often do. Those were mostly happy times.

Until I was sent away to train with the Druids.

That was the first step on a path that would take me to the throne of our tribe and later to become the warlord of Britannia and sworn enemy of Rome. And it happened because of Bladocus, my Druid mentor. Without him, I would never have become king.

I was eleven years old. It was a pale grey morning, late in the autumn. The ground was slick with churned mud and a thin haze of woodsmoke hung in the air as I made my way across the royal enclosure towards the great hall. Adminius and Togodumnus trudged alongside me, the quagmire squelching beneath our leather boots. We had spent a few hours playing in a shallow dell beyond the enclosure. A short time later, one of our father's retainers had summoned us back to the hall for our daily instruction with Bladocus – one of the last survivors of the Gallic branch of the Druid cult.

'Let's hope the old goat keeps it short today,' Adminius muttered as we passed the stables. 'It'll be another story about dead kings and magic spells, no doubt.'

'What's wrong with that?' I asked.

'It's boring, that's what.' Adminius snorted contemptuously. 'Waste of time. We should be learning to fight, not listening to that stinking Gaul.'

The lessons had been our father's idea. He had insisted that as sons of the king we must receive a good education, as soon as we were old enough to commence our studies. Each morning at the third hour, I gathered in the hall with Adminius and Togodumnus, along with the sons of Camulodunum's wealthy nobles, to study under the tutelage of Bladocus. The Druids were our most learned men, the practitioners of our sacred rites and the guardians of the wisdom of the ancients, trained in the ways of magic, healing, tongues, the histories of our tribes and the ways of the gods. Our kings and elders entrusted them with passing on their learning to their children, so that they might

29

bestow them with the knowledge they would need one day to lead their people.

I loved these lessons under Bladocus, particularly the histories of our ancestors and the many great battles they had fought. They spoke of a time when the Celts ruled over half the known world, and Rome trembled before the vast armies of our forebears. But Adminius and Togodumnus hated them. They preferred wild pranks and playing games with their friends to listening to stories of the past.

'Don't know why Father makes us go to these lessons,' Adminius went on sullenly. 'All that talk of golden chariots and cattle raiding. It's bloody nonsense.'

'It's the story of our past,' I said. 'Our people. It's important. Besides, the stories are fun.'

'For you, perhaps.'

'If you feel that strongly, why bother to attend?' I challenged him. Adminius had skipped several lessons lately, preferring to spend his mornings charming the younger daughters of the local nobility.

'I promised Father,' he said glumly. 'He told me he'd beat me if I didn't go.' He paused. 'Maybe I should have taken the beating instead. Anything's better than listening to that miserable Druid.'

'Bladocus isn't that bad.'

'He's a bore. His breath stinks of onions. And he's as ugly as an old crone's teeth.'

'Don't say that!' Togodumnus cried anxiously. 'You'll get in trouble. The Druids can hear everything you say.'

Adminius rounded on our younger brother and frowned. 'Says who?'

'Uncle Epaticcus. He says it's one of their special powers. The Druids can see and hear as well as any of the gods, he says. Any child who curses them is turned blind, and all their hair falls out.'

Adminius let out a cruel laugh. 'And you believe that? You're thicker than you look, brother.'

'Shut up!'

'You shut up, turd-face.'

'He's right,' I said to Adminius. 'You shouldn't make fun

30

of Bladocus. He's a Druid of the third ring. That makes him power-ful.'

'Maybe so. But he's still a miserable Gaul. Face it, you only like him because you're his favourite. His star student.' Adminius glared accusingly at me. 'Teacher's pet. That's what you are.'

'At least I'm learning something,' I responded with feeling. 'Unlike you.'

'What's the point?' Adminius shook his head bitterly. 'Studying history and poetry won't do us much good, whatever Father thinks. Not if Verica keeps causing trouble,' he added quietly.

I pursed my lips and looked away. Verica was king of the Atrebates, a powerful tribe based in the rich lands to the south-west of our territory. He had seized the Atrebatan throne some years ago from his older brother, Eppillus, with the help of Roman silver used to bribe many of the tribe's nobles. Eppillus had fled the tribal capital at Calleva to take refuge in the east. Verica had allowed Roman merchants to set up trading posts along the coast and rivers of his kingdom in exchange for their silver, and many tribes feared that where Roman merchants ventured, their legions would one day follow. Now Verica was turning his attention to our territory. A month ago, we had received word that he was stirring things up, courting the support of exiled Trinovantian nobles and encouraging them to rise up against their Catuvellaunian overlords. The news had greatly alarmed the royal court. Although Camulodunum was secure enough, several of the outlying settlements had been bitterly contested by our tribes for generations, and many feared a costly war if Verica continued to support the exiles.

I looked up as we neared the entrance to the hall. A pair of bodyguards dressed in bright blue tunics stood in front of the doorway, their spears grounded as they gazed idly across the near-deserted enclosure. Next to them the banner of our tribe, the sacred stag, flapped like a serpent's tongue in the faint morning breeze. The guards nodded a respectful greeting at the sight of us, then quickly stepped aside before we passed through the porch into the clammy atmosphere of the interior.

The hall was quiet that morning. My father had departed a short time earlier to inspect the latest improvements to Camulodunum's defences, and only a handful of lesser nobles and warriors remained seated on the benches either side of the wide central avenue. In the middle of the hall, a servant poked and prodded at the logs burning in the fire-pit. Nearby, a bitch and several puppies lay sprawled on the flagstone floor, basking in the warmth of the flames. In the far corner my little brothers, Vodenius and Maridius, sat with the other Catuvellaunian infants while a female house servant told them a story.

A space had been cleared in front of the nearest trestle tables. A dozen children, the offspring of Camulodunum's nobility, sat on padded stools arranged in a rough circle as they chatted and joked amongst themselves. In the middle of the circle sat a tall, black-robed figure with wild hair: Bladocus, my father's adviser. At the sound of our approaching footsteps, he stood up and turned towards us.

'Ah, the young princes. At last,' he announced in his soft Gallic accent. He glanced at Adminius with a look of surprise. 'Even Adminius has deigned to join us today, I see.'

Adminius shrugged. 'I promised Father I'd attend, Master Bladocus.'

'Well. That is uncommonly good of you.' Bladocus smiled, displaying stained teeth. 'Now that you're here, perhaps you will endeavour to learn a thing or two.'

'Or get bored to death, more like,' Adminius muttered under his breath.

The Druid's eyes narrowed to dagger points. 'Did you say something?'

'No, Master.'

Bladocus continued to stare coldly at him. 'I am pleased that you have committed to attending these lessons. But while you're here, I expect you to apply yourself. If you misbehave or create trouble, I won't hesitate to inform your father. Is that clear?'

'Yes, Master,' Adminius replied, bowing his head slightly.

'Good.'

As I sat down at one of the spare stools, I studied Bladocus. To a stranger, I suppose he must have looked more like a beggar than a wizened Druid. He was thin and reedy, with skin the colour of cow's milk and eyes as black as stones set deep into his gaunt skull.

Like all those of his cult, he had a plaited beard and tattoos inked on his forehead and hands. Magic charms of twisted horsehair and animal teeth adorned his wrists. He waited until we were all seated, then cleared his throat as he prepared to address the class.

'Today we shall continue with the history of your great ancestor, Cassivellaunus.'

A few groans went up around the circle, my brothers amongst the moaners. I listened with rapt attention as Bladocus went on.

'Yesterday we ended with Cassivellaunus rising to the throne of your tribe after enduring many great struggles. He had fought traitors in his own court and vanquished enemy tribes. But now he found himself up against his greatest foe of all: Caesar, the barbarous slayer of Celts and the brutal conqueror of my own people, the Gauls. The Romans invaded at a time of great strife and anarchy among the peoples of Britannia. The crops had failed that year. Women and children were dying of hunger, and there was widespread unrest. Only King Cassivellaunus stood between the tribes and annihilation . . .'

Bladocus was a Druid by training, but he knew how to weave a tale better than any of Father's obsequious bards. I listened attentively as he recited every detail of the old king's life, but Adminius barely paid any attention and as the Druid carried on, I glimpsed my older brother whispering to the curly-haired boy sitting next to him, the spoilt son of a Trinovantian noble. Bladocus glowered at them, and they quickly fell silent.

'Now, then,' he said as he searched the faces of my fellow students. 'Who here can tell me the names of the five tribes who surrendered to Caesar and betrayed King Cassivellaunus to the Romans? Anyone?'

Silence descended over our group. The other boys shifted or stared at their feet, but none dared to reply. Bladocus slid his gaze towards me.

'Caratacus. Perhaps you can enlighten us?'

I felt the eyes of the other students on me. It often seemed that Bladocus deliberately picked on me during our lessons, singling me out for the most challenging questions. Sometimes it was almost as if he wanted to see me make a mistake. But I refused to be bested and his constant examinations of my knowledge only motivated me to study even harder.

'Of course, Master,' I replied confidently. 'The names of the tribes are the Bibroci, the Cenimagni, the Ancalites, the Segontiaci, and the Cassi.'

'Correct.' Bladocus regarded me thoughtfully for a moment. 'Excellent.'

'Thank you, Master.'

'If only some of your peers showed as much devotion to their studies.'

Out of the corner of my eye, I caught sight of Adminius muttering something to the boy with the blond curly hair. They both started giggling. In the next instant Bladocus snapped round and glared at my brother.

'You have something you wish to share with us, Adminius?'

'No, Master.'

'Really?' Bladocus indicated the boy at his side. 'Your friend Moxius certainly seems to find something amusing. Perhaps you'd care to share your joke with the rest of us?'

'But I didn't say anything, Master. You're mistaken.'

A dark expression crept like a shadow across the Druid's face. 'Don't try to deceive me. You haven't been listening to a word I've said. You've been joking with your friend here.'

'I haven't, I swear it!'

Bladocus smiled cruelly. 'In that case, prove it. Tell me which of our kings conquered Verulam. Since you've been paying such close attention, the question shouldn't be too difficult for you.'

My brother's cheeks flushed as the rest of the class turned towards him. He glanced round, as if hoping someone else might spare him further embarrassment.

'Come on, brother,' I said. 'This is easy!'

'Quiet there! Let him answer!' Bladocus snapped. He took a step towards Adminius and spread his hands. Moxius fidgeted nervously and stared at the ground.

'I'm still waiting,' the Druid said.

Adminius bit his lip. 'Is it . . . King Ludnus, Master?'

Bladocus shook his head. 'No.'

'It's Tasciovanus,' I interposed. 'The answer is King Tasciovanus. Everyone knows that. Lud, even a halfwit could have got that one right.'

Some of the other children chuckled amongst themselves. Bladocus held up a hand. 'That's enough. I think you've made your point.'

Looking back across more than half a lifetime, I realise my mistake now. I should have heeded the Druid's warning. But I didn't. Instead, I went on, eager to raise a few more laughs. For months Adminius had teased me over my love of history and poetry. Now I seized the chance to make fun of him.

'I'm just saying, Master. He should pay more attention.' I cocked my head at Adminius. 'If you spent half as much time on your studies as your hair, you might learn a thing or two.'

A ripple of laughter echoed through the hall as the rest of the students shared in my amusement, and I felt a strange thrill at provoking their reaction. Some of them joined in, throwing insults of their own. Adminius hunched his shoulders and lowered his head, avoiding the gaze of his peers.

'Silence!' Bladocus thundered. 'All of you!'

The others quickly fell quiet, and an uncomfortable silence lingered in the hall, broken only by the occasional cough and the distant sounds of the slaves toiling away in the adjacent kitchen. Bladocus stared darkly at me before he turned to my brother.

'I believe what Caratacus was trying to say is that the pursuit of knowledge requires discipline and concentration. The point is a valid one, if rather clumsily made.' He paused to glare at me again, then nodded at Adminius. 'You would do well to follow your brother's example, if not his manners. Do you understand, boy?'

'Yes, Master,' Adminius mumbled.

'Good. Then we shall resume the lesson . . .'

As the morning wore on, I looked up a few times to catch sight of Adminius glowering at me, his lips set in a hard line. It had been a mistake to make fun of him in front of the group. There had always been bad blood between us as we competed with one another for our father's approval. I was the more accomplished scholar, whereas Adminius was more popular, with his good looks and easy manner. But by mocking him in exchange for the amusement of myself and the others present, I had only succeeded in hurting his pride.

The animosity would only worsen now, I realised. Adminius would not forget his public humiliation. He would surely seek his revenge. It was only a matter of time.

CHAPTER FOUR

The following afternoon, our small class gathered on the training ground for our daily weapon practice. A chill autumn wind whispered across the enclosure as we fought in pairs with wooden staves crudely fashioned to resemble swords under the watchful eye of my uncle. Epaticcus was the commander of one of our father's war-bands and he knew how to fight as well as anyone in the kingdom. Those of us old enough to wield a stave fought against evenly matched opponents, while the smaller children played with toy swords in the muddy area closer to the hall. On the far side of the space, several veteran warriors unleashed a flurry of blows against a line of stout timber posts.

'Call that a bloody strike?' my uncle thundered at me as I lunged feebly at my training partner. 'You're supposed to cut your opponent down, not tickle him, for Lud's sake.'

I paused to catch my breath, gripping my stave tightly as I faced my opponent. Brigos was the younger son of a Trinovantian aristocrat who had switched sides after his king had fled into exile. He was several months older than me but shorter by a few inches, with dark hair and a chubby, round face. Around us, the air was filled with a series of sharp cracks as the other boys competed against each other.

'Come on, Caratacus!' Epaticcus roared at me. 'What are you waiting for, an invitation? Attack!'

I filled my lungs and thrust at Brigos, this time aiming at his midriff. Brigos hastily blocked the blow, feinted and slashed crosswise, catching me on the forearm. I staggered backwards, then made another ragged thrust. Epaticcus groaned in disapproval.

'Not like that!' he growled. He marched over and thrust out a hand at Brigos. 'Right. You. Tub of lard. Give me your stick. I'll take it from here.'

Brigos reluctantly handed over his stave before retreating to a safe distance. Epaticcus stared at me while he held the stave in his huge hand. With his drooping moustache, bright blue eyes and blond hair badly thinned after years of washing it in lime water, my uncle had the look of a true Celt. His face was nicked with scars and he looked old to me then, even though he was still in his thirties. But all men look old when you are a child. Epaticcus was proud and arrogant and foul-mouthed, with a quick temper and a seemingly endless thirst for beer. He was also the bravest man I knew, and I loved him as much as my own father. Perhaps more so.

'When you fight with a long sword, it's all about the edge,' he said, tapping the length of the stave. 'That's how our fathers fought, and their fathers before them. And do you know why?'

I shook my head slowly. 'No, Uncle.'

'Because it's a bloody powerful attack, that's why.' His face creased into a broad grin. 'In a one-on-one fight, an effective blow with an edged weapon is one of the most devastating attacks you can inflict. Get it right, master the technique, and you can shatter a man's collarbone, slice through tendons and muscle . . . and even cut off his head with one clean blow.'

He stepped back from me, tensing his muscles as he dropped into a low crouch.

'Attack me, and I'll show you what I mean.'

'Uncle?'

Epaticcus laughed. 'Don't worry. I won't hurt you.'

I took a deep breath and sprang forward, hoping to catch my uncle with a sharp stab to his chest. Epaticcus deftly parried the move, driving the weapon up and away from his chest. He shifted round to my right, moving nimbly on his feet, and I winced as he struck me on my side with the hard edge of the stave. Epaticcus watched me retreat and grinned.

'You see? With a well-aimed slash, you can hit your opponent high . . . or low. Now, again!'

Epaticcus calmly waited for me to attack. Shaking my head clear,

I lunged at my uncle once more. Epaticcus easily sidestepped the thrust and slashed downward, gently catching me on the thigh. The momentum carried me helplessly forward and I felt a soft tap against my spine as he struck me on the back with the blunt tip. I stumbled on, tripped and fell to the ground with a weak groan. Across the training ground some of the older boys pointed and laughed. Epaticcus yelled at them to return to their training, then extended a hand to me.

'Ignore them,' he muttered. 'They were beginners once, too. You might be raw, but you've got guts. That's the main thing.'

I accepted his hand and climbed slowly to my feet.

'Bravery, lad,' Epaticcus said. 'That's what makes a true Celt. Any idiot can be taught how to hold a sword or throw a spear, but he can't be taught to stand his ground when his enemy is charging towards him. That's what makes us who we are. Our courage. Don't forget that.'

'I won't,' I said.

He looked me hard in the eye. 'Remember: slashing with a long sword is the quickest way to win a fight. A single blow will kill your enemy, and it'll terrify his mates. And it looks a lot more impressive than those women in the Roman legions with their dainty little blades. And you know what they say about a man with a small sword, don't you?'

I stared at him blankly. 'No, Uncle?'

Epaticcus shook his head. 'Never mind. Now, pay attention.'

He stepped back, adopted a fighting stance and effortlessly swung the stave as if it weighed no more than a feather. Then he brought the stave crashing down in a sudden blur of motion. He repeated the move more slowly to demonstrate the technique.

'The trick to attacking with the edge is to let the blade do the work. Use the strength and momentum of your whole body when you attack. Bend slightly at the knees, keep your shoulder relaxed and aim for the head, neck or lower torso. Those are the vulnerable areas, so you'll do the most damage there.'

'What if he's wearing armour? Or a helmet?'

'You'll still knock the fight out of him. Even if the first blow doesn't kill a man outright, it'll strike him down faster than a dog's fart can clear out a roundhouse. Then you can finish him off while he's writhing on the ground with a nice quick stab to the guts. Or better yet, you can part his head from his shoulders and display it as a trophy.' He winked at me. 'Catuvellaunian women like a man with a few famous heads nailed to the front of his home. Means he's a good warrior.'

'I want to try!' Togodumnus shouted as he looked on. 'I want to fight too!'

'And I'd like to have a nice plump princess for a wife. But we can't have everything we want, can we?'

A look of disappointment crossed my brother's freckled face. Epaticcus turned back towards me, his face suddenly serious once more.

'Remember, edge first, then stab if you need to finish him off. It takes skill and strength to fight that way, but once you've got the hang of it, you'll never lose. The Celts have been doing the same thing for centuries, and there's no surer way of defeating your enemy on the field of battle.'

'What about the Gauls?' I asked.

'What about 'em?'

'They fought with their long swords against Caesar under King Vercingetorix, and they still lost.'

Epaticcus frowned. 'Know your history, don't you?'

'Just what Bladocus teaches us.'

My uncle wrinkled his nose in disgust. 'I don't care what the Druids say. The Gauls lost because they're a bunch of wine-drinking surrender goats. Those cowards would run scared from an old crone. They might have been crushed by the Romans, but it'd be a different story if those red-crested turds tried their luck here.'

'Maybe.' I nodded uncertainly, wishing I shared my uncle's confidence. But even at that young age, Bladocus had told me enough about the legions for me to fear them.

'Do you think the Romans will come back here?' I asked.

'How should I know? I'm just a simple warrior.' Epaticcus tapped a finger against the side of his head. 'Now your father, he's the one who does all the thinking. That's why he's the king.'

'Father says the Romans won't rest until they've conquered all the world.'

'That sounds about right. The Romans are greedy swine if nothing else.' Epaticcus knelt down beside me and rested a hand on my shoulder. 'But if they do ever return, we'll give their soldiers a bloody good kicking. Mark my words. They'd shit their breeches before they could get off their fucking ships.'

I stared at him.

'What?' Epaticcus demanded.

'You swore.'

He rolled his eyes. 'For Danu's sake, don't tell your mother. You know what she's like. I'll never hear the end of it.'

'That tongue of yours will get you in trouble one of these days, brother,' a familiar voice called out.

Epaticcus straightened up and looked towards the great hall. I glanced in the same direction and saw a tall, broad-shouldered figure emerging from the entrance. My father, Cunobelinus, High King of the Catuvellaunians and the Trinovantes.

My father wore his usual attire of a finely woven tunic, coarse trousers, leather shoes and a thick woollen cloak with a fur trim. A decorative gold torc as thick as an adder gleamed around his neck. A small entourage followed a few paces behind him: a loose throng of attendants, nobles and Druids in their dark flowing robes. Bladocus was among them, a dark cowl covering his head. A large brindled hunting dog trotted dutifully alongside my father. It sniffed at the dirt while Epaticcus bowed his head.

'Sire.'

At a signal from Epaticcus the other children stopped practising and bowed their heads towards the king.

'I thought I might see how my sons are getting on,' my father said. 'I didn't realise teaching them colourful language was part of the training.'

The king's steady gaze rested on me briefly. Although they were separated by only a few years, my father looked much older than Epaticcus. He had been on the throne for eight years, and the burden of leading our people was starting to take its toll on his body. His trimmed beard was speckled with grey, and crow's feet had formed at the corners of his eyes.

My uncle's cheeks flushed. 'Sorry, sire. It won't happen again.'

My father's mouth twitched. 'I'm sure it's nothing the boys haven't heard before.'

Epaticcus started to reply but the king cut him off with a curt wave of his hand.

'I'm preparing my sons to become great warriors,' he said, 'not fawning bards. I can hardly expect to shield them from the language of the battlefield for ever, can I?'

'I suppose not.'

'How are my sons progressing?'

'Well enough.' Epaticcus nodded at my older brother. 'Adminius is improving every day. His footwork needs to be lighter, and he's guilty of showing off sometimes, but he's getting there.'

'And Caratacus? How does he fare?'

Epaticcus scratched his jaw as he considered. 'It's early days. He's only had a few training lessons and he makes plenty of mistakes.'

'So did we, at the same age.'

'True enough.' Epaticcus grinned. 'But he's tough and willing, and he's a quick learner. Quicker than most, I'd say. Reminds me of you, come to think of it.'

My father regarded me curiously but continued to address Epaticcus. 'He shows promise, then?'

'I reckon so, aye. With the right instruction, he'll be a skilled warrior. As good as his brother, perhaps.'

Adminius snorted his contempt. 'This puny weakling? You can't be serious, Uncle. He'll never make a decent warrior. Look at him! Skinny as a shepherd's crook, he is.'

'He might be slender, but size isn't everything,' Epaticcus said.

'Slender?' Adminius laughed. 'He's nothing but a streak of piss. You should stick to your history lessons, brother. Leave the fighting to the big boys.'

'I could beat you,' I said.

'You're a scrawny runt,' Adminius sneered. 'You couldn't beat a blind old man in a sword fight.'

A few of the older children chuckled amongst themselves. I clenched my jaw and felt a hot spark of anger flare inside my chest.

'Shut your mouth,' I said in a low voice.

42

Adminius threw back his head and laughed. 'Or what? You'll make me?'

'I might.'

Adminius edged closer to me, his face twisted into a snarl. 'Little runts shouldn't make empty threats,' he said. 'They might get more than they wished for.'

I looked steadily at my brother. 'I'm not afraid of you.'

'If you think you're so tough, why don't you come over here and prove it?' he taunted. 'I'd crush you with one hand tied behind my back.'

The adults gathered around the confrontation chuckled in amusement.

'You're both bloody idiots,' Epaticcus muttered, rolling his eyes. 'When are you going to stop behaving like a couple of brats? Always squabbling, the pair of you.'

'Let us see them fight, Epaticcus,' the king said.

My uncle arched his eyebrows in surprise. 'Fight?'

'The boys are in disagreement. They can settle their differences in single combat, in the old ways of our people. It will be a wonderful opportunity to test their skills.'

'But it wouldn't be a fair contest,' Epaticcus protested. 'Adminius is four years older. He's a head taller at least, and much more developed.'

'They're both children. And they fight all the time. They're always challenging one another. You just said so yourself.'

Epaticcus shook his head forcefully. 'There's a big difference between squabbling children and individual combat. Adminius has been training for years. Caratacus has only had a few lessons. He won't stand a chance.'

'They will only be using practice weapons,' the king pointed out. 'They're not likely to do each other any real harm.'

'But Caratacus could get badly hurt, even if they're just using staves.'

'Then it will teach him a valuable lesson,' my father said coldly.

'What lesson is that?' Epaticcus threw up his arms. 'How to get his arse kicked by someone much bigger than him?'

'Caratacus has issued a threat against his older brother,' the king stated. 'A challenge has been made, Epaticcus. The boy must understand that a warrior who cannot back his words with his actions is unworthy.'

'The lad didn't mean it, my lord,' Epaticcus replied. 'It's just a couple of young pups trading insults.'

'Perhaps he should have thought before he opened his mouth.' The king's expression tightened. 'Words have power. Caratacus must learn to choose them wisely or suffer the consequences.'

'This is wrong.'

My father's expression hardened. 'You forget yourself, Epaticcus. I am the king. I have decided that my sons shall fight, and that is the end of the matter. Now, you will do as I say and prepare them. Is that clear?'

Epaticcus opened his mouth as if to protest once more but thought better of it and dipped his head in a slight bow.

'Yes, my lord.'

'Good.'

There was a bustle of activity as my father's entourage formed a rough circle around us. At the same time the handful of warriors on the other side of the training ground set down their weapons and marched over, keen to watch the contest. Adminius stepped forward, and we took up our positions facing each other in the middle of the circle. Epaticcus stood between us, acting as the umpire for the occasion. Some of the older boys in the crowd loudly cheered their support for Adminius. He acknowledged his friends with a curt nod, and I saw a wicked gleam in his eyes as he prepared to fight me.

'Now it's your turn to suffer,' he hissed under his breath. 'You made me look like a fool yesterday. You'll be sorry for that.'

'We'll see,' I replied tersely.

He smirked. 'Your Druid tutor won't be able to save you now. By the time I'm done with you, you'll be begging for mercy.'

'All right, you two.' Epaticcus looked both of us in the eye. 'This is a training fight, so keep it clean. That means no cheating or trying to seriously harm each other. The winner is the first one to force his opponent out of the circle or deprive him of his weapon. Got it?'

'Yes, Uncle,' we both replied.

I took in a breath, bending my knees and keeping my sword arm out from my side, just as Epaticcus had taught me. Then my uncle stepped back and bellowed for the fight to begin. Adminius let out a roar as he charged forward. The long hours spent on the training ground had honed his muscles and the ferocity of his attack caught me by surprise as he brought his stave crashing down towards my neck. There was a splintering crack as I parried the blow, and before I could recover Adminius hurled himself at me again, raining down a succession of violent blows, which I blocked with difficulty as his supporters in the crowd enthusiastically urged him on.

Adminius came forward once more, slashing furiously. I lacked his strength, but I was lighter on my feet and I flung myself to the right, evading the attack then striking at a low angle, hitting him on the shin bone. Adminius hissed in pain but the blow merely seemed to enrage him. He swung down at my head, as if chopping wood. I saw the move a fraction too late and gasped in agony as the stave crashed down on my shoulder. I stumbled back again, almost losing my balance. Adminius paused to bask in the adulation of his supporters.

'Finish him off!' one of his friends shouted.

'Crush him!' another called out.

My shoulder throbbed viciously. My breathing came in short, erratic gasps. I knew I was in trouble. There was no way I could hope to match my brother's skill or strength. Unless I could find some other way of beating him, or at least forcing a draw, I was in danger of getting severely injured.

I tensed my muscles and took a breath, forcing myself to ignore the searing pain in my shoulder.

'Is that the best you can do, Adminius?' I yelled. 'Call yourself a warrior? I've seen infants fight better than you. You can't even knock down your little brother!'

A few of the onlookers chuckled heartily. The taunt enraged Adminius. His face screwed up in anger as he threw himself at me, hurling blow after savage blow. My weapon shuddered with the impact of each attack as he gradually forced me further back. I glanced quickly over my shoulder and realised I had almost reached the edge of the circle.

'Got you now,' Adminius sneered.

He raised his stave high above his head, ready to slash downward at my skull. The action momentarily exposed his torso, and I took him by surprise with an attack of my own, slamming my weapon against his ribs. Adminius gasped in shock. I dived to the right as he swung wildly, evading the blow, then sprang up on the balls of my feet and struck a second time. The wooden edge smashed into the side of my brother's jaw with a jarring crunch, whipping his head to the side. His arms slackened and he fell away, his weapon tumbling from his grip. The crowd looked on in stunned silence as my brother lay writhing on the ground, pawing in agony at his face.

'Adminius loses his weapon! Caratacus is the winner!' my uncle exclaimed.

Togodumnus gleefully cheered my name. After a few moments several other spectators joined in, and soon most of the crowd was cheering my victory. As their shouts carried across the air, I saw my father gesturing to a couple of his followers.

'You two! Take him inside the hall,' he ordered, pointing at my stricken brother. 'Get him cleaned up.'

They rushed forward and helped Adminius to his feet. He slowly lifted his head and spat out a gout of blood and a broken tooth.

'Not fair,' he rasped. 'I had him cornered, Father. The fight was mine to win. I demand another bout.'

'There are no second chances in single battle,' our father responded sharply. 'You underestimated your opponent, Adminius. That is a grave mistake, one you would do well to learn from. A better swordsman would have knocked you out cold.'

'It was a lucky hit, that's all.' Adminius pointed to the circle. 'Let us fight again. Best of three, Father. I'll crush the little turd-face next time.'

'No! My decision is final.' He glared at Adminius. 'You've lost. Now you will accept the result with the good grace befitting a Catuvellaunian prince. Am I clear?'

'Yes, Father.'

Adminius limped off towards the hall with the king's attendants, closely followed by a handful of his friends. My father smiled faintly at me. 'You fought well, Caratacus. If rather unconventionally. A fine victory.'

'Thank you, Father.'

He smiled again and tipped his head at Epaticcus. 'I think I've seen enough for one day. You may resume your lesson.'

'Yes, my lord.'

My father gestured to his entourage and set off towards the hall, a steady trickle of nobles and servants following him, while the warriors began drifting back to their timber posts on the other side of the practice ground. Epaticcus barked an order at the rest of the children, and they slowly returned to their positions with their training partners. I turned to join the others and spotted Bladocus beckoning to me. He studied me with a calculating expression as I approached.

'That was nicely done,' he said. 'But you were lucky your brother lost his head near the end, so to speak. On another day, he might have defeated you.'

I shook my head. 'Luck had nothing to do with it, Master.'

Bladocus looked at me questioningly. 'No?'

'I knew I didn't stand a chance against Adminius. Not in an equal contest. I had to anger him. Force him to act rashly and hope that he'd make a mistake.'

'That's why you goaded him?'

'Adminius is thin-skinned,' I said, rubbing my sore shoulder. 'He has pride. I knew if I insulted him in front of his friends, he'd react that way. He can't help it.'

The Druid inclined his head at me and frowned. 'Not many children your age would think that strategically.'

'It was the only way I could win.'

'Yes. I suppose so.' He laced his fingers together. 'Still, you wouldn't have had to fight Adminius at all if you had handled him more carefully yesterday. That was foolish of you.'

'But I didn't do anything.'

'We both know that's a lie. A halfwit, I believe was the term you used to describe your brother.'

'He gave the wrong answer. It's not my fault he can't be bothered to study.'

'Perhaps not. But there are other ways of dealing with people,' Bladocus chided me. 'You must learn to point out their errors gently, without turning them against you. Your behaviour yesterday morning was unacceptable.'

47

I felt a wave of anger towards the Druid. I had just proved myself in a contest against a much stronger opponent, and instead of offering his congratulations he was upbraiding me.

I said, 'If Adminius thinks I hurt his feelings, that's his problem. Not mine.'

'Sometimes it's not just about being right. It is more important to get others to see things your way, make them think it was their own idea. That way, you can turn their mistakes to your advantage. You were right, yes. But making fun of your brother left him with no choice but to respond in the way he did. Do you see?'

'Maybe I shouldn't have embarrassed him,' I admitted.

Bladocus gave me a searching look. 'You're a promising scholar. And you know how to fight. But you won't get far unless you learn how to win people over. A good king gains his victories by guile and persuasion, as well as by courage on the field of battle.'

I shook my head. 'I'm not going to be a king. Adminius will take over the throne one day. Everyone knows that.'

'Perhaps.' He smiled strangely. 'You may return to your training.'

'Thank you, Master.'

I turned and started back across the training ground. A short distance away Epaticcus stood watching me, his thick arms folded across his chest. 'What did he want?' he asked, nodding at the Druid as the latter strode towards the hall.

'Nothing,' I said. 'Just wanted to ask me a few questions.'

'Questions.' He sniffed. 'I'd watch yourself around him if I were you.'

I glanced at my uncle, furrowing my brow. Like almost everyone in our kingdom, Epaticcus had a paralysing fear of Druids, and he tried to steer clear of them at all costs.

'What do you mean?'

'He's a Gaul.'

'So? They're Celts, the same as us.'

Epaticcus made a noise in his throat. 'They might speak the same language and worship the same gods, but that's it. They don't understand our tribes, or our way of life.'

'Father trusts him.'

'Your father tolerates him. There's a big difference. And that's only because he needs the support of the Druids to stay on the throne. But if the Gaul is taking an interest in you, he'll have his reasons.'

'Why?' I asked. 'What does he want with me?'

'I don't know. Only he can answer that. They see things other men cannot see. That's why they're chosen by the gods as their servants. Just be careful, do you hear?'

'Yes, Uncle.'

'Back to your training, then.'

I marched over to Brigos, my joy at winning the fight quickly giving way to a gnawing unease. Beating Adminius would only deepen his enmity towards me, I knew. And now I had to worry about the Druid. Bladocus had begun watching me closely over the past few weeks, often observing me from afar during my training sessions with Epaticcus and questioning me after our evening meals in the hall. Now I started to wonder why.

I shook my head, pushing my anxieties to the back of my mind. There was no point worrying about the Druid's motives now. Whatever he wanted with me, I would find out soon enough.

CHAPTER FIVE

It has often seemed to me that the gods have a wicked sense of humour. More than once they have taken pleasure in rescuing me from the depths of despair, only to throw me headlong into some crueller torment. Out of the cauldron and into the fire-pit, as my father used to say. Perhaps that is unfair, but then life is neither fair nor good – and neither are the gods. I only know that whenever Lud saved me from disaster, the respite was only temporary. Some other threat always lurked unseen, like the snake sheltering in the shadow of a fallen tree.

I spent the days after the fight looking anxiously over my shoulder. My victory had only increased Adminius's hostility towards me, as I had feared. I tried my best to avoid him, but every so often I would look up and see him scowling at me, his jaw bruised purple and his lip badly swollen. It was inevitable that he would confront me sooner or later, and I knew I wouldn't stand a chance against him the next time. There was no way Adminius would fall for the same trick twice.

My situation seemed hopeless. Until, late one afternoon, I was summoned to the great hall.

Our group had finished our weapon practice a short while earlier. The servants had cleared away the training weapons, and I was playing with Togodumnus and his friends in the thinning light of the training ground, re-enacting the famous battles of our ancestors.

'Look!' I cried at the other children, pointing my toy sword at imaginary foes. 'Here comes Caesar and his Roman dogs! They're landing on the beach!'

'I can smell them from here!' Togodumnus yelled excitedly. 'They stink worse than the Druid's breath! Stinking Romans!'

'Get them! On me! CHARGE!'

Our screaming rabble rushed towards the far palisade, waving our swords and shouting the battle cries of our tribe as we tore giddily into the invisible Roman soldiers. Amid the melee I heard a gruff voice calling out across the training ground.

'Caratacus!'

I stopped, looked up and saw one of my father's bodyguards marching over from the direction of the great hall, a dark-haired man with a prominent scar running down his cheek. He drew to a halt a few paces away and nodded briskly at me.

'Follow me.'

'What for?' I asked.

'The king wants to see you. In the hall.'

'Now?'

'If you don't mind.' He glanced at Togodumnus. 'Or I can tell your father you're too busy to see him.'

'Fine,' I grumbled. 'Let's go.'

'But you said you'd play with us,' Togodumnus moaned. 'You promised.'

'I will.' I ruffled his hair playfully. 'I won't be long. Soon as I'm finished with Father, I'll come right back. I swear.'

Togodumnus looked doubtfully at me. 'You'd better.'

I hurried after the bodyguard as he crossed the bare dirt ground towards the rear entrance. He led me through the timber doorway and past the king's private quarters and storerooms to the main chamber. In the wavering orange glow of the torches, I spotted a small crowd of nobles standing to one side of the stone dais, Epaticcus amongst them. My father sat above them on his carved wooden throne, a splendid black hunting dog nestling at his feet. Bladocus stood to one side of the king, the cowl pulled back to reveal his pale, scarred face. A pair of bodyguards stood further away near the edge of the dais.

'Ah, Caratacus!' my father beamed. 'There you are, my son.'

He dismissed the bodyguard at my side with a brisk wave of his hand. The man bowed stiffly, then headed for the front of the hall while my father signalled for me to approach.

'You wished to see me, Father?' I asked.

He nodded curtly. 'I've asked my advisers to join us, since this matter concerns the future of our family – of our tribe. It's important they hear what I have to say, before we make a formal announcement to my people.'

'Announcement, Master?'

'Yes.' My father flashed a brief smile. 'You have been chosen by the Druids.'

I puckered my face into a frown. 'I don't understand.'

'I've been talking with Bladocus,' my father said. 'He tells me that you've become an exemplary student over these past few months. A scholar of rare talent, apparently.'

I glanced sidelong and noticed several of the nobles regarding Bladocus with looks of suspicion and unease. I was not surprised. It was well known that many of my father's advisers resented the presence of an outsider at the royal court, and they frequently ridiculed his Gallic ancestry.

'Not only have you impressed Bladocus in your studies,' my father continued, 'but you clearly have promise as a young warrior. As we all saw the other day.'

'Yes, Master,' I said, because I did not know what else to say. I wondered again why he had ordered me to the hall. My father gently stroked the hound's neck as he carried on.

'Bladocus feels that your education would best be served elsewhere. I am inclined to agree.'

'Elsewhere, Master?'

My father nodded. 'Bladocus has requested that you be taken into the care of the Druids. I have given my consent.'

A low murmur of surprise went up among the nobles. This was a singular honour for a boy of my age. I stared at my father, dumbfounded.

'I am to . . . train with the Druids?' I asked, my mind racing.

'For a while, yes.'

'Where?'

Now Bladocus addressed me. 'There is a sacred place of learning, my child. Some of the wisest Druids in all of Britannia are to be found at this sanctuary. You will continue your studies there, under my supervision.'

My frown deepened. 'Is it far, Master?'

'Very far. To the west, not far from Merladion, the capital of the Silures.'

'The Silurians?' Epaticcus shook his head. 'But those backwater savages live on the other side of the island. The arse-end of Britannia.'

Bladocus glanced at my uncle. 'So?'

'Why send Caratacus to the west? Why not have him study somewhere closer to our kingdom? Somewhere we could keep an eye on him?'

Bladocus smiled. 'I spent some time as a novice at Merladion when I first came over from the lands of my people in Gaul. All the knowledge of the Celts is to be found among the Druids who reside at the sanctuary. There is no better place for Caratacus to learn.'

I swallowed hard. 'How long will I be gone?'

My father glanced at Bladocus, as if deferring to him.

'The training will be long and difficult,' the latter responded matter-of-factly. 'You will have to learn the laws, rituals and customs of each tribe, the histories of our great ancestors, and the deeds of every king and warrior hero in Britannia, both living and dead. In addition, you will study astrology, the meaning of the calendars and the tongues of the many other tribes of the lands. All of this you shall commit to memory, so that you may recite any part of it without a moment's hesitation.'

Epaticcus puffed out his cheeks and exhaled. 'Sounds like a lot of bloody hard work.'

'It is not easy,' Bladocus agreed. 'It normally takes a minimum of seven years for a young scholar to complete their initiation into the first ring. Those that reach the standard have the choice of continuing their training, or returning to their people to apply what they have learned.'

'Seven years!' I gasped.

'At a minimum. It is not unheard of for a curate to spend fifteen or even twenty years in training before he is ready to become a Druid.'

A thin, grey-haired noble dressed in a fine purple tunic stepped forward. 'I have a question, sire.'

'Of course, Orenus. Speak your mind.'

Orenus pointed a long finger at me. 'Why him? Why not his older brother?'

'Adminius has many talents. However, only the most promising scholars are permitted to study at the sanctuary. Bladocus has made it clear that Caratacus is the outstanding candidate.'

'And what of Adminius, sire?'

'He will remain here at my side, observing the royal court and learning about the demands of the throne. That is a more fitting education for a future king.'

'What about the boy's combat training?' Epaticcus pointed out. 'Who will teach him to fight while he's away? He can't be allowed to neglect his swordsmanship.'

'Bladocus tells me that the sanctuary is under the protection of the nearest tribal chief,' my father said. 'The Druids have an agreement with this man to train up the novices in all aspects of warfare. The boy will be billeted at the capital for the duration of his training. Along with the other scholars.'

'And why in Lud's name would the chief agree to that?'

'I know the chief well,' Bladocus said in his harsh voice. 'He is one of the Druids' most dedicated allies and a fine warrior. He is sworn to obey us.'

'The Silurians are not ruled by any one king,' my father said. 'Each chief swears an oath of allegiance to their Druid overlords. Bladocus has explained that the Druids have complete authority over the locals at Merladion. They supply the sanctuary with food, ale, bodyguards, slaves . . . whatever they need. In return the Druids ward off evil spirits and arbitrate any disputes and treaties between the chiefs.'

'Sounds like a good deal for the Druids,' Epaticcus muttered.

Bladocus shot him an evil look. 'It is a mutually beneficial arrangement. The Silurians have never complained.'

'In any case, their chief will provide Caratacus with whatever he needs while he is away from us,' my father interjected. 'As an added incentive, I intend to provide the chief with a generous gift of silver coin, to compensate him for his time and trouble.'

My father must have seen the anxious look on my face, because he leaned forward and smiled reassuringly.

'You will not be alone, if that is what you're worried about,' he said. 'Bladocus will stay with you during your time at Merladion, as your private mentor, until you are ready to return home. That is the custom for novices, I understand,' he added, glancing at Bladocus.

'Correct, sire,' the Druid said.

I tried to smile. But I could think only of the dread prospect of leaving behind my family and friends and the familiar surroundings of my childhood. Although I did not fear the Druids as much as my uncle or brothers did, I had no great desire to live among their kind, or their Silurian followers. I had heard a little of their people: a hardy bunch of ferocious warriors who struck fear into the hearts of every other tribe in Britannia.

'And who will oversee the instruction of the other boys while Bladocus is away?' asked my uncle.

'Another Druid will take my place,' Bladocus replied. 'I've already sent word for him. He should arrive in a few days.'

Then Orenus spoke up. 'Forgive me, sire, but I cannot help but wonder if we are missing a valuable opportunity with regard to our wider tribal interests.'

My father frowned. 'How so?'

'If Caratacus is to be sent anywhere then why not entrust him to one of our neighbouring rulers? The Iceni, perhaps. Or the house of the Corieltauvi to the north. An exchange of young princes between royal families would be most welcome, as a guarantee of peace and friendship between our tribes.'

'I have no intention of allowing my son to be raised by a bunch of gutless potters and craftsmen,' my father responded harshly. 'Besides, I have already given my word to Bladocus.'

'An education with the Druids is a great privilege, of course. But I fear our need for allies is even greater, sire. Especially with the recent worrying news about Verica.'

The king fixed his gaze on the noble. 'You disagree with my decision, Orenus?'

The noble shifted his weight onto his other foot. 'Sire, we all know that Verica has been making trouble to the south. Recruiting disgraced Trinovantian nobles to his cause and courting Roman merchants.'

'Yes. So?'

'Verica's intentions are clear enough, are they not? He is determined to expand his influence north. He wishes to supplant our tribe as the greatest power in the land.'

'*My* tribe,' my father pointed out. 'Not yours, Orenus. You are a Trinovantian noble by birth. Or have you forgotten your own bloodline in your hurry to enrich yourself at my court?'

Orenus lowered his head. 'I am loyal to no one but you, sire. I have given you my word, since the day you became king.'

My father raised his hand, cutting him off. 'Enough talk of your loyalty,' he said irritably. 'Come to your point.'

'I merely wish to suggest that with the Atrebates growing stronger, it might be wise to seek out new friends among the tribes. We will need them, to guard against future attack.'

'Verica would not dare launch an assault on our territory,' my father said. 'He doesn't have the numbers, for a start. Many of his men have fled east to join Eppillus, and the handful of warriors left under Verica's command are hardly worthy of the name. It takes years to recruit and train a disciplined war-band, as you well know. Verica poses no immediate threat.'

'Not yet. But in time, he might cause us problems.'

'Then we will deal with him accordingly.'

'And in the meantime, sire? Are we to do nothing to protect our interests?'

'Verica's position is not as assured as it might seem. My spies in Calleva tell me that many nobles are opposed to his rule, especially since he's begun encouraging Roman traders to settle in his lands. He will have his hands full consolidating his grip on power. Of course, the day may come when we have no choice but to stand up to the Atrebatan usurper.'

'Quite so, sire,' said Bladocus. 'Particularly if Verica continues to court his new Roman friends. That would spell disaster for the tribes of this island. Britannia could go the same way as Gaul, if we are not wise to the threat.'

Orenus sniffed. 'Britannia is not Gaul.'

'No. But I have seen what happens when tribal chiefs, blinded by power and wealth, seek to ally themselves with the emperor. I have heard the stories of how Rome preyed on the weakness and division of our people in Gaul, how our tribes failed to set aside their differences, even as the legions laid waste to our lands, enslaved our peoples and destroyed our hill forts. If we are to defend ourselves against the red crests, we must build a coalition under the standard of the Catuvellaunians, strong enough to resist Verica and his Roman allies. Only if we build up our forces and fight together will we stand a chance against the legions.'

'Assuming Rome returns to these shores.'

'It will happen, Orenus. I am certain of it.'

'And what if Verica does try to attack us?'

'Then we'll crush the bastard,' Epaticcus said.

'But if he's so weak, then why not attack him now?' Orenus pressed. 'Nip the threat in the bud, so to speak.'

'Out of the question,' my father said. 'Our forces are badly stretched as it is, defending our kingdom. As you well know. We simply cannot spare the men for an invasion of his kingdom.'

Orenus shook his head. 'But, sire—'

'I've made my decision,' my father snapped. 'The matter is not up for discussion.'

'Yes, my lord.'

My father lowered his gaze to me. 'Do you have any questions?'

'When do I leave?' I asked anxiously.

'Two days from now,' replied Bladocus. 'All new scholars must present themselves at Merladion two days before the seed-fall, in ten days' time. Lessons begin at the sanctuary the day after.'

'The road west is dangerous, my lord,' Epaticcus said, spreading his hands wide. 'It will take the boy through the lands of the Dobunni. There are brigands in those parts, and Durotrigan raiders.'

'Which is why you will accompany him. Along with a small escort from my personal bodyguard.'

Epaticcus rubbed his jaw. 'I'll need good men for the job.'

'How many?'

'Four should be enough.'

'As you wish. I leave the particulars to you.'

My father looked round the chamber. 'Now, if there is nothing else . . . ?'

No one else said a word. After a moment my father rose from his throne. The hound stirred at his feet and yawned.

'We shall hold a feast tomorrow night,' he declared. 'I will make an announcement to my people then. The great and good of Camulodunum can join us in celebration.'

'A wonderful suggestion, my lord,' Orenus said.

My father looked down at me with a heavily furrowed brow. 'Is there a problem?'

'No, Master,' I managed to reply. A smile spread across my father's lips.

'This is a great day, my boy. You should be excited. To be chosen by the Druids is a rare privilege.'

I departed Camulodunum two days later. It was a fine autumn morning, bright and clear, and the air was thick with midges. Bladocus, Epaticcus and the other four men from the royal bodyguard stood beside the town gate, looking on while my father bade me farewell. The Druids announced that they had seen a raven flying west, which we all took to be a good omen. Then I climbed onto my mount, the gate opened, Epaticcus shouted at his men, and we trotted out of the settlement, following the rutted track running between the steep-sided defensive earthworks.

In front of me lay an uncertain path in a land I did not know, in the company of a Druid I did not trust. But there was no turning back. As we followed the track I took one final glance back at Camulodunum.

It was the last time I would see my home for many years.

CHAPTER SIX

I have promised you a candid tale, Roman. So I must confess that as we set off I felt a rising sense of terror in my chest. I did not want to leave the comforts of Camulodunum; I hated the Druid for choosing me and if I had been given any say in the matter, I would have stayed put at the royal court. The threat of Adminius and his bullying friends was nothing compared to my fear at the prospect of spending the next seven years among the Druids in the furthest reaches of our island.

The weather held for the next few days as we rode west. I have seen much of your city and its environs, but the greatest splendours of Rome cannot match the beauty of the Britannic countryside on a warm afternoon in the autumn, when the sun bathes the land in a golden hue, the leaves of the forest glow yellow and red, the air is rich with the earthy tang of damp earth, and one can hear the melodic songs of the birds.

In the evenings we rested at isolated farmsteads along the way, sitting around the hearth-fire while we filled our bellies with pork stew, coarse bread and a little cheese. Epaticcus always insisted on giving the poor farmers some coin for their kindness, and they always refused to accept, as is the proud custom of our tribes. You might think our people are barbaric and war-like, and perhaps in some ways you are right. But at night in an unfamiliar land, far from home, there is no more welcome sight for a stranger than the hospitality of a Celt.

On the third afternoon we crossed into the territory of the Dobunni, and my mood lifted. It was the first time in my life I had ventured outside my father's kingdom. I felt a thrill of exhilaration as we passed through wide, fertile valleys, rolling green hills and immense stone circles said to have been placed there by the giants who once roamed our lands. The Dobunni were at peace with our tribe at that time, but the farmer who welcomed us into his roundhouse that evening did so with uneasy glances at my bodyguards, and when he smiled at us there was no warmth in his eyes. Later that night, he sat in grim-faced silence beside the fire, watching me warily as I mopped up the dregs of my stew with a hunk of bread. In one corner of the hut, his fat wife rocked a wailing infant on her knee.

'Something troubles you?' Bladocus asked, noticing my puzzled expression.

'The farmer. He doesn't seem to like us,' I replied quietly.

'Of course not. You're Catuvellaunian.'

I frowned. 'What has that got to do with anything?'

'Your tribe is not popular in these parts. The people fear your father's warriors.'

'But we are friends of the Dobunni,' I said. 'We wish them no harm. Tell him that, Master.'

Bladocus muttered something to the man in the local dialect. Although our tribes shared a common Celtic language, there was a bewildering number of regional accents and dialects, and I found this particular tongue almost unintelligible.

The farmer grunted and shook his head, then responded in the same guttural-sounding tongue. Both men chuckled heartily.

'What did he say?' I asked.

'He thanks you for your kind words, prince. But he says the friends of the Catuvellaunians have a strange habit of becoming slaves, or worse.'

'He's lucky we're on friendly terms,' Epaticcus said. 'Otherwise, I'd gut the ungrateful bastard.'

'Rather proves his point, wouldn't you say?' Bladocus said drily.

Epaticcus wiped his greasy fingers on his tunic. 'Typical bloody Dobunnians. Always mouthing off about how we sell our souls to traders from Gaul, but they're happy enough to buy the foreign wines and trinkets that pass through our trading posts.'

'A trade that profits both sides considerably, I believe.'

Epaticcus tilted his head at the Druid. 'Whose side are you on?'

'None. I answer only to the greater needs of our people.'

'You're an adviser to the king. You'd do well to remember that.'

'Loyalty is not the same as blindness.'

My uncle scoffed at that and helped himself to another cup of warm beer. I looked inquisitively at Bladocus. 'How many tongues can you speak, Master?'

'I'm fluent in all the dialects of these isles. I can speak some Greek and Latin, too.'

'Latin? Where did you learn that?'

'In Gaul. My grandfather taught me. He was a Druid, too. One of the senior men in our tribe, the Carnutes. He had the foresight to realise that Rome would one day come to our lands and we needed to learn the language of our enemies.'

I frowned. 'I thought the Romans wiped out the Druids in Gaul.'

Bladocus gave a bitter laugh. 'The legions tried, child. My grandfather and several other Druids lived in the caves, deep in a forest. They continued to practise their beliefs there, passing their sacred knowledge on to the younger generation, including me. But each year, it became more dangerous to cling to the old ways. When our tribe rose up against our foreign masters, the soldiers put many of our men to the sword, including my father. My grandfather and I fled to Britannia.'

'Don't you want to return home, Master?'

'Return to what? All that I knew had been destroyed by Rome. My grandfather passed on to the Otherworld a few years after we arrived here. My family were dead. Gaul is nothing but a land of defeated people these days. This place is my home now.'

I fell silent for a few moments and stared at the flames. Something had been puzzling me ever since my father's announcement in the great hall. Now I decided to put the question to Bladocus.

'Why did you choose me?' I asked.

'Because you're a gifted student. As I explained to your father.'

I considered, then shook my head. 'Some of the other children were talented scholars as well. I wasn't the only one. There's got to be more to it than that.'

'Must there be?'

I considered. 'You're going to be away from my father's side for years. You wouldn't do that. Not unless there was a good reason.'

Bladocus shrugged. 'There is a reason for everything, child. In the way the wind whispers through the trees, in the merest ripple on the surface of the lake.'

'I'm not sure I follow, Master.'

The Druid sighed. 'Do you believe in fate?'

I thought a moment and nodded and he continued.

'The gods tell us prophecies. Warnings of things to come. But a prophecy is no more certain than the flight of a bird. The gods demand that we embrace the plans they have made for us. Do you see?'

I shook my head. 'The gods have a plan for me?'

'The gods have plans for all of us. The only question is whether you choose to accept.'

'I still don't understand,' I protested. 'What do you want with me?'

'When you are ready you will know,' Bladocus responded sharply. 'Now finish your supper. You will need your strength for the rest of the journey.'

We reached Gobannium five days later. It was a bleak, unremarkable place. The streets were strewn with stinking piles of rubbish and ordure, and a pall of smoke from the bloomeries hung in the air. We rested for the night at the quarters of the local chief, a dark-haired man who wore a permanent scowl. The following morning, at the first pale hint of dawn, our small party set off for the final stretch of our journey to Merladion.

The weather turned that day. The sky darkened with thick grey clouds, carrying the threat of rain, and a sharp wind whipped across the land as we continued west at a steady trot. After a while we forded a shallow river and walked our horses through a cultivated region of small farms and scattered flocks of sheep. In the distance, a range of mountains rose like dark fists out of the earth, their forbidding peaks wreathed in shreds of mist. The first hint of winter was in the air and I could feel the wind tugging at my cloak as Bladocus led our party deeper into the valley. As the morning wore on, the wind faded, the sun broke through a gap in the clouds, and we climbed a hillock covered with bracken and patches of gorse.

'How much further, Master?' I asked as we began the steep climb.

'Not far now, my child,' Bladocus replied.

'Let's bloody hope so,' Epaticcus muttered. He took a pull from his waterskin and wiped his lips. 'This sanctuary of yours is in the middle of nowhere.'

'Of course. The sanctuary is a place of seclusion and peace, where one may turn one's thoughts inward, free from the unpleasant distractions of the world beyond.'

'Sounds boring if you ask me.'

'Not at all. It is the centre of Druidic learning, a place of wonder and knowledge. Some of the most important questions of our faith are debated there.'

Epaticcus rolled his eyes. 'Speak for yourself. As long as there's a jug of warm beer and a hunk of roasted pork waiting for me, I'll be happy.'

A short time later we approached the crest of the hillock. Bladocus continued ahead of us until he reached a small clearing just beyond the treeline. Then he stopped and pointed to the secluded vale below.

'There,' he said, catching his breath. 'That's the place. Merladion.'

I gazed down, straining my eyes in the weak afternoon light. A narrow river valley stretched out before me, dotted with farms and woodland and hemmed in on both sides by the barren slopes of the mountains. In the centre of the vale, a sprawling settlement occupied the summit of a low hill enclosed behind a high earthen rampart and a palisade. Beyond the gateway I spotted the usual muddle of thatch and timber roundhouses, along with a larger, separate enclosure I took to be the chief's dwelling. Red kites flew lazily overhead, tracing imaginary patterns in the sky.

'Where's the sanctuary?' I asked.

Bladocus indicated a separate palisaded enclosure no more than a quarter of a mile beyond the hill, built on raised ground beside a river. A pair of guards stood in front of the entrance to the compound. Inside I descried a handful of stone roundhouses and a circle of gnarled oak trees. A winding track led from the compound to the main settlement.

'What's that place?' I pointed to a massive timber structure set in the middle of the Druids' sanctuary.

'That is the sacred shrine,' Bladocus explained. 'It is known in our faith as the Shrine of the Twelve Skulls. The shrine is protected by the Druids' most loyal bodyguards. Each warrior takes an oath to defend the place with their lives.'

'Must be important, for that lot to risk their necks guarding it,' Epaticcus observed.

Bladocus gave him a mirthless look. 'It is built on the most sacred soil in Siluria. It is said that this spot marks the entrance to the Otherworld. Once a year Lud sounds his war-horn, and all the souls of the warriors that have died since the last ceremony arrive to begin their journey to the afterlife. The Silurians make offerings at the shrine, whenever they win a great battle. Many priceless treasures are kept inside.'

'What if anyone tries to steal them?' I asked.

'They would not dare. They would suffer the severest punishment.'

'They're put to death?'

'Worse. Any thieves are flayed alive, their bodies impaled on stakes and left for the crows to feed on.'

I suppressed a shiver and followed Bladocus as he set off at a gentle trot down the hill. We crossed a shallow stream running along the valley floor and followed the track across the open ground for a mile or so until we reached the foot of the hill. Then we made our way up the slope towards the Silurian fortress, picking our way past the clumps of heather and blackthorn. As we neared the timber gateway a sentinel appeared on the rampart and bellowed an order. Bladocus threw up a hand, signalling for our party to stop. There was a brief pause before the gate groaned open, and then we entered the capital.

We were met a few paces beyond the gate by a trio of guards wrapped in furs. One of them stepped forward: a short, hairy-chested man with a thick beard. His two comrades watched us warily, their hands clasped around the shafts of their long thrusting spears, while the bearded man exchanged a few words with Bladocus in the rich, harmonious dialect beloved of the peoples in this part of our island. Although I couldn't understand what they were saying, I formed the distinct impression that the Silurians were afraid of the Druid.

Bladocus gestured to me and said something to the guard, drawing a look of surprise from the Silurian. He shrugged, glanced over his shoulder and barked at one of his comrades. The latter hurried back down the thoroughfare towards the larger enclosure. Several moments later, a tall figure in a black cloak emerged and marched briskly over to the gate. A small retinue followed the Silurian chief, a pair of Druids among them, with their distinctive dark robes and wild, unkempt hair. As they drew near, Bladocus swung round and dropped down from his horse, and the rest of our party swiftly dismounted. The chief greeted Bladocus, and they spoke for a while before the latter turned to us.

'This is Vortagus,' he said. 'Chief of Merladion. He welcomes you to his capital. He says it is a great honour that King Cunobelinus has entrusted his son to the care of his tribe.'

'Tell him I am most grateful,' I said.

Vortagus slanted his gaze towards me and grinned. He was tall and well-built, with long, greasy hair and a bristly moustache. His woollen cloak was spattered with mud, I noticed, and his crooked teeth reminded me of the ruined stone circles I had seen a few days before.

'So, you're the Catuvellaunian prince,' he said in a thick accent I struggled to comprehend. 'Little on the young side, aren't you?'

'Vortagus trained as an initiate for a while, before he became chief of this place,' Bladocus put in. 'He spent some time at one of our sacred groves to the east, in your father's kingdom.'

'You know our lands well, then?' I asked.

'Well enough,' Vortagus replied. 'I've travelled through Verlamion and a few other places. But I wouldn't go back there, not for all the silver in Britannia.'

'Why not?'

'No hills. Country that way is as flat as a witch's tit. And the women! They drink more than the Brigantes.' He shuddered at the memory. 'No, give me the fresh mountain air any day of the month.'

'Bunch of bloody goat shaggers,' Epaticcus muttered.

Vortagus didn't appear to have heard the remark. He stared at me and stroked his chin, sizing me up like a farmer at a cattle market. 'I thought all you easterners were supposed to be big ugly bastards. Like him,' he added, pointing a thick finger at my uncle. 'You look like you'd fall over in a gentle breeze, boy.'

I felt my face burning with anger. 'I might be young, but I can fight as well as anyone.'

'Is that so?' The Silurian chief laughed again. 'Those are bold words. At least you sound like a true Catuvellaunian warrior, even if you don't look like one.'

'Which reminds me,' Epaticcus put in. 'The boy needs an instructor while he's here. Someone who can teach him to fight. I'm told you lot are in charge of training up the youngsters.'

'Of course.'

Vortagus barked an order, and a swarthy-looking warrior with greying hair stepped forward from his retinue.

'This is Mendax,' he said. 'The commander of my bodyguard. He's in charge of instructing the young initiates. Sword-trained from childhood. He knows how to whip any youth into shape. Even a lanky wretch such as yourself.'

He directed the last statement at me. Mendax looked me up and down with something approaching contempt. His hands were the size of pork knuckles and his breath reeked of stale beer. Two of the fingers on his left hand were missing, I noticed.

'Mendax is one of my finest warriors,' Vortagus went on. 'He has led my war-band to many great victories over our enemies.' He grinned. 'I'm afraid he doesn't care much for your tribe. But you won't find a better trainer in the whole of Siluria.'

The bodyguard stared at me for a long moment. Then he spat on the ground and muttered something to his comrades in the local dialect. A chorus of laughs erupted among the other warriors.

'What's so funny?' my uncle demanded.

Mendax smirked. 'I was just telling my comrades that the Trinovantes must have been ruled by women and children, if the Catuvellaunians were able to conquer them with such scrawny princes in their household.'

'That's rich, coming from a ponytailed Silurian prick.'

A dark look flashed across the bodyguard's face. 'At least I have hair. Better than suffering the humiliation of becoming as bald as a new-born babe.'

His fellow warriors roared with laughter. Epaticcus tensed his muscles, his nostrils flaring with rage.

'Think you're funny, do you? You won't be laughing so hard when I've kicked the bollocks out of you.'

'Quiet!' Bladocus snapped. 'That's enough!'

'Don't look at me. This idiot started it.'

'I don't care.' The Druid dropped his voice to an undertone. 'We are guests of this tribe, and you behave accordingly. Is that understood?'

He stared hard at my uncle, daring the latter to defy him. 'Fine,' Epaticcus replied grudgingly. 'Have it your way.'

'Good.' Bladocus nodded at the Silurian chief. 'We have travelled many miles today. The prince's bodyguard will need to rest and feed their horses. I trust you can provide them with shelter for the night, before they return east in the morning.'

'Of course. There's room in the guest quarters for your friends.' The chief cocked his chin at Epaticcus. 'You'll join us tonight in the hall for the feast? We have plenty of good Silurian ale to go around.'

'Beer?' My uncle's eyes lit up. 'Why didn't you say so?'

Vortagus tipped his head at his chief bodyguard. 'Mendax will show you to your lodgings,' he said to me. 'You'll be billeted with the other young scholars.'

'Are there many novices here?' I asked.

'A few.' Vortagus scratched his bristly jaw. 'We've had nine boys arrive for this year's group, including yourself. A few others may yet show up. Most of 'em are highborn princes. There are a few sons of lesser nobles as well. You'll get on fine with them, I'm sure. Assuming you don't change your mind about your place here.'

'What's that supposed to mean?'

He shrugged indifferently. 'Some of the initiates can't tolerate life at Merladion. You wouldn't be the first to quit and head home at the first sign of hardship. Or the last.'

'I'm not afraid of hard work.'

'They all say that.' He smiled mockingly. 'Any questions, boy?'

'When do I begin my training?'

'Tomorrow morning. The Druids will take you and the other new students down to the sanctuary at first light. Once you've finished your studies, you'll return here in the afternoon to practise your fighting skills. Then we'll see what you're really made of.'

He uttered a few words to his chief bodyguard, then wheeled

round and started back up the path to his private enclosure. Epaticcus followed him closely behind with the rest of the royal escort, smacking his lips at the prospect of helping himself to a jug of ale. Mendax shouted an order, and the two other bodyguards hurried over and led our mounts over to the stables erected close to the main gateway. Then the chief bodyguard said something to Bladocus and motioned for me to follow him down the main thoroughfare. Bladocus turned to me and nodded slightly.

'Go with Mendax. He'll show you to your quarters.'

I frowned. 'Where are you going?'

He flapped a hand in the direction of the chief's hall. 'To talk with Vortagus and his associates. The chief will need to be properly compensated in return for providing for you while you're his guest. I'll see you later.'

'When?'

'At the feast. Now, run along. And Caratacus?'

'Yes, Master?'

'Try to get some rest before this evening's entertainment. You're going to need it. You've got a big day ahead of you tomorrow.'

CHAPTER SEVEN

Rome, AD 61

There was a stretch of silence in the study. I glanced up from my notebook and saw Caratacus leaning back in his chair, his calloused hands resting in his lap while his eyes gazed at a point on the honeycomb shelf behind me. The hour was late. Night had descended on our city, with all its attendant iniquities and horrors. The house was dark and quiet now, except for the faint trickle of water from a fountain in the overgrown rear garden. Further away, in the street outside, I could hear the drunken carousing of revellers at a nearby tavern. A dog barked; someone yelled at the beast to shut up. I waited for Caratacus to go on, but the old fellow seemed lost in his thoughts. I cleared my throat.

'That must have been terrifying for you,' I said in an attempt to break the spell and steer him back to the narrative. 'Being trained by the Druids, I mean.'

Caratacus snapped his gaze back to me. He tilted his head slightly and his brow crinkled into a frown. 'What makes you think that?'

I hesitated, anxious not to offend my host with some disparaging remark about his faith, however distasteful I found it personally. 'It's well known that the Druids indulge in some rather, ah, questionable practices. Any child training with that lot would likely be scared witless.'

'You are referring to our ritual of human sacrifice, I presume?'

'Among other things, yes.'

'Do you believe such tales?'

I glanced down at my notebook and considered. Like many of my fellow historians, I had read a little about the Druids over the years in various treatises and biographies. Most of it was sensational material, admittedly, with graphic reports of condemned criminals shot full of arrows or burned alive in giant wicker men, and dark-robed Druids in eerie oak groves, consulting their gods through the inspection of human viscera. All gruesome stuff, no doubt exaggerated somewhat by the authors to shock their delicate readers. But the volume of accounts suggested there was, at the very least, a kernel of truth to their lurid claims.

'I suppose I do, yes,' I said. 'I see no reason to doubt their veracity.'

Caratacus smiled sadly. 'You shouldn't believe everything you read.'

'You aren't claiming that the stories of human sacrifice are false, surely? Gods, you'd have an easier time convincing me of the literary merit of the emperor's poetry.'

He shook his head. 'The practice is true enough. But there is more to our religion than what is written in your books. Far more. You ought to know that better than anyone.'

'How do you mean?' I asked, frowning heavily.

The old king paused while he reached forward and poured himself another cup of beer. 'You're a historian. You know that scribes are not dispassionate observers of events. Every writer has an agenda . . . even you, Felicitus.'

I decided to ignore that comment. 'What does that have to do with the Druids?'

'You find our doctrine abhorrent, but that's because you've only heard one side of the tale, twisted to suit the political needs of your generals and emperors.' He leaned forward. 'Or do you really believe that our Druids are the monsters of popular imagination?'

'Perhaps not,' I replied. 'Maybe the Druids have been misunderstood by some, as you claim. But that doesn't change the fact that they oversee and conduct human sacrifices. That's monstrous enough. Some might say,' I added hastily.

'And what of the slaves and criminals you send to their deaths in the arena? Does that not strike you as an equally gruesome practice?'

'Actually, I find the spectacles quite sickening. Haven't been in years myself. Can't stand the sight of blood.'

Caratacus looked at me in surprise. 'Then you're a rare breed in this city. I've had the pleasure of attending the games a few times, if you can call it a pleasure to watch men get torn apart by wild beasts for the satisfaction of the mob. At least when our Druids sacrifice someone, there is great honour in being chosen by them to appease the fury of our gods. Yet you Romans kill for mere amusement and you dare to accuse us of barbarity.'

'Not everyone takes such a dim view of your religion,' I pointed out. 'It's fashionable to admire the Druids in certain circles these days, you know. Some of our philosophers speak openly in favour of their wisdom.'

The smile stretched across his weathered face. 'Yes, I've met a few such men. Humourless Stoics who think that our tribes existed in some sort of savage Arcadia, unsullied by the corrupting influences of civilisation.' He took a long gulp of beer. 'They should try living in a Silurian village for a month.'

'What were the Druids really like, then?' I enquired. 'You were there. Tell me what it was like to train with them.'

Caratacus shook his head. 'You're a Roman. You wouldn't understand.'

'I'd like to try.'

'Why? Why do you care what I think about the Druids? It's not going to change the opinions of your readers.' He laughed drily. 'There's more chance of Rome burning to the ground, I should think.'

'That's as maybe. But if I am to properly capture your voice, I need to know the truth. This is your tale, not mine. Telling me about the Druids will help me to understand your mindset.'

The King of the Britons looked away. 'I don't know. Perhaps it is easier if we don't dwell on my time at the sanctuary.'

'You promised to give me a full and honest account of your life,' I responded, surprising us both with the feeling in my voice. 'You spent many years with the Druids. It's an important part of your story, and it needs to be told in detail. The work simply won't be complete without it.'

I was acting out of pure selfishness in my appeal to Caratacus, naturally. I'm not ashamed to admit it. Why should I be? A writer is always hunting for literary gold. Gods know we spend enough time sifting through the dross in search of it. I felt certain that some fresh material on the Druids would be bound to stir up a little controversy. Druids are like sea monsters or Greek pornography, you see. They never go out of fashion. I'm not sure why our citizens are so fascinated by this distant and obscure religious order; I only knew that my biography would be much more likely to gain attention if it contained some appropriately gruesome scenes of human sacrifice and sacred groves. Even if I had to wait several years before it could be officially published.

Caratacus set down his drinking cup and exhaled wearily. The lines in his face seemed as deep and black as gorges in the flickering glow of the oil lamps. He had a peculiar faraway look in his eyes that reminded me of the destitute and crippled veterans one often sees on the streets around the Forum, begging for coins from passers-by.

'I had no idea,' he said at last, still looking at the wall, as if addressing the piles of scrolls stacked along the shelving. 'No idea of the scale of the task in front of me. The challenge was formidable.'

'At Merladion?' I asked.

Caratacus nodded slowly. 'I had to learn fast. It wasn't just about studying laws and tongues. I had to learn how to survive. It was tougher than anything I had expected.' His watery eyes met my gaze. 'There are things I saw that you wouldn't believe.'

'What things?'

He didn't answer the question directly. 'The Druids are nothing like the evil sorcerers you have read about, Roman. The truth is very different.'

'How?'

I gripped my stylus and eagerly waited for him to continue. But then Caratacus slumped back in his chair, overcome with fatigue. He looked up at me with heavily lidded eyes and called for his doorman. A few moments passed before I heard the dull patter of feet crossing the atrium as the slave approached. Caratacus levered himself up from his chair with considerable effort.

'It's late,' he said. 'We shall continue this discussion tomorrow. Davos will find a trusted linkboy. I'll have one of my household slaves accompany you home.'

I rose to my feet. 'Where shall I meet you?'

'Come back here tomorrow morning. At the third hour. Then I'll tell you about my time with the Druids.'

I left him there, alone in that dimly lit study with his scrolls and his thoughts. The doorman guided me back down the hallway and I waited in the decaying front garden while he sent a burly household slave outside to fetch a linkboy to light the way. As I sat listening to the clattering of the nightly delivery carts rolling through the streets, I thought about what Caratacus had said to me about the Druids. Clearly, something significant had happened to him during his time at the sanctuary. Something that had ultimately set him on the path to becoming a feared warlord, and the fiercest enemy Rome had encountered on that benighted island. But what?

Tomorrow, I told myself, I would find out the truth.

PART TWO

THE DRUIDS' LAIR

CHAPTER EIGHT

Rome, AD 61

In the morning I returned to the house of Caratacus at the appointed hour. It had rained heavily during the night and the sky remained grey and overcast, but even the vile weather couldn't dampen my mood, and as I made my way through the puddled streets I felt a keen stirring of excitement at the prospect of my next interview. My initial conversation with Caratacus had gone well, better than I had dared to hope. I had rushed home the previous evening to write up the notes I had taken, working feverishly at my desk by the wan glow of a bronze oil lamp. As I scribbled away, I felt surer than ever that I, Caius Placonius Felicitus, minor historian and scribe to the Roman aristocracy, had stumbled upon the project that would preserve my name for posterity.

Along with that of Caratacus, of course.

I had spent years recording the mainly dull lives of senators and knights. Now I finally had the opportunity to tell a worthier tale. The life of Caratacus, I was certain, would be read through the ages. I didn't dwell too long on the fact that the only sincere account of the invasion of Britannia would be the one told by an exiled barbarian. Quite what that says about our glorious empire, I'm not sure.

His home on the Aventine appeared even more decrepit in the harsh light of the day than it had done the night before. The surly doorman, Davos, admitted me with a disapproving grunt and as we passed through the inner courtyard I noticed a small boy and girl playing with a set of wooden toy figures while a woman stood nearby watching over them. I dipped my head in a greeting but she received me with a look so cold it belonged in a frigidarium.

'My lady, please allow me to introduce myself,' I said. 'My name is—'

'Yes, I know who you are. Felicitus something-or-other. You're that historian. The one my husband has been talking to. The Roman.'

She spoke in harsh, heavily accented Latin and it took me a moment to understand what she was saying. 'I'm sorry. You are?'

'Mardicca,' she replied flatly. 'His wife.'

I studied her closely. She was in her fifties, with fierce green eyes and long red hair streaked with grey. She was undeniably a Celt: she was dressed in the fashion of her backward culture, with a colourful tunic beneath a plaited cloak fastened with a brooch. The golden torc around her neck was decorated at both ends with a pair of serpents' heads. The wife of Caratacus looked nothing like a highborn Roman woman, but in her own way she had clearly once been quite beautiful.

'A pleasure, my lady,' I said.

'Yours, perhaps. It certainly isn't mine.'

I was so taken aback by the bluntness of her manner that for a moment I didn't know how to respond. 'F-forgive me,' I stuttered. 'Have I done something to offend you?'

'You're a Roman, aren't you? That's bad enough, where I come from.'

'Sorry?'

'Never mind.' She cocked her head. 'This is a terrible idea, you know. This biography of yours. No good will come of it.'

I knitted my brow in puzzlement. 'Caratacus is a great man. A true hero of his people. His story deserves to be told.'

'He's also my husband, the father of my children and the grandfather of these two.' She nodded at the children. 'Telling his story is going to bring us nothing but strife once your audience reads an account that flies in the face of the vainglorious falsehoods of the Roman version. You know it, and so do I. Don't pretend otherwise.'

I held up my hands in mock surrender. 'I have vowed to your husband not to publish a word until he is deceased. He made me swear to it. His story won't bring him any harm, my lady. I assure you.'

'And what about the rest of us? Have you thought about that?'

I admitted that I had not, and muttered something to the effect that the biography would make people aware of her husband's heroic deeds and perhaps go some way towards restoring his reputation after death, which could only help his family's cause. If I'm honest, I didn't really believe the argument myself.

'You give your fellow citizens too much credit,' Mardicca sniffed. 'Your emperor thinks we're nothing but barbarians, and the rest have an even lower opinion of us. What makes you think you can change their minds?'

'People are fickle. Opinions change.'

'Not when it comes to us Britons, they don't.' She nodded in the direction of the street beyond the perimeter wall. 'Ten years we've been living here, and still people hurl abuse at us. They call us all sorts: milk-drinkers, torc-wearing scum, and a lot more besides. It's been even worse since this business with Boudica. Hardly a day goes by without someone insulting my family in the street. Last month some idiots even scrawled graffiti on the front door telling us to go home. I won't repeat the other vile message they left for us.'

'I'm sorry to hear all that.'

Mardicca shook her head. 'I can deal with it. Lud knows, I've put up with far worse in my life. But the children have done nothing wrong. Why should they get punished?'

'I'm just trying to help, my lady.' I shuffled my feet awkwardly and searched for some grain of comfort I could offer her. 'Perhaps the book will bring attention to your family's plight. It might persuade the emperor to raise a modest pension for you and your children once Caratacus is no more.'

She laughed at that. 'You don't know Nero very well, do you? He'd sooner see us all rot.'

'Yes,' I admitted quietly. 'I suspect you're right.'

'Look,' Mardicca said, 'if you really want to help us, then leave my family alone. My husband has suffered enough at the hands of Rome. We all have. He should be dedicating himself to securing a future for his offspring, not sitting in his study wallowing in the past.'

'This is not just some idle biography, my lady. It's far more important than that. We're telling the truth about his life and the invasion. This is the story of how it really happened.' She laughed bitterly and I frowned. 'What's so amusing?'

'My husband said something similar to me last night. I couldn't persuade him to change his mind, and it seems you're just as stubborn. Clearly, I'm wasting my breath. Just promise me one thing.'

'Yes, my lady?'

'You're well connected, I hear. Friends in high places. Is that true?'

'I have a few acquaintances in the Senate, yes.'

She nodded. 'When the time comes, if my family should ever be in trouble, promise me you'll help us out. Don't abandon us.'

'Why would you be in danger?'

Mardicca made a face. 'This is Rome. I'm not stupid. I know the emperor dares not move against us as long as my husband is alive and well. He's a living demonstration of Roman benevolence, and far too valuable to your precious imperial prestige. But once he's gone, our family will be vulnerable. I want your word that you'll help if anything should happen to Caratacus.'

'But of course,' I replied sincerely. 'I swear to it.'

'I hope you are a man of your word.' She stepped to one side and folded her arms across her belted chest. 'Well, you'd better go and find him. He'll be waiting for you.'

'Where is he?'

'His study. Where he spends most of his time these days. Teaching one of his grandchildren.'

I bowed again and headed for the study, pausing beside the entrance. Caratacus was pacing the length of the room, his hands behind his back. A fair-haired boy no older than seven or eight years of age sat on one of the padded stools, reciting a few words in some ghastly foreign tongue. I cleared my throat noisily, they both stopped and glanced up, and then Caratacus placed a hand on the child's shoulder and smiled.

'That's it for today,' he said in Latin. 'Excellent work. Now run along and play with your little brother and sister, there's a good boy.'

'Yes, sire,' the boy replied.

He hurried past me and scurried off towards the front of the house. I watched him leave, then looked at Caratacus in surprise. 'What language was that? I've never heard it before.'

He smiled sadly. 'Catuvellaunian. Tongue of our kingdom,

although few people speak it now. The boy's a natural. Very advanced for his age.'

There was something tragic about this aged Briton clinging to his old values even after ten years of exile.

'My grandchildren are the descendants of a king,' he continued. 'They should learn to be proud of their ancestry. Whatever Rome might think of us.'

'What else do you teach them?'

'Some of our customs, the history of our tribes, the names of our gods. It helps to keep our traditions alive in some modest way.' He dropped his voice to a murmur. 'Not that my daughter-in-law agrees.'

'She doesn't approve of their education?'

He grunted. 'She thinks my grandchildren should learn to become more like their Roman betters. She tells me I should stop trying to teach them the old ways of our tribes.'

'She may have a point.' I spread my hands in front of me. 'This place is their home now.'

Caratacus glared at me, his voice trembling as he replied. 'We may be prisoners of your emperor, but my family will never consider this city as their home. Never.'

'But they can't go back to Britannia. You said so yourself. Who knows? They might even be conferred with Roman citizenship one of these days. If they married into a Roman family, or entered into military service—'

'Nero has already offered my children citizenship,' Caratacus interrupted. 'In return for publicly denouncing their barbaric origins and praising Rome's glorious civilisation. Even in exile, it seems your emperor is determined to shame me and my family.'

I could see that I had touched a raw nerve, so I stayed quiet while Caratacus eased himself down into his chair and gestured for me to take a seat. 'Now,' he began. 'Where were we?'

I sat down, rested my wax writing book on my lap and looked down at my notes. 'The Druids. You had told me how your father had sent you to train under them at their sanctuary in Siluria. You had just arrived at the Silurian capital, Merladion.'

'Ah. Yes. I remember.' Something gleamed in his eyes as he leaned across the desk and pointed a finger at me. 'The first thing you must realise is that the Roman idea of the Druids is completely wrong. The tales written about them are nothing more than crude caricatures. Do you know why?'

I shook my head.

'Because they're a threat,' he went on. 'The Druids are a powerful force, more so than any of our kings. Since my arrest, they have been the only group capable of uniting our tribes against the legions. Romans have a habit of making monsters out of the things they fear most.'

'But that's all in the past,' I countered. 'Their spiritual home on the isle of Mona was destroyed shortly before the Boudican revolt. Everyone heard the announcement in the Forum. General Suetonius Paulinus and his men overran the defenders and their Druid commanders and cut down their sacred groves. The cults are finished, they say.'

Caratacus smiled wryly. 'If you believe that, you're more foolish than you look. The Druids have other hiding places, ones your generals do not know about. They will continue to thrive in the shadows, as they have done in the past.'

'Maybe so, but they can't hide for ever. The emperor has vowed to suppress them once and for all.'

'A hollow threat. The Druids will not be so easily wiped out, no matter how many groves your soldiers burn to the ground. General Paulinus has made the same mistake as his predecessors. He thinks the Druids rule the tribes through ignorance and fear. If he had bothered to understand them, he'd realise the futility of his policy.'

'So what did you really think of them?' I asked.

Caratacus went quiet for a moment as he gazed out of the window at the crumbling ruins of the garden. Then he spoke again.

'The Druids were many things to our tribes,' he said. 'They practised the sacrifice of humans and animals to the gods, it is true, but they did much else besides.'

'Like what?'

'We knew them firstly as wise men. We were afraid of the Druids, yes, but we also respected them. They were prophets, arbiters, healers and scholars. They knew the secrets of the stars and the most distant histories of the Celts . . . they had even mastered the art of magic.'

'Magic?' I barely suppressed a laugh.

Caratacus narrowed his eyes. 'You don't believe me?'

'Oh, I'm sure your Druids knew a clever trick or two,' I replied. 'You can find plenty of Phoenician conjurers in the Forum with a similar talent for deception.'

The wily old Briton shook his head. 'The Druids are different. They have powers far beyond anything you can imagine. That is one of the first things I learned at their sanctuary. The first of many . . .'

CHAPTER NINE

Britannia, AD 18

My time at Merladion did not begin happily. Shortly after my arrival at the Silurian capital, I was taken to my lodgings in a compound housing the initiates. As the last rays of the setting sun sank behind the distant mountain peaks, Mendax, the commander of the chief's bodyguard, led me past the densely packed roundhouses and animal pens, until we reached the gateway at the front of the enclosure. We passed through the open gate and entered a wide space with several low huts arranged in a semicircle. A dozen older-looking novices sat nearby, dressed in plain brown tunics made from coarse wool. Their heads were closely shaven and the tattoo of a sickle adorned each boy's cheek. A few stopped to stare at me, but most of them appeared to be engrossed in their studies, reciting their lessons with their Druid masters.

Mendax led me over to one of the huts and stopped in front of the timber-framed entrance. From within I could hear the hubbub of excited voices.

'In here,' he growled.

I stepped through the opening and entered a gloomy interior faintly illuminated by the glow from several tallow candles set on a pair of oak tables. On the other side of the hut I spotted a number of bedrolls furnished with blankets. In the centre the dirt floor sloped towards a small hearth. A handful of wooden platters lay beside it, along with a set of clay drinking cups and a stave bucket filled with water. Several students sat on their beds, while three other boys sat around one of the tables playing a board game with carved wooden figurines.

'You'll sleep here,' Mendax explained in his singsong accent. He pointed to a bare space on the floor next to the bedrolls. 'This is your home in this place now. Tomorrow you meet the High Druid. You and the other novices. Then you'll train.'

I felt my heart sink as I glanced round. It was a long way from the comforts I had known back home in Camulodunum, but I was determined not to show my disappointment in front of the truculent Silurian.

'Where's my bedroll?' I asked. 'It's missing.'

'New scholars supply their own bedding. Rules of the sanctuary.'

'But I don't have any,' I said. 'You can't expect me to sleep on the floor like a dog, surely?'

Mendax shrugged. 'Not my problem.'

'Could I have something to eat, at least? I'm starving. I haven't had a morsel all day.'

'Later,' he replied. 'You eat tonight. In the hall. With the other scholars.'

'But that's hours away.'

'Tough.'

'I demand to speak to your chief. This is unacceptable.'

Mendax laughed. 'I don't think so. You're not in Camulodunum any more. You belong to us now, prince.'

'This isn't fair!'

Mendax didn't reply. Instead he turned and marched stiffly out of the hut. I sat down on the space on the floor I had been allocated and sighed heavily. As soon as he had disappeared from sight one of the boys sitting at the table rose to his feet and walked over to me.

'Take no notice of him,' the boy said cheerfully. 'Mendax treats all of us the same way. Thinks he's in charge of a military training camp instead of a load of Druid scholars.'

'I'm beginning to realise that.'

The other boy smiled a friendly greeting. 'I'm Sediacus, by the way. From the lands of the Dobunni. Pleased to meet you.'

I looked him up and down. Sediacus was a year or two older than me, I guessed. He was lean and gangly, with close-cropped fair hair and freckled cheeks. He spoke with a slight Dobunnian accent, no doubt softened by his noble upbringing. He was certainly easier to understand than the farmers I had encountered on my journey west.

'I hear that you're a prince?' he added.

I nodded. 'I'm Caratacus. Son of Cunobelinus.'

He stared at me with widened eyes. 'The High King of the Catuvellaunians and the Trinovantes? That's your father?'

'Yes,' I replied warily. 'You've heard of him?'

'Why, of course. Everyone has heard of your father. He's just about the most powerful ruler in the land. And the most feared, I should think.' He paused. 'First time away from home?'

I nodded. 'I've spent most of my life at Camulodunum. Never really left the place, except for a few summer trips to our cousin's estate in Verlamion. I didn't know it would be like this.'

He smiled sympathetically. 'It's hard at first, especially when you miss your family and friends. But it will get better. You'll see.'

'Have you been here long?'

'A year. I can still remember my first day here. Terrifying.' Sediacus pursed his lips. 'Although I'm sure it must be worse for you, my dear fellow. Being the son of Cunobelinus and all.'

I asked Sediacus what he meant, and he shrugged apologetically.

'Some of the other scholars come from tribes who have fought against your father in the past. They won't take kindly to your presence here.'

'Then their tribes should have put up a better fight against our war-bands,' I said. 'If anyone has a problem with my father, they can tell me to my face. I'll set them straight.'

'That would not be wise. Our less enlightened students are not exactly the debating types, if you know what I mean.'

I looked at him. 'And what about your people? Do you hate us?'

'We're no different to any other tribe in the land, I suppose. We're wary of your father. My uncle is afraid of him, or so I hear.'

I wrinkled my brow. 'Your uncle?'

'Antedius,' he said. 'Chief of our people. Perhaps you've heard of him. He's not as famous as your own king, obviously.'

I nodded. I knew a little of the Dobunnians and their history from my earlier lessons with Bladocus. I vaguely recalled that Antedius had taken over as ruler a few years before and had recently become a close ally of my father's. I also knew that our own people tended to look down on the Dobunnians, regarding our neighbours

86

as little more than a bunch of backward farmers and bog-dwelling simpletons entirely lacking in cultural sophistication or military accomplishments. I decided against mentioning any of this to Sediacus.

'What about you, my friend?' he asked. 'What's your story?'

'There isn't much to tell,' I said. 'My Druid master, Bladocus, told my father that I should continue my education here in the west. Father agreed. That's all.'

'And your father was happy to let you go? He didn't wish for you to stay at home and learn how to rule the kingdom instead?'

I shook my head. 'My older brother, Adminius, is my father's favourite. He'll inherit the throne of our tribe, not me.'

'What are you supposed to do, then?'

'I must find another role in life, Father says. Perhaps I'll take my vows and join our Druid cult.'

Sediacus clicked his tongue. 'If you say so. Though I rather doubt it would suit you.'

'Why do you say that?'

'You're Catuvellaunian. Everyone knows you're a warlike people. Fighting is in your blood. You wouldn't last long as a greybeard.'

'What's a greybeard?'

'It's what we call our Druid teachers,' Sediacus said. 'I've been taught by plenty of them since I've been here, and you don't strike me as the type to enter the order.'

His pointed remark irritated me, although I tried not to show it. 'And yourself? Do you want to join the Druids eventually?'

Sediacus laughed. 'Not a chance. I'll study here for as long as it takes to get admitted to the first ring, but then I'm off. I've no wish to spend the rest of my life bottled up in some remote grove, inspecting sheep livers in order to find out the will of the gods.'

'What would you do instead?'

'I don't know. Haven't given it any thought. Maybe I'll fight in one of my uncle's war-bands. All I know is, I'd rather be a warrior than a Druid any day of the month. All that celibacy and abstinence.' He visibly shuddered at the thought.

I decided to change the subject. 'What can you tell me about the High Druid?'

Sediacus considered for a moment. 'He's a hard taskmaster. But fair. You've got to watch yourself around him, though. He sees everything. He's a master of magic, too.'

'Says who?'

'Some of the Druids, for a start. They reckon he has the power to take on the form of any animal, bend the weather to his will and even make himself invisible to others.'

I looked at him sceptically. 'Do you really believe that?'

'The High Druid is chosen by the gods as their representative in this world. Who's to say what powers they might bestow on such a man?'

'My brother says magic doesn't exist. Adminius reckons it's all an illusion.'

'He'd soon change his mind if he trained under the High Druid. Trust me, I've seen his powers with my own eyes.'

I blinked in surprise. 'You've seen him practise magic?'

'More than once. Anyway, you'll see for yourself soon enough. At tomorrow's initiation ceremony.'

I looked at him with raised eyebrows. 'What's that?'

'Didn't you know? All the new scholars are required to take an oath before the High Druid, on the first day of their lessons. The High Druid performs the initiation rites at the sanctuary in front of the other tutors and scholars.'

'What do I have to do?'

'Oh, nothing much. It's a formality, really. Lots of chanting and divining, followed by a bit of sacrifice. Then you'll get marked.'

'Marked?' I repeated.

Sediacus pointed to the tattoo on his cheek. 'All the initiates must shave their heads and accept the initiation mark before they are allowed to begin their training.'

I felt my guts squirm. 'Does it hurt?'

'It's not exactly pleasant. Once the Druids bring out the bone needles, you'll see what I mean.' He paused. 'But I'd be more worried about the training if I were you.'

'Is it really that tough?'

'Very. The hours of study are long, the combat training is sickening and the weather in these parts is generally terrible. And that's without having to worry about the bad food and the rats scavenging around the huts all the time. Half of the boys in my year have left this place for one reason or another, and I'm told hardly any scholars make it past the initiation to the second ring.'

'I see,' I said quietly. I was beginning to wish that the Druid had never decided to bring me to Merladion.

Sediacus saw my uneasy expression and looked me in the eye. 'Word to the wise,' he said. 'Whatever you do, don't cross the High Druid. Stay out of trouble, do exactly as he says, keep your head down and you'll do all right.'

'I'll try to bear that in mind. Thanks.'

'Thank me another time.' He patted me on the back and waved a hand at the other scholars. 'Now, allow me to introduce you to some of the lads.'

A steady trickle of new scholars arrived at Merladion on the same day as me. Each new boy was shown into our hut and given a space on the dirt floor. A few introduced themselves to the older students, but most of them sat anxiously on the floor and stayed quiet. Later that evening one of the chief's attendants called us to the hall, and we left the enclosure and made our way down a trail for the feast in honour of our arrival. We swept through the entrance to the chief's enclosure and I followed Sediacus and the other novices into a high-roofed hall lit up by dozens of flickering torches fixed to brackets on the stone walls. Skulls of the slain enemies of the Silures decorated niches in the walls. Chief Vortagus, his tribal elders and warriors occupied the trestle tables nearest the dais, while a servant led our party over to a few tables in a separate corner of the cavernous space.

While the rest of the novices took their places I made my way over to the nearest bench and sat down next to Sediacus. The rich aroma of roasted meat wafted into the hall from the adjacent kitchen, and my belly growled at the prospect of finally tucking into a hearty meal after my long journey to Merladion. Just then an older scholar marched over to our bench and stood over me.

'You're in my place, I believe,' he said. 'Get up.'

I froze and looked up at the student. He was perhaps two or three years older than me and several inches taller, with greasy dark hair and a pockmarked face. Behind him, two more older novices stared at me with hostile expressions.

'Are you deaf?' the dark-haired student snapped. 'I'm talking to you, slug.'

The novices sitting opposite me hastily shuffled away to the far end of the bench without saying a word. Beside me, Sediacus stared down at the floor and said nothing.

'We sat here first,' I said. 'There's plenty of other free spaces.'

'I don't care. This is my seat. Move yourself, slug. You and your friend. This table is for the stags. Slugs sit with their own kind.'

He spoke in a smooth, highborn accent, but his voice was laced with the threat of violence. I was about to reply when I felt Sediacus clasping a hand around my bicep. 'Come on, Caratacus. Let's find another bench.'

'Caratacus?' The boy stepped closer to me, and something like recognition flashed behind his eyes. 'Why, you're the son of that wild dog, Cunobelinus.'

I took a sharp breath and replied icily, 'Don't you dare talk about my father that way.'

'I'll talk about him however I want, you little prick.' He frowned. 'How in Lud's name did you get chosen for this place? I've heard that Catuvellaunians are as stupid as the beasts they herd.'

'I'm not stupid,' I protested lamely.

'No?' He laughed. 'Could have fooled me. Your kind are scum. Uncultured boors. Thick as doorposts. Isn't that right, lads?'

His companions nodded and murmured their agreement. I said nothing as the dark-haired boy tilted his head and regarded me with a sly grin.

'You don't look much like a warrior prince to me. Skin and bone. I've seen scarier turds than you.'

'I am the son of a king,' I replied as firmly as I could manage. 'And you shall treat me accordingly.'

The boy let out an ugly laugh. 'You're the son of a shepherd with ideas far above his station. Now fuck off.'

The dark-haired boy took a step closer. He seemed to tower over me and I had to force myself to meet his menacing gaze.

'Move,' he said. 'Before I make you. Go on. Wriggle out my way, slug.'

'Don't argue with him,' Sediacus muttered under his breath. 'It's not worth it.'

The older boy smiled thinly. 'Listen to your friend, new boy. He's giving you some very shrewd advice.'

I clenched my teeth and shot him a final look. Then I stood up and started towards another table. Before I could move away the dark-haired boy intercepted me, a threatening glare in his eyes.

'You should watch yourself. You might be the son of a king, but around here you're just another slug. There's no royal bodyguard to protect you here.' He grinned. 'Now piss off out of my sight.'

I shuffled away with Sediacus and we found a couple of spaces at a nearby table with some of the younger scholars. As we sat down I looked across and saw the older-looking boy and his friends chuckling as they chewed on chunks of bread.

'Don't take it personally,' Sediacus said. 'Eboricus is a bully. I'm afraid he picks on all the slugs.'

'Slugs?'

Sediacus smiled apologetically. 'It's what we call the new arrivals. Eboricus has made it something of a habit to pick on them each year. Although he has a particular dislike of the Catuvellaunians for some reason.'

'Who is he?'

'Eboricus? No one terribly important. The nephew of Verica, the new king of the Atrebates. One of many nephews, I'm told. Twelfth in line to the throne or some such. A rather coarse and unpleasant fellow, as you can probably tell. I'm still amazed he was allowed to study here. But then I suppose even the Druids make mistakes. Most of the other students are terrified of him.'

'Why don't they say anything to the Druids?'

'They're too afraid. If they spilled their guts to their mentors, Eboricus and his comrades would find out and rough them up.'

I shook my head angrily. 'Someone should do something about him and his friends. They shouldn't be allowed to treat us like that.'

Sediacus made a helpless gesture. 'Eboricus is one of the stags.' He saw the blank look on my face and rolled his eyes. 'The senior novices.'

'So?'

'The stags enjoy certain privileges over us. And from what I hear, Verica has made some very generous donations to the lodge recently. The High Druid wouldn't want to upset him by punishing his nephew too harshly.'

'So what? We're supposed to walk around in fear of him?'

Sediacus shrugged. 'That's just how it is. There's nothing we can do about it.' He glanced round and lowered his voice. 'You seem like a nice fellow, so listen carefully. Steer clear of Eboricus from now on. Don't aggravate him.'

'How am I supposed to do that?'

'Keep your head down and don't go looking for trouble. Trust me, you'll have enough problems here without making any enemies.'

As he spoke the servants brought out the roasted pigs, followed by several mouth-watering platters of cheese and bread, and I licked my lips in anticipation as they began serving the food to the higher-ups at the other tables first. The chief and his coterie of advisers helped themselves to the choicest portions, heaping their plates with cuts of steaming hot meat and hunks of fine bread. Once they had taken their helpings the servants carried the remnants of the feast over to our corner of the hall so that Eboricus and the older novices could pick over the lesser cuts. Only then did they bring the platters to our table. I handed my plate to one of the servants and watched in despair as he dumped a few scraps of gristle and bone on my plate.

'What's this?' I asked.

'What d'you think it is? That's your supper. Enjoy.'

I stared at the miserable morsels of toughened meat and fat. My bread was speckled with mould, I noticed. 'But there's hardly any meat here. How am I supposed to live on this?'

'That's all you get, boy. Scraps for slugs. You don't like it, don't eat it.'

I turned to Sediacus and saw him chewing furiously, his brow furrowed in concentration as his teeth worked on a strip of meat. Across the hall, Eboricus and the senior initiates laughed at a joke as they feasted on their tender hunks, meat juices running down their chins.

'Something wrong?' Sediacus asked through a mouthful of food.

'This food. I can't eat this. We throw these cuts out to the dogs at home.'

'It's not so bad. You'll get used to it. You'll see.'

I picked up a small chunk of meat from my plate, eyed it suspiciously, and nibbled on it. The roasted flesh was tasteless, and as tough and dry as old leather. I managed another bite and washed it down with a gulp of water.

'You, er, going to eat that?' Sediacus asked, nodding at the chunk of gristle on my plate.

I shook my head. 'Help yourself.'

Sediacus reached over and grabbed the stringy fat, a hungry look in his eyes. Just then Vortagus levered himself up from his throne. The guests stopped tearing at their food and listened obediently as the chief prepared to make a short speech.

'There are some new faces here tonight,' he began, raising his drinking horn in our direction. 'To them, I say welcome. I imagine you are missing your homes. Some of you will be anxious about what lies ahead, no doubt. So you should be. Your childhood is over now. You will endure hardship and hunger. Only those who are strong of heart, tough and quick thinking will see their training through to the end. As for the rest? They will be sent home in shame if they fail to meet the standard required by the Druids.'

Vortagus paused, and I was sure he was staring directly at me as he went on.

'Be certain of this, children. Many are brought here. Almost all fail. Those that endure are the chosen men of the gods. I wish each of you the best of luck. You are going to need it if you are to survive for long. And now . . . enjoy the rest of your meal.'

He sat down again and gestured to one of his slaves. A pair of bards on the gallery above the dais began reciting a long-winded verse poem celebrating the generosity and heroic deeds of Vortagus, while I picked at the pitiful scraps that remained of the feast.

Conversation with the other new initiates was difficult. There were eleven of us in total: the finest young scholars drawn from the many tribes of our land. A few of them were clearly afraid of my father's reputation and asked if it was really true that he stood as tall as a giant and walked around with the severed heads of his enemies hanging around his neck. The others seemed wary or downright hostile towards me, and I was quietly relieved when we were ordered back to our huts at the end of the feast.

As I lay on the cold bare floor that night, in a room full of strangers, I felt an overwhelming sense of homesickness. I missed my family and friends dearly, and to make matters worse I had to worry about avoiding Eboricus and his friends. I endlessly replayed the incident in the hall in my head, wishing I had responded in some other way. Now I would have to watch my back in case he tried to target me again. I tossed and turned for hours until I eventually slipped into a troubled sleep.

CHAPTER TEN

I t was still dark when we were awoken by the shouts of Mendax and the other guards before the following dawn. I stumbled out of bed and rubbed my eyes as a guard thrust a plain brown tunic at me.

'What's this?' I asked groggily.

'Your clothes, new boy. All novices wear the same. Rules of the sanctuary. Now, get dressed.'

I hurriedly put on the tunic and laced my leather boots while a man brought us a wicker basket filled with leavened bread and a pitcher of fresh drinking water. We ate standing around the tables; a short time later I trudged out of the enclosure with the other initiates in the murky grey light of pre-dawn and followed the guards down the trail towards the gateway at the far end of the capital. Bladocus and the other Druid masters stood waiting beside the gate, their black robes rippling in the strengthening breeze. I glanced back over my shoulder, straining my eyes as I searched the chief's enclosure for any sign of my uncle Epaticcus, but at this hour the area was deserted.

Bladocus greeted me with a stern expression. 'Is something the matter?'

'My uncle,' I said. 'I wish to bid him farewell, Master. Before he heads back east with the bodyguard.'

The grey-bearded Druid shook his head firmly. 'There is no time. We must leave for the sanctuary. The High Druid is waiting to see you all.'

'But I promised him, Master. I gave Epaticcus my word.'

'Forget your uncle. You belong to us now,' Bladocus snapped coldly. 'Your old life in Camulodunum is over. Understood?'

I lowered my head. 'Yes, Master,' I muttered.

95

At a command from Mendax the guards on duty opened the gate, and our group started down the wooded hill towards the sanctuary. The first faint rays of light glimmered behind the mountain peaks as we descended towards a patch of gloomy forest. We followed the rough track through the tangled undergrowth, crossed a narrow timber bridge over a stretch of rapids where spray burst over glistening rocks, and a short time later we emerged from the treeline. Ahead of us I saw the Druids' enclosure, situated on a spur of land above a gentle river. A pair of guards stiffened to attention at our approach, a shout went up, and the gate swung open. Then I followed the other novices and our mentors into the stockaded compound.

We entered a wide space with a pathway flanked by crude columns of stone inscribed with lines of runes. At the far end of the avenue was the Druids' sacred shrine: a timber-roofed structure with an oak-framed entrance surmounted by the biggest pair of antlers I had ever seen. Then I lifted my gaze and stopped dead in my tracks. A dozen human skulls had been placed in niches along the length of the wooden lintel above the doorway. Beyond the entrance I glimpsed a vast pile of bent swords, gleaming bronze shields and helmets arranged in a shallow pit in the middle of the paved floor, reflecting the light from several bracketed torches.

To the right of the building there was a separate ditched enclosure with a series of deep pits filled with what appeared to be animal skulls, along with a smaller animal pen. On the far side of the sanctuary a set of steps led up to a platform with a large dais ringed by several jagged stone columns. At the end of the dais there was a giant limestone altar. Gnarled oak trees surrounded the platform, their ancient boughs creaking and groaning in the stiff breeze that moaned across the hilltop.

'What do you think, child?' Bladocus whispered.

I gazed up at the huge shrine and felt a sense of awe. 'I've never seen anything like it.'

He grinned. 'I told you this was a special place.'

'Who lives there?' I asked, pointing to a small group of roundhouses set close to the main gate.

'The High Druid and his most senior companions,' Bladocus explained. 'All men of the fifth ring. Only those who attain the highest standard of training are permitted to live among the spirits of the Otherworld.'

'How long does it take to reach the fifth ring?'

'Many years,' said Bladocus. 'Some men spend their entire lives trying to attain such a level of wisdom.'

As he spoke a group of dark-robed figures emerged from one of the huts and walked over to us. One of them, a shrivelled man gripping a long stave with a small sickle fitted to the end, muttered a few words to Bladocus and the other mentors.

'Welcome to the sanctuary of the Twelve Skulls, children,' he said, turning to address the new arrivals. 'My name is Segorix. I am one of the senior Druids here. Follow me, please.'

He wheeled round and led our group across the pathway and up the stone steps to the elevated platform. We stopped in front of the dais, and then the older boys and their masters spread out in a loose circle. Above them I saw the dark outlines of several crows in the trees, cawing as they stared down at our group.

Once everyone had taken up their positions, Segorix, the sickle-wielding Druid, raised his hands to the sky and began chanting in a tongue I didn't understand.

'What's happening?' I asked.

'The Druids are calling on the gods to witness the initiation ceremony,' Bladocus said. 'They must seek Lud's approval before the rites may be conducted.'

Segorix ceased his chanting and one of his companions stepped into the middle of the platform: a tall man in a flowing white robe, with a gold chain around his neck. In his right hand he clutched several iron rods, each one as long as an arrow shaft and engraved with a series of peculiar markings. The man bellowed an incantation before he cast the rods, and they scattered across the ground with a metallic clatter. The other scholars looked on as the white-robed Druid bent down to inspect the symbols.

'What is he doing?' I whispered to Bladocus. 'What are those sticks?'

'Divination rods,' Bladocus replied softly. 'Quiet, boy.'

There was a tense stillness as the Druid studied the markings. A moment later the man stood upright and made an announcement in the same strange dialect. Then several of the other Druids banged their staffs against the floor in unison.

'What did he say?' I asked.

'The seer says the omens are highly favourable. Lud has given his consent. The ceremony may proceed.'

'Now what?'

'Now, we wait.'

Some of the older novices muttered to one another in hushed voices. Segorix stamped the butt of his stave against the stone floor, calling for silence. An eerie quiet fell over the sanctuary. For a moment there was no sound except the faint breath of wind rustling the leaves of the surrounding oak trees.

'Where is he? Where's the High Druid?' I muttered, craning my neck.

'Quiet!' Bladocus hissed sharply.

In the next instant the wind faded to a whisper, then died off, and dark clouds began to gather overhead, pressing low in the sky. The silence was abruptly broken by a fluttering noise in the trees. One of the boys shouted and pointed a finger at the sky as a murder of crows took to the air and swirled overhead, croaking wildly. We gazed up at the spectacle, our attention momentarily diverted.

'Welcome, children,' a rasping voice called out from the altar.

We shifted our attention back across. A robed figure in an antlered headpiece stood in front of us, as if he had suddenly materialised from thin air. Despite his modest stature there was an intensity about the man. His eyes were deep set beneath thick eyebrows and gleamed like wet coals. Angular bones defined his face over which the creased skin looked grey. He raised a bony arm, and the audience promptly fell silent.

'My name is Lugracus,' he went on. 'High Druid of the Silurian tribes and keeper of the Shrine of the Twelve Skulls. From now on you will call me "High Master". Do you understand?'

'Yes, High Master,' we replied in unison.

The High Druid parted his lips into a smile. I saw that his incisors had been filed into sharpened points.

'Novices,' he went on in a harsh tone, 'your Druid mentors have brought you here to study for your initiation into the first ring of our order. That is a great honour. Each of you has been selected because of your intellectual promise, your desire for knowledge and your potential for reading the signs of our gods. Few are chosen. Far fewer succeed.

'Your past achievements count for nothing at Merladion. You will be required to work harder than you have ever done before. Each day, you will be pushed to the very limits of mental and physical endurance. There will be times when you feel you cannot go on any longer. But there is no place for weakness here. Strength and discipline are all. To succeed, you must learn to master your mind and body.

'There are three things I demand of any novice. Diligence, hard work and obedience. Follow these rules, and you may eventually become wise in the ways of the Druid cult. For those of you who are chosen to continue their training beyond the first ring, you will learn the secrets of prophecy and even magic. But it will take many years of study to attain such powers. Very few of our novitiates ever make it that far . . . Very few.'

Lugracus paused again, making sure he had our full attention before he carried on.

'You will report here each day at the first hour with your mentors. From then until the noon-hour you will attend lessons with your tutors. At the end of each month you shall be examined on a particular subject in front of your fellows. Those of you who do not meet the required standard will be sent away.'

He pointed at our personal mentors: the Druids who had individually accompanied us to Merladion.

'Your Druid masters will oversee your training. They are your guides on this journey, and it is essential that you heed their teachings and follow their commands at all times. Understood?'

'Yes, High Master,' we replied.

'Excellent.' Lugracus nodded and pressed his hands together. 'There is a code we live by. Each of you will strictly adhere to this code or face the harshest punishment for disobedience. Our order does not tolerate theft, drunkenness or consorting with women. This sanctuary frowns upon the tradition of duelling. It is forbidden for a novice to demand satisfaction except in certain instances touching upon personal honour. Besides your studies here, the chief's bodyguards will train you in the use of weapons. You shall obey your trainers as you obey your mentors; I will personally discipline any students who neglect their military instruction.' He raised a hand and pointed at each of us in turn. 'Does any of you wish to ask a question?'

I glanced round at the other novices but no one said a word.

'Then we proceed with the initiation rites.'

The High Druid turned to his comrades and signalled to a man holding a sickle. The latter shouted an order, and a gap opened up in the circle as a pair of Druids climbed the steps, leading a bleating white goat by a rope tied around its neck. Behind them walked another Druid bearing a large bowl. He stopped at the edge of the platform and waited while his two comrades led the goat towards the stone altar.

'Lud requires an offering,' Bladocus explained to me. 'To accept the new initiates and to ask the gods to guide you favourably in your studies.'

The two Druids untied the rope from around the goat's neck and hoisted it up onto the altar. At the same time the High Druid produced a small dagger from beneath the folds of his flowing robes. He approached the altar and held up the dagger to the sky, and the tip glinted beneath the rising sun as he chanted a phrase in a tongue I had not heard before. The other two Druids fought with the goat, pinning the struggling animal on its side. Then the High Druid lowered the gleaming blade to the goat and slashed open its throat in a brutal cutting motion.

The animal made a hideous noise, spasming wildly as a pained gurgle escaped its gashed windpipe. The Druid with the clay bowl hastened over and knelt down beside the altar, filling the vessel with the dark blood spurting out of the beast's neck. After a brief struggle the goat stopped writhing and its head flopped lifelessly back. The High Druid raised his bloodstained hands to the sky and bellowed at the top of his voice.

'Lud, Lord of the Otherworld! Accept this humble gift from your servants! Protect these boys and guide them as they begin their journey to the inner rings of the Druid cult!'

He lowered his hands, stepped back from the altar and wiped the dagger blade against his blood-splattered robes. A moment later an attendant walked over to our group holding several wreaths of mistletoe. A second attendant followed close behind clutching a large drinking cup. The latter approached the altar. He set the cup down and poured the goat's blood into the drinking vessel, filling it to the brim, and sprinkled some dried herbs and grasses on top. Then he brought the cup over and offered it to me.

'Drink,' Bladocus whispered.

I looked down at the contents and wrinkled my nose in disgust. 'Do I have to, Master?'

'You must, child. It will protect you from evil spirits.'

I reached out and accepted the cup, fighting the urge to retch.

'Do not spit it out,' Bladocus warned. 'Otherwise the High Druid will take it as a sign that your soul is corrupted.'

I drew in a breath and pressed the cup to my lips, forcing down the warm goat's blood. Then I handed the cup back to the attendant, trying to ignore the rancid taste in my mouth. He moved further along the line of initiates, forcing each one to imbibe in turn. When he had finished, his comrade crowned each of us with a mistletoe wreath; then the High Druid beckoned us forward. We stood nervously before him as he took the blood-filled bowl from the man standing nearby and dipped his finger into the dark liquid. He dabbed each of our foreheads with blood, muttering an incantation under his breath. He set the bowl down on the altar beside the slaughtered beast and pressed his hands together.

'Now, children, repeat after me,' he said. 'I swear before the gods of the Otherworld and their servants . . .'

He paused while we repeated the words slowly. I will not say the words of the rest of the oath. It is a secret known only to the Druids and those they train. To repeat the oath is to invite eternal torment at the hands of the gods. Suffice to say the oath ends with the words:

'I vow never to set down in writing any of the wisdom imparted to me by my tutors, and I shall guard the secret mysteries of the order with my life . . .'

Once we had finished reciting the oath, the High Druid nodded at us.

'It is done,' he announced. 'Lud has borne witness. The oath has been taken, the sacred rites have been performed. Each of you now belongs to the Druids, body and soul, from this day until you depart our sanctuary. And now your training can begin.'

As soon as the initiation ceremony had finished we left the altar and made our way back down the steps to the space in front of the shrine. The older students made off to begin their daily instruction with their respective tutors, while I followed the other young novices as Lugracus and Segorix led us towards a separate corner of the sanctuary. A few moments later three Druids marched over, one of them clutching a wooden tray with a set of sharpened bone needles, bronze razors and shears, and a small clay pot filled with pigment. The Druids called us forward in turn, shaved our hair and then pricked the skin on our cheeks with the bone needle, marking each of us in the same way. Once we had all received our tattoos, we gathered around a gaunt-faced Druid and spent the rest of the morning memorising the basic tenets of the cult before we paired off with our individual mentors to better understand the tribal dialects. As the sun reached its zenith the High Druid announced that our instruction had ended for the day, and we made the short journey back up the hill to the capital to begin our weapon training.

A couple of Silurian guards stood waiting for us at the gate. They greeted us wordlessly and led us across the settlement to a large training area situated next to the chief's hut. While the older students immediately began hacking away at a row of timber training posts under the stern gaze of their trainers, Mendax ordered the new arrivals to form up in front of a bare patch of dirt. The maimed warrior folded his hairy arms across his chest and prepared to speak. Bladocus stood close by with the rest of the Druid masters, observing the lesson keenly.

'Now, then,' Mendax began in his hoarse tone of voice. 'How many of you have trained with a sword before? Or a training weapon?'

Most of us thrust our arms into the air. A few did not. Mendax spread his lips into a lopsided grin.

'Perfect. Well, you can forget whatever nonsense you've been taught in the past. From now on, you're going to learn how to fight like true warriors. Like Silurians!'

His voice echoed across the barren training ground. I glanced sidelong at my companions and saw them staring at Mendax with a mixture of curiosity and apprehension.

'As you know,' the bodyguard went on, 'we are a mountain people. We're also the toughest tribe in the land. Unlike most, we have never been conquered by outsiders. Do any of you know how we've managed it?'

The question was met with silence. Mendax glared at us, waiting for a reply. When none came, he swept an arm in the direction of the mist-wreathed mountains that towered over both sides of the vale.

'Look around you,' he growled. 'See them bloody great big hills? That's how we repel the invaders. Not by charging at the enemy pell-mell in an open field like a load of idiots. We win by using the landscape to our advantage.'

My ears pricked at that. I waited for Mendax to go on.

'Out here we don't fight our enemies in big battles, hacking at each other with sword and spear,' he said. 'Here, we fight with stealth and guile. We use the natural cover of the hills and forests to take the enemy by surprise, at a time and place of our choosing. We hit them hard, gut the bastards and then melt away again before the other side knows what's hit 'em. That's how we have defeated our foes for centuries, even when they've had the advantage of numbers.'

I listened with fascination. The type of combat Mendax was describing was completely foreign to the warriors of my own people. I had been raised to believe that individual fighting tactics and single combat were the best ways of triumphing on the battlefield, with each warrior measuring his skill and bravery in close quarters against a worthy opponent. Such an approach emphasised prestige and personal glory above all things. But Mendax was suggesting something very different.

'Each of you will be trained in our fighting style during your time here,' he continued. 'That means learning everything there is to know about ambushes, raids and concealment. Over the next few years you will become proficient in climbing, marching long distances over some of the toughest terrain in the land, using swords, spears, slings, bows and all aspects of our warfare. By the end of your stay at Merladion, you'll be as capable as any of our fine warriors.' He paused and nodded at me. 'Even you, prince weakling.'

Around me, a few of the children broke into laughter. Mendax waited until they had fallen silent before he spoke again.

'Any questions?'

I thrust my arm into the air. 'Where are our training swords, Master?'

Mendax shook his head. 'No weapons. We won't be using 'em yet. Not for a few months, at least.'

A low chorus of groans echoed across the training ground. 'But most of us have used weapons before,' I countered.

Mendax strutted over to me. 'Are you questioning my judgement, son?' he said, jabbing a meaty finger at me. 'Think you know better than me, do you?'

'No, Master.'

'Perhaps you'd like to take over the training session? Show us all how it's done, eh?'

'No, Master.'

'I should fucking hope not. I don't care what you did with those shepherds in your tribe. You're in Merladion now, and you'll do exactly as I say, when I say. If I tell you no weapons, then you'll bloody well accept it. Is that clear?'

'Yes, Master.'

'Right then. Are you going to let me get on with my lesson, son? No other clever questions?'

'No, Master.'

He stepped back and turned to address the rest of the group.

'As I was saying. Before you learn how to fight, each of you must learn to move like a Silurian warrior. There's no point ambushing the enemy if you're too weary to hold a sword properly when you get to the fight.'

He pointed towards the patch of dirt behind him. A rough track ran around the perimeter of the training ground, while the more experienced novices practised at their wooden posts to one side.

'We'll start off with something nice and easy. Twenty laps of the training ground.' His lips stretched into a sadistic grin. 'Whoever finishes last will spend the next week cleaning up the lodgings. Get moving!'

★ ★ ★

Mendax pushed us hard during the rest of the afternoon. After we had completed the laps of the training ground the Silurian marched us through the gates of the capital and forced us to run repeatedly up and down one of the surrounding hills, with each novice carrying a woven sack weighed down with rocks. It was backbreaking work, harder than anything I'd endured back home in Camulodunum, and by the time we had finished, every muscle in my body ached appallingly. An hour later, as the sky faded into dusk, I followed the other exhausted trainees back down the trail towards our enclosure. While the rest of the initiates took the opportunity to rest until supper, joking with one another or playing their favourite games, I fashioned some makeshift bedding out of a few twigs and the bracken I'd carried back with me from the hill.

'How was your training with Mendax?' Sediacus asked as he wandered over.

'Tough,' I muttered, grimacing at the throbbing pain in my legs. 'Is it like this every day?'

Sediacus laughed. 'Oh, it gets worse, my friend. Much worse. Trust me, Mendax is as hard as they come. Some of his sessions are so brutal you'll be throwing up at the end.'

'Wonderful. Something else to look forward to.'

'I did warn you.'

'I know,' I replied quietly.

He saw the despondent look on my face and slapped me on the back. 'Cheer up. It's not so bad here.'

'Isn't it?' I asked miserably as I regarded my crude bed of sticks. 'I don't have a decent place to sleep. The training is physically exhausting, Mendax is a bully. And as for the food . . .' I shook my head. 'The foul scraps they feed us at supper aren't fit for slaves.'

'The food's all right, once you get a taste for it. And things will get better. You'll see,' Sediacus said. 'I'm a second-year Druid initiate. I've been trained in the powers of divination, you know.'

'Really?'

'Oh yes. In matter of fact, right now, I'm divining that you are about to sneak into the kitchen in the great hall and steal some of the chief's best mead for us to share.'

'I can't do that!'

'You must, child.' Sediacus adopted the slow, harsh voice of the High Druid and pointed a crooked finger at me. 'It is foretold!'

He looked at me seriously for a moment, then erupted into a fit of laughter, and I laughed along with him before a sudden silence fell over the hut. I glanced up at the entrance just in time to see Eboricus swagger through the opening, accompanied by the two other boys I had seen at the feast the previous night. One of them was a short, stocky youth with a pinkish scar above his upper lip. The other boy stood at least a head taller than Eboricus. He had short red hair and his lips were as thin as a knife blade.

'Shit,' Sediacus muttered.

'What does he want now?' I asked.

'The same thing the stags always want,' Sediacus muttered disconsolately. 'To make our lives miserable.'

The younger novices sat very quiet and still as Eboricus swept his eyes across the interior of the hut. His gaze settled on me and an ugly smirk spread across his lips as he marched over. His two friends lingered beside the entrance, glowering at me.

'Well, well, Sediacus,' Eboricus said. 'Making friends, are we? With the village idiot, no less. What were you two laughing about?'

I stood up and looked levelly at him. 'Mind your own business.'

Eboricus stared at me in mock horror. 'Is that how you talk to your betters? Here I am, a senior novitiate and the son of a respected Atrebatan noble, and you're addressing me as if I'm some worthless farmhand.' He tut-tutted. 'What manners are they teaching the sons of the nobility in Camulodunum these days, I wonder?'

'Leave him, Eboricus,' Sediacus cut in. 'He's new. He doesn't mean any harm.'

'I'll be the judge of that, country boy. Not you. Or perhaps we'll bash your thick head in for a laugh.'

Sediacus said nothing. Eboricus slid his gaze back to me and the corners of his lips curled upwards as something caught his eye. He pointed to the golden ring on my left hand. The one given to me by my father as a sign of my royal lineage.

'That's a nice piece you've got there. Very nice indeed.' His grin widened. 'I'll be having that.'

I shook my head fiercely. 'No. It's a gift. From my father.'

'I don't care if it's from Lud himself. You'll hand it over, new boy. Consider it a form of compensation.'

'Compensation? What for?'

'Failing to treat your superiors with the proper respect when you're addressing them.' Eboricus extended his hand. 'Now give it to me, slug.'

'No,' I replied firmly.

'I'll make this very simple. Either you hand over that ring, or me and my friends will beat the shit out of you.' He jerked a thumb in the direction of his companions. 'Once we're finished, you'll be pissing blood for the next month.'

I clenched my fists and edged backwards. Eboricus cocked his head at his friends. 'Durrus, give us a hand. Vegorix, keep a lookout. Make sure no one disturbs us.'

The short, thickset boy hastened over while the taller youth guarded the entrance. Eboricus drew closer to me, bunching his hands into tight fists. 'You'll thank me for this, new boy. I'm about to give you a valuable lesson in respecting your elders.'

He lunged forward, dropping his shoulder as he shaped to deliver a powerful strike to my face. I read the move, remembering the lessons Epaticcus had taught me, and jerked to the right, sidestepping the blow before I slammed my fist into his ribs in the same ragged blur of movement. Eboricus was much bigger than me but even so the impact stunned him and he let out an enraged grunt as he swung again. This time I snapped my head back out of range before aiming a kick at his groin. Eboricus staggered backwards, groaning as he cupped his hands to his balls.

Before I could strike out at him again, Durrus sprang forward with a maddened yell. I spun round to face my new adversary, saw him throwing a punch at my cheek and instinctively put up my hands to protect my face. Then Durrus aimed low, and I gasped in pain as his knuckles smashed into the wall of my stomach, driving the air from my lungs. I doubled up and sank to my knees, gasping as Durrus dropped down beside me. Sediacus came rushing over to help me but the taller boy, Vegorix, moved forward and intercepted him, holding him back.

Durrus threw me down on my front, pinning me to the dirt floor with his knee. I fought wildly, kicking out as I tried to wriggle free, but I couldn't move with the weight of his heavyset frame pressing down on me. Eboricus stumbled over and knelt down beside me, still gasping for breath after the blow to his groin. He clamped a hand around my left wrist and began prising the ring free from my index finger.

'Get off me!' I cried.

'Shut up!' Eboricus hissed. 'Hold him down, Durrus!'

As he fought to yank the ring free, a familiar rasping voice abruptly split the air. 'That's enough!'

Eboricus and Durrus automatically froze. Their hands fell away from me at once, and I looked up at the entrance and saw Bladocus standing a few paces inside the hut, wearing a severe expression. He silently took in the scene in front of him, glancing at the other initiates in turn, before he directed his gaze at Eboricus.

'What's going on here?' he demanded.

Eboricus and Durrus both scrambled to their feet while I fought to catch my breath. 'Sorry, Master,' Eboricus said, bowing his head before the Druid. 'We were just play-fighting. Weren't we, lads?'

Durrus and Vegorix murmured their agreement.

'Really?' Bladocus arched a thin eyebrow. 'It doesn't seem very playful from where I'm standing.'

Eboricus patted me on the back. 'He's fine, Master. We just got a bit carried away. Ask any of the lads here, they'll tell you the same thing. Ask the boy if you don't believe us.'

Bladocus searched my face. 'Is that so, child?'

'Yes, Master.' I hated to lie to Bladocus, but I also knew that if I told him the truth about Eboricus and his friends, it would only make things worse. It would be my word against his, and the other boys would be sure to take his side. Moreover, I would be branded as a tell-tale, and such a reputation was unlikely to endear me to my fellow students.

'You're quite sure?' Bladocus asked.

I nodded. 'Me and Eboricus were wrestling for fun, and it got a bit out of hand.' I noticed Eboricus staring at me keenly as I spoke. 'It's my fault, really. No harm done.'

'I see.' Bladocus stood up straight and smoothed a fold in his robes. 'Well, get up. You need to come with me.'

'Now, Master?'

'Yes, now. On your feet, child. Come.'

He spun away from me and ducked out of the hut. I scraped myself off the floor and made for the entrance, but Eboricus moved quickly forward, blocking my path.

'I'll be seeing you around, boy,' he said in a low hiss. 'You might have got away today, but I'll find you again. Mark my words. And the next time, there won't be anyone to save you.'

He shifted out of my way but continued glowering at me as I hastened through the opening. Bladocus stood waiting for me beside the gate, his hands behind his back. He looked up at me as I approached, his brow heavily furrowed.

'What happened back there? Tell me.'

'Nothing, Master. Honestly. It's fine.'

The Druid stared at me for a moment longer. Then his face relaxed and he sighed. 'Well, let's go. You've wasted enough time fooling about for one afternoon.'

'Where are we going?' I asked.

'To the great hall. We have another lesson to cover before supper. We can find a quiet corner to study there.'

'But our training has finished for the day. Mendax said so.'

Bladocus spun round and shot me a dark glare. 'I am in charge of your training here. No one else. You answer to me and me alone. Your work finishes when I say so, and if I tell you that we must study further, you will obey me without question.'

'Why do I have to study while the others get to rest?'

'Because I said so. That is reason enough.' A cold smile crossed his scarred lips. 'It is not your place to question my authority. Or perhaps you would prefer to do another twenty laps of the training ground instead? Your choice.'

I started to protest, but then I caught sight of the icy look in the Druid's eyes and I pressed my lips shut again. It would be pointless to press my argument any further.

'No, Master,' I muttered.

'I thought not. Now come along. We've got to start your Latin instruction, and there's a lot of ground to cover before we're done for the day.'

'Latin?' I stopped mid-stride. 'Why the tongue of the Romans?'

Bladocus's smiled faded. 'Because one day they will be our enemy, and a wise man needs to know their ways before he can hope to defeat them.'

CHAPTER ELEVEN

The first few weeks at Merladion passed in a blur of pain and exhaustion. Each day began with the guards waking us at the first hint of dawn, followed by long hours of instruction at the sanctuary with our Druid mentors. In the afternoons Mendax took us on a series of long and brutal runs up and down the surrounding hills, carrying increasingly heavy loads on our backs. Once he judged that we had built up our strength and endurance, we progressed to weapon practice, training with wooden swords, lightweight throwing spears and bows in the fields outside Merladion. I had used a bow before at Camulodunum and I swiftly established myself as the most talented shot in our group, consistently hitting the centre of the target during our sessions. But my skills went unremarked by Mendax. If anything, it only seemed to increase his determination to mark me out for special treatment. By the time I reported to Bladocus for my extra tuition in the evening my entire body ached with fatigue. The workload was punishing, but the Druid showed no sympathy towards me and insisted on continuing my education until an hour before supper.

'Another hard day, my good fellow?' Sediacus asked as I slumped down on my makeshift bedroll. My back ached terribly after weeks of sleeping on a layer of sticks and ferns, and I'd asked Mendax if he might be able to provide me with a worn bedroll from the chief's supplies. I had even promised him that my father would reimburse him for the cost. But the Silurian had laughed and told me that if I complained again he'd make me sleep with the animals.

'Something like that,' I muttered. That evening Bladocus had tested me on my Latin. At the end of my examination the Druid had escorted me to the training ground and ordered me to run twelve laps, one for each incorrect answer I had given. By the time I had completed my punishment I could barely drag myself back to my lodgings.

Sediacus squatted down beside the wooden bucket next to the hearth. He filled a cup with fresh water from the communal butt and handed it to me. 'Here,' he said. 'Drink up. Looks like you need it.'

I took the cup and drank thirstily. 'Thanks,' I said.

Sediacus stared at me with a concerned expression on his face. 'That Druid master of yours has been pushing you hard again, hasn't he?'

'That's putting it mildly.'

'Any idea why he's so tough on you? None of the other novices are given such a hard time. It's almost as if he's picking on you deliberately. Him and Mendax both.'

'Bladocus reckons the extra training is for my own good. That's all he tells me.'

'Strange.' Sediacus stroked his jaw. 'Your mentor must have his reasons, I suppose. Perhaps he sees something in you.'

'Or maybe he wants to break me.'

'Do you really think so?'

'Sometimes I wonder why he bothered bringing me here at all,' I said gloomily. 'All he does is berate me and punish me, even when I make the slightest mistake. I can't seem to do right in his eyes.'

Sediacus paused and bit his lip. 'At least there's one benefit to all this extra work.'

'Really?' I laughed drily. 'What's that?'

'It's keeping you away from Eboricus. As long as you're studying with your Druid, he can't harm you.'

I looked down at my empty cup and felt an invisible weight pressing down on me. I had tried my best to avoid Eboricus around the sanctuary. To my relief he made no further attempts to take my princely ring from me after our confrontation in the hut, but despite my efforts he had continued to torment me whenever the Druids weren't watching, muttering or mocking my father in front of the other novices. At the evening meals in the hall he took a perverse pleasure in gorging himself on his serving of honeyed cake while the rest of us subsisted on scraps. Sometimes he forced me to hand over my food to the chief's hunting dogs. On one occasion I had refused to comply, half-starved from the exhaustion of our training. Later on, Eboricus and his lickspittles had marched into our hut and dunked my head in the communal butt while the rest of the scholars pretended to look the other way. At other times, Eboricus ignored me and picked on the other slugs, spitting in their broth or pummelling anyone who looked at him the wrong way.

At night I lay on my bed, filled with black misery. In my darker moments, I considered fleeing from Merladion, making my way to a nearby village and persuading the locals to return me to my family. Only the shame of that kept me from seeing it through. To run away would blacken my name for ever in the eyes of my people, and I would rather suffer at the hands of Eboricus and his toadies than be thought of as a coward. But I privately wondered how much more I could bear before the temptation became irresistible.

'It doesn't matter,' I replied despondently. 'I can't hide from Eboricus for ever. Anyway, he seems to be perfectly capable of making my life a misery even when I'm not around.'

'You're not the only one he's been picking on,' Sediacus reminded me. 'He reduced Cadrus to tears yesterday.'

'I know. I was there.'

I grimaced at the memory. The previous afternoon I had been playing the stick-and-ball game in the open space in front of the huts with Sediacus and a few of the other boys, using a pair of folded woollen cloaks for goalposts. Our side had been heroically defending a slender lead against the five other boys, when the leather ball landed at the feet of Cadrus, the affable but clumsy son of a minor Cantiaci noble.

I sprinted desperately back to our goal as Cadrus struck awkwardly at the ball with his bladed wooden stick and sent it flying through the air at terrific speed. The ball had sailed hopelessly wide of the makeshift goal and instead thumped into the back of Eboricus as he sat nearby with the other stags.

Silence had dropped like a stone across the enclosure. Eboricus stretched to his full height and turned round, then spotted the ball at his feet. He slowly lifted his gaze to the playing area, his face pinched into a frown. Everyone stood rooted to the spot as Eboricus scooped up the ball and held it up for us to see.

'Who hit this?' he demanded.

No one replied. Eboricus stormed over to the nearest player and stepped into his face. 'You! Tell me, boy.'

The player hesitated, his lips quivering. Eboricus grabbed the youth by the fold of his tunic and pulled him closer.

'Give me a name or so help me Lud I'll knock your brains out of your skull,' he said.

'It was him,' the boy replied anxiously, nodding at Cadrus. 'He's the one who did it.'

Eboricus refocused his gaze on Cadrus. He strode over to the younger boy. The latter looked around forlornly for help, but none of us dared to get involved.

'Whack a ball at me, will you?' Eboricus spat. 'Are you trying to insult me?'

'No!' Cadrus had made a pleading gesture. 'I didn't mean it,' he said nervously. 'It was an a–a–accident, Eboricus. H–h–honest.'

'A–a–accident, eh?' Eboricus had pulled a face. 'Then you should be more fucking careful. Someone might get seriously hurt, smashing balls all over the place like that.'

Cadrus nodded hastily. 'Y–y–yes, Eboricus. Sorry.'

'Sorry isn't good enough. You hit me, fatso.' His face darkened. 'You'll have to pay for that.'

The smaller boy's eyes widened. 'But it was an accident.'

'I don't give a toss,' Eboricus said.

He unloaded a punch into Cadrus's midriff, badly winding the boy. Cadrus sank to his knees and then Eboricus shoved the youth to the ground and kicked out at him, landing a blow on his ribs. Cadrus screamed, pleading for mercy as Eboricus grabbed hold of the fallen stick and beat him with it, while the rest of the players looked on in horror. I gritted my teeth and took a step towards Eboricus, intending to shout at him to stop, but Sediacus read my intention and shook his head, subtly indicating the presence of Vegorix and Durrus several paces away, ready to attack anyone who dared to interfere. Eboricus unleashed a final blow at Cadrus, striking him in the face with the blunt end of the stick, and then he tossed it aside as the boy lay curled on the ground, groaning and snatching at the thin air.

'Hit me again, will you?' Eboricus demanded.

'N-n-no, Eboricus!' Cadrus pleaded. 'I swear! P-please!'

'You'd better not, fat slug,' the older boy said in a low growl. 'Next time, I'll break every bone in your worthless body.'

He spat on Cadrus. Then he spun round and headed off towards his hut with his companions following close behind, leaving Cadrus crumpled in a heap on the muddy ground. The rest of us had abandoned our game after that. Later that night, in the darkness of our hut, I heard Cadrus weeping softly to himself.

'It isn't right,' I said, bristling with anger. 'We shouldn't have to put up with this. Why doesn't anyone do anything about him?'

'Such as what?' asked Sediacus.

'We could tell the Druids,' I suggested. 'Tell them what Eboricus and his friends did to Cadrus. This time they'd have to take action, surely. They can't permit bullying at the sanctuary.'

'There's no proof. The older boys would back up Eboricus's version of events, and the Druids wouldn't believe us. Besides, if you snitched on Eboricus, he'd find out about it. Then you'd be in trouble.'

'Someone should challenge him, then. Teach him a lesson.'

'How? Eboricus is much bigger than any of us.'

I suggested that confronting Eboricus had to be preferable to enduring months, if not years, of bullying and humiliation at the hands of the brute and his accomplices. I had seen my older brother, Adminius, picking on some of the smaller children back at Camulodunum, and I knew that the only way to deal with bullies was to challenge them. Trying to appease such aggressors only served to embolden them, I explained. But if we joined forces and squared up to Eboricus together, we might force him to back down. Sediacus listened patiently to my argument, then shook his head.

'It wouldn't work, my dear fellow.'

'Why not?'

'As I said, the other boys are scared of Eboricus. Even the stags. None of them would stand up to him. They wouldn't dare.'

'Maybe not now,' I replied softly. 'But if one of us stands up to

Eboricus, that might inspire the others to make a stand too.'

'A worthy sentiment, but misguided. You've seen what happens if you cross him. Anyone who dares to defy Eboricus and his cronies gets beaten to a pulp.'

'We can't let him get away with this, Sediacus.'

'I agree. But you're ignoring the bigger problem. Sooner or later, Eboricus is going to confront you. And you'll end up getting the same treatment as Cadrus.' He saw the expression on my face and held up his hands. 'Sorry, my friend. I hate it as much as you. But it's the truth.'

'I know,' I replied through gritted teeth.

Sediacus looked at me with a strained expression. 'What are you going to do?'

I shrugged. 'I don't know. Maybe I should go and fight him by myself. Have it out with him once and for all.'

'Forget it,' Sediacus said, shaking his head. 'You wouldn't stand a chance. Vegorix and Durrus follow him everywhere. They're as tight as strands on a torc, those three. If you confronted him, they'd beat you rotten.'

I threw up my arms in despair. 'There must be another way of dealing with him. There has to be.'

Sediacus shook his head again. 'There isn't, my friend. Trust me. Other boys have been in your position before.'

I looked up at him searchingly. 'What others?'

Sediacus hesitated. Then he said, 'Eboricus has forced several novices to leave Merladion in the past. He marks one of the boys out for special punishment every year. I've seen it happen.'

'And I'm his victim this year?'

'Something like that.' Sediacus lifted his eyes to me and made a pained face. 'I'm sorry. Eboricus won't rest until he's broken you. If you can't avoid him, or find a way to defeat him, then I fear your days here will be numbered.'

CHAPTER TWELVE

A few days later, I joined the other novices in the vale outside Merladion for our afternoon training session. Mendax stood in front of our group, at the edge of a bare field ringed with a wide dirt track. A crude wicker target in the shape of a man had been erected in the middle of the field. A few paces away from us, several of the older novices waited beside a pair of richly decorated chariots, Eboricus and Sediacus among them. Nearby a huddle of Druids had gathered to watch the afternoon's chariot-riding practice. Bladocus and the other mentors looked on while the two charioteers, hand-picked for their expert driving skills, inspected their vehicles, checking the iron-rimmed wheels and the harnesses.

Mendax cleared his throat as he prepared to address us. 'Today, lads,' he began in his usual gruff tone, 'the older novices will be giving you a demonstration on the uses and limitations of one of our oldest weapons: the chariot.'

A babble of eager voices went up around me, and there was a palpable sense of excitement in the air as we waited for the bulky old warrior to go on.

'Now, as some of you might know, the chariot isn't as popular as it used to be. Matter of fact, the Gauls stopped using chariots many years ago, and some of our tribes no longer employ them either. There are good reasons for that. They make a lot of noise, they're costly to maintain, and in a pitched battle, they're about as useful as a wooden cauldron. Having said that, they still have advantages in certain types of warfare.' He pointed at me. 'You. Weakling. Why would we still use chariots nowadays?'

'Er . . . for hit and run attacks, Master?' I replied hesitantly.

117

Mendax pretended to look shocked. 'Fuck me. That's actually right. Perhaps you're not as dumb as you look or sound.'

He walked over to the nearest chariot. The polished wooden spokes on the wheels glinted dully in the thinning afternoon light. Both horses wore sturdy harnesses and a central wooden pole connected the yoke to the chariot bed. The finely groomed horses snorted as Mendax continued.

'The slug is right. The chariot is still useful in an ambush, for one simple reason: it's the fastest way of transporting warriors to and from the skirmish. That's why our ancestors deployed 'em to harass that wretched swine Caesar all those years ago. Used in a coordinated fashion, chariots can bring a band of hardened warriors into a battle and ferry them out of harm's way again quicker than a Gaul can finish a jug of wine.' He grinned. 'Plus, they impress the womenfolk. Trust me. Riding one of these things is bound to catch the eye of any fair maiden you encounter.'

Several giggles rippled through our group. Mendax patted the iron-rimmed wheel of the chariot as he went on.

'Not so long ago, your ancestors would have raced into battle on a chariot with their trusted driver. Nowadays you'll do most of your fighting from horseback, or even on foot, but learning how to ride on a chariot is still a valuable test of skill and nerve for any highborn warrior. That means knowing how to throw a spear while moving at speed across the battlefield, directing your charioteer and mastering the art of jumping down from a moving vehicle without breaking an ankle or making a complete arse of yourself. Now pay attention.'

He turned away from us and gestured to the trainer in charge of the older initiates. The latter beckoned forward one of the students, a lithe Durotrigan prince. We watched closely as the Durotrigan clambered onto the platform and took up a position behind the charioteer, his right knee braced against the bent wooden loop on the side panel to provide stability. The trainer passed him a light throwing spear with an iron spike fixed to the base. The charioteer dropped to a crouch and jabbed the horses with the tip of a metal goad, spurring them into a gentle trot. The air was filled with the chink of horse-bits, the creak of their harnesses and the steady clop of the hoofs as the vehicle set off down the track.

'Eboricus!' the trainer called out.

The Atrebatan strode forward from his comrades. 'Yes, Master?'

'You'll be up next.' The trainer indicated the other chariot. 'We all know you're a skilled rider. Show us how it's done, d'you hear?'

Eboricus flashed a smug grin. 'As you command, Master.'

Our attention turned back to the field as the charioteer bellowed a command and flicked the reins, urging the horses to go faster. At once they lurched into a gallop and the chariot quickly gained speed, the wheels clattering over the uneven ground as the charioteer expertly steered around the track. Behind him the Durotrigan youth bent slightly at the knees and drew back his right arm, aiming for the wicker man in the centre of the field. He sighted the target, using his left hand to steady himself, and awkwardly released the spear as the chariot bounced over a divot in the earth. The missile cut through the air on a low trajectory before it dipped down and the narrow iron tip fell short, striking the ground three paces from the target. Eboricus and his friends shared a laugh at the Durotrigan's efforts.

Just then I noticed a movement in the periphery of my vision. I glanced sidelong and spotted Cadrus lingering beside the second chariot. He watched the older novices and their instructors for a moment, making sure no one was looking in his direction. The rest of the crowd had focused their attention on the Durotrigan prince and were unaware of the portly youth behind them.

I kept glancing across as Cadrus knelt down beside the carriage and began loosening the leather thongs fixing the standing platform to one of the looped side panels. He worked quickly, before moving round to the back of the spectators. A few moments later the Durotrigan and his charioteer completed their circuit of the field and the latter snapped on the reins, easing the horses to a halt beside us.

'Good work,' Mendax said. He spun round and barked an order. 'Eboricus! You're up. Let's see what you've got, son. Show the young cubs how it's done.'

'With pleasure, Master.'

Eboricus manoeuvred round to the back of the second chariot and climbed onto the main platform while his charioteer took up the slack reins. Before they could set off, I called out to Mendax.

'Master!'

He shot me a puzzled look. 'Yes, weakling?'

For a fleeting moment, I thought about alerting Mendax to the tampered chariot. Then I closed my mouth and reconsidered. Here was a prime opportunity to humiliate Eboricus in front of his companions. Perhaps the sight of the bully suffering an accident would cause him to lose face in the eyes of his peers. Given the bad blood between us, Eboricus would surely suspect that I was responsible for meddling with his chariot. In which case, I might be able to manoeuvre him into challenging me in front of the others, giving me the opportunity to settle things between us once and for all . . .

'Well?' Mendax asked testily. 'What is it?'

'Let me ride in his place,' I replied, knowing full well that such a request was bound to be dismissed.

Mendax eyed me curiously, before his expression shifted to a flinty glare. 'You cannot run before you can walk, boy. Don't waste any more of my time.'

'Apologies, Master.'

'Right then.' He straightened up and nodded at Eboricus. 'Off you go.'

Eboricus clasped his hand around the shaft of his spear and tapped his charioteer on the shoulder, giving the signal for the bare-chested man to set off. He jerked on the reins and the vehicle creaked and groaned as the horses broke into a trot. Vegorix and Durrus shouted their encouragement and the horses swiftly increased their speed to a thunderous gallop, their hoofs churning up clods of earth. Eboricus braced his legs and twisted slightly at the torso before launching his spear in a graceful motion at the man-sized target. The projectile struck the wicker figure at chest-height, drawing several loud whoops and cheers from the Atrebatan's loyal supporters.

'Bloody show-off,' the boy next to me muttered.

I glanced again at Cadrus; he was watching the chariot with keen expectation. Across the field, Eboricus had started to perform a series of tricks for the amusement of the crowd. The charioteer edged forward on bare feet along the timber shaft connected to the yoke, his long hair sweeping behind him, while Eboricus stood fully upright on the rear platform and struck a muscular pose, raising his arms and flexing his impressive biceps.

There was a sudden shout as the straps on either side of the platform snapped apart and several members of the crowd gasped in horror as the panels collapsed. Eboricus fell backwards and crashed to the ground behind the vehicle with a cry of pain. In the same moment the charioteer lost his balance and tumbled off the central pole. He landed on his back and rolled in the dirt, narrowly avoiding being crushed under the wheels as the horses ran on with the wrecked carriage trailing behind them.

'Get the horses!' Mendax shouted. 'Move yourselves!'

Two of the other trainers rushed over to the horses, snatching up the reins and shouting commands at the beasts as they fought to bring them under control. Mendax ran over to the charioteer and another instructor dropped down beside Eboricus to check on him. He offered the youth his hand but Eboricus angrily swatted it away and shook his head clear before rising unsteadily to his feet. He staggered back over to our group, rubbing his bruised ribs. The other instructors steered the chariot over to the side of the field; one of them began inspecting it for signs of damage while a crowd of Druids and students formed around us.

'What happened?' Mendax demanded.

The trainer scratched the back of his head. 'Looks like the panel straps came apart,' he said, indicating the thongs. 'Must have been a bit loose before the practice.'

'Impossible!' the charioteer said in a nasal tone as he tried to staunch the flow of blood from his nose. 'I checked them myself beforehand. They were as tight as a drum.'

'So how did they come loose?' Mendax said.

'Maybe they were worn?' the trainer suggested.

The charioteer shook his head ferociously. 'Someone must have deliberately loosened them when we weren't looking. It's the only explanation.'

Eboricus locked eyes on me and marched over, his nostrils flared, his facial muscles twitching with rage. 'You,' he seethed. 'It was you, wasn't it? You did this.'

I feigned a look of surprise. 'I don't know what you're talking about.'

'Bloody slug.' Eboricus spat.

121

He lunged at me with a maddened yell, arms swinging. I jerked backwards, moving out of range to the cheers of the other boys. Eboricus cursed and charged at me again, but before he could throw another punch Mendax barged his way through the crowd and stepped between us. He held the two of us apart while Bladocus hurried over and glared at us in turn.

'What in the name of Lud is going on here?' he hissed sharply.

'This slug messed around with the chariot while no one was looking,' Eboricus seethed. 'He set me up. It was Caratacus, I know it.'

I stood my ground and addressed him calmly. 'Are you calling me a liar?'

Eboricus regarded me with a contemptuous sneer. 'Bloody right I am.'

I drew in a deep breath, sensing that this was the moment I had been waiting for. For weeks Eboricus had been inflicting torment and misery on the new initiates. Now I had the chance to finally put an end to his reign of terror.

'A public assault has been made on my honour,' I said. 'In which case there must be a duel.'

A laugh escaped Eboricus's mouth. 'You're not serious.'

'You are accusing me of rigging your chariot,' I said coolly. 'I claim my right to a contest to resolve the dispute, using a weapon of my choice.'

'You can't do that.'

Bladocus said, 'A serious accusation has been made. Caratacus's honour has been called into question. He is therefore entitled to seek a duel, according to the rules of the sanctuary. Unless you wish to apologise instead?'

'Fuck off!' Eboricus growled. 'This slug tampered with my vehicle. I'd rather chew on a turd than apologise to him.'

'Then we are left with no alternative,' Bladocus said. 'The two of you will fight tomorrow, at first light. Until the appointed hour you shall conduct yourselves in a respectable manner around one another. How do you wish to fight, Caratacus? The conditions and choice of weapon are yours, as the wronged party in this matter.'

'I've made up my mind,' I said boldly. 'We shall shoot arrows at each other. At twenty paces.'

'Arrows?' Eboricus frowned. A shadow of concern crossed his face, before he swiftly composed his expression. 'Makes no difference to me. I'll beat you all the same, slug.'

'Arrows it is.' Bladocus nodded solemnly. 'That is a most unusual request, but, of course, the choice is yours. You shall fight tomorrow at dawn. One of the other Druids will make the necessary arrangements. In the meantime, I want no further trouble from either of you. And may the gods defend the right boy.'

Eboricus gave his back to me and promptly marched over to his companions. Mendax growled an order, and one of the Silurian instructors slung an arm around the injured charioteer's back to support him and the two men hobbled off in the direction of the settlement. As the crowd thinned out Sediacus drew up alongside me.

'What in the name of the gods are you playing at?' he asked in a low voice. 'Have you lost your mind?'

'It's a question of honour. I can't let him get away with insulting me. Surely you understand that.'

'But arrows! Gods below. You could get killed.'

'I'm well aware of that,' I said through gritted teeth. 'But I don't have a choice. Either I take him on, or he's going to keep picking on me. And the rest of the new boys. At least this way I've got a chance of beating him.'

'Do you really think you can win?'

I let out a bitter sigh. 'If we fought bare-fisted or with swords, Eboricus would have the advantage in strength and skill. I wouldn't stand a chance against him. But I've got a certain knack with the bow. My uncle taught me how to use it in Camulodunum.' I managed a smile. 'Trust me. I know what I'm doing.'

Sediacus glanced back in the direction of Eboricus and made a strained sound in his throat.

'I hope so, my friend,' he said quietly.

CHAPTER THIRTEEN

We spent the rest of the afternoon watching the older boys demonstrate the basics of chariot riding, taking turns to jump up and down from the back of a moving vehicle and learning how to stay upright wielding a sword and shield while the charioteer sped round the field at a fast gallop. Later on, Mendax took us for a long run across the hills. I struggled to pay attention, and as the day wore on my mind kept drifting ahead to my impending fight with Eboricus. I had never confronted the possibility of death before, and with each passing hour my anxiety steadily worsened. That evening I sat in the great hall, picking at my food scraps, while those around me talked excitedly of the duel and the respective prowess of both Eboricus and myself. Some even placed bets on the outcome. Unsurprisingly the vast majority of the novices seemed to favour my Atrebatan opponent.

I slept little that night and awoke long before dawn with a sick feeling of dread. Perhaps I had acted too rashly in demanding a duel. I was eleven years old; I had no great desire to join my ancestors in the Otherworld at such a tender age, and yet I was about to foolishly stake my life in order to settle a quarrel with a bully. But it was too late to go back now. Shortly before first light Mendax marched into the darkness of the hut, snapping me out of my ruminations.

'Up you get, boy!' he barked. 'It's time!'

My body was trembling with nerves and I struggled into my boots with some difficulty. One of the servants offered me a piece of coarse bread and some salted pork, but the thought of food turned my stomach and I politely declined.

'You sure, lad?' he asked. 'Could be your last meal in this world before you join Lud.'

'I'm fine, thank you,' I managed.

The servant shrugged indifferently. 'Please yourself.'

'The others are already waiting for us,' Mendax explained as I finished getting dressed. 'One of the senior Druids has chosen the location for the duel.'

'Where is it?' I asked.

'A clearing in the vale. Not far from here. Eboricus and his party have gone ahead already.'

'What about my Druid? Where is he?'

'Your mentor is there. Eboricus's too, lad.' Mendax regarded me with a curious mixture of sympathy and admiration. 'You'd better hurry up. Don't want to keep them Druids waiting for too long.'

The Silurian turned on his heel and strode out of the hut. I turned to follow him and saw Sediacus staring at me with a grave expression.

'Do you really mean to go through with this?' he asked.

I shook my head slowly. 'I can't back out. Not now. It's a matter of personal honour.'

'I know that, for Lud's sake. But is it worth getting killed over some spat with Eboricus?'

'Would you prefer me to be a coward and run away?'

Sediacus held up his hands. 'I'm not questioning your courage. No one can accuse you of lacking in bravery. I just hope you know what you're doing, that's all.'

I sighed. 'If I don't confront Eboricus this morning, he'll go on making our lives unbearable. At least this way I've got a reasonable chance of defeating him, even if it means risking my neck. Unless you've got a better plan?'

'No. Sadly not.'

'Eboricus has been allowed to push us around for long enough,' I said, surprising myself with the steadiness of my voice despite the tightening knot of dread in my chest. 'It's time someone stood up to him.'

Sediacus shrugged. 'Come on then. We'd better get moving.'

The enclosure was almost deserted as we emerged into the cool of the dawn, most of the novices having gone ahead to get the best view of the action. A thin mist hung over the land as Mendax led us out of the gates and we set off down the slope towards the valley floor. We headed through the forest and I was keenly aware that I might be entering the last moments of my life. In a short time, Eboricus might fire an arrow into my chest, and my lifeless body would be returned to Camulodunum for burial according to the customs of our people. I shoved that grim thought aside and reminded myself that I would need a steady hand if I was to have any hope of seeing another dawn.

We navigated a dirt trail roughly following the course of a shallow stream. After a quarter of a mile we reached a wide clearing enclosed by a ring of contorted oak trees. The rosy dawn crept across the sky; the last pallid shreds of mist rapidly cleared. It seemed cruel that it was such a beautiful morning, a last gift from the gods before my life was snatched away.

Eboricus stood in the centre of the clearing, alongside a tall Druid with a gleaming gold neck chain. I recognised him as Segorix, the man who had greeted us at the initiation ceremony weeks ago. Nearby, two attendants inspected the hunting bows. Further away, Vortagus and his entourage observed the proceedings from a safe distance, flanked by a throng of bodyguards, Druids and tribal warriors. I briefly scanned their faces, searching for the face of my Druid. Bladocus stood slightly apart from the others, watching me intensely.

Sediacus wished me luck and walked across the clearing to take his place with the rest of the novices. A hush fell over them as I advanced towards my opponent. I forced myself to move at a calm pace and prayed that my face did not betray my nerves. Then I stopped at a sword's length from Eboricus while Segorix, acting as umpire for the occasion, looked at me with a stern expression.

'Are you resolved to go through with this deadly business?' he asked us in turn. 'This is your last chance to settle the matter peacefully.'

I breathed in deeply and said, 'Eboricus has made a serious attack on my personal dignity. If he is prepared to withdraw his accusation and apologise to me before all those gathered here, I will drop my challenge.'

'Never!' Eboricus glared at me with an arrogant sneer, but I detected the slightest flicker of unease in his voice.

'Then the duel must proceed,' Segorix announced. 'Attendants!'

The two men hastened over with the hunting bows. I selected one of the weapons, testing its weight. The bow was made of yew and felt heavy in my grip. The attendant handed the other bow to Eboricus, and then the second man gave us each one shaft from the quiver.

'Now, boys, the rules,' Segorix went on. 'At my command you will take up your respective positions, ten paces away from each other. You shall not take aim at your opponent until I have given the signal. Once I give the word, you are free to shoot as you please. If one duellist misses, he must stand his ground and wait for the other to take his shot. If both shots miss, the contest will be declared a draw and honour will have been restored on both sides.'

For a brief moment I met Eboricus's gaze. He looked tense and impatient.

'Do you understand the rules?' Segorix asked.

'Yes, Master,' I replied.

'Let's get it over with,' Eboricus snapped.

Segorix ordered me to stand directly on the spot marked by a coloured flag, while Eboricus took up his place beside the other mark, twenty paces away from me. Once Segorix was satisfied with the arrangements, he nodded to the attendants and they withdrew to the edge of the clearing. Then the Druid took several steps back from us and raised his voice so that all could hear him.

'Are you ready?' he called out.

'Yes, Master,' I said.

'Ready,' Eboricus nodded.

My mouth was dry. My breath felt trapped in my throat. In my imagination twenty paces had seemed a reasonable distance. But as I stood there, confronting Eboricus, the range was so short it seemed almost impossible to miss.

'You may shoot after my signal,' Segorix continued.

We both waited for the Druid. He raised his staff and held it up for what felt like a very long time. Then he brought it crashing down with a dull thud.

'Shoot!'

As soon as the word left his mouth Eboricus took up his arrow and notched it, pulling back on the bowstring before I even had a chance to sight my own weapon. There was a snap as the Atrebatan hastily released his arrow, and I stood frozen in terror as the shaft shot towards me in a low arc. For an awful moment I couldn't move, and I felt my heart pounding ferociously in my chest as cold dread seized every part of my body. Then, incredibly, the arrow whipped past me, missing by several inches. Eboricus looked on aghast.

'No! It can't be!' he cried.

'Silence!' Segorix shouted at him. 'You must stand your ground until the challenger has made his shot. Caratacus, when you are ready.'

A look of panic flashed across my opponent's face as he realised the gravity of his mistake. In his desperation to shoot first he had rushed his shot, spoiling his aim. Now he was powerless to do anything except wait for me to reply.

I nocked my arrow, steadied my breathing and calmly sighted my opponent, drawing the shaft level with his torso. Eboricus stood stock-still, looking deathly pale while I took aim. There was a moment of unbearable tension as he waited for me to shoot. Then he let out a sharp cry of panic and threw himself aside, apparently overcome with terror.

For a fleeting instant, as I recalled the appalling humiliations Eboricus had inflicted on me, I considered aiming at his prone figure. It would have been easy enough to kill my tormentor. Then I deliberately lowered my aim, away from Eboricus, and loosed my bowstring; the arrow fell short, harmlessly striking the ground between us. Some of the spectators, who had no doubt been hoping for a more violent end to our confrontation, rounded on me and jeered.

A moment later Segorix strode hurriedly towards the middle of the clearing, waving his staff to signal the end of the duel. He looked at Eboricus with contempt before he intoned, 'I declare Caratacus the victor.'

A handful of the spectators cheered the decision. Eboricus's cronies rushed forward to lift the dazed bully to his feet. He shook his head, angrily tore himself free of his companions and stormed over to the Druid. To the side of the clearing Vortagus and a number of the Druids stared at Eboricus with ill-disguised scorn. His own supporters looked on unhappily as he jabbed a finger at Segorix.

'The duel isn't over,' he said. 'I demand another shot, Master.'

Segorix looked at him with a rigid expression. 'Out of the question.

You failed to receive your opponent's shot in an honourable manner. Therefore you have failed the test of courage.'

'But this slug took too long to shoot. He cheated.'

'A duellist is permitted to take as long as he wants to make his shot. Caratacus had the right to delay until he was ready. Perhaps you would have hit the target if you had exhibited the same control.'

Eboricus glowered at me, his eyes blazing with impotent rage. 'I'm not finished with you yet, slug. Face me again, if you dare. I'll show you who's the best shot this time.'

'There will be no second contest,' Segorix replied flatly. 'The matter has been decided. It is over, boy.'

He turned his back on Eboricus and barked an order at the attendants. One of them cupped his hands to his mouth and shouted at the crowd, announcing the end of the spectacle, while the other man collected our bows and fallen arrows. At once the onlookers began to leave the clearing. A few initiates paused to make mocking faces at Eboricus, but most of the boys ignored him and walked away as he continued to loudly insist on a rematch. I set off after them and found Sediacus waiting for me at the edge of the clearing.

'Looks like you had the luck of the gods on your side this morning.' He smiled with evident relief. 'Thank Lud. For a moment there I thought you were done for.'

'So did I,' I croaked.

Perhaps I should have felt elated at winning the duel. But in truth, I felt nothing but a hollowness in my stomach and a tiredness in my bones. The gnawing anxiety of the past several hours had exacted a heavy toll on my body, and I craved nothing but rest. I suppose your gladiators must feel something like that, after their lives have been spared in some blood-soaked encounter in the arena.

Sediacus said ruefully, 'It's a pity your skills deserted you this morning. If your aim had been true you would have shut up Eboricus permanently.'

I shook my head and explained how I had missed my target on purpose. Sediacus stared at me in amazement, then frowned.

'What the hell did you do that for? You would have done us all a favour if you had killed him.'

I said, 'There was no need. Eboricus had humiliated himself when he threw himself to the ground. If I had struck him then, I would have looked cruel and vengeful. This way, Eboricus will have to live with the knowledge that he lacked the courage to face a shot from his opponent, and the contempt of the other students and Druids. That is a just punishment for his actions.'

'Well, one thing's for sure,' Sediacus said. 'He won't be bothering anyone else from now on. Not after word of his humiliation gets around.'

Later that afternoon, I was taken aside by one of the Druids at the end of our training and summoned to the High Druid's private quarters. I followed the man to the sanctuary and through the gates until we stopped in front of the largest roundhouse. The Druid told me to wait outside while he drew back the animal skins covering the entrance and ducked under the human skulls nailed to the lintel. I stood in the growing dusk, listening to the murmur of voices from within the hut. A few moments later the Druid reappeared and gestured for me to step through the entrance. I hesitated, fearful of what awaited me inside, before the Druid nudged me forward and I stumbled into the gloom.

I entered a wide space lit up by several decorated bronze oil lamps. Animal skulls and charms hung from iron nails fitted to the timber support posts on either side of an oak-framed bed. The High Druid sat behind a massive table, set with a platter of juicy boar meat, loaves of bread and a lump of cheese. After weeks of living on scraps, the sight of the feast made my belly growl painfully with hunger.

Bladocus stood to one side of the High Druid, his hands laced together in front of him. He watched me intently as Lugracus waved me forward. I slowly approached the table and stood in nervous silence while the High Druid grazed on a tender cut of meat. He chewed noisily, washed his food down with a sip of mead from a silver cup and let out a satisfied belch. Then he dabbed at his beard with a cloth and eased back in his chair as he scrutinised me.

'Bladocus has told me about your duel,' he began in his rasping tone. 'I must say, I wasn't entirely surprised at the outcome.'

130

'No, High Master?' I asked in surprise.

Lugracus smiled. 'You think I don't know my own students? Eboricus is a clever boy. Cunning, certainly. And ruthless. But he wouldn't throw away his life for the sake of a perceived insult.'

The High Druid popped another morsel of roasted boar into his mouth and touched the cloth to his lips before he went on.

'I'm told that Eboricus has requested another contest. He has been making his demands to me via his Druid mentor. You've heard about this, I suppose?'

'Yes, High Master,' I replied.

'I've discussed the matter with your mentor. There will be no further duelling. I have told Eboricus the same. If he continues to press his claim, I'll see to it that his privileges as a senior novice will be withdrawn.'

I stared at him in shock. To have his privileges taken away was the severest punishment an older novice could suffer. Eboricus would lose his place at the top table at mealtimes and his choice of the finest cuts, along with his fine bedroll and the countless other comforts that made life at Merladion slightly more tolerable.

'You have conducted yourself well, I understand,' the High Druid added, glancing at Bladocus. 'Nevertheless, I do not expect any more trouble from you from now on.' I tried to protest, but he cut me off with a wave of his hand. 'I accept that you had no choice but to seek a duel, once Eboricus had questioned your honour in front of your companions. But a wise warrior chooses his fights carefully. You will learn that yourself, in due course.'

'Yes, High Master.'

'However, I do have one question.'

'Yes, High Master?'

Lugracus leaned forward and looked me in the eye.

'Eboricus accused you of rigging his chariot. You denied the accusation and since you were willing to stake your life on the claim, I am sure you're innocent. So who sabotaged his vehicle?'

I stole a glance at Bladocus then shook my head. 'I don't know, High Master.'

'Come now. Surely you must have seen something? You were there at the time. Speak truthfully, child.'

Lugracus eased back and waited for a reply, drumming his fingers on the table. I ground my teeth and stared at him, torn between the need to tell the truth and my desire to protect Cadrus from punishment.

'I'm sorry, High Master,' I said at last. 'I was too busy watching the chariot practice. Like the rest of the novices. I'm afraid I didn't see anything.'

In the corner of my eye, I caught sight of Bladocus fixing me with a curious expression. Lugracus stroked his beard for a moment before he rested his wrinkled hands on the table in front of him.

'Well, I suppose the identity of the miscreant will come to light soon enough. Nothing stays secret here for long. That's something else you will realise, in time.'

'Yes, High Master.'

The High Druid cleared his throat. 'That is all, Caratacus. You may return to your training. I expect you to rededicate yourself to your studies from now on.'

'Yes, High Master.' I nodded determinedly. 'I will.'

'Let us hope so. Your mentor tells me you have shown great promise. It would be a shame to allow yourself to get distracted by petty squabbles while you're here.'

Darkness was beginning to encroach as I followed Bladocus out of the roundhouse. Across the sanctuary a group of Druids squatted on the ground beside one of the huts, helping themselves to bowls of steaming hot broth while others chatted in muted voices. After we had walked a few paces from the roundhouse Bladocus halted and looked down at me, frowning.

'Why did you lie to the High Druid, child?'

The question startled me. I stopped in my tracks and glanced up at him. 'Master?'

'I was watching you yesterday,' Bladocus replied. 'At the chariot practice. I saw the other novice untying the knots on Eboricus's vehicle. That podgy child, Cadrus. And I saw you watching him as well. You saw what happened, didn't you? And yet you chose not to tell the High Druid of his role in the matter. Why?'

I hung my head and confessed that I had wanted to avoid landing Cadrus in any more trouble, even if it meant hiding the truth from the High Druid. I told him how Cadrus had been bullied by Eboricus for weeks beforehand, like many of us, until it had reached a point where he had decided to take his revenge at the chariot practice. How I had seen an opportunity to manipulate Eboricus into fighting a duel, by getting him to accuse me in front of the other scholars. Bladocus listened closely, his frown lines deepening.

'But you could have lost the duel,' he pointed out. 'Your decision to challenge him could have resulted in your death.'

I shook my head. 'I had a decent chance of beating him. I've used a bow plenty of times. Epaticcus taught me how to shoot with it. Anyway, I didn't have a choice. I had to settle things between us, Master.'

Bladocus stared down at me, and for a moment I thought he might berate me. Then he let out a sigh.

'You did well,' he said approvingly, catching me by surprise. 'Your actions demonstrated courage and guile.'

'Thank you, Master.'

'Perhaps you are going to fulfil the plans I have for you after all.'

Now it was my turn to frown. 'What do you mean?'

Bladocus spread his hands. 'You are a boy of rare potential. With the right guidance and tuition, I believe you are capable of achieving great things among your tribe. Your response to the threat from Eboricus proves as much.'

I shuffled my feet uncertainly. 'Is that why you brought me here?'

'You are an outstanding scholar. That is first and foremost why I chose you. But I believe you have something else, too. Something the other novices lack. The ability to think strategically. That is unusual in one so young.'

I shrugged. 'I was just trying to survive, Master.'

'Maybe so. But I have taught enough children of the aristocracy to know that many of them are lazy and self-indulgent wastrels concerned only with stuffing their faces and jealously guarding their own privileges. Most of them can't see further than their own noses. But you are different. If the gods are on your side, you might become a great warrior, or perhaps even king of your people.'

I scoffed at that. 'You're forgetting about my brother. Father wants Adminius to inherit his throne. He's made that plain enough.'

'For now. But that might change.'

'What makes you think that?'

Bladocus gazed out across the sanctuary. 'Adminius has his charm, but he lacks the necessary talents to rule the kingdom. In time, your father may come to realise that.' He paused. 'But if you wish to become king one day, you must be prepared to suffer for it.'

A sudden realisation struck me like a fist. 'That's why you've been pushing me all this time, isn't it? To test me?'

The Druid's black eyes gleamed like dagger points. 'The hard work you have endured so far is nothing compared to the challenges that lie ahead, boy. Especially if the legions return to our shores.'

I gave him a doubtful look. 'You think they're going to come back here?'

Bladocus nodded. 'I believe it is only a matter of time.'

'I don't understand. Why would they invade again? They haven't bothered us for decades.'

'The Romans have a thirst for conquest. A thirst that can never be quenched.' He pointed to the ground and then jabbed a finger at the sky. 'They believe all of this belongs to them as much as the soil of Rome itself. Sooner or later, they will train their gaze on our lands once more. And when they do come back, we must be ready.'

'Even if you're right, that could be years away,' I argued. 'Or longer. Decades, even.'

'It is never too early to prepare. And that includes training the possible future leaders of our kingdoms. Your father won't be around for ever, you know.'

I frowned at the Druid, my mind racing. I could hardly believe what he was telling me. For weeks I had resented Bladocus for making me endure hours of extra work at the sanctuary. Now, suddenly, I understood. He hadn't been picking on me. Instead he had been testing me to see how much I could take, to judge whether I was capable of realising his longer-term plans. Plans he had kept from me until now.

'If you want to achieve greatness, you must trust me and do as I say, without question. But I must warn you. The training will be even harder from now on. What you have suffered so far at Merladion is nothing compared to the pain you will feel. Submit yourself fully to my demands, however, and in return I will give you the guidance and wisdom you require. Only then will you be ready to one day assume your father's throne.'

He stood back and inclined his head to one side. Anticipation and excitement swirled inside me.

'Well, Caratacus?' he said. 'Are you ready to truly begin your work?'

CHAPTER FOURTEEN

Rome, AD 61

'I accepted the Druid's offer, of course,' Caratacus said as we sat in his cluttered study. He smiled ruefully. 'I was a fool. I was ignorant of the dangers lurking ahead of me.'

'How do you mean?' I asked.

Caratacus didn't answer. He stood up, circled round his desk and pulled back the pleated curtain separating the room from the rear courtyard. Bright sunshine poured in through the opening, revealing the patina of dust coating every surface in the study. Small motes drifted idly through the air, like tiny flakes of snow. Caratacus cleared a path through the stacks of old volumes on the floor and gestured for me to step outside.

'Let's stretch our legs,' he said. 'I'm afraid I can't sit down for too long these days. At my age your bones start to rust.'

I closed my writing book, rose from my stool and followed him into the garden. The stagnant fishpond released a putrid odour that reminded me of the filthy slums of the Suburra. Dead leaves and rotted stems were strewn across the path. The central fountain still worked, but the basin was cracked and a pool of water had collected beneath it. For a moment I considered using the scene as a neat symbol of Caratacus's tragic decline, but I dismissed the thought. This was not some crude picaresque penned by one of Nero's dissolute courtiers to titillate the literary salons of Rome. I was aspiring to something far more important.

We walked around the portico in silence. In my experience, it is best to let the client go at their own pace. The secret is to let your subject feel as if they are in control. If you press them like some hard-nosed interrogator at the imperial palace, you will only succeed in provoking a defensive reaction. Rather, it is my job to hold the subject's hand as we stroll down the familiar routes of their past. As we were doing at that precise moment.

'Things improved at the sanctuary after that,' Caratacus said finally. 'The other initiates no longer lived in fear of Eboricus. Everyone knew that he was a coward.'

'Aren't all bullies?'

Caratacus stopped and thought a moment. 'Yes, I suppose they are.'

'What happened to Eboricus? Presumably he endured a rather torrid time of it after your dawn duel?'

'Eboricus was never quite the same. Most of his friends abandoned him. I remember him as a pathetic creature, eating alone at supper. He was banished from the sanctuary a year later.'

'On what grounds?' I asked, pretending that I gave a fig about the fate of some minor tribal aristocrat. It never hurts to show an interest in the smallest details of your client's life, I have found. Especially if you wish to earn their confidence. 'Did he bully someone else?'

Caratacus shook his head and gave a wry smile. 'He broke the oath of celibacy. The fool was caught in bed with the daughter of Vortagus. After that the Druids had no choice but to kick him out. Even Eboricus's uncle couldn't save him.'

We walked on, moving at a slow pace around the courtyard as Caratacus gathered his thoughts. From within the house I could hear Mardicca yelling at her grandchildren. A child's shrill voice pierced the air, pleading his innocence. It sounded like any other family house in our city. Perhaps these unruly Celts were not so different from us after all. Caratacus stared in the direction of the house and waited until the screaming had stopped before he turned to me.

'Rome is no good for my family,' he said. 'Living here, it makes the children soft and ill-disciplined. They are losing touch with our traditional values.'

'Perhaps they could benefit from a Roman education,' I pointed out.

Caratacus fixed me with his pale gaze. There was a quiet fury in his voice as he replied. 'You agree with my daughter-in-law, then?

You think my grandchildren should be tutored by my enemies? The same wretches who seized my lands and titles?'

'I'm merely suggesting that they might learn a thing or two from a private teacher. Analysing verse. Writing in Latin and Greek. Rhetoric. That sort of thing.' I paused a moment before inspiration struck and I continued smoothly. 'If you have taught me anything so far it is that you should know the ways of your enemy. I can arrange for one of my acquaintances to offer their services, if you'd like.'

'My grandchildren are Celts. That is not how our people are taught. We keep our stories up here.' The Briton tapped at the side of his head. 'Our poetry, our histories, our stories are far richer than anything they would find in most of the dusty scrolls that I have read during my time in Rome. Our stories and legends live in our souls. Are they to surrender their proud heritage, for the dubious privilege of reading the works of some dead Greeks?'

'Many of your countrymen would give their right arm for a chance to have their progeny schooled here,' I said.

Caratacus rounded on me. 'Don't tell me about my countrymen, Roman,' he replied tetchily. 'I am well aware of their attitudes towards our conquerors. Those worthless nobles who sided with Rome are always finding new ways to ingratiate themselves with the enemy. They might have surrendered their values in favour of wine and togas, but I won't be so easily cowed.'

There was something admirable about the way this old king fought to hold on to the ways of the past. How differently might things have turned out, I wondered, if the other British tribal leaders had resisted the legions as fiercely as Caratacus. Instead, many of their kings had been quick to throw themselves at the feet of their new masters almost as soon as the first soldiers landed on that distant windswept island.

'Would you have preferred your children to train at a Druid sanctuary?' I asked, half in jest. 'Life there was hardly easy, from what you've told me so far.'

He smiled. 'Perhaps you're right. But studying there taught me the importance of discipline and hard work. Without that, I doubt I would have ever become king.'

'So what happened next?' I said. 'After the Druid told you about his plans for you?'

Caratacus gave a weary shrug. 'There isn't much to tell. I knuckled down to my studies and trained hard with the Silurians. The work was unforgiving, as Bladocus had promised it would be. I had to work harder than I could ever have imagined, but I was determined not to fail my mentor. The seasons passed, one year gave way to another, and eventually I completed my initiation.'

'And when was this?'

He frowned in thought. 'Seven years after I had arrived at Merladion. I had just turned eighteen.'

'What happened then?'

'Looking for some grisly details, Felicitus?' Caratacus grinned. 'There was no wicker man full of criminals waiting to be sacrificed to the gods, if that's what you're thinking.'

'How many of you were admitted?'

'Only a handful of us. Myself, Cadrus. One or two others. Sediacus had passed out the year before and returned to his uncle's court.'

He looked relaxed now, and I judged the moment was right to press him again on his earlier remark. 'You said there were dangers lurking ahead of you,' I reminded him. 'What did you mean?'

We had stopped beside a stone bench. Caratacus planted himself down and motioned for me to sit beside him. I chose my spot carefully, taking care to avoid the dried bird shit spattering the surface. The Briton rested his hands in his lap and we sat in the quiet of the garden, listening to the steady trickle of the fountain. At last, he made his reply.

'After the initiation, each scholar had to decide whether to continue their studies at Merladion or go back to their tribes. I had already made up my mind to stay on.'

I struggled to mask my puzzlement. 'But I thought you hated it there? Didn't you miss your family? Your people?'

'Very much so. But Bladocus felt that I could benefit from remaining at the sanctuary for at least another year or two, and I had agreed to obey him without hesitation. That was the plan, anyway,' he reflected. 'As things turned out, my studies were cut short. That was when the trouble began. When it all started.'

I sat upright. 'What trouble?'

'The conflict between my family and King Verica.'

'The ruler of the Atrebates, you mean? The one who had knocked his uncle on the head and seized the throne at Calleva?'

His bushy eyebrows rose. 'You surprise me, Roman. You're becoming quite the expert on Britannic tribal quarrels.'

'I try my best.'

Caratacus smiled briefly, then the pensive expression returned to his face. 'There had been bad blood between our tribe and the Atrebates for many years,' he said. 'Father and Verica never saw eye to eye. But the situation became much worse soon after I had started my training for the second ring. That was when the tension between our peoples erupted into a violent conflict. We had no idea at the time that it would lead to the downfall of both our kingdoms.'

'Why? What happened?'

Caratacus abruptly stood up from the ruined bench and said, 'I'm tired of this place. Too many ghosts. Let's talk somewhere else.'

'Certainly,' I said, grabbing my notebook and stylus. 'Did you have somewhere in mind?'

'There's a tavern lower down the Aventine. The Drunken Boar. It's supposed to serve authentic Celtic dishes, although that's stretching the truth somewhat. But the beer is passable, and I know the owner. He'll find us a quiet spot. We can talk there later.'

'When?'

'The ninth hour. After I've finished at the gym. Then I'll tell you of the war between our tribes, Roman. The war that ultimately sealed the fate of our island.'

PART THREE

THE WAR PRINCE

CHAPTER FIFTEEN

Rome, AD 61

I arrived in the afternoon at the tavern Caratacus had chosen for our next interview. It stood on the corner of one of the main streets of the lower Aventine, rubbing shoulders with a crumbling apartment block of the type that dominates this squalid corner of the city. From the outside, the Drunken Boar didn't seem a particularly welcoming establishment. The plaster on the exterior walls had cracked in places, revealing the brickwork beneath, and someone had scrawled lewd graffiti below one of the windows. A painted sign hanging above the gloomy entrance promised 'Warm Food and Drink'. Which was setting the bar rather low, I thought, heated wine and victuals being the very least one might reasonably expect from any half-decent watering hole.

I threaded my way through the throng of degenerates that haunted the lower reaches of the Aventine and stepped through the entrance. A stale odour of beer and human sweat hung in the air. At that early hour the tavern was quiet. The labourers and stevedores in the nearby docks had yet to finish work for the day and I counted no more than half a dozen old sweats seated at the trestle tables. Glancing round, I noted that a crude attempt had been made to recreate the world of the Celts. Swirling patterns decorated the walls, along with bucolic scenes: kings riding their chariots, children playing in front of a roundhouse, bare-chested men painted in woad hunting a boar. A bronze war-trumpet with an animal head hung from the wall behind the counter.

I pulled up a stool at the nearest empty table and waved to the thickset barman, making the universal sign for a drink. He set aside the plates he had been rinsing, wiped his hands on a rag and came over to my table.

143

'What'll it be?' he asked in a gravelly voice. I presumed the man was from Gaul. One of the more recent arrivals in our city, perhaps, given the coarseness of his accent.

'Do you have any Gallic wine?' I asked. 'Something cheap, preferably.'

The barman grunted. 'No Gallic. But we've got some Britannic stuff that's just come in, if you're interested. Fresh off the wagon.'

I curled up my lips in horror. 'Britannic wine?'

'That's right. From the estate of Cogidubnus himself. He's got an extensive vineyard these days, so they say.'

'An acquired taste, no doubt,' I said, recalling the name from several of the military memoirs I had read for research. Cogidubnus was a minor British noble who had been guaranteed his kingdom in the former lands of the Atrebates in return for his enthusiastic support for Rome.

'It's a touch on the rough side,' the barman admitted. 'But it's all the rage with the quality up on the Caelian. They can't get enough of the stuff.'

If that was true, then standards had plummeted amongst those who lived in that district.

'Another time, maybe.' Drinking wine from the estate of a Roman puppet king was hardly going to endear me to Caratacus. 'Do you have any Etruscan?'

The barman shook his head firmly. 'Britannic wine. Or we've got ale. That's your choice, friend.'

'Gods, what sort of establishment is this?' I asked incredulously.

'Most of our customers are Celts looking for a reminder of home. We're not here to cater to outsiders. Although we do get more of your sort these days.'

'My sort?' I looked at him quizzically.

The barman nodded. 'Young Roman gentlemen, looking to sample the delights of our native food and drink. Something to brag to their mates about, I suppose. Demonstrate their exotic tastes. You'd be surprised how many of them have acquired a thirst for British beer.'

'Is business good?' I asked.

'We do all right.' He scratched his scraggly beard. 'Though some of the regulars ain't happy about it.'

'Why not?'

He shrugged. 'They'd prefer it if the Romans stuck to their own haunts.'

I thought about making an arch remark about the Celts and their famous hospitality towards strangers, but something in the barman's expression told me that he shared his patrons' dislike of me and my fellow citizens.

'I'll take the Britannic, then,' I said.

'As you wish. Something to eat, too? We serve lots of good Celtic fare.' He pointed to a menu on the wall. 'Chef's special today is rabbit stew.'

'Just the wine for now. And make it two cups.'

The barman shrugged and walked over to the counter. He returned carrying a pitcher and a pair of chipped Samian cups and set them down carelessly on the stained table.

'That'll be three sestertii.'

I winced at the price, fished out a handful of coins from the leather purse tied to my belt and set them down on the table. The barman made no move to scoop them up, so I reluctantly added a small tip and wondered how I would explain this latest frivolous expense to Aelia. My dear wife had upbraided me earlier that afternoon at our cramped apartment, questioning my decision to write Caratacus's story while she cradled our screaming infant son, Lucius.

'A Briton!' she had exclaimed. 'Of all the foolish things you've done in your life, Caius. Why on earth would you agree to write his memoirs?'

'It was my idea, actually.'

'Even worse!' Aelia had shouted over the baby's hysterical cries. 'Is work so hard to come by that you're reduced to writing for exiled barbarians? What about all your connections in the Senate?'

'It's nothing to do with that. There are plenty of commissions to be had. I just wanted to tell an exciting history for a change. And one that's actually true. The fellow has lived an extraordinary life.'

Aelia snorted. 'I should hope Cara-docos, or however you

145

pronounce his barbaric name, is compensating you handsomely for your time.'

'I'm afraid there's no money involved, my dear,' I had told her. '*Caratacus* has been treated rather shabbily by the emperor and can't afford to pay me anything.'

Aelia had given me one of her icy looks, the kind that could frighten the hide off a cow. 'You're working for this man for *free*, Caius?'

'Yes, but that's beside the point. Don't you see? This is the great untold story of our time, my dearest. It's sure to attract much more interest than those stuffy family histories I've written in the past. This could open new doors for me . . . for us both,' I corrected hastily. 'If this is as successful as I hope, we'll be able to move to a place on the Caelian, just like you always wanted.'

'Don't be a fool, Caius!' Aelia replied, making no attempt to hide her derision. 'Do you honestly think you can make your fortune from writing about some wrinkled old Briton?'

'If you heard his story, you'd understand,' I replied defensively. 'His tale is quite unlike anything I've ever heard before. This work could become one of the greatest histories of the age. I'm convinced of it.'

'Wonderful. All our dreams are about to come true thanks to Caratacus, it seems. And how do you propose to pay the bills in the meantime, dearest husband?'

'I've still got some silver banked from the last commission,' I pointed out. 'That should keep us for a little while, if it's money you're worried about.'

'That's not the point,' Aelia scolded me. 'You have a son now, Caius. You can't afford to indulge your whims any more. You should be out winning friends in the imperial court, not wasting your time with some long-forgotten king no one cares about.'

The memory of our argument rankled, but I tried to shrug it off as I reached for the pitcher and poured myself a generous measure of wine. I took a tentative sip and choked as the acidic liquid burned the back of my throat. I was poised to call over the barman to complain about paying for such poison when I spotted a dishevelled fellow approaching me from a gloomy corner of the room.

'Felicitus! Caius Placonius Felicitus!' he slurred, wine splashing from his cup onto the hay-strewn floor as he stumbled over to my table. 'I'll be damned!'

I stared at the man in bemusement, wondering how on earth this tramp knew my name. He looked at least a decade older than me, with thinning, untamed hair and a scraggly grey beard, and his brown tunic was frayed with age. He was oddly familiar, but I couldn't recall where I'd seen him before. Then he drew nearer, and I sat up with a start as I suddenly recognised his face.

'By Jupiter! Decius Tuscus!'

Decius Spurinnus Tuscus was a minor historian who had ingratiated himself with the previous emperor's inner circle by writing slavish hagiographies of his allies. Despite fawning on Nero, his career was on the slide. The rumour was that some of the protagonists of his previous works had fallen out of favour. Fatally, in some cases. Mud sticks to those who surround such characters. We had first met at some tedious dinner party a year ago and spent a few hours discussing the relative merits of Ennius and Naevius. I had thought him a dull fellow, another of the imperial family's toadies who relied on the strength of their connections rather than any great skill with the stylus. Our paths had crossed once or twice since, but in recent months Tuscus had been conspicuous by his absence at the palace. The shock of seeing his face in such miserable surroundings left me momentarily stunned.

'What a pleasant surprise,' I lied, recomposing my face. 'How, ah, unexpected.'

'Do you mind?' Tuscus gestured to the stool opposite and planted himself on it before I could reply, spilling wine across the table as he set his cup down. The man was clearly inebriated. His breath reeked of cheap wine, his face was bloated, and his eyes had the glaze of a veteran drunk. He looked almost unrecognisable; nothing like the smooth, well-dressed bore I had dined with several months ago. I made a heroic effort to mask my annoyance at his intrusion and smiled a greeting.

'What are you doing here?' I asked. 'Researching the haunts of the plebs for some new Menippean satire, perhaps?'

Tuscus shook his head and jerked a fat thumb in the direction of the dilapidated block I had passed on my way to the tavern. 'I live round the corner,' he said, pausing to let out a belch. 'On the fourth floor. Up with the pigeons, as they say.'

'Oh.' Somehow I managed to disguise my horror.

'This is my local. The wine's awful, but the company is pleasant enough. And you don't run into many familiar faces,' he went on, as if trying to justify his choice of watering hole. 'Anyway, what brings you here?'

'I'm meeting someone,' I said guardedly.

'A friend?'

'More of an acquaintance, you might say.'

There was a twinkle in his eye as he grinned. 'Still getting generous commissions from those worthies in the Senate? Who's your new client? Someone I know?'

'I really can't talk about it,' I replied, recalling that Tuscus had a reputation as an insatiable gossip. If I let slip about my project with Caratacus, every hack in Rome would know about it before sunset. 'And you? How are you faring these days?'

A dark look clouded the aged historian's face, and he snorted angrily.

'No such luck,' he muttered. 'I haven't had a scrap of work in months, thanks to someone uncovering an unflattering poem I wrote years ago about Emperor Claudius and handing a copy to Nero. My career is in ruins.'

He took a swig of wine and stared miserably at the floor. I can't say I felt too sorry for the old codger. If you are going to write *ad hominem* doggerel, then pick a target you can afford to mock. What goes around comes around, you might say. But for all that I found his unkempt appearance more than a little disturbing.

'It can't be as bad as that,' I said. 'You've got plenty of friends in high places. They can't all have abandoned you, surely?'

That drew a mirthless smile from Tuscus. 'You don't know what Nero is capable of. He might have abolished the treason trials, but he's as wicked as they come. Everyone's afraid of him. He's made it known that anyone who associates with me will pay a high price.'

I shifted and sat in uncomfortable silence while Tuscus drained the rest of his cup. It was hardly a secret that Nero disliked personal criticism, and one always trod carefully around the imperial set, but Tuscus was suggesting something far more sinister. I knew enough of my history to remember the dark days of Claudius; I had read the accounts of how the so-called enemies of the emperor had been seized from their homes in the night to face secret trials in the bowels of the palace. Nero had claimed to be cut from a different cloth, publicly declaring his support for the Senate, but then again, hadn't his predecessors made the same hollow promises?

'It's not just the emperor,' Tuscus went on. 'That commander of the Praetorian Guard is a nasty piece of work. He made it his business to destroy my reputation.'

'Burrus?'

Tuscus nodded. 'That's the one. He's a vicious bastard. Even worse than Nero, some say.'

I grimaced at the name. I had seen Sextus Afranius Burrus at the imperial banquet the other night and knew a little of the man. As the commander of the Praetorian Guard he was closer to Nero than anyone, except perhaps Seneca. There were also rumours that Burrus had helped to do away with Nero's mother, Agrippina, although it would be unwise to air such thoughts aloud.

I glanced around, gripped by a fear that one of the emperor's spies might be watching me share a drink with an out-of-favour writer.

'What are you going to do?' I asked quietly.

'What can I do?' Tuscus shrugged. 'Without the emperor's approval I can't get the necessary patronage to continue my work. I have a small income as a private tutor, teaching the sons of warehouse owners and traders, but it barely covers the rent.'

'I'm sorry to hear that,' I said, suppressing a shudder. After all, we writers endure a career that is vulnerable to the vague whims of fashion and the shifting sands of politics. One can't help feeling a certain degree of sympathy for those who fall out of favour; even the ones who write the basest sort of doggerel.

He dismissed my concerns with a flap of his hand. 'I got off lightly compared to some. Last month Burrus and his heavies seized Saloninus.'

My mouth sagged. 'The playwright?'

Tuscus nodded gravely. 'The guards arrested him at his house in the middle of the night. They took him to the palace, beat him to within an inch of his life and forced him to hand over his property in Campania.'

'On what grounds?'

'Including a thinly veiled criticism of Nero in his latest interminable tragedy.' Tuscus rolled his eyes. 'Apparently someone in the audience reported their concerns back to Burrus. No doubt that someone is already planning the new kitchen at his place in Campania.'

'That's terrible,' I replied distractedly, glancing at the entrance in the hope that Caratacus might show up and spare me from listening to any more of his depressing tale. 'Listen, I'd love to chat further, but—'

Tuscus suddenly thrust an arm across the table. He clamped his clammy hand around my wrist and looked at me with a desperate expression. For a dreadful moment I thought he was going to embarrass us both by asking to borrow some money, or, gods forbid, asking me to plead his case with my contacts in the Senate – fat lot of good that would do. But instead he leaned across the table and spoke to me in an undertone.

'Look here, Felicitus,' he said. 'You're a smart fellow. Take my advice and watch yourself. Nero might seem ridiculous, with his artistic affectations, but he's dangerous. Him and the rest of his inner circle. If you cross them, you can expect no mercy. Even if it's no fault of your own.'

I laughed nervously. 'I doubt the emperor and his cronies would bother with the likes of me. I'm hardly important. Gods, I doubt Nero even knows I exist.'

'I thought the same thing, once,' Tuscus said. 'Look what happened to me.'

I reached for my cup and took a swig of rancid wine, feeling a little queasy. In my rush of excitement to tell Caratacus's story, I had given no thought to how the palace might react. Nero's dislike for the old British warlord was well known; might he seek to censor the work, or even suppress publication? I had no idea. I was at the mercy of the powerful forces of imperial politics, and for the first time

I had the troubling notion that writing the life of Caratacus might not be as rewarding as I had hoped.

Just then Tuscus looked up at the entrance and froze. I glanced in the same direction and saw a tall, lean figure with tattooed cheeks and long grey hair approaching from the street. The man stopped just inside the tavern and scanned the faces of the patrons. Tuscus squinted at him.

'Hello,' he remarked. 'Isn't that Caratacus?'

Before I could reply, the one-time King of the Britons met my gaze and swerved towards our table. He halted a couple of steps away and turned his puzzled gaze on Tuscus, while the latter stared at him in surprise. I stood up, my stool scraping across the floor as I nodded quickly at the old historian.

'Yes. Well.' I paused and coughed. 'Lovely to see you again, Decius Tuscus. Really. Great to catch up. I'd love to talk more. Another time, perhaps?'

Mercifully, Tuscus still had his wits about him despite being three sheets to the wind. He composed his features, slapped his hands on his knees and rose from the stool with as much dignity as he could muster. 'Of course. I was, er, just on my way. Take care of yourself, Felicitus.'

'You too.'

He bowed his head at Caratacus, wished us both a good evening and shuffled off towards the entrance. Tuscus paused beside the corner of the street and glanced back in our direction, and for the briefest moment a knowing glint flashed in his eyes. Then he turned and disappeared into the crowd.

Caratacus looked curiously at me. 'Friend of yours?'

'Just an old acquaintance,' I said.

The Briton arched an eyebrow. 'I didn't know Roman writers befriended the unfortunate beggars of their city.'

'We don't. He was a fellow historian, actually.' Caratacus looked at me curiously. 'It's a long story,' I added. 'I'll tell you another time.'

He shrugged and signalled to the barman as soon as he caught his eye. The barman finished wiping down one of the tables and ducked into a room behind the counter. A few moments later a broad-shouldered man with long dark hair and a scarred chin emerged from the space and limped over to our table. He glanced at me with interest, then beamed at Caratacus. The two men clasped arms and exchanged a warm greeting in their guttural dialect.

'This is Lugnus,' Caratacus said in Latin as he waved a hand at the huge figure standing beside him. 'An old friend of mine. He owns this place.'

'Are you from Britannia as well?' I asked.

Lugnus let out a roar of laughter. 'You must be joking. I've never set foot on that island of hairy bastards, thank Lud.'

'Lugnus is from Gaul,' Caratacus explained. 'From the tribe of the Arverni. He was a great boxer in his youth. He fought against some of the toughest pugilists in the Empire.'

'Indeed?' I asked, feigning interest. The Celts, I knew, had a rich tradition of boxing, and many of the champions of our third favourite sport (after hacking one another to bits in the arena or racing in absurdly fragile chariots) hailed from their lands.

'"The King of the Celts", they called me,' Lugnus said with a clear note of pride in his voice. 'Never lost a bout, mind you. Settled down here after I retired and sank my hard-earned winnings into this place. It's not much, I know, but it's mine.'

'Lugnus helped my family out when we were new to the city,' Caratacus said. 'He knows every Celt in Rome. Without him, we would have found it even more difficult to adapt to this place.'

I frowned. 'I thought the Gauls and Britons were rivals?'

'Aye, that's true,' Lugnus replied with a grin. 'Most of the time we can't stand the sight of one another. But there ain't many of us Celts in this city. We have a duty to stick together. It's not as if the Romans are going to do us any favours, is it?'

'No,' I replied. 'I suppose not.'

Lugnus peered at me. 'Caratacus tells me you're writing his memoirs?' I nodded, and the huge Gaul made a sound deep in his throat. 'What makes you think any Romans will want to read about the life of one of us, eh? You lot spend most of your time looking down your noses at our people.'

'True,' I conceded. 'But we also come to your taverns to drink your beer and gorge ourselves on Celtic dishes. We're a contradictory nation, if nothing else.'

He grinned, revealing a set of rotten teeth. 'Fair point.' He gave me a playful tap on the shoulder. 'Perhaps when you're done, you could write my biography. I've got more than a few tales to tell.'

'I'm sure,' I replied diplomatically.

Caratacus said, 'My friend and I would like to talk in private, Lugnus. Away from prying eyes.'

'Of course. Right this way.'

Lugnus led us across to a table in a separate corner of the tavern, away from the other drinkers. He snapped at the barman, and the latter hurriedly fetched the pitcher and cups from the other table and brought them over to us. I offered to pour Caratacus a cup of wine but he shook his head and asked the barman to bring him a pot of ale instead. The man returned with a tankard filled with the dark brew, politely refused the payment Caratacus offered and retreated to the counter.

'What do you think?' Caratacus asked, indicating our surroundings with a broad sweep of his tattooed arm.

'It has a certain charm,' I said, groping for a compliment for this depressing hovel. 'I take it you're a regular patron?'

Caratacus nodded. 'I come here once or twice a week, usually. Partly for the comforts, but mainly for the gossip. There's always someone here with news from Britannia. That's how I stay informed about the old land.'

'Why don't you just read the gazettes posted in the Forum each week, like everyone else? They mention Britannia often enough.'

Caratacus smiled faintly. 'Do you think they tell the whole story, Roman?'

As he spoke, I was struck again by the tragedy of his existence in Rome. Cut off from his old tribal kingdom, living in a dilapidated townhouse and reduced to foraging for scraps of information about the territory he had once ruled from strangers in a tavern. I supposed he missed the land of his forefathers terribly, and I muttered something to that effect.

'There is nothing there for my family now,' Caratacus said grimly. 'Our kingdoms have fallen to your legions, our Druid altars razed to the ground. Those of us opposed to Rome have been put to the sword or enslaved, while the likes of Cogidubnus prostrate themselves at the feet of their new masters. Perhaps things would have been different if Boudica's rebellion had succeeded, or if the Brigantes hadn't betrayed me . . .' His voice trailed off, before he shook his head firmly. 'It doesn't matter. All of that is lost now. Soon our whole way of life will disappear. When that day comes, all we will have left is places like this.'

'And your recollections,' I reminded him. 'Don't forget that. The published account of your life will last longer than any building in our city.'

He gave a bitter smile. 'Are you sure it is my name you wish to go down in history? Or yours?'

The discomfort I was feeling must have shown on my face. Caratacus smiled and said, 'Let us be honest with one another, Roman. You have your own reasons for wanting to tell my tale. We need not pretend that you're doing this out of sympathy for the plight of my people.'

'I'm doing this to tell the story of a true hero of our times. That's all.'

He laughed. 'You're a historian. You crave literary recognition as much as the next writer. In a way, you're not so different to the rulers of our tribes, determined to have their stories honoured in song by all the great bards in the lands. The difference is that they perform the deeds while you writers are the fleas who live off their blood.'

'Maybe so,' I said as I took out my waxed tablet notebook. 'But you still need me to write your story.'

'And you need my cooperation to tell the heroic tale that will win you the adulation of the literary salons of Rome.'

After my dispiriting conversation with Tuscus, I was not so sure that the work would be welcomed by Rome's higher-ups, but I decided not to share that concern with Caratacus.

'True,' I said. 'So what's your point?'

'From the beginning, I have insisted on an honest account of the invasion,' Caratacus replied forcefully. 'I hope your motivation won't be swayed by your own ambitions, Felicitus. After all, a sanitised account would surely be more acceptable to your friends in the palace. And, no doubt, aid your career.'

'Not at all,' I said. 'I gave you my word this story would be truthful. I intend to honour it.'

'Glad to hear it.' He took a swig from his tankard and eased back. 'Now, let us continue my tale.'

I glanced down at the notes I had scrawled on my writing tablet. 'You had started talking about the conflict between your own tribe and the Atrebates, under King Verica.'

The British king nodded and folded his scarred hands together. 'Yes, I remember. No one knew it at the time, of course, but that struggle was the beginning of the end for us.'

'How so?'

'Your fellow historians write that we were a quarrelsome people, and they're not wrong. The truth is, we were always at each other's throats, forever splitting hairs that gave rise to constant conflict. If we had known how it might end, perhaps we might have been able to act differently, and Rome might never have invaded us, or conquered our lands.'

'Do you really think so?' I challenged him. 'Or is that just a comfortable lie to tell yourself?'

Caratacus gave me a hard look. 'Rome's victory in Britannia was not guaranteed, whatever your smug histories might say. If our tribes had been able to unite, instead of fighting one another, the outcome might have been different. But the war between our tribe and Verica made that impossible.'

'And how did that come about?' I asked.

'The way such things always started between the tribes. A heated dispute, made much worse by a few obstinate fools who mistook compromise for weakness.'

I gripped my stylus and waited for Caratacus to go on. There was a faraway look in his eyes as he gazed past my shoulder, his sharp mind recalling events that had happened half a lifetime ago.

'I was eighteen when it began,' he went on. 'I was training with the Druids at the time, and I had made up my mind to continue my studies at the sanctuary, at least for a few more years. But all that changed one afternoon . . .'

CHAPTER SIXTEEN

Britannia, AD 25

The course of history is often altered by the smallest of actions. You might disagree, but I can only tell you the truth as I have seen in it. All I know is this: the seeds of our downfall were sown long before the legions returned to our shores, and it happened because of a minor Britannic prince you Romans have never heard of. If it hadn't been for Trigomaris, the long and costly war between our great tribes might never have occurred, and the fate of our island might have been very different. Perhaps the invasion would never have taken place at all. But then again, only the gods can know such things for certain.

The trouble began in my last year at the sanctuary. Many of the other scholars had returned to their families by then. My good friend Sediacus had left the sanctuary the year before. We had become as close as brothers during our time together, and I was sad to see him go. But I understood his relief at the decision. Sediacus disliked the ascetic way of life practised by the Druids and he had long desired to return home, no doubt to work his considerable charms on the fair women of the Dobunni. Even so, I missed him terribly.

The few of us who had decided to stay on at Merladion submitted ourselves to a gruelling routine of lore study, weapon practice and religious instruction. The pace was relentless, but whenever I felt too exhausted to go on I would remember the vow I had made to my Druid mentor years before. I had sworn to Bladocus that I would endure any hardship and pain without complaint, accepting his guidance whenever he offered it. Only then, he had told me, through hard work and the guidance of the gods, would I stand a chance of one day succeeding my father to the throne of my tribe.

Towards the end of the autumn, I undertook my initiation into the first ring. On that day, those of us who had completed our studies were brought before the High Druid at the sanctuary. The Druids, their bodyguards and the other remaining scholars had gathered near the altar to witness the ceremony. A guard stoked an iron shaft in the embers of a glowing brazier, while we all swore an oath that I cannot repeat. We drank a potion of fresh goat's blood mixed with herbs picked by the left hand of a Druid healer, and then we received the brands signifying our admission to the ring. The guard wrapped a woollen cloth around the end of the shaft and pulled it free from the brazier. Then he walked steadily over to me, the tip glowing white with heat, and shoved the tip against my forehead. I gasped as a searing pain wracked my body. It lasted for several agonising moments before the guard snatched the poker away, and then I collapsed to the ground, tears streaming down my face.

To be branded in this manner is a great honour among our tribes. Those who carry the mark of the first ring are held in high regard by their tribespeople. It is a symbol of the knowledge they have gained at the feet of the Druids, the wisest of all men. It remains one of the proudest days of my life, and I was ready to commit myself to years of further study for the second ring. Then one evening a novice overheard the guards discussing my father's annexation of Cantium. Their ruler, King Eppillus, had united the quarrelling princes of that kingdom and marched north to seize Camulodunum from our family. My father had led a large war-band against the king and defeated him at a great battle. Many warriors had died on both sides. Eppillus himself had been slain during the fighting. There were rumours that my father planned to gift the Cantiaci throne to my older brother, Adminius, in order to prepare him for one day ruling our people. The months passed, and I began to doubt the Druid's prophecy would ever come true.

Later, we heard further news from a group of travelling bards and storytellers. The ill feeling between our tribe and the Atrebates had been getting steadily worse, and Verica, in search of new allies to shore up his position, was said to have encouraged deeper ties with Rome.

For decades after Caesar's invasion the tribes had existed under a delicate balance of power overseen by the council of Druids, and some people feared that the growing rivalry between our people and the Atrebates threatened to upset that arrangement. Few, however, believed it would lead to outright war. Both sides had much to lose through such a conflict. But the ominous news continued to trickle down to Merladion all through that hard winter.

As the days grew longer, I redoubled my weapon training under my Silurian instructor. Mendax pushed me hard, until I was strong enough to march for twenty miles a day, up and down the steep hills of the vale, shouldering heavy loads of rocks on my back. With his encouragement I learned the secrets of concealment, moving soundlessly at night, establishing weapons caches, planning ambushes, and all other aspects of mountain warfare. I became proficient, too, in the use of the sling, bow and long sword. I toiled for hours on the training ground, even in the worst weather, striking repeated blows against the sturdy timber post with my blade until my forearm muscles burned with the effort.

Sometimes I grew frustrated with the unending grind of life under the close scrutiny of the Druids. I resented having to endure the harsh conditions at Merladion, while my brothers grew up in the comfort of the royal court at Camulodunum. In my darkest moments, I wondered if I would ever see my home again.

And then, one afternoon in the early autumn, my uncle arrived at Merladion.

It had been a particularly gruelling day and I had returned to the cramped roundhouse I shared with the other scholars to rest for a while before supper. A short time later, I was sitting on the blankets on my bedroll, reciting the lessons we had been taught earlier that morning, when a thickset guard yanked back the heavy leather curtain covering the entrance. He stepped inside the hut, caught sight of me and called out.

'On your feet, prince. Now. You're wanted. Chief's hall.'

'Right now?'

'That's what Vortagus said.'

I sat up and felt a tightening sensation in my chest. A summons from the chief of Merladion was highly unusual. Vortagus rarely took an interest in the lives of the Druid scholars he hosted at his tribal capital, except for the odd occasion when he attended our sword practice, or the weekly stick-and-ball matches we played against the sons of the local aristocrats.

'What's this about?' I asked.

The guard gave a shrug of his huge shoulders. 'How the fuck should I know? I ain't a seer. Now hurry up.'

I stood up and followed the guard out of the entrance. A sharp gust of wind blasted across the vale as I emerged from the round-house, stabbing my skin like a thousand bone needles. It was bitterly cold and damp, and within moments I was shivering in my coarse tunic.

'Bloody weather,' the guard muttered as he scowled at the grey skies. 'We're in for a foul spell, from the looks of it. The vale will be waterlogged before the autumn is out.'

We swept through the open gate leading into the chief's compound. A pair of bored-looking warriors leaned against a cart to one side of the covered porch, taking swigs from a jug of ale. They spared me a disinterested glance, nodded at the guard and waved us through.

A rich smell of woodsmoke filled my nostrils as I entered the hall. The guard led me towards the dais at the far end, where I saw Vortagus sitting on his wooden throne, his stern gaze already fixed on me. A pair of bodyguards lingered at his side, tightly gripping their long thrusting spears. Bladocus stood below the dais, his cowl pulled back to reveal his pale, gaunt face. My Druid master acknowledged my presence with a curt nod.

A broad-shouldered figure stood to his right, dressed in a thick woollen cloak. He turned towards me as I drew near. In the wan glow of the fire I didn't recognise him. Then his features became clearer, and I abruptly halted, my mouth slack with surprise.

'Uncle!' I cried.

'Hello, lad,' Epaticcus said. I grinned happily as I hurried over to him and we clasped forearms.

'By Lud, you've grown some,' he went on. 'What have they been feeding you out here?'

At first I was overcome with joy at seeing my uncle after eight long years. Then I saw the tense expression on his face, and I instantly knew something was wrong. 'What are you doing here?'

Before he could reply, Vortagus leaned forward in his throne and said, 'It appears, Caratacus, that your time with us has come to an end.'

I stared at him in surprise, momentarily lost for words. Then I snapped my gaze back to Epaticcus. 'Is this true?'

'It is so.' My uncle had aged considerably since I had last seen him. His blond hair was now almost fully grey, and his brow was heavily lined with wrinkles. 'I'm to escort you back east,' he continued. 'You and the Druid. Your father's orders.'

'What about my studies?' I said falteringly. 'I'm training for the second ring. I've already begun my instruction.'

'Sorry, lad. But it can't be helped. The king has ordered me to bring you home, and that's the end of it. I've already told your mentor about the situation. He agrees it's for the best.'

'But . . . why?'

'There's trouble,' he explained. 'Between our people and those southern swine, the Atrebates.'

I frowned. 'What trouble?'

He hesitated and glanced sidelong at Bladocus. Then he said, 'Prince Trigomaris is dead.'

'Trigomaris?' I frowned. 'The ruler of Lhandain?'

'Aye. That's the one.'

My frown deepened as I digested the news. I knew a little of Trigomaris from my Druid teachers. He was the ruler of a small but wealthy kingdom on the banks of the Tamesis, on the border between our tribe and the Atrebates. Although Lhandain was independent, the territory had once belonged to our tribe, in the days of King Cassivellaunus; their people spoke our dialect and we shared many of the same customs. In recent years Lhandain had flourished under the prince's reign, becoming a wealthy trading post used by Roman merchants and other traders. But the royal court itself remained fiercely divided between two factions, one loyal to our tribe and the other supporting the Atrebates, who also sought control of the lucrative trade along the river.

'What happened?' I asked.

'There was an accident while Trigomaris was out hunting, three days before the last full moon. Apparently one of the nobles in his entourage struck him with an arrow.'

'By mistake?'

'That's what I've heard. I don't know the full details.'

'But what has that got to do with me?' I asked. 'Or my father?'

'As you probably know, Trigomaris had no children. His wife perished three winters ago, and the prince died without naming a successor. Which means our tribe should rightfully inherit his lands.'

I nodded, vaguely recalling the details. Two generations earlier an agreement had been brokered by the Druids, between our tribe and the ruling house of Lhandain. The latter, fearful of the growing power of the Atrebates to the south, had agreed to return Lhandain to our side in the event that the royal line produced no heir. 'But it's not as simple as that,' Epaticcus continued.

'What do you mean?'

'There was a revolt at Lhandain,' he said. 'After the prince's death was announced. One of the nobles on the Atrebatan side declared himself the rightful ruler.'

'Who?' I asked.

'Some weasel by the name of Moricanus. The prince's cousin. Spent most of his childhood in the court at Calleva, so you can imagine where his loyalties lie.' I could hear the anger in my uncle's voice as he went on. 'After the prince's death, Moricanus called a meeting of the council of elders. He denounced the alliance with our tribe and claimed that Lhandain rightfully belonged to him. Then he demanded that the elders recognise him as the new ruler. Some of the nobles protested the decision and a fight broke out, but Moricanus had the support of the royal bodyguard and he had the rebels arrested and put to death. Now he's pledged his allegiance to Verica.'

'How did you come to hear of it?'

'A few of the nobles loyal to our tribe managed to escape Lhandain before they could be rounded up by Moricanus's guards. They went straight to Camulodunum with the news.'

'Where does Verica stand in all of this?' I asked.

'Where do you think?' Epaticcus seethed. 'He's backing

Moricanus's claim to the throne. Verica has made it known that if anyone tries to interfere with Lhandain's internal politics, he'll regard it as an attack on Calleva itself and retaliate in force.'

'But our tribes had a treaty. Binding on both sides. The Druids witnessed it. Surely that must count for something, Uncle? Besides, it's our land. The territory is on our side of the river. The people are our kinsmen. Always have been.'

'That is not how Moricanus sees it,' Bladocus said. 'He claims he has an agreement with Prince Trigomaris. Moreover, he says he has proof supporting his right to the throne.'

I frowned. 'What proof?'

Epaticcus shook his head. 'It doesn't matter. This isn't about Moricanus. This is about his ally Verica. That Roman–boot-licking cur has been trying for years to expand his influence north across the river.' He smacked a clenched fist against his thigh. 'Now he's going to snatch Lhandain from right under our noses.'

Bladocus said, 'If Verica is allowed to expand into Lhandain, Rome will gain an interest in one of the key ports in Britannia. Lhandain would be crawling with Roman merchants and imperial agents before long. Once they infest the land, it will be too late to stop them. The legions would follow them soon enough, once they realise how vulnerable these lands are to attack. They will destroy the cults, impose their swingeing taxes on the tribes, enslave the women and children, and lay waste to all those who defy them. It happened once before, in Gaul; it will happen here, too, before long, if we do not stop the Atrebates.'

I looked at Epaticcus. 'Do you really think Verica will try to annex Lhandain?'

'I'd bet my right bollock on it. Trust me, it'll be the standard of the Atrebates flying over the place before long.'

'Moricanus might object to that,' Vortagus pointed out.

Epaticcus laughed. 'He's the puppet ruler of a small trading settlement with a handful of warriors under his command. If Moricanus tries to resist, Verica will remove him at the point of a sword and stick another man in his place. But I doubt it'll come to that. Most likely Verica will keep him on the throne for as long as he's useful. Once things have settled down, he'll quietly grab the land and pension Moricanus off with an estate in the south.'

I considered for a long moment. 'What does my father have to say about this?'

'He insists the terms of the original treaty should stand, since both sides made the deal in good faith. But if the Atrebates are allowed to gain Lhandain, it'll be a costly defeat for us. Verica will control the trade flowing along the river, and the profits from it.'

'Not just that,' I said, my mind racing ahead of me. 'It'll give him control of the passage over the Tamesis, too.'

'Either way, this means trouble,' Epaticcus said.

'Will Father go to war?'

My uncle shook his head slowly. 'Not yet. He's worried about provoking the Romans.'

Bladocus, who had been listening to our exchange, broke his silence. 'There is a substantial trading community at Lhandain, including an influential group of Romans. If your father declares war on Moricanus and his Atrebatan allies, there's a chance they might try to encourage Roman interest in the outcome of the struggle.'

I looked at him. 'Do you really think Verica would go to the Romans for support, Master?'

'It cannot be ruled out. Other kings have pleaded their cause to the Empire in the past, despite the obvious risk of further Roman influence in the affairs of this island. And we know that Verica has welcomed Roman trade in his own territory.'

'That's putting it mildly,' Epaticcus put in. 'I hear that snake has even laid down a street grid in Calleva, just like those Roman towns across the sea.' He screwed up his face in disgust at the thought.

'So what is to be done?' I asked.

Epaticcus scratched his chin. 'Your father has called on the Council of Druids to adjudicate. His advisers support the decision. The king wants to try to resolve this dispute without bloodshed if possible.' He paused. 'And he wants you to sit in on the talks.'

'Why me?'

'You've studied under the Druids for almost eight years. You know the details of tribal law as well as anyone, and it'll be useful to have you on hand to advise the king to help secure a favourable outcome.'

'I will not be able to assist your father in this matter,' Bladocus said. 'As a member of the Druid High Council, I am required to travel to Lhandain to meet with the others ahead of the gathering. We will need guidance from the gods before we hear from each party and make our judgement, and there are rituals to be carried out. So the responsibility for advising your father must fall to you.'

'Besides, you're a young man now,' Epaticcus added. 'Second in line to the Catuvellaunian throne. Your father reckons you've learned enough about Druid ways for one lifetime. It's time you started learning how to be a king.'

The tone of his voice suggested Epaticcus strongly approved of the conclusion of my studies at Merladion.

'When and where is this gathering?' I asked.

'Ten days from now. At a sacred grove, a few miles north of Lhandain. All three parties have been invited to attend the gathering and present their arguments to the Druid council.'

'Three?' I repeated.

My uncle nodded. 'Verica has insisted on attending the meeting, given the Atrebatan interest in the territory.'

'The council must reach a clear majority for their ruling to carry weight,' Bladocus reminded us.

'And if they can't reach a decision?' I asked.

'Then it's war. Plain and simple.'

'Has Verica agreed to let the Druids adjudicate?'

Epaticcus said, 'He doesn't have a choice. He can hardly go against the wishes of the Druid council, can he? He'll offend every other tribe in Britannia. At least this way, we'll have a chance to put forward our case. If the Druids have got any sense, they'll see the danger posed by letting Lhandain fall into the hands of the Atrebates and their Roman friends and vote in favour of returning the land to our tribe.'

'What if the decision goes against us?' I asked.

'It won't. Not if the Druids play fair. But either way, your father wants you at his side, and we're going to need all the warriors we can get if this turns ugly. Besides, you look like you know how to swing a sword.' He nodded approvingly at me. 'The last time I was here, you were as skinny as a scythe. Now look at you.' He grinned.

'Perhaps these hairy Silurian bastards know a thing or two about fighting after all.'

'Where's my father now?'

'At Camulodunum, with the rest of the royal household. He's ordered the Catuvellaunian chiefs to assemble there ahead of the meeting. We'll meet the others at Camulodunum and ride down together to the meeting with the Druid council.'

'I shall travel with you as far as Verlamion,' Bladocus said. 'But from there I will make my own way to Lhandain.'

I turned to Epaticcus. 'When do we leave?'

'Tomorrow morning. At first light. Two warriors from the royal bodyguard have travelled here with me.' He turned to Vortagus. 'We'll need a couple of mounts for these two. Enough food for five men, and feed for the horses.'

'Of course,' Vortagus replied. 'I assume your king will reimburse me.'

Epaticcus shot him a dark look. 'I thought you were a friend of our tribe?'

'I am.' A thin smile flickered across the chief's lips. 'But I'm also no fool. I don't want to be seen to be doing the Catuvellaunians any favours. The other tribes might get the wrong impression and assume we're taking your side in this dispute.'

Epaticcus snorted in contempt. 'The Silurians and their famous neutrality, eh? You lot might live in the arse-end of the world, but you'll have to pick sides one of these days.'

'Perhaps so. But until then, we'll let you pig-headed easterners hack each other to bits.'

Bladocus saw the dark expression on my uncle's face and stepped forward. 'I'll ensure you are properly compensated,' he said, addressing himself to Vortagus. 'You shall receive a fair price for the horses and the supplies. You have my word.'

'Glad to hear it.'

Epaticcus nodded gravely at Bladocus. 'Let's hope your Druid friends settle this matter in our favour. Because if they don't, there's going to be trouble. Not even the gods will be able to stop war from breaking out.'

CHAPTER SEVENTEEN

The next day, shortly after dawn had broken, our small party rode out of Merladion. It was unusually warm for autumn, and the sun pulsed in the bright blue dome of sky, burnishing the bare slopes of the surrounding hills and burning up the milky wisps of mist clinging to the ground. I felt no relief at leaving the sanctuary after eight long years. Instead, as we carried on down the rutted track heading east, I thought only of the growing turmoil waiting for me at home.

That evening we rested at a village on the frontier with the Dobunni tribe. Epaticcus bartered with the headman and traded a few coins for a finespun tunic, patterned cape and leggings to replace the tattered tunic I had worn at the sanctuary. The following day we crossed over into the lands of the Dobunni. They were our nominal allies, but I could see the anxiety written into the features of our hosts when we stopped for shelter each night. In their capital, a familiar face greeted me at the main gate. It was Sediacus. I was delighted to see him again, but the threat of war loomed large during the short time we spent together that evening.

'The tribal chiefs are all saying the same thing,' he said as we ate in the royal hall with his uncle, King Antedius.

'And what is that?' I asked.

Sediacus lowered his voice so Bladocus would not overhear. 'The Druids' assembly will solve nothing. It's a waste of time.'

'Then your chiefs are better at prophecy than the Druids themselves, it seems.' I smiled at my own feeble joke. But I didn't really believe in the prospect of a peaceful resolution. The enmity between our people and the Atrebates ran so deep I doubted even the Druid council could resolve the quarrel between our tribes.

'Will your uncle really support us, if it's war?' I asked, filling the silence.

'The king will do what is best for the Dobunni.' Sediacus smiled weakly.

'What does that mean?'

'Your father has put him in a difficult position. My uncle has no interest in getting involved in what he sees as a feud between your people and the Atrebates. Some of the chiefs are already questioning the wisdom of seeking an alliance with the Catuvellaunians, if we are to be dragged into a conflict.'

'But he's agreed to back our claim.'

'Quite so. And if it comes to it, we shall honour the treaty and fight alongside your father, within reason. Many won't like that, of course.'

'Verica is our common enemy,' I pressed him. 'You share a border with him as well. If he's willing to steal our lands, what is there to stop him from invading your territory?'

'You're right, but the chiefs won't see it that way. They only care about their own villages. They'll have to supply their quota of men for the war-bands, which means there will be no one to gather the harvest if the conflict endures too long. Crops will be left to rot; it will be a hard winter for our tribe. It will cost my uncle much silver to raise, feed and equip his army. Money the royal court can ill afford to spare.'

I suddenly felt very tired. 'Does any tribe in Britannia look beyond their own narrow interests?'

'Why should they, my friend, when our rulers are so fond of war? If your farm is under threat from your neighbours across the river, you do not trouble yourself with the concerns of distant kings. Or die in their wars.'

'Then let us hope it doesn't come to that,' I replied.

We left the capital the next day, and on the third afternoon we arrived at Abondun, a sprawling settlement set in a valley beside the confluence of two rivers, enclosed on the landward approaches by a series of huge defensive earthworks. Abondun had once been a small village but with the growth of the Roman interest in Lhandain and the lands surrounding it a small number of foreign merchants had settled in the area, keen to take advantage of the Roman thirst for our goods. Some of the townsfolk had grown rich from this trade, and a few of the newcomers had spied an opportunity to exploit the inhabitants. As a result, a handful of Roman-style taverns had opened their doors in Abondun, offering a selection of imported wines as well as some traditional ales bartered for jewellery, furs and suchlike for those who lacked coin. After a few hours in the company of the local chief and his family, Epaticcus had suggested sampling the drink on offer at one of these taverns; a place recommended by a warrior back in Camulodunum. I had agreed, since I had nothing better to do. Bladocus, however, took a dim view of such establishments and had decided to remain at the chief's hall for the evening, along with the two other warriors.

We stumbled through the darkened alleys for a while before we finally found the place we had been looking for: a squalid timber-built structure on the fringes of Abondun, close to the sprawl of workshops, forges and store houses. A crude symbol of a vine leaf had been painted on a board above the doorframe. From within, I could hear the hubbub of voices, interspersed with peals of drunken laughter. As we drew nearer the door flew open and a portly man in a patterned tunic stumbled outside. He staggered on for a few paces, then doubled over and vomited onto the ground.

'Someone recommended this place . . .' I shot a sceptical look at Epaticcus.

'My friend says it is the best on offer.'

I looked at him with raised eyebrows. 'There are worse ones than this?'

'Sounds lively enough to me. Anyway, it's got to be better than listening to the chief and his cronies blathering on all night.'

Epaticcus marched up to the entrance and wrenched open the door. I followed him into the clammy warmth of the tavern, squinting as my eyes adjusted to the flickering apricot glow from the hearth-fire and oil lamps. A dozen or so drinkers sat at the tables around the room, knocking back cups of wine and beer. Many of them wore the patterned tunics, leggings and golden torcs of the local warrior-caste, their arms and faces adorned with swirling tattoos.

A few paused to look in our direction as we approached the counter.

Epaticcus signalled to the barman, a shaggy-bearded fellow in a drab brown tunic. He shuffled over, his heavily lidded eyes watching us closely. 'What can I get for you?'

'Give us a jug of ale,' Epaticcus said. 'Two cups.'

The barman nodded and produced a jug and a pair of chipped clay cups from somewhere behind the counter. He slid them across to us, extended his palm and named an exorbitant price. Epaticcus snorted with outrage. 'You are joking. I'm not paying that.'

'Don't blame me,' the barman countered. He spoke our tongue with a strong Gallic accent which made him difficult to understand. 'It's all this trouble down in Lhandain, disrupting the trade in goods up the river. We haven't had a decent shipment in weeks, and the ones I do get are costing me twice as much.'

'That's not our problem.'

'It is, if you wish to enjoy my fine establishment,' the Gaul said, without a hint of irony.

'At the prices you're charging, you must be making a killing.'

The barman shrugged. 'Pay up, or piss off and stop wasting my time. Makes no difference to me.'

'Uncle, don't,' I said quietly. 'We don't want to make trouble.'

Epaticcus glared back angrily. I saw his fists clench at his sides, and for an instant I thought he might swing a punch at the other man. Then the dark look passed from his face and he reached for his leather purse and fished out a few silver coins.

Amid the smoke and hubbub of loud voices and laughter my eye was drawn to a cluster of burly-looking figures seated at a pair of trestle tables near the hearth.

'Who are they?' I asked, gesturing towards the group.

The Gaul wrinkled up his face. 'That lot are with a noble from up north. Travelled in here a week ago on the orders of King Antedius himself.'

'Why? Is Abondun under threat?'

The Gaul gave me a funny look. 'We're on the border with both the Atrebates and the Catuvellaunians. The king's worried that Verica might decide to attack us too if this situation with Lhandain gets any worse. Use it as a pretext for taking over our trading posts. Not that

169

this lot would stand a chance against Verica's men. They spend most of their time drinking and brawling instead of training.'

'Must be good for business.'

He shrugged. 'Good in some ways. Bad in others.'

'Meaning?'

'Some of my regulars have been scared away by this mob.' He sounded bitter. 'They prefer to do their drinking somewhere a little less rowdy.'

'Why is that a problem?' Epaticcus said. 'You've got plenty of customers, from the look of it.'

'I make a better profit on the wine. The local quality can't get enough of the stuff. They'd sell their own mothers for a jar of it. The margin on the beer, sadly, is nowhere near as good. I barely make a profit on it.'

'Liar.' Epaticcus slapped the coins down on the counter and glowered at the Gaul. He grabbed the jug and drinking vessels, then marched over to the nearest spare table.

'Bloody Gauls,' he muttered. 'Thieves, the lot of 'em.'

We planted ourselves on the crudely constructed bench, giving ourselves a good view of the tavern. Epaticcus lifted the jug and poured the amber liquid into both cups, filling them to the brim. He handed one to me. 'Here. Get this down your neck.'

I took the cup and gulped down a mouthful of ale. Across the table, Epaticcus smacked his lips approvingly.

'Not bad, eh? The Dobunnians might be a bunch of lazy farmers, but they know a thing or two about brewing beer.'

I glanced round the tavern. 'Looks like this is a popular spot.'

Epaticcus scoffed. 'It's a passing fashion. Drinking in taverns will never catch on. Why sit with a bunch of strangers when you can booze in the comfort of your own roundhouse? Doesn't make any sense.'

'We're drinking here,' I pointed out.

'That's different. And we're not getting pissed on skinfuls of foreign wine, unlike this lot.' He cocked his chin at the others. 'Look at them. They'll be wearing togas and speaking Latin next. And they're supposed to be our allies.'

'I didn't realise that Roman influence had spread so far inland.'

My uncle laughed bitterly. 'If you thought things were bad here, you should see Calleva.'

I asked him what he meant. He said, 'From what travellers tells us, the town is crawling with Roman merchants these days. Verica has even taken to entertaining them at banquets, would you believe. And it gets worse. A bunch of Romans have set themselves up in Camulodunum too. Spreading their tentacles across our lands, like some bloody sea monster.'

I frowned. There had always been a few Gaulish traders living at our tribal capital, but this was something else. 'Father tolerates this?'

'He doesn't have a choice. Some of the elders have grown rich from their dealings with the merchants, and plenty of them have started indulging themselves with Roman wine and other luxuries. Including your older brother.'

'Adminius? He has a taste for wine these days?'

My uncle nodded. 'Not just that. Adminius has made friends with a few of the merchants. I've seen one or two of them hanging around the royal court lately.'

'I can't imagine Father approves, given his own views on Rome.'

'What can he say?' Epaticcus shifted his weight on the bench. 'Things are complicated at home, lad. Your father has fought hard to resist the growing encroachment of Rome in the affairs of our people. But he's also realistic enough to know that we can't risk pissing off the Romans or their friends among the Catuvellaunian nobility. So he allows a handful of merchants to operate on our soil, as long as they keep their noses out of our politics and don't stir up any trouble. It's a fine line, and up to now that approach has kept everyone content. But this business over Lhandain has got the court divided.'

I asked my uncle what he meant.

'Some of the elders are concerned about your father's insistence on claiming Lhandain by whatever means possible. They reckon Lhandain is more trouble than it's worth, especially if Rome gets dragged into the struggle.'

'But the land is ours. It was promised to us. Our ancestors shook hands over it.'

'I agree. But some of the elders see things differently. They won't

171

say so publicly, but they worry that your father is overestimating the significance of Lhandain.'

I shook my head. 'Father cannot let the territory fall into the hands of the Atrebates. It would mean a pro-Roman kingdom gaining control of a lucrative trading post, right on our doorstep.'

'I know. But we're not the ones having to make the tough decisions. Your father has got to balance the competing interests of the nobles.' Epaticcus briefly contemplated his cup. 'Between you and me, the situation is taking its toll on him.'

'How so?'

'He's growing tired. And cautious. He knows that this dispute could split the tribe if he handles it in the wrong way. He can't afford to have powerful nobles or the men of the wise council turn against him.'

'It doesn't matter what they think,' I said. 'If the Druids can't resolve the situation, every warrior in the tribe will be demanding Verica's head.'

'I hope you're right. But there's one thing I do know.'

'What's that?'

'If we have to go to war, it'll be a tough fight. Verica has spent years strengthening his war-bands.'

He swallowed the dregs of his beer, golden drops dribbling down his chin. Then he reached for the jug and refilled both our cups. 'Right. Enough talk of politics. Let's celebrate.'

I frowned. 'What are we celebrating?'

'The end of your studies, you idiot. What else?' He slapped me cheerfully on the shoulder. 'Bet you're glad to get away from that shithole!'

I groaned inwardly, remembering my uncle's fearsome capacity for drink. There was no way I could hope to keep up with him, so I tried to pace myself with small sips of the warm, spicy brew. But after several beers a dense fog began to settle behind my eyes, and I found it hard to focus on Epaticcus as he regaled me with another one of his old war stories. A while later he emptied the last few drops from the jug into his cup and chucked a few coins onto the table.

'Here. Get another round in,' he said.

I looked up at him. 'Why me?'

'Because I fucking said so, that's why.'

He gave me a flinty look. I scooped up the coins and made my way to the counter, my head swimming. Walking was even worse than sitting down, and I had to concentrate on the simple act of putting one foot in front of the other. The tavern was heaving with drinkers at that late hour, and a crowd of warriors stood beside the counter, laughing and chatting in the familiar guttural dialect of the Dobunnians. As I blundered forward a stocky figure carrying a cup of dark ale turned away from his comrades and knocked into me, spilling his drink down my fresh tunic.

'Watch it, you clumsy bastard!' the man growled.

I stopped and focused my drunken gaze on the man. He was dressed in a pair of colourful leggings and a striped tunic fastened at the waist with a leather belt, and his long hair had been plaited into a pigtail in the fashion of the Dobunni warriors. Tattoos adorned his muscular arms. The pinkish scars on his knuckles and face hinted at his fighting experience. His eyes bulged with anger as he took a step towards me and stabbed a finger at my chest.

'You just made me spill my beer,' the Dobunnian said, thrusting his heavily scarred face to within inches of mine. His speech was thickened with drink, and I could smell the rancid tang of ale on his breath. 'You owe me another one.'

My jaw tensed. I felt the anger pounding in my veins, mixing with the beer. 'I don't owe you a thing. Look at my tunic. It's soaked! It's you that owes me a drink.'

'Bollocks,' the Dobunnian snarled. 'Ain't my fault. You should have looked where you were going.' He spat on the hay-strewn floor. 'Now pay up.'

'No.'

The Dobunnian set down his cup on the counter and took another step towards me, his hands balled into tight fists. The conversation among his companions ceased as they turned towards us, sensing the mood turning hostile. The warrior glared at me with a contemptuous sneer.

'I ain't asking nicely again,' he growled.

I tensed my muscles and forced myself to stand up to the warrior. 'If that's how you want to settle it, my friend . . .'

As I edged closer, I saw a blur of movement in the corner of my eye as Epaticcus marched over. 'What's going on here? What's the fucking problem?'

'Stay out of this, old man,' the Dobunnian slurred. 'This doesn't involve you. It's between me and this stinking turd.'

My uncle held up his hands. 'There's no need for this, lads. You've had too much to drink, the pair of you. Stop acting like idiots.'

'The only idiot around here is this piece of shit,' I replied between gritted teeth.

The Dobunnian glared savagely at me. 'Is that a fact?'

I started to reply, but then the barman swept round the counter and hurried over to us, waving his arms furiously.

'Not in here, gentlemen!' He pointed to a small door at the rear of the tavern. 'If you've got a problem, take it out back. I'll have no fighting inside.'

The warrior's thick lips curled up at the corners in a drunken grin. 'Fine by me. One place is just as good as another.'

'Let's get on with it,' I snarled back.

'Fight! Everyone outside!' one of the drinkers shouted gleefully.

There was a dull scraping of benches and stools across the floor as the customers shot to their feet and swept towards the door at the back of the room. Some carried their drinks with them, while others talked in excited voices about the unexpected but welcome addition to the evening's entertainment. From the fragments of conversation I overheard, most of the drinkers seemed to favour the Dobunnian's chances. Epaticcus saw me wobbling towards the doorway, tutted and shook his head.

'Is this really necessary?' he asked in a low voice.

'What do you mean?' I slurred. 'You're always getting into scraps, Uncle. You said so yourself.'

'Not when I'm three sheets to the wind, I ain't. Look at you, lad. You're in no fit condition to fight. Lud, you can barely even stand up.'

'You saw it. The oaf's to blame,' I protested sourly. 'If he wants a fight, I'll give him one.'

I followed Epaticcus through the doorway and emerged into a cramped alley contained on three sides by stone-built sheds. Piles of rubbish had been dumped outside the tavern, and a fetid stench of dung and woodsmoke hung thick in the air. The ground was an expanse of churned-up dark mud, squelching underfoot as I made my way across the makeshift circle. I took up my position three paces from the warrior, while two of the drinkers carried out pitch torches taken from inside the tavern. Their wavering orange glow lit up the scene as the rest of the spectators gathered round.

A short warrior with spiked hair had taken it upon himself to act as umpire. My eyes kept spiralling round and I struggled to listen as he addressed us.

'Keep it honest, gentlemen,' he said, shouting to make himself heard above the din of the rowdy onlookers. 'First to yield loses the fight. Ready?' We both nodded and I felt my legs swaying beneath me. 'Then begin!'

He jumped back as the huge warrior staggered towards me in a wild charge. He dropped his shoulder and took a ragged swing at me with his right arm, aiming for my jaw. The Dobunnian misjudged the distance and cursed as his fist sailed harmlessly through the air, missing me by several inches while the spectators laughed.

'Come on, Lugovesus!' one of the spectators called out. 'You can do better than that!'

'Try hitting him next time!' another drinker urged.

I shook my groggy head, frantically trying to clear the fog behind my eyes. Then I lunged forward, throwing a punch at my opponent's midriff. I had spent countless hours at the training ground at Merladion, learning how to fight under the guidance of Mendax, but now my limbs felt heavy and slow, as if I was moving through deep snow, and the warrior easily evaded the attack, staggering back towards the stone wall. Voices in the crowd urged us to fight. Several others chuckled at our pitiful attempts to land a blow. I came forward once more and took another clumsy swipe at the warrior, aiming for his chin. The Dobunnian threw himself to my left at the last moment and I struck the wall immediately behind him, scraping my knuckles against the stonework, prompting another chorus of raucous laughter.

'Call this a fight?' someone bellowed hoarsely. 'Someone punch someone, for Lud's sake!'

I wobbled round to face the Dobunnian and almost lost my balance. Then I refocused just in time to see the warrior lurching forwards, moving like a demented bull as he shaped to punch me in the head. I stood frozen, but before he could strike me the Dobunnian gave a sudden cry of surprise as he slipped on a dark puddle and pitched forward, arms flailing. He splattered into the mud a few paces away, his head planted face-down in the puddle.

There was a silent pause before my opponent slowly picked himself up, his face and tunic splattered with filth. For an instant I thought he might charge towards me again. Then I caught the man's eye, and the absurdity of the fight dawned on both of us. The Dobunnian's chest started to heave up and down with laughter. I smiled, and soon we were both roaring as the crowd looked on in bewilderment. After a few moments the warrior staggered over to me and offered his hand in drunken friendship.

'I suggest, brother, that we call it a draw,' he said. 'Before we both make even bigger arses of ourselves.'

'I couldn't agree more.'

We clasped forearms, and then the umpire strode briskly into the ring as he called out to the spectators. 'That's it, everyone! Fight's over! Back to your drinks!'

The crowd quickly thinned out, some of them grumbling about the disappointing contest as they trudged back into the tavern. Epaticcus stayed behind in the alley to wait for me, along with two of the warrior's drinking companions.

'Name's Lugovesus,' the Dobunnian said to me. 'And you are?'

'Caratacus,' I replied. 'Of the Catuvellaunian tribe.'

The warrior's mouth fell open. 'Fuck the gods! You're the son of . . . King Cunobelinus?' he stammered.

I nodded and showed him the gold ring I wore, denoting my status as a prince of the Catuvellaunian royal household. He stared at it, and then his face quickly flushed with embarrassment. He stepped back and dipped his head before me.

'Forgive me, lord,' he said. 'If I had known, I wouldn't have dared to challenge—'

I cut him off with a wave of my hand. 'You've no need to apologise, Lugovesus. The fault was mine as well as yours.'

'Aye, that's true.' The Dobunnian rubbed the nape of his neck. 'I, er, didn't mean all of them things I said before, lord. About you being a stinking turd and all.'

I smiled. 'I spent the best part of eight years living with the Silures. I've been called much worse, believe me. But you should be more careful with that tongue of yours in the future, brother. You never know who you're talking to.'

'Yes, lord.'

I canted my head in the direction of the tavern. 'Join us for a drink? My uncle's buying.'

Lugovesus's face brightened. 'Now you're talking.'

We strolled back into the tavern and shared a jug of ale with Lugovesus and his comrades. An hour or so later, we parted company and the three Dobunnians left in search of the entertainments on offer at one of the more dubious drinking holes in Abondun. Lugovesus bade me farewell with a lopsided grin, and then the giant warrior followed the others outside, lowering his head as he ducked under the low timber doorframe.

'Big lad, that one,' Epaticcus said. He scratched his elbow and burped loudly. 'Solid as a standing stone. You're lucky you didn't have to fight him sober.'

My gaze floated across to my uncle. 'What's that supposed to mean? I can handle myself.'

'I don't doubt it. But that fellow is huge. Reckon he could give Taranis himself a good licking. At least he looks like he'd be handy in a scrap. Which is more than I can say about the rest of his people.'

'You don't think the Dobunnians can fight?'

'What, this mob?' Epaticcus laughed. 'They're nothing but a bunch of plough-hands and potters for the most part. Haven't fought a proper war in years. Most of them probably couldn't tell one end of a sword from the other. If we end up against Verica, it'll be our side doing most of the fighting, not this lot.'

I suspected that my uncle's opinion of the Dobunnians was yet another example of the antipathy that governed relations between our tribes, even those we considered our allies. He gulped down the rest of his beer and slammed his cup on the table. 'Now, then,' he added. 'Hurry up and finish your drink.'

'What for? I thought we were staying here?'

'There's another place nearby, according to your new friend. With a different type of hand-to-hand combat on offer, courtesy of a few nice tarts.' He grinned. 'Who knows? Maybe there's a future in these taverns after all . . .'

CHAPTER EIGHTEEN

On the fifth day, we reached the old tribal capital at Verlamion. The settlement occupied a plateau overlooking a low valley by the river, partially enclosed by a series of steep grassy banks topped with a low stockade. Outside the imposing earthworks, the landscape was studded with isolated farmsteads and cattle. Further away, beyond the thickly wooded valleys surrounding the plateau, I could see the faint outline of the fortress where King Cassivellaunus had once made his defiant stand against Caesar's legions. It had stood empty ever since, a ghostly reminder of that fearful time when Rome had threatened to overrun the tribes of Britannia. I always felt a chill whenever I set eyes on that place.

Although it was no longer the seat of power of our tribe, Verlamion had continued to flourish in the years after my father had moved the royal court east to Camulodunum, benefiting from its strategic position on the main trade routes. The nobility had grown rich from the tax on goods passing through the valley, but the looming threat of war with Verica had provoked unease amongst the townsfolk and the settlement was in a state of panic.

Their anxiety was understandable. If Moricanus and his Atrebatan allies succeeded in their claim, they would gain control of the lucrative flow of trade along the Tamesis. The Atrebates could then cut off the supply of goods to Verlamion, or even attempt to take the camp by force. The capture of our former tribal stronghold would be a significant victory for the Atrebates. From Verlamion, they could launch raids deep into our territory, perhaps even threatening Camulodunum itself.

I tried to shake off this gloomy train of thought as we set off again the next morning. Bladocus left us to join his fellow council members in Lhandain, while the rest of our party continued towards Camulodunum. Two days later we arrived at the great capital of our tribe. A pair of guards greeted us in front of the outer ditch and led us through the timber gateway into the sprawling settlement. As we dismounted, I noticed a miserable-looking crowd occupying the ground in front of the royal stables. Some of them had erected crude tents; others lay on beds of bracken and rushes. A group of them stared at us, talking amongst themselves in muted voices. They cut a pitiful sight. I saw mothers comforting their wailing infants, scrawny children dressed in tattered rags.

Epaticcus beckoned to one of the guards standing near the gatehouse, a short, stocky warrior dressed in bright-blue leggings, who marched over and dipped his head before him in greeting. 'Yes, lord?'

'Who are these people?' Epaticcus asked, jabbing a thumb in the direction of the bedraggled multitude in front of the stables.

'Refugees, lord,' the guard said. 'From Lhandain.'

'What are they doing here?'

The guard looked at us in surprise. 'Haven't you heard the news? Moricanus has booted the Catuvellaunians out of Lhandain. We've had hundreds of the buggers arriving over the past few days. The locals aren't too happy, as you can imagine.'

My uncle clenched his jaw. 'That bastard Moricanus . . . Most of these people have lived in Lhandain for generations.'

The guard shrugged. 'I'm just telling you what I know, my lord.'

'How did Moricanus manage to turf all these people out of their homes?' I asked. 'I wouldn't have thought he'd have enough men for the job.'

'Verica sent one of his war-bands up to Lhandain. To protect the independence of the settlement, he claimed.' The guard spat with contempt. 'His men seized the lands of everyone with Catuvellaunian blood and ordered them to leave at once.'

'And those who refused?'

'Put to death, so I heard.'

'Where's the king now?' Epaticcus asked.

180

The man pointed towards a separate enclosure at the far end of the settlement. 'The royal compound, lord.'

We left our mounts with the warriors from my father's bodyguard and set off down the rough track leading through the settlement. Camulodunum had changed in the years since I had left to train with the Druids. Ramshackle taverns had been erected in the filthy alleys between the densely packed roundhouses. There were many more warriors present than usual, seated on the benches outside the drinking establishments, laughing and arguing with each other as they passed round jugs of wine, while others gambled their possessions on games of dice. A line of timber warehouses and workshops stretched along the bank of the river, while a team of slaves unloaded goods from several moored boats. A bustling marketplace offered Roman goods to those who wished to indulge their appetite for foreign wine or fine cloth. Close by, on the fringes of the settlement, stood a cluster of dwellings belonging to the handful of traders who had recently settled in our territory.

We strode past the taverns towards the large compound at the far end of the town. The guards waved us through the gateway before resuming their idle chatter. I followed Epaticcus into the great hall, and we marched briskly past the rows of empty trestle tables and headed straight for the doorway at the far end of the cavernous space. A series of splintering cracks and thuds filled the air as we emerged into the training area behind the hall. To the left, a dozen or so warriors from my father's royal bodyguard practised at the wooden posts, delivering vicious hacks and slashes with their long swords. My father stood close by, flanked by his advisers and nobles. As we drew nearer, one of his aides glanced in our direction and pointed us out to my father. The King of the Catuvellaunians abruptly turned away from the training ground and moved forward to greet me, shadowed by his entourage. A smile beamed across his face.

'Caratacus! My son. Welcome home.'

As he approached I was struck by how much older my father looked. The crow's feet at the corners of his eyes were more prominent now, and his beard was more white than grey. But the cold blue eyes were still as restless and calculating as ever. I noticed a pair of youths standing dutifully at his side. The older boy looked no older than ten or eleven. He was pale-skinned, with round freckled cheeks and bright blue eyes. The other child was two or three years younger. He had fair curly hair, and he wore a silver charm around his neck. They both watched me keenly as I bowed before the king.

'Hello, Father.'

Cunobelinus gripped my shoulders and took in my appearance. 'You look well, my boy. Lean, but tough. By Lud, I hardly recognise you. You've become quite the man since I last saw you.'

'Thank you, Father.'

'How was your journey?' he asked in the gruff tone he always used when addressing his children.

I shared a quick look with Epaticcus. 'Uneventful.'

'Good, good.' My father looked tired, I thought. 'I'm told that you thrived in your studies under the Druids,' he said. 'An initiate of the first ring, no less.'

I said that was so, and my father nodded. 'Your mother would have been proud. She was always a devoted follower of the ways of the Druids, as you know.'

'Yes, Father.'

'Perhaps your achievements will inspire these lads to greater efforts.' He placed a hand on the shoulder of the freckly boy. 'You remember Maridius? He's become a strong young fellow now. And Vodenius, too,' he added, gesturing towards the younger boy.

The last time I had seen my little brothers, they had been mere infants. They regarded me shyly and I smiled warmly at them. 'Hello, my brothers.'

'I assume your uncle has explained the reasons for your return to us,' my father said, changing the subject. 'I imagine you were reluctant to abandon your studies, but you must understand the urgency of the situation in Lhandain. A remote Druid sanctuary is no place for a prince at such a critical time.'

'Looks like things have got worse since I left.' Epaticcus waved in the direction of the stables and the people camped out in the open.

'Yes.' My father grimaced. 'It seems Verica is determined to expel any dissenting elements from Lhandain.'

'We should make him pay for that,' Epaticcus said. 'Him and that backstabbing prick, Moricanus. They cannot be allowed to get away with treating our people like dogs.'

My father shot him a dark look. 'We will look to the Druids to resolve this situation, brother. As we have discussed.'

'Yes, sire.'

As he spoke a sinewy figure swaggered over from the direction of the training ground. His bare torso rippled with honed muscle and his light brown hair hung down in thick braids about his broad shoulders. Sweat glossed his body. He stood taller than me by a few inches, I noted. I recognised him at once, despite the long years I had spent away from my family.

'Togodumnus!' I cried.

My younger brother grinned. 'By the gods of the Otherworld. Caratacus! It's really you!'

He extended a muscular forearm, and I grasped it keenly. I stared at him in astonishment, hardly able to believe that the headstrong little brother I had known back in Camulodunum had grown into this powerful warrior. 'It's good to see you, brother.'

'Likewise.' He punched me lightly on the shoulder. 'About time, too. A warrior's place is here, among his people, not sitting at the feet of some bearded hermit in a sacred grove. Let us hope you haven't forgotten how to fight like a true Catuvellaunian, while you were out there learning your tongues and spells.'

'Can you really cast spells?' Vodenius asked. He looked up at me wide-eyed.

I chuckled. 'Not yet. You have to study for many years to learn the secrets of magic. But I know a lot of stories and histories. I can recite the history and lores of the tribes in Britannia in many tongues.'

Vodenius looked disappointed. 'Sounds boring.'

'I'd like to hear a story about Druids,' said Maridius. 'Can you tell me one, Caratacus? Please?'

'Maybe later,' our father cut in. 'Your brother has travelled a long way. He must be tired.'

Just then a slender, handsome figure with close-cropped blond hair walked over from the direction of the king's hall. It took a moment before I recognised my older brother. Adminius wore a patterned tunic of Roman design, a pair of purple leggings and leather boots. Gold rings gleamed on some of his fingers, and a dagger with an ornate handle inlaid with a silver design hung from his belt. Behind him trailed several smooth-faced young men. I knew the type at once. The sycophantic sons of minor nobles and advisers to the court, aligning themselves with the presumptive heir to my father's throne in the hopes of one day sharing in the fruits of his reign.

Adminius thrust out an arm in greeting and parted his lips into a thin smile, revealing a set of perfect white teeth.

'My dear brother. How wonderful it is to see you.' His smile widened fractionally but there was an insincerity in his eyes, and I knew then that the bitter jealousy he felt towards me had not dulled in the years since I had been away from home.

'Likewise, brother,' I said.

Adminius peered at the intricate tattoos on my face and arms. 'You've acquired some rather interesting new markings, I see. And what, pray tell, is *that*?'

He pointed to the brand on my forehead, the mark of my initiation into the first ring.

'Tell me,' he went on, 'are all the Druid scholars branded like the wretched slaves they sell in the markets of Gaul?'

A few of the young followers in his entourage laughed drily. I looked evenly at him. 'You might have found that out for yourself,' I said. 'If you had dedicated yourself to your studies, instead of drinking with your cronies. You could have shown more ambition.'

'Ambition? You mean the chance to live among some savage tribes in the mountains? Honestly, I think I prefer the more civilised parts of our island.'

'The Silures are no savages.'

'Really?' Adminius sniffed the air. 'You certainly stink like one, brother.'

Our father stepped between us and placed a hand on both our shoulders.

'I'm sure Adminius is only teasing. He's delighted to see you, my boy. Isn't that so?'

Adminius curled his lips up at the corners into a cynical smile. 'Yes, Father,' he said. 'Of course.'

'Good.' My father nodded briskly at us both. 'There will be a feast tonight, in celebration of your return, Caratacus. In the meantime, Parvilius will show you to your quarters.' He indicated the commander of the royal bodyguard. 'Come to the hall at dusk. We shall talk further then. There is much to discuss.'

CHAPTER NINETEEN

Later that afternoon, as dusk crept over the valley, I made my way towards the great hall and strode down the centre to my father's private chamber at the rear of the building. A wary bodyguard stood in front of the doorway, gripping a short thrusting spear in his right hand. At my approach the man banged his fist against the doorframe and announced my arrival to the king. A moment later, my father's stentorian voice called out from behind the leather curtain. The bodyguard pulled back the heavy animal skin and I stepped into my father's private quarters. A hearth crackled in one corner of the room, and the flagstoned floor was partially covered in furs. Animal skulls, trophies from the many hunts my father had enjoyed in his prime, adorned the walls.

He sat at the head of the great council table to the left of his luxurious upholstered bed. Epaticcus, Togodumnus and Adminius were seated round the table, along with a number of minor chiefs and nobles. Most of their faces were familiar from my youth, but others I had not seen before. Some wore Roman clothing: a sure sign of Rome's growing influence. There were several silver jugs filled with wine and beer, but unlike the others my father was not drinking. He always liked to think with a clear head. That was one of the reasons he had survived for so much longer than many other kings.

'Ah, there you are, Caratacus!' he said. He indicated the empty stool next to my uncle. 'Join us, please.'

I took my seat, and my father made a brief round of introductions before he addressed us all.

'I have called you here, gentlemen, to put you in the picture before we meet with the Council of Druids,' he said. 'As you know,

I fear we are on the cusp of a great war between our tribes. There are no guarantees that the talks will succeed, but I am determined to seek a peaceful solution.'

He paused to let his words sink in, and I glanced round at the other members of the king's council. Several of them were highly regarded warriors who had marched alongside my father when he had fought against the Trinovantes and the Cantiaci. Others were smooth-faced aristocrats, men who owned large tracts of land and through their wealth had amassed sizable client followings of their own. Some commanded the loyalty of hundreds of warriors and other bondsmen. These were some of the most powerful men in the kingdom, I knew: for although my father was a great ruler, he needed the support of his nobles and the wise council in all important matters.

'The Druids have summoned us to the sacred ring at Senomagus, about fifty miles from here, just outside of Lhandain,' he continued. 'The meeting will take place in three days' time. The Druids will hear the claims of both sides before putting the decision to a vote among their members. Moricanus will be there, along with Verica and his retinue. I'll be accompanied by all of you, and my bodyguard. There will be an additional force of picked men escorting us.'

Epaticcus lifted an eyebrow. 'Do you suspect a trap, sire?'

'An ambush on sacred soil?' My father permitted himself a slight chuckle. 'I doubt even Verica would consider such disgraceful tactics. But I don't intend to take any chances.'

'What about weapons, sire?' asked Bellocatus, a stocky bearded figure who commanded one of my father's war-bands. He was a proud warrior with a fiery temper and a prickly sense of pride, the sort of fellow who believed in the warrior traditions of our tribe.

'The Druids have permitted us to carry our weapons during the talks, but I have given assurances that we will keep our swords sheathed at all times.' The king paused again while he looked round at the faces of his council. 'Understand this, gentlemen: there will be no violence at this meeting. We shall show respect to the other side at all times.'

Bellocatus bowed his head. 'As you wish, sire.'

One of the older nobles cleared his throat noisily. It was Orenus, a thin-faced man with wrinkled skin and silvery hair. He had served the old king of the Trinovantes, before switching his allegiance to my father after our tribe had captured Camulodunum. He was an opportunist and I did not trust him.

'Yes, Orenus?' my father said. 'You may speak freely.'

'Sire.' Orenus laced his hands together and leaned forward. 'Forgive me, but how likely is it that the Druid members will vote in our favour?'

The king tipped his head in my direction. 'Caratacus has spent eight years living and training with the Druids. He has studied at one of their most sacred sanctuaries, he has committed their laws to memory. He knows their ways better than any of us. I have brought him here so he may advise us on how to approach the council.'

'I see.' Orenus's greying eyes skated over to me. 'Well? Are the Druids going to support our cause?'

I pursed my lips for a moment. 'It's hard to say. There are a number of different cults with members on the council. Some come from tribes who are no friends of the Catuvellaunians. That said, their first loyalty is to their cult rather than their tribe. They have sworn an oath to be impartial in their dealings with the tribes. I am confident that many will see that justice is on our side. But others will be harder to persuade.'

'Surely the council must accept our case?' Bellocatus spread his hands across the table. 'Lhandain belongs to our side. Moricanus and his cronies are trampling over the treaty that guarantees our right to Lhandain. They are breaking their word, and nothing is more sacred to the tribes than the sworn word of their rulers.'

His remark prompted a murmur of agreement from several of the more senior nobles. I waited for silence before I replied. 'It is not simply a matter of law. There are those among the Druids who fear the rising power of our tribe. Such men will not be easy to win over.'

'Then what are we to do?'

'We must make certain our case is compelling,' my father said. 'We must persuade the more reluctant members of the council to support our cause.'

'But how, sire?' Bellocatus asked. 'From what your son says, many of the Druids would rather see us frustrated than resolve the matter fairly.'

My father smiled. 'There are ways to win over men without using a long sword, Bellocatus. A point you would do well to understand.'

Orenus looked sceptical. 'And what of this supposed evidence Moricanus has vowed to produce, supporting his claim to Lhandain, sire? Do we know anything of it?'

'I am afraid not.'

Epaticcus snorted. 'Whatever it is, it won't sway the council. We have a sacred oath between our tribes, witnessed by the Druids. There's nothing stronger than that.'

'And if we lose the argument?' Orenus asked my father. 'Are you seriously suggesting that we abandon Lhandain to Moricanus and his Atrebatan overlords?'

'That is the point of the arbitration, Orenus,' the king replied. 'All parties must abide by the council's decision. Assuming they can reach one.'

The other attendees shifted uncomfortably. There was no higher power in our land than the Council of Druids: men of the innermost ring of each cult, chosen by the gods to adjudicate in all legal matters in our lands. Anyone who defied their judgements would become outcasts in their own kingdoms.

Bellocatus shook his head. 'But if the vote is likely to be split, as Caratacus implies, then why are we even bothering to talk to the Atrebates at all? Why don't we march on Lhandain at once, sire, before Verica has a chance to send up more of his men and strengthen his position?'

'And drive Verica scuttling to the Romans for help?' Adminius threw up his arms. 'Do you really wish to provoke a fight with Rome, over some trading post?'

Bellocatus did not hide his contempt. 'The Catuvellaunians never run from a fight. Especially when our cause is just and our enemy is in the wrong, my lord.'

'Enemy is a rather strong word. We are not at war with the Atrebates, or Rome.'

189

'Not yet, perhaps.'

My father said, 'We know that Verica has been seeking closer ties with Rome. There are even rumours he may seek a formal alliance with the emperor. If our warriors seize Lhandain, it is almost certain that the Romans will take his side in any conflict.'

'All the more reason to hit him now.' Bellocatus hammered a fist into the palm of his hand. 'My war-band stands ready to fight, sire. Give the word and I swear by the gods, my men will put Moricanus to the sword.'

'That is enough!' My father sighed wearily. 'We have been over this already, many times. We must not do anything that risks drawing Rome into this struggle . . . At the very least not before we have exhausted every opportunity of peace.' Bellocatus went to speak again, but my father cut him off abruptly. 'If the Druids are unable to reach a clear majority, then and only then shall we commit ourselves to action. Is that perfectly clear?'

'Yes, sire,' Bellocatus replied quietly.

'Then let us continue. And do not question my judgement again.'

Some time later, my father rose stiffly to his feet and called an end to the meeting. I followed the rest of the council members out of the king's chamber and found Togodumnus waiting for me in the gathering darkness outside the hall. 'A few of the lads are going for a drink,' he said. 'Care to join us?'

I was briefly tempted, but the day had been long, I was tired after the long journey from Merladion and I needed some time to think. 'Another evening, maybe.'

'Suit yourself.' Togodumnus glanced round to make sure no one was within earshot. 'What do you make of all that talking?'

I hesitated. 'Uncle was right. The council is badly divided. This business over Lhandain means trouble.'

My brother puffed out his cheeks. 'You don't know the half of it. Ever since Moricanus claimed the throne, the council has been split over the issue. It's got so bad that half of father's advisers won't even sit at the same table as the other lot to feast. It's a wonder they didn't come to blows just now.'

'I know . . . It seems that many of the nobles are wary of provoking Rome.'

'Can you blame them? Things have changed while you've been away, brother. And not for the better. Plenty of the elders at Camulodunum have acquired a taste for Roman wine and trinkets. Even Adminius has taken to their ways lately.'

'So I've seen.'

Togodumnus looked troubled. 'Do you think the Druids will fail us?'

'I hope not. But if I was going to bet coin on it, I'd say the most likely outcome is a split vote, with no clear winner.'

Togodumnus sighed. 'Well, if the Druids can't agree on the issue, then it's war. Like Father said.'

'Yes, it's as likely as not. And if it comes to that, then we cannot afford to fight amongst ourselves. If that happens, Verica is going to be the least of our problems.'

My father held a feast that night, in honour of my ascension to manhood and my return from the sanctuary. After the ceremonial toasts had been made my father beckoned me to his seat atop the stone dais and reached for a long, thin parcel bound in fine cloth.

'A young noble warrior is in need of a suitable weapon,' he said, unwrapping the fabric to reveal a richly decorated long sword. He smiled as he passed it to me.

'It is the sword of Tasciovanus,' he said. 'This belonged to your grandfather once. He wielded it at the Battle of Verlamion, and this very same sword cut down the Trinovantian king Ariovistus in single combat. Now it is yours. A gift, to celebrate the completion of your studies.'

I clasped my hand around the jewelled grip and tested the weight and balance. The sword was surprisingly light compared to the heavy wooden sticks I had trained with in Siluria. I bowed my head to my father while Adminius looked on with ill-disguised jealousy.

The drink flowed freely as the night wore on. The guests mingled with one another, sharing jokes and recounting old tales of heroism against hardened foes. Our feasts were boisterous affairs, compared to the sedate formality of Roman gatherings. A small crowd cheered on two men as they traded punches in a corner of the hall. Nearby, an older warrior vomited on the flagstoned floor while his companion groped one of the serving girls. I drank heavily that night, for in our tribe a young aristocrat's character is measured in part by his capacity to consume fearsome quantities of ale.

At length, I looked blearily round the hall and realised that many of the guests had left or were slumped over their tables or against the wall, sleeping. In one corner the two warriors had resumed their exchange of blows as their cronies cheered them on. Only a few small groups of men were still carousing or talking quietly. Among them I spotted a young woman sitting alone while she sipped from her drinking horn. She was around my age, tall and fair-skinned, with round cheeks and shoulder-length red hair. Her bright green tunic matched the colour of her eyes, and she wore a heavy golden torc around her slender neck, denoting her status as a noblewoman. She was strikingly beautiful. I had noticed her around the royal household earlier that day, but with all the other business to attend to there had been no time to introduce myself.

'Are you enjoying the feast, my lady?' I slurred as I wandered over to her table.

She smiled wryly. 'Not as much as some, lord.'

'My lady?'

The noblewoman tipped her drinking horn in my direction. 'It appears you have been celebrating rather enthusiastically tonight. My congratulations, lord. I'm amazed you can stand upright.'

She smiled again, in a way that suggested she was mildly amused rather than offended by my inebriated state.

'You needn't worry, lord. I grew up in a household full of warriors. I'm used to their drunken antics.'

'May I introduce myself, my lady,' I stammered. 'I am—'

'Caratacus. Yes, I know who you are. The Druid scholar. Quite the achievement, I gather. For someone from your tribe.'

I frowned. 'What's that supposed to mean?'

'Let's just say that some of your kinfolk have a reputation for boorish behaviour.'

'That's hardly fair.'

'Isn't it? What about your companions over there?' she asked, indicating the brawling warriors. 'Rather proves my point, don't you think?'

'Not all of us are like that, my lady.'

'No. I suppose not.' She smiled at me again, and I felt something warm stir in my chest. 'What about you, lord? Did you enjoy your studies with the Druids?'

I nodded. 'It was difficult at first, being so far from home and my family, and the training was demanding. But I grew to love it. I had much to learn from them – much I still have to learn.'

'Why didn't you stay there?'

'It was not to be.' I shrugged. 'The will of the gods is sometimes hard for us to comprehend.'

She gave me a considered look. 'Do you believe in that, Caratacus? The will of the gods?'

'I believe in what the Druids teach us,' I said carefully. 'The gods may guide us to the water's edge—'

'But we must make the crossing ourselves, even when the way is perilous,' she interrupted. 'Yes, I know the line. From the saga of Beranius.'

I looked at her in amazement. 'How did you know that?'

'My father thought I should have a proper education,' she explained. 'He had several tutors brought over from Gaul at great expense to teach me what they knew. He always said that one must seek knowledge, if you wish to distinguish truth from falsehood.'

'He sounds like a wise man.'

'He was.'

A faraway look clouded her eyes before she sank the rest of her ale and stood up. 'It was nice to meet you. I hope your head isn't too sore tomorrow.'

'You're leaving, my lady?' I asked clumsily.

'It's late, and I'm tired.' On the other side of the room, the spectators roared with excitement as one of the warriors caught his opponent on the jaw with a savage uppercut and sent him crashing back into the table, knocking over a load of platters and clay cups. 'And I'd like to retire to my chamber before these louts start breaking up the furniture.'

'I didn't catch your name.'

'That's because I didn't give it.' She smiled playfully. 'I'm Mardicca.'

'Goodnight, my lady.'

'Goodnight, lord.'

I watched her leave. I couldn't explain why – not at the time – but something about Mardicca intrigued me, and I found myself wanting to know more about her. Then Togodumnus stumbled over, grinning drunkenly as he threw an arm around my shoulder.

'Making friends, brother?'

'Who is she?' I asked. 'I don't remember seeing her around the court before.'

'Mardicca?' He hiccupped. 'She's the daughter of King Eppillus.'

I bit my lip, recalling the news I'd heard the previous winter about our tribe's victory over the Cantiaci at the Battle of Durovernum. Eppillus had died in battle, cut down by my father in front of his bodyguards as our forces stormed the royal compound.

'What's she doing here?'

'Father took her into the household,' Togodumnus explained. 'After the Cantiaci elders surrendered to our side. Mardicca had no family in Durovernum, and her grandmother was a Catuvellaunian noble, so Father took pity on her and allowed her to live with us.'

'Why would he do that?'

'Father has plans for her. He wants to use her to secure an alliance with another tribe through marriage.'

'Of course he does.'

'If you ask me, we're better off without her,' Togodumnus continued.

'Oh? Why's that?' I asked.

'She's too clever by half, and she dislikes most of our kin.'

'After what happened to her family, can you blame her?'

Togodumnus pondered the question. 'Perhaps not,' he said at last. 'But I prefer a good Catuvellaunian woman any day. All those Atrebatan ladies think they're better than us.' He curled up his face in disgust. 'Frankly I'd rather face a horde of Iceni warriors than marry her.'

CHAPTER TWENTY

It was a clear autumn morning when we departed for the assembly at the sacred ring. A small crowd had gathered in front of the main gate to watch our delegation leave. The mood among the locals was subdued and anxious, with none of the usual cheers of support for the king, and I was relieved when we had passed beyond the gate and started down the track leading south towards Lhandain. Our party numbered more than a hundred men. The royal bodyguards formed the head of the column. I rode behind them, alongside my father, Adminius, Togodumnus and the rest of the king's entourage. Our youngest brothers, Vodenius and Maridius, had been ordered to remain at Camulodunum, much to their disappointment. Behind us rode the various minor chiefs of the Catuvellaunians, followed by their retinues. Each man wore his individually styled torc and carried a long sword or a dagger. The sword of Tasciovanus hung by my side, looped through the metal belt fastened around my waist.

We travelled south through a series of low valleys and lush meadows. Men sang as they toiled in the fields. Scrawny children raced out of their huts to watch us pass, some excitedly running alongside our horses, while others begged for food or silver coin. Young women smiled coyly at the bodyguards. At that moment war seemed distant.

'The old man looks tired,' Togodumnus muttered as he drew up alongside me. He pointed with his eyes at our father. The king rode a short distance ahead of us, scanning the horizon with a strained expression, Adminius at his side.

'Are you surprised?' I said. 'He's carrying the fate of the kingdom on his shoulders.'

'Father shouldn't worry. Even if this goes badly, our war-bands will crush the Atrebates like vermin. We can look forward to the day the bards sing of our glorious victories over Verica's men.'

'Glorious victories?' I arched an eyebrow. 'The Atrebates are some of the toughest warriors in the land, brother. What makes you think it'll be easy to defeat them?'

'It'll be a hard struggle,' Togodumnus conceded. 'But fighting is in our blood. That's what makes us Catuvellaunians.' He gripped his reins and spat on the ground. 'Anyway, I'd rather settle this dispute with cold steel instead of talking like old men.'

'You think Father was wrong to take the matter to the Druid council?'

Togodumnus chewed his lip. 'No. He wants to try and spare bloodshed on both sides, and I respect his decision. But perhaps it is for the best if the talks do not succeed. At least with a war, we can win Lhandain with honour and put paid to any ambitions Verica may have to undermine our place above the other tribes.'

'Maybe so . . .' I thought a moment before I continued. 'Even if we do defeat Verica as easily as you say, then such a victory might cause its own dangers. There are some Druid cults who fear the growing power of the Catuvellaunians. They regard the Atrebates as a counterbalance. If we defeat them then our people will be more powerful than ever. I wonder how long it will take the other tribes to ally against us to protect themselves?'

Togodumnus chuckled. 'I think you overestimate the willingness of Celts to cooperate, brother.'

I shrugged. 'There's always a first time. If only we could harness such a common will there would be nothing that could stand before the might of the people of this island.'

'Not even Rome?' Togodumnus glanced at me with amusement.

'Perhaps,' I ventured. 'I can see a time coming when we may have to answer that question. Sooner than we are prepared for. If we do crush the Atrebates then we face the prospect of them running to the Romans for support. Who knows where that will lead us?' I shook my head bitterly. 'The whole situation is a mess. I do not envy Father.'

'You can say that again. Sometimes I wonder whether being a king is worth all the trouble.'

'Adminius doesn't appear to share that belief,' I said quietly.

'No.' Togodumnus's expression hardened. 'He's made his ambitions plain enough. Smug bastard acts like Father is merely keeping the throne warm for him.'

'What does Father think?'

Togodumnus gave a shrug of his huge shoulders. 'He's always favoured Adminius as his chosen successor. But he doesn't approve of some of Adminius's habits. Especially his new friends.'

'The Roman merchants, you mean?'

He nodded, then dropped his voice. 'The two of them rarely see eye to eye these days. And it's been worse since this trouble with Lhandain began. Father has been insisting to the wise council that we have to gain control of Lhandain by whatever means possible, but Adminius argues that we shouldn't go to war with the Atrebates. He's worried it will draw Rome in.'

'Adminius is right about that much,' I said.

Togodumnus smiled grimly. 'Better pray to the gods these talks succeed then, brother.'

I fell silent and looked away, gripped by an acute sense of frustration. The hostility between our kingdom and the Atrebates was threatening to lead us into a potentially ruinous war, at great cost to both sides. Even the Druids seemed powerless to prevent it from happening.

We camped beside a pebbly river that evening and set off again at first light. On the second afternoon, we reached a small village not far from the border with the kingdom of Lhandain. My father called our column to a halt and hastily summoned his advisers while our horses were watered at a nearby stream.

'Senomagus is only two miles away,' he said. 'The conference is set to begin at nightfall. We'll head straight to the henge. The Druids should be there already. Once all sides have arrived, they will perform the ceremonial rituals. Then the talks will begin.'

'How long will this thing take, sire?' Epaticcus asked.

'It depends on how long each side argues their case before the issue is put to a vote. Either way, we'll return here as soon as the matter has been decided. We'll sleep in the village. It's the twelfth day of the moon, so there will be plenty of light to guide us on our way back.'

We rested briefly at the village and helped ourselves to a light meal of bread and cheese, while the headman came out to pay his respects to the king. He was an old fellow, with a face like coarse leather and a grey wispy beard that clung to his chin like cobwebs. Like many of the locals he had heard of the gathering from passing travellers, and he expressed his sincere hopes that the Druids would avert a war between the tribes.

'Why?' I asked him. The headman wrung his hands and nodded in a southerly direction. 'My people do business with the Roman agents in Lhandain. They buy our grain and ship it across the sea.' He grinned, revealing a handful of stained teeth. 'The legions on the Rhine are hungry.'

I shot him a cold look. 'You are feeding the bellies of soldiers who may one day come and steal your land.'

He shrugged. 'The Romans pay a good price. I have mouths of my own to feed.'

I had nothing else to say to him. We were a maddening people sometimes.

We set off again a short time later and followed the track towards Senomagus, passing through a shallow vale fringed on both sides with dense, gloomy woodland. We were in the territory of Lhandain now. The atmosphere was oppressive, and I glanced warily at the treeline, looking for any sign of a lurking enemy amid the shadows. Then I forced myself to relax. Moricanus and his allies had sworn to respect the rules of the gathering. They were unlikely to break the oath, and risk incurring the wrath of the Druids by launching an ambush on our delegation.

Half an hour later we passed through a small coppice and the track abruptly steepened as it climbed towards the crest of a grassy hillock pocked with felled trees. We steered our tired mounts towards the top of the mound and then, in the approaching dusk, I caught my first sight of Senomagus. The Druids' sacred enclosure was below us, in the middle of a sprawling plain. A flat strip of grass, roughly half a mile long and lined at regular intervals with stone posts, ran towards an open gateway at the western edge of a vast circular enclosure surrounded by a low earthen bank and a ditch.

A short distance beyond the timber gateway stood a wide circle of around sixty stones topped with horizontal lintels, surrounded by an outer ring of flickering torches. On the southern side of the ring there was a smaller entrance and avenue leading down to the bank of the Tamesis three miles away. Beyond the enclosure the landscape was dotted with burial mounds belonging to the local chieftains and renowned warriors, each one the size of a small hill. Fires glowed in the spaces between the markers along both avenues, illuminating the scene for miles in every direction. The flames meant the Druids were making the ground ready for the ceremonies. There are rituals to be performed before such gatherings, but I shall not describe them here as they are sacred to our people and the gods would punish me for sharing the details with any Romans who read this account of my life.

'Quite a sight,' Togodumnus remarked.

'That's one way of putting it,' Epaticcus said. 'This place gives me the fucking chills.'

'Who built this, I wonder?' Togodumnus asked.

'Giants. Who else? The same ones who used to roam these lands, hundreds of years ago.'

'It seems our Atrebatan friends have already arrived,' my father said. He pointed towards a large crowd of figures and horses mingling on the open ground close to the main avenue. I guessed there had to be at least two hundred of them in total.

'Looks like Verica has brought along every noble in the land.' Epaticcus spat.

'It's a show of strength,' I said. 'Verica wants us to see what we're up against if we have to go to war with Moricanus and his allies. It's a clever move.'

'He won't look so clever when my sword is buried in his stomach.'

My father scowled. 'There will be no threats made to the other side during these talks. We must present our case to the council with calm heads, without resorting to insults. Such tactics will only turn the Druids against us. Come.' He tugged on his reins. 'Let's get this over with.'

We spurred on our mounts and continued down the slope as the sun dipped fully below the horizon, smothering the valley in a gloomy dusk. At length we reached the stretch of levelled ground in front of the fire-lit avenue, and at my father's command we drew to a halt and slid from our horses. Ahead of us, the Atrebatan delegation had started making their way inside the henge, accompanied by their warriors and advisers. A separate cluster of retainers, guards and servants waited near the edge of the enclosure, watching over their masters' horses. Close by, I spotted a smaller group of Druid bodyguards standing beside a pack of ponies.

A trio of Druids strode briskly over to us from the direction of the entrance, dressed in black robes. Bladocus was among them, I noticed. The Druids stopped a few paces away, and then one of them, a short, fat man with a cowl pulled over his tattooed head, stepped forward and bowed slightly in front of my father.

'Welcome.' He spoke our tongue in a vile accent. 'Please leave your horses here and follow me. We must go inside now. The High Council of the orders is ready to begin the ceremony.'

He wheeled round and started down the avenue at a quick pace, while my father ordered his servants to wait with the mounts. At the same time the rest of our party joined the remaining trickle of Atrebatans hastening down the avenue towards the main gateway. As we started to follow them towards the enclosure, Bladocus fell into step alongside me. He kept a close eye on the other Druids as they marched several paces ahead of us.

'Listen carefully,' he said, speaking to me in a hushed voice. 'There's something you should know.'

There was an urgency to my mentor's voice I had never heard before. 'What is it, Master?'

Bladocus stayed silent while a Druid bodyguard hurried past. As soon as the other man had moved out of earshot, he said, 'Someone attempted to bribe me in Lhandain.'

I paused mid-stride and looked at him. 'Who?'

Bladocus gestured for me to keep moving as he continued. 'A Roman merchant. He gave me no name, but he claimed to be acting on behalf of a group of concerned traders at the settlement. He wanted me to vote in favour of an Atrebatan outcome.'

'When was this?'

'Two days ago. Shortly after the High Council arrived.'

Unease ran through me like a knife. I asked the obvious question. 'Has anyone else on the High Council been approached?'

'I believe so, yes.'

I swallowed. 'Then we must bring this to the attention of the other Druids. At once.'

'That would not be wise.'

'Why not, Master?'

Bladocus licked his lips and glanced quickly round. 'I fear that some of the other council members might have been less principled in their dealings with the Roman than myself.'

I was startled. 'You think others have taken the bribe?'

'Some Druids are not immune to the temptations of Roman wine and coin,' he replied bitterly.

A chill slithered down my spine, and I suddenly felt cold in spite of the warmth of the fires either side of the stone avenue.

'Do we have any proof?' I asked.

Bladocus shook his head. 'Not yet.'

'Then what is to be done, Master?'

There was no time to reply as we approached the crowd milling about just inside the gateway. Dozens of human skulls had been nailed to the immense timber columns either side of the entrance, victims of the sacrificial offerings made to our gods. Beyond the entrance, the inner ditch had been filled with the bones of slaughtered animals. The whole place carried the unmistakable stench of death.

Several Druid attendants were busy directing the latest arrivals to their positions around the ring. One approached and gestured to us. We followed him past the ring of fire until we reached the sacred stones, each one as tall as three men and covered with patches of lichen. We took up our places on the left side of the stone circle, while Bladocus and the other Druids joined the rest of the council members standing either side of a large stone altar stained with dried blood. The Atrebatan delegates stood in a large group on the right side of the ring, their warriors easily identifiable from their hairstyles, torcs and patterned cloaks. Many of them glowered at us with expressions of silent hostility.

'Can't say I'm happy about the odds here,' Epaticcus muttered. 'We're badly outnumbered. If it all kicks off, we're going to be in trouble.'

'Don't be ridiculous,' Adminius snapped irritably. 'Even Verica and his friends wouldn't be foolish enough to fight us on sacred ground.'

'Quiet!' my father hissed.

As soon as everyone had taken up their positions, a Druid wielding a bronze sickle stepped forward, calling for silence. For a moment there was no sound except for the sharp crackle of the surrounding fires, and the distant churring of the nightjars. Then a white-bearded Druid emerged from the dense blackness beyond the stones. The bull-horned headpiece denoted his station as the High Druid, Lud's chosen representative in our world, bestowed with the powers to communicate with the gods. The man stopped beside the altar and swept his gaze around the ranks of the royals, nobles, warriors and Druids standing before him.

'Before we begin, all those present must swear an oath,' he said, his frail voice echoing off the stones around us. 'Each of you must vow to respect any judgement passed by this council before the gods. Anyone who refuses to abide by the decisions made tonight shall suffer the shame of the dishonoured and be forever an outcast of the tribes. Now, repeat the oath after me.'

We placed our right hands on our sheathed swords and repeated the words chanted by the High Druid. Then he turned to my father. 'Do you have the offering for the gods?'

'I do.'

The king said something to Parvilius. The commander of the royal bodyguard beckoned to two of his men, and they dragged forward a skeletal figure dressed in a pair of threadbare leggings. His hands had been bound with rope behind his back, and his bare chest was covered in painful-looking welts and scars.

The man in question was a cattle thief: one of the lowest types of malefactor in our tribe. Now he was to be sacrificed to the gods by the Druids. Perhaps, Roman, you are appalled by this custom, and you would not be alone. I have heard many of your countrymen express their disgust at our practices, even as they excitedly discuss the latest orgy of bloodshed at the amphitheatre here in Rome. But I must tell you the story of what really happened, however distasteful you may find it. And the truth is, the gods of our lands must be appeased before such meetings. To conduct the assembly without their consent, on sacred ground, would only incite their fury and bring misery on our people.

The High Druid accepted a dagger from one of his attendants. He closed his eyes and chanted the words sacred to our faith, while the guards thrust the prisoner onto his knees. The man did not protest or plead for his life. He did not dare, for only those who boldly embrace death are permitted to join Lud in the great hall in the Otherworld, feasting on the choicest meat and the finest beer. To give the prisoner strength for his journey, one of the Druids' attendants handed him a drink made from the juice of sloe flowers mixed with herbs and the blood of a slain white bull. The man drained the cup, and then he ate the bowl of mushrooms given to him by a second attendant.

When he had finished, the High Druid began another incantation. Then he raised the dagger above his head, and I saw the tip reflecting the blazing light of the fires a moment before he plunged the blade down, stabbing the prisoner in the back of the neck. The man spasmed and gave out a gurgle as he fell forward, slumping to the ground. As the prisoner lay writhing, the Druids swiftly crowded round him, stooping to inspect the twitching of his limbs and observing the flow of blood pulsing out from his wound to determine the will of the gods.

At last the prisoner drew his final breath. The attendants dragged his corpse away, and then the High Druid stretched to his full height as he turned to address both delegations.

'The death throes are propitious,' he declared. 'Lud has accepted this gift brought by the petitioner in his honour. The meeting may commence.'

The High Druid passed the bloodstained dagger to one of his servants. Then he folded his hands behind his back and continued to address the crowd gathered around the circle of fire and stone.

'We are here tonight to resolve the competing claims to the kingdom of Lhandain, lately ruled by Prince Trigomaris. Among us we have representatives from the royal court at Lhandain, from their allies the Atrebates and from the Catuvellaunians. We shall presently hear from both sides regarding their claims. Once the arguments have been heard, each member of the council will cast their vote. As the petitioners, the Catuvellaunian delegation shall go first.'

My father stepped forward and trained his gaze on the Druids by the altar, addressing his appeal directly to the council.

'Wise men of the High Council,' my father began. 'I am Cunobelinus, High King of the Catuvellaunians, Trinovantes and Cantiaci. I thank you for giving us this opportunity to make our argument. I shall keep my comments short, but do not mistake brevity for lack of substance. For the facts of the case are plain to see. Lhandain belongs to our side. There is, truthfully, no claim stronger than ours.'

He paused, his hands folded behind his back, keeping his eyes firmly fixed on the Druids and making sure he had their full attention. Never once did he so much as glance at the Atrebatan contingent. In doing so, he rendered them almost irrelevant to the debate. My father knew how to make a speech as well as any would-be Cicero in the law courts of Rome.

'There was, as you all know, an agreement between our tribe and the grandfather of the late, honourable Prince Trigomaris, which clearly stated that his lands would pass to our kingdom in the event he died without male issue. This agreement, I might add, was accepted by all the council of nobles in Lhandain. Indeed, this venerable council witnessed the treaty at the time.'

The High Druid rested his chin on his balled fist as he pondered. 'But that treaty is no longer valid. Moricanus claims that the land was promised to him, by Trigomaris himself.'

'That is a lie, issued from the lips of the treacherous usurper Moricanus,' my father countered. 'Trigomaris publicly declared his intention never to let his lands fall into the hands of the Atrebates. He would never agree to renege on our treaty.'

'That is an opinion contested by several members of the Atrebatan side,' the High Druid stated. 'Do you have any other grounds to support your claim, Cunobelinus, other than some half-remembered treaty agreed generations ago, with not one witness alive to confirm your version of events?'

'I have the claim of ancestry and bloodline.' My father swept an arm around him, indicating the surrounding valley. 'Gentlemen, look around you. This land has been home to our kinfolk for generations. It once belonged to my ancestor, Cassivellaunus. The people of this kingdom speak our tongue, practise our customs and marry into our families. Many have fought in our war-bands. Lhandain is, and always will be, Catuvellaunian in all but name.'

The High Druid said, 'That is hardly an indisputable claim. Tribes cannot annex lands simply because a few of the inhabitants braid their hair in the same fashion.'

'Whose fucking side is he on?' Epaticcus whispered.

'Not ours,' I muttered. 'That's for sure.'

My father shook his head vigorously. 'The ties between Lhandain and our tribe are far deeper than that. They are blood brothers of our tribe. But there is another reason to award the territory to our side. Perhaps the most important reason of all, even more so than the treaty between our tribes.'

'Do go on, Cunobelinus,' the High Druid said.

'Rome's influence is stealthily creeping across our land. We all know this to be true. Some among us have tried to resist their encroachment wherever possible, trading with the foreigners while keeping them at arm's length. This has not always been easy. But others have taken a different path, seeking ever closer ties with the Romans. Men such as Verica. If you allow the kingdom to fall into the hands of Prince Moricanus and his Atrebatan allies, they will surely encourage further Roman interest in our lands. Is that what we want?'

'The king makes an excellent point,' Bladocus said. 'We all know what happened when Rome interfered in the tribal affairs of Gaul, brothers. Untold numbers of massacred warriors, the land reduced to waste, the womenfolk and children of the most noble families condemned to the depredations of slavery.'

The High Druid rolled his eyes. 'Come now, Bladocus. A few Roman merchants do not constitute a grave threat. Foreigners have traded in the settlements of our tribes for generations without any trouble.'

'This is different.' My father was warming to his theme now, and there was a note of anger in his voice as he continued. 'For many years, it is true, we have lived without fear of reprisal or invasion from our hated foes across the sea. But I fear that time is now behind us. The legions have crushed the Germanic tribes, their leaders have been exiled or put to the sword, and the frontier along the Rhenus is all but secure. How long before Rome turns her greedy eye towards us again? We must act now to stop the poison of Rome seeping into our lands. And the only way to do that is to award Lhandain to our tribe. Only the Catuvellaunians have the power to prevent the great calamity that threatens the tribes of our island.'

It was an eloquent speech, more so than my description can convey. But as I scanned the cautious expressions on the faces of the Druids, I wondered if we had been able to sway enough of them in our favour.

There was a long pause of silence before the High Druid spoke again. 'Do you have anything else to add, King Cunobelinus?'

'I do not.'

'Then, if you please, we may hear from the other party.'

My father stepped back from the middle of the circle while the High Druid signalled for the Atrebatan camp to present their case. And a tall, lean man in his middle years stepped forward. His beard was neatly trimmed, and he wore a wool tunic of the finest quality, intricately threaded with gold designs. His features reminded me of a hawk, and there was a steely glint in his eyes as he glanced round the figures crowding the circle. Even then, I could see he was a dangerous man, and one you could trust about as far as you could spit a rock.

'King Verica wishes to speak,' the High Druid said.

'Thank you, wise men of the High Council.' Verica looked round the circle. 'All of you know my name. I am Verica, brother of Eppillus, brother of Tincomarus, son of Commius. My people can trace our ancestry back to the great tribes of Gaul. I speak to you here tonight as a friend of Prince Moricanus, the rightful heir to the throne of Lhandain.'

He paused and indicated a slightly built man with dark curly hair, smooth cheeks and a short Roman-style tunic beneath his brightly patterned cloak. Beside Moricanus stood a tough-looking bodyguard with a leather haversack slung over his shoulder.

'I seek peace and prosperity for all,' Verica continued. 'It is my fervent desire that we avoid war with the Catuvellaunians. We have heard some strong words from our dear friend Cunobelinus. He accuses my people of establishing ties with Rome and damns us for doing so. But what is the alternative, I ask you? Should we refuse to sell our goods to their merchants, and impoverish ourselves instead? Would rebuffing Roman merchants not merely invite conquest instead? At least this way, we may enjoy the fruits of a mutually beneficial relationship. Rome desires peaceful relations with our tribes.'

'Peace, Verica?' my father sniffed. 'Tell that to the butchered peoples of Gaul and Hispania. Aye, friends, there is such a thing as Roman peace. It is delivered at the point of a sword, and if we welcome the enemy with open arms, as Verica suggests, we will be the architects of our own destruction.'

'You speak of a time long ago, Cunobelinus. Times have changed. Rome has no more appetite for conquest now.'

'And why should we believe you, Verica?' my father called out. 'You who claim to be for peace, but who counts a murderer among his friends.'

Verica's eyes narrowed to slits. 'Explain yourself!'

'Friends,' my father replied, pointing at Moricanus, 'we have all heard the rumours surrounding the death of Trigomaris. Killed in a hunting accident by an arrow fired by one of his nobles, we are told. And yet the man in question was highly skilled with a bow. Now he too has died in suspicious circumstances. Stabbed in the neck three days after the prince's death.'

Verica sneered. 'You suggest foul play, Cunobelinus?'

'I suggest nothing, Verica. The facts speak for themselves, do they not?'

'Enough!' the High Druid yelled at the top of his voice. 'You shall refrain from making any more baseless accusations in front of the council. Verica, please continue.'

The Atrebatan nodded and turned to address himself directly to the Druids.

'As I was saying, wise ones. Rome has no reason to attack our lands. At present, she enjoys the benefits of trade with our tribes, without the crippling burden of military occupation. Why would she abandon the status quo in order to send in the legions? But there is, in fact, another threat facing us. One much closer to home. And which threatens all our interests. I speak of the Catuvellaunians.'

There was silence as Verica stepped towards the middle of the ring and waved at the throng of nobles on our side.

'These men, under their warmongering king, have conquered the lands of the Trinovantes, and the many divided kingdoms of the Cantiaci, and yet we have done nothing to stop them. They are the true aggressors, not Rome!' he thundered, his voice echoing off the tall stones. 'Give Cunobelinus control of Lhandain, and he will have a free hand to sweep across the lands of every tribe in the southern reaches of our island. None will be safe from his war-bands.'

'It is better that our people are ruled by their own kind, than a stooge of Rome,' Epaticcus shouted to a chorus of chortles from our side.

My father said, 'This is not about other lands. We are here to discuss the rightful ownership of Lhandain. Do not distract us from the issue at hand, Verica.'

'On the contrary, Verica makes a cogent point,' the High Druid said. 'Might I remind my fellow members that this council has always sought to balance the powers of the many tribes of this fair island. We all appreciate the risks of allowing any one tribe to become too powerful. Are we to abandon that policy in order to satisfy the questionable claims of King Cunobelinus and his supporters?'

Bladocus cleared his throat. 'High Lord, if I may.'

'Yes, Bladocus?'

'It is true that in the past this council has been guided by the principle of achieving a balance of power between the tribes. But I wonder if such a policy is still the wisest course, given Rome's growing interest in our affairs.'

'How so, Bladocus?'

'High Lord, we have heard King Cunobelinus talk about the threat we may one day face from our old enemies across the sea. It is a threat I know all too well.'

The High Druid smiled indulgently. 'We are all familiar with your Gaulish roots, Bladocus. Get to your point.'

'Our tribes were crushed by the Romans because we were too busy squabbling amongst ourselves, when we should have been putting our differences aside. By the time our leaders recognised the seriousness of the threat and pledged their allegiance to Vercingetorix, it was too late. That should serve as a warning to all of us here to-night. If we remain divided, our resistance will crumble in the face of the Roman legions. Only by uniting will we stand a chance against them.'

'You believe we should let the Catuvellaunians freely subjugate their neighbours?'

'I believe, High Lord, in the idea of a single powerful tribal alliance, with the strength to resist its enemies. That would serve the interests of all sides. It is, in any case, surely preferable to splitting hairs over tiny kingdoms.'

'A single alliance dominated by a single king?'

'It is not without precedent, High Lord. The tribes formed an alliance under Cassivellaunus when Caesar invaded.'

The High Druid made a face as if he'd sipped curdled milk. 'And look how that turned out, Bladocus! You fellows might have done things differently in Gaul, but here we have a rich tradition of tribal independence.'

'Too bloody right,' Epaticcus muttered.

'No,' I whispered in reply. 'What Bladocus says makes sense.'

'Pffff! You're only saying that because he's your mentor. And the tribes would never agree to set aside their differences.'

'For now, perhaps. But if Rome threatens our lands, it might be a different story.'

'You don't know the tribes, lad. Look at 'em.' He nodded at the surly Atrebatans. 'This mob would rather gouge out their own eyeballs than fight alongside us.'

The High Druid stared coldly at Bladocus, and a note of irritation crept into his voice as he spoke. 'This is not the time to address your particular designs. I suggest you focus your attention on the question at hand, Bladocus. You may continue, Verica.'

I saw something flash behind the Atrebatan king's eyes. 'Thank you, High Lord.' He paused and turned to address the other council members. 'Cunobelinus claims that Lhandain belongs to his tribe, as you have heard. But I have irrefutable proof that the lands were in fact left to our ally, Prince Moricanus.'

He signalled to Moricanus. The prince turned to his bodyguard: the latter withdrew a papyrus scroll from his leather haversack. He handed it to Verica. My father traded a questioning look with Epaticcus while the Atrebatan king held up the scroll for all to see.

'I have here a written agreement, bearing the mark of Trigomaris, confirming his dying wish to see his lands transferred to Moricanus,' he declared. 'This is a legally binding document, gentlemen. Its veracity cannot be denied.'

A murmur of surprise rippled through the gathered nobles at the sight of the scroll. This was something new. We had, of course, no written language of our own; our codes and judgements were passed down from one generation to the next; a man's word was considered as sacred as an oath sworn to Lud himself.

'The document is written in Latin,' Verica went on. 'It states Trigomaris's wishes clearly, as anyone literate in the Latin tongue can see for themselves. Lhandain is to be awarded to Prince Moricanus.'

'You make a mockery of our laws, Verica,' my father said accusingly. 'A scroll in the language of our enemies? This carries no meaning in our society. The esteemed members of the council will surely treat this evidence with the contempt it deserves.'

'We had no choice. Trigomaris was gravely ill after his hunting accident,' Moricanus added in his grating voice. 'Given the circumstances, we had to transcribe his wishes at short notice. A Roman merchant who had previously trained as a clerk offered to draft the document and witness the signatures, so there could be no misunderstanding as to the prince's intentions.'

Verica extended his hand. 'Don't believe it, Cunobelinus? Here. See for yourself.'

My father nodded at me. I alone among our representatives could read Latin, having studied the language of the Romans for many years at Merladion. I took the scroll from Verica, unspooled it from the bottom and skimmed through the neat text. The document had been written in terse legal language. At the bottom three separate marks had been made.

'What does it say?' Cunobelinus asked impatiently.

I swallowed. 'It is as Verica says, Father. This is a signed agreement between Trigomaris and Moricanus, witnessed by a Roman merchant by the name of Bassianus, stipulating that Lhandain and its environs are to go to Moricanus.'

Verica turned his attention to the Druids. 'This document is all the evidence you need to make your decision, gentlemen. I am sure you will agree that it is far more reliable than some vague verbal agreement struck long before any of us were born.'

My father shook his head. 'This is ridiculous. Trigomaris couldn't read Latin. He couldn't possibly have any idea what he was signing. The Druids cannot accept this.'

Verica affected a look of outrage. 'Are you suggesting we deceived him? Really, such accusations ought to be beneath you, Cunobelinus.'

The arguments continued. The Druids took turns to present their thoughts. As the crescent moon rose above the trees the High Druid raised his hand, signalling an end to the debate. 'We have heard enough,' he announced. 'Now, brothers, we must vote. Let us conclude this business.'

I felt the tension in the night air as both delegations trained their gazes on the Druids and awaited their verdict.

The High Druid stood before the council and said in a commanding voice, 'All those in favour of awarding the kingdom of Lhandain to the Catuvellaunians, show your hands.'

A small number of Druids raised their arms. I counted them and felt my heart sink. Less than a third of the council had voted in favour of our side. There were groans of disappointment and muttered curses among some of the nobles on our side as the High Druid called on all those in favour of a pro-Atrebatan outcome to show their hands, and a larger group lifted their arms above their heads, including the High Druid himself. At my side, Epaticcus swore under his breath.

'Shit. I don't believe it.'

'The issue is settled,' the High Druid declared. 'There is a clear majority in favour of Prince Moricanus. He shall henceforth be recognised as the legitimate ruler of Lhandain, and the Catuvellaunians shall agree to drop any further claim to his lands. It is the will of the High Council.'

The Atrebatan delegation broke out in celebration, cheering and slapping each other on the back. To my left, I saw my father staring at them, the rage etched into his features under the glow of the flames. Then, without warning, Bladocus stepped away from the altar and moved swiftly towards the edge of the henge. I craned my neck, straining to look past the sea of delegates as Bladocus shouted at one of the Druid bodyguards near the entrance. The latter turned and hurried down the avenue of fire at a quick trot. He returned several moments later, leading a fine white pony with a pair of leather saddlebags hanging down from the cantle. Bladocus snatched the reins from the bodyguard and guided the beast past the ancient stones, towards the bare ground in the middle of the ring.

'Brothers of the High Council!' he cried.

At once the noise from the Atrebatan camp ceased as both delegations looked towards Bladocus. A short distance away, the High Druid stood rigid, his face clouded with confusion.

'What in Lud's name do you think you're doing?' he demanded.

Bladocus ignored the question and indicated the pony at his side. 'For the benefit of those present, can you confirm that this is your mount, High Lord?'

'Of course it is,' the High Druid snapped impatiently. 'What is the meaning of this?'

'What the fuck is going on?' Epaticcus whispered.

'I don't know,' I said. But I felt a cold tremor ripple down my spine.

The crowd watched as Bladocus untied the leather straps on one of the saddlebags. I glanced at the High Druid and saw a look of alarm flashing across his pockmarked face.

'What do you think you're doing?' he demanded. 'Leave that alone, you damned fool!'

Before he could protest any further, Bladocus grabbed the bag and tipped out the contents. A shower of freshly minted silver coins

212

cascaded onto the ground at his feet, to the stunned silence of the gathered nobles and warriors. For a moment, we were all too shocked to react. Then my father approached the gleaming pile of coins. He bent down, scooped up a fistful and squinted at them in the glow of the fires.

'These coins bear the likeness of Emperor Tiberius,' he said.

Bladocus nodded. 'Two days ago, my lord, I was approached by a Roman trader in Lhandain. This man claimed to be acting on behalf of imperial agents who wished to guarantee a pro-Atrebatan outcome for the kingdom. I refused his offer of silver coin, but when I went to report my suspicions the next morning I spied the same trader leaving the High Druid's private quarters.'

'Lies!' the High Druid rasped, spittle flecking out of the corners of his mouth. 'Baseless lies!'

'It is the truth,' Bladocus said, speaking to my father but training his gaze on the High Druid.

'Why didn't you bring this to our attention before?' my father demanded.

'I had my suspicions, but I could not be sure. And I did not wish to jeopardise my position on the council by openly favouring one side before the debate. But when our esteemed leader supported the weaker Atrebatan claim, I knew he had taken the Roman coin.' He glowered at his companions beside the altar. 'I suspect he is not the only one among us who has done so.'

Several of the Druids who had voted on our side glared accusingly at their companions. The High Druid looked down at the coins and licked his lips.

'This is an outrage!' my father cried.

As the shouts of protest and anger echoed across the henge, Verica moved towards the middle of the ring, raising his hands in a placating gesture.

'Surely this is some trick, my friends?' he said smoothly. 'Why, one of the Catuvellaunian servants could have planted the saddlebag while we have been standing here. This is obviously a brazen attempt to blacken the High Lord of the Druids' good name.'

'Do you really expect us to believe that?' Cunobelinus looked at him scornfully, his voice quivering with rage. 'You stole the vote,

213

Verica. Like the cheap thief that you are. You and your Roman friends. Scum!'

Then he hurled the coins at Verica's face.

And all hell broke loose.

CHAPTER TWENTY-ONE

W hat happened next has long been disputed by both tribes. For what it's worth, Verica later claimed that he first saw my father and his bodyguards reaching for their sheathed swords and screamed at his men to defend him. My father always insisted that our warriors only drew their weapons *after* Verica had bellowed an order at his bodyguards. In which case, Verica was responsible for starting the Battle of the Henge. There are several competing versions of the events of that night, none of which agree on the smallest details, and even I can't be quite sure of how it happened – and I was there, Roman.

But what I do know is that a moment after my father had thrown the coins in Verica's face, a series of rasping hisses filled the air as both sides tore their swords free and charged towards the middle of the circle to defend their kings. At around the same time Epaticcus and the handful of warriors nearest to my father, already wise to the danger, poured forward to confront the Atrebatan horde, bellowing the fearsome battle cries of our tribe. They met in a sea of flickering steel blades, and they were swiftly joined by the rest of the warriors on both sides. Above their voices I heard some of the Druids imploring us not to fight on consecrated ground, but their pleas fell on deaf ears as both sides tore into each other with savage intent.

Amid the melee one of Verica's bodyguards shouted a challenge as he bore down on me, slashing wildly, the edge of his long sword gleaming in the reflected glow of the fire. I wrenched my sword from my scabbard and threw up my arm, hastily blocking his attacks as I edged backwards, gritting my teeth through the burning pain running up my arm. The warrior snarled and charged at me again. This time

I parried his attack and delivered a swiping blow to my opponent, cutting deep across his exposed midriff. The man howled in agony as the blade ripped open his stomach, like a knife tearing through a bulging sack of grain, and he fell away screaming and clawing at his bowels.

'That's it!' Epaticcus roared as he slashed furiously at another Atrebatan. 'Kill them! Cut them down!'

The fighting had swiftly spread across the henge. In the histories, we are told that battles are tidy affairs, with neat columns of men engaging on open ground, but this was nothing like that. Glancing round, I saw only a tight press of bodies hacking insensibly at one another, accompanied by the demented cries of the injured and dying, the grunts of fighting men, and the sharp ringing of steel against steel. It was impossible to tell who was winning.

Several paces away I spied the High Druid kneeling beside the heap of silver coins, frantically shovelling fistfuls of them into his saddlebag while the fighting raged all around him. The white pony lay sprawled on its side nearby, the shaft of a thrusting spear protruding from its flank, its agonising whinnies splitting the night air. A moment later one of our warriors grabbed the Druid by his robes and threw him roughly to the ground. The Druid held up his hands, screaming for mercy, and then his cries were silenced for ever as the warrior brought his sword crashing down with such force that he almost cleaved the Druid's head in half.

A flicker of movement caused me to turn. I looked ahead and saw a bare-chested warrior with a long, drooping moustache driving towards me, the sharpened edge of his blade sweeping towards my head. I had no time to evade the attack. I threw up my right arm, absorbed the blow on my sword and edged backwards as the warrior followed up with a succession of brutal hacks and slashes. I could feel my arm muscles throbbing from the effort of absorbing his attacks, and I knew I couldn't defend against him for much longer.

The warrior snarled in frustration and threw himself forward again. This time I took him by surprise and feinted towards him, aiming for his chest and then angling down at the last instant, catching him on the thigh. The man hissed through gritted teeth as the edge sliced through his flesh, cutting into muscle and tendon. He staggered back out of sword range, uttering a string of curses as blood pumped out of the deep wound. Then I pressed home my advantage, unleashing a series of swingeing blows at the Atrebatan, driving him backwards.

I swung again, slashing just below his guard, and followed it up with a quick stab at his head. The man flinched and jumped backwards, then let out a cry as he tripped over the corpse of one of Verica's bodyguards. He fell heavily to the ground, the sword tumbling from his grip. Then he disappeared from view, trampled beneath the swarm of warriors tearing into one another across the circle.

By now the ground was slick with gore. There was also the piss and shit from the voided bowels of the dead and badly wounded. I caught my breath, looked over my shoulder and felt my stomach drop. Both sides were locked in a series of individual battles across the henge, but although our men were fighting bravely we were in danger of being overrun by the enemy. Everywhere I looked our warriors were being forced back to the edges of the henge, steadily yielding ground to the combined forces of Verica and Moricanus. In one corner of the ring I saw an Atrebatan noble clubbing a warrior to death with the head of an axe, dashing the man's brains across the ground.

'Too many of the bastards!' Bellocatus seethed.

Just then I caught a glimmer of movement in my peripheral vision. I snapped my gaze round, beyond the ring of fire, and saw several figures charging through the main gateway as the small number of Atrebatan guards who had been waiting outside the henge raced forward to join the struggle. They tore into the nearest Catuvellaunian warriors, slashing manically and cutting down several of them before they could turn to defend themselves. Scores of Druids fled for their lives, running in every direction to escape the slaughter.

I glanced round, frantically searching for my father amid the dense press of bodies. Togodumnus, Adminius and a handful of bodyguards were fighting beside him near the fringes of the ring. Around them, the earth was carpeted with broken bodies, abandoned swords and glistening entrails. By this point at least half our men had been cut down by the enemy. The fighting had spread beyond the confines of the ring and a few of our tribesmen, sensing imminent defeat, fell back towards the rampart, but they were cut down by the enemy before they could escape. In a few moments, I realised, we would be overwhelmed.

'Father! We've got to make for the horses!' I shouted as I hastened over. 'Before we're all done for!'

'He's fucking right,' Epaticcus growled. His face was smeared with blood, though whether it was his or someone else's, I couldn't tell. 'We stay here and we're dead.'

My father nodded in grim understanding. He called out to my brothers, his voice barely audible above the raging sounds of the fight. At once they broke away from the ring and started towards the main gateway, swiftly followed by Bellocatus and the bulk of the bodyguards. I hurried along several paces further back, gripping my sword in my right hand while Epaticcus and the remaining warriors continued to hack away at the enemy, keeping them at bay for as long as possible.

'Come on, Uncle!' I bellowed. 'We're leaving! Now!'

Epaticcus and the last few warriors turned and hurried after us as we picked our way past the outer circle of fire. Some of these men were wounded and those of us who remained unscathed helped them along as they limped through the gateway. Most of the Atrebatans were locked in individual struggles with their opponents and the few who tried to attack us were swiftly cut down by my father's bodyguards. As we neared the entrance I glanced over my shoulder, looking for any sign of Bladocus amidst the pockets of tribesmen still holding out against the Atrebatans, but he was nowhere to be seen.

I forced myself to carry on as we stumbled through the gateway with Epaticcus and the other stragglers. A short distance ahead I could see my father and brothers, accompanied by a cluster of royal bodyguards. Half a mile away the avenue opened out to the wide patch of bare earth along the valley floor. Our only hope, I knew, was to race clear of the henge, deal with any Atrebatans lurking outside and make good our escape on the horses. From there, we could ride back to Camulodunum, using the cover of darkness to give any pursuing forces the slip. There, at least, we would be safe from the Atrebates, free to plot our revenge over our enemies. If we survived for that long.

After a quarter of a mile I heard a panicked shout from one of the warriors. I looked over my shoulder and saw a blur of movement at the gateway as a small party of Atrebatans came charging down the avenue, armed with a variety of short thrusting spears, battleaxes and swords. I clenched my jaw through the burning pain in my muscles and willed on the man limping along at my side, but the injured warriors in our party were slowing us down, and when I glanced back again I realised with a pang of dread that the Atrebatans had swiftly gained on us.

I pushed on, my heart beating fast. At the far end of the avenue, my father and the others had almost reached their mounts. Another darting look to the rear told me that the pursuing Atrebatans were less than fifty paces away now, and I knew that we weren't going to reach the horses before they could close with us. Then I heard a war cry at my back, and I wheeled round to see the Atrebatans falling upon us in a shimmer of flickering sword points and spear tips.

One of the Atrebatans, a skinny man wielding a spear, lunged at me, his yellow teeth bared in a snarl. I shoved aside my wounded comrade, throwing him out of harm's way, then jerked backwards from the spearman as the latter aimed at my stomach. I felt a searing hot pain as the tip caught me on my flank, tearing through the fabric of my tunic and grazing against my ribs. I gritted my teeth and staggered back out of range as the spearman growled and thrust at me again, aiming higher. I read his intentions, saw the leaf-shaped tip driving towards me and dropped to my haunches. The spear murmured through the air, narrowly missing my head, and before he could retreat I sprang forward, slashing down at an angle. I did not care where I struck my opponent. I knew only that I must land a blow before he attacked again, or I would die. The sword edge bit deep into the Atrebatan's ankle, cutting through muscle and tendon and shattering bone. He let out a hideous cry and landed on his back, clawing at his almost-severed foot. He looked up at me as I shaped to kill him, and there was animal fear in his eyes as he pleaded for his life. I killed him anyway, slashing open his throat. The Atrebatan cursed me, a moment before his words were lost in the gurgled noise he made as he choked on his own blood.

The fighting raged for what seemed like a long time. I saw one of my father's bodyguards picking up his severed hand from the blood-soaked earth. An Atrebatan howled in agony as his opponent piked him in the groin with his spear, lacerating his vitals. Another Catuvellaunian fell away with a battleaxe buried between his shoulder blades. Men were shouting taunts at their opponents, audible even above the groans of the mortally wounded. At some point I looked across and saw Epaticcus several paces away, blood flowing freely out of a shallow cut on his arm as he frantically fended off a spearman and a second Atrebatan wielding a sword. Epaticcus caught the spearman with a vicious blow to the stomach, but even as the man sank to his knees the second Atrebatan sprang forward, slashing downward and tearing through the side of my uncle's tunic. Epaticcus stumbled backwards, almost slipping on a pool of blood as the swordman came at him again.

I rushed forward, shoving aside a Catuvellaunian guard with a bloodied stump where his left forearm had once been, and bore down on the Atrebatan. He must have heard my shouts because he whipped round before he could cut Epaticcus down, and his face formed a look of surprise and horror a moment before my sword blade punched into his abdomen. His mouth slackened as he made a light moaning noise in the back of his throat.

I tore my weapon free from the dying Atrebatan and dropped down beside my uncle. He had sunk onto his knees, his eyes clenched shut in agony as the blood gushed out of the large wound he had taken to his flank, staining his tunic. I hauled Epaticcus to his feet and slipped an arm around his waist while Togodumnus charged towards us from the direction of the horses, roaring madly. He fell upon the nearest Atrebatan, cutting the man down in a torrent of quick cuts and slashes. At the same time several guards came racing to join in the struggle. They made short work of the outnumbered enemy; within a short time the remaining Atrebatans had been killed with a succession of brutal hacks and thrusts.

'Come on!' Togodumnus yelled at me. 'Let's go!'

More enemies were sprinting down the avenue now, bellowing in anger as they rushed forward to stop us from escaping the killing frenzy. Togodumnus wrapped his arm around my uncle, supporting his weight from the other side, and then we set off towards the mounts at a quick walk. The colour had drained from his face, his breathing was erratic, and I worried that he would lose consciousness before long. Behind us, the rest of the guards were helping along the walking wounded. Those less fortunate were left behind. Some of those broken souls screamed at us to kill them instead of allowing them to fall into the hands of the enemy, but there was nothing we could do for them.

After another hundred paces or so we reached the horses. I glanced back and saw that our pursuers were perhaps twice that distance behind us but closing fast. We led Epaticcus over to one of the spare mounts and lifted him up to the saddle, holding him upright while the others ran over to their respective steeds. Epaticcus was swaying heavily, and from his whitened complexion I judged that he had already lost a significant amount of blood.

I called over two of my father's guards and instructed them to ride either side of Epaticcus to keep him upright.

'Whatever you do, don't let him fall,' I told them, struggling to keep the strain out of my voice. 'Understood?'

'Don't worry about me,' Epaticcus groaned weakly as he pressed a hand to his bloodstained tunic. 'I'm not about to die here, lad. Not in this fucking place.'

I raced over to my horse and climbed up into the saddle, while Togodumnus made for his own steed. Adminius was already galloping ahead with my father and his senior bodyguards. I gripped the reins and urged my horse towards the distant foothills while my brother and uncle set off at a quick trot alongside me. Further down the avenue, the Atrebatans were running towards us for all they were worth. Some of them stopped to hurl their spears at our fleeing party in a last bid to prevent our flight. Spears hissed through the air, thudding into the dirt behind us. Most landed well short, but one struck a horse on its flank before the guard could spur it forward. The wounded beast reared up and squealed in agony before it lurched to one side, crushing the rider beneath it. I stole another glance over my shoulder and saw the guard struggling to crawl free from under the weight of the dying horse. A pair of Atrebatans dashed forward, brandishing their battleaxes, and the guard's pitiful screams split the night as they hacked at his trapped body.

Their comrades started towards their individual mounts, hoisting themselves up to their saddles as they scrambled to give chase. They were soon lost to the impenetrable darkness as we pulled clear of the henge, but we kept a close watch on our rear as we pushed the horses hard up the slopes. Twice that night we had to set up hasty ambushes when we heard the thud of hooves behind us. On both occasions we put the enemy to the sword, suffering only light wounds to two of our men. Soon after the second attack we crossed the border, at which point the Atrebatans abandoned their pursuit, and we urged our horses on to the safety of the nearest sizable village. There we rested our blown horses, and the headman summoned his strongest men to guard the camp while we tended to our wounded.

Epaticcus had grown progressively weaker since our escape; by the time we helped him down from his saddle he was barely conscious. We transferred him to a cart, along with the other badly injured. Bellocatus tore off a strip of cloth from his tunic and tied it around his waist to help stem the bleeding, but there was little else we could do for him until we returned to Camulodunum. My father bristled with rage at the sight of his brother's bloodstained form and for the only time in my life, I saw tears welling in his eyes.

'Will he live?' I asked as Bellocatus fastened the makeshift dressing.

Bellocatus paused to wipe the blood from his hands on his filthy leggings. He looked exhausted. 'I don't know, lord. I've seen men recover from such wounds. But others . . .'

His voice trailed off, but we all understood what he meant. For a short time no one said anything. We stood in the darkness outside the headman's quarters, listening to the agonised groans of our injured comrades. Servants brought us water and food, but though we were fatigued no one had an appetite. By my estimation, no more than thirty of us had escaped the slaughter at the henge, less than a third of the delegation that had left Camulodunum. I wondered again what fate had befallen Bladocus and those left behind. I made a silent prayer to Lud that he might protect them from our enemies.

Then Bellocatus looked to my father. 'What are your orders, sire?'

'Have the men ready to move out at first light. We'll make for Camulodunum. Ask the headman to provide victuals for thirty men, and feed for the horses.'

'Yes, sire.'

'We'll make Verica regret this,' my father said. He spoke to no one in particular but stared into the immense blackness beyond the palisade. His hands were clenched into tight fists at his sides.

'I'll cut his heart out for what he's done tonight,' he went on in a trembling voice. 'The Atrebates are going to suffer. Every last one of them. This I swear.'

CHAPTER TWENTY-TWO

Rome, AD 61

'Our party left the village at dawn and rode back to Camulodunum as fast as we could,' Caratacus said. 'The headman sent some of his warriors to accompany us, in case we came under attack. But the main tracks remained mercifully clear of enemy forces. We stopped for nothing, only to water and rest the horses, and we reached Camulodunum on the second afternoon. Not long after we arrived, Bladocus reached the town gates. He told us that he had managed to escape from the bloodbath on foot with a handful of other survivors; after giving the enemy the slip they had journeyed through the night to our capital. From him we learned that those left behind had been killed. The Atrebatans had taken no prisoners.'

'And your uncle?' I asked the Briton. 'What of him?'

'By that time, Epaticcus was drifting in and out of consciousness from the loss of blood,' Caratacus said. 'Father put him in the care of the royal healer. He was not the only one in a bad way. Many of the seriously wounded succumbed to their injuries over the next few days. These we buried, as is the custom of our people.'

I suppressed a shiver, having quite forgotten that the Britons, like their brethren in Gaul, insisted on interring the dead in the ground near their settlements, instead of cremating them in the manner of the more civilised peoples of the world. All very distasteful, you'll agree, and another reason why almost no one in Rome mourned the passing of the Celts and their benighted culture.

Caratacus drifted into one of his habitual silences. He stared past me, into some indefinable point in the distance, as if his mind was transporting him back to that mist-wreathed island of his youth. I waited for him to continue.

'That is how it all began,' he said at last. 'The trouble between our people and the Atrebates. Though I'm sure you will depict these events with greater skill than I. You must forgive my own poor attempt to describe them.' He smiled wryly. 'I am afraid I lack your talent for words, Felicitus.'

'Far from it. I think you've told it rather well. And your powers of recollection are extraordinary. I never knew one could vividly recall every detail of a battle fought half a lifetime ago.'

'Do you doubt the veracity of my account?'

'Not at all. I'm merely making an observation.'

'You can depend on my memory, if that's your concern,' Caratacus said. 'I was trained by the Druids, remember. It is quite impossible to flourish under their instruction unless you have a skill for memorising a vast wealth of knowledge. Besides, one tends to remember the defining moments of one's life in vivid detail. It must be so. How else do you explain how your fellow historians can recall the speeches given by your generals on the eve of battle?'

I blushed at that. It was one of the worst kept secrets among the Roman literary class that the long speeches put into the mouths of our commanders and our enemies were entirely made up. Presumably, Caratacus suspected as much, and I mumbled something about artistic licence, and the need to convey the emotional truth of the moment to the reader, even if the words themselves were not entirely true.

'I sincerely hope you won't feel the need to add any colourful fictions to this project of ours,' he said.

'Absolutely not.'

'Good.' He smiled. 'At any rate, I know my story is in the care of an accomplished scribe. Your history of the clan of Macrinus proves as much.'

'You've read my works?' I tried to disguise my startled reaction, although I should have anticipated that Caratacus might seek out some of my earlier commissions, given his passion for the written word.

'Some of them,' Caratacus said. 'The hagiographies of the better-known senators, and one or two minor projects.'

I couldn't help myself from asking the obvious question. 'What did you think?'

'You have a clearly refined tone, particularly in your earlier works. Sober and sturdy, with none of the fustian prose one finds in the poorer sort of works distributed in the Argiletum. I'm confident my story is in the hands of an accomplished scribe.'

'Thank you,' I replied awkwardly. I didn't know what else to say. I was not used to being complimented on points of style by a barbaric Briton.

I had the sense that Caratacus was attempting to flatter me. The fellow had shown no previous interest in my qualities as a writer, yet now he was showering me with praise. Could it be that he wanted me to present his tale in a certain light? Perhaps he wished to make sure that I depicted him in suitably heroic form, so that future readers would see the Caratacus that he wanted them to see.

I wondered again about his reasons for telling his story. In my profession, the motives of my clients are usually plain enough: a desire to burnish their family credentials ahead of an election campaign to the Senate, or to impress powerful friends with influence in the imperial palace. I've even accepted commissions to write histories purportedly authored by the clients themselves (which happens more often than you might think. Nothing helps one's career more than claiming to have penned an exhaustive history of one of the minor Etruscan kings). Perhaps naïvely, I had assumed that Caratacus had decided to tell his tale out of a simple desire to preserve the history of his island. But now I started to suspect that there was another reason.

It was late. A bustling crowd of stevedores and labourers had descended on the tavern, eager to fritter away their hard-earned wages on jugs of wine and games of dice. In one corner, two men were arguing over the respective qualities of the Blues and the Greens. Outside, in the faint glow provided by the light from the doorway of a tavern across the street, a pair of gaudily dressed tarts called out to a drunken passer-by, shouting the prices for their dubious (and, to my ear, anatomically impossible) services. Rome at night isn't to the taste of many of the worthier residents of our city, but I'll say this much: it's a lot less dull than the dinner parties up on the Caelian Hill.

'So what happened then?' I asked, eager to press on with our narrative. 'After you returned to your capital?'

Caratacus took a sip of beer. 'War was inevitable. My father had to begin preparations for the coming months. There were meetings to hold, men to recruit for the war-bands.'

'What about the elders?'

'What of them?'

'You said that some of them had Roman sympathies. Or at least, they didn't want any disruption to their trade with the Empire. Did they oppose your father's plans?'

Caratacus shook his head. 'The battle at the henge changed everything. My father made them understand that the days when they could maintain an ambiguous relationship with the Romans were over, and he challenged them to pick a side. He knew, of course, that there was no way they would take Rome's side over their own people. From that point on, they had no choice but to support my father.'

'Even those who had been arguing against seizing Lhandain at all costs?'

'Yes.'

'Then a cynic might say that the battle came at a convenient moment for your father.'

'In what way?' Caratacus asked.

'You stated that the court at Camulodunum was badly divided before the gathering with the Druids, and your father needed a way of uniting the squabbling factions.' I shrugged. 'Verica's actions at the henge played right into his hands.'

'Maybe so. But that was not my father's intention. And the peace between the factions did not last for long.'

I remembered something I had read in one of the military memoirs about the invasion. 'General Plautius prefaced his *Account of the Late Conquest of Britannia* with a brief history of the tribes. He claimed Camulodunum was a flourishing trading post in the years before the legions first arrived in Britannia.'

'So?'

'Your tribe must have maintained some sort of friendly contact with the trading community,' I suggested. 'Your father can't have cut off the Romans completely after the battle.'

'Of course not.' He chuckled. 'Our tribe flourished in part thanks to the trade across the sea. It would hardly have served our purposes to drive the merchants out of Camulodunum.'

'I'm just trying to understand your tribe's policy towards Rome. You say your father despised us, to the point where he was prepared to go to war to keep Lhandain from falling under Roman influence. And yet you continued to profit from the trade with us. That seems rather contradictory.'

He nodded. 'There is a saying in our tribe, Felicitus. "If you wish to keep the wolf out of the sheepfold, you must throw him meat."'

I noted that he had taken to calling me by my cognomen. Another sign of his growing trust in me, perhaps. Or more likely another subtle attempt to win my friendship so that I would write the account he wanted. 'I'm not sure I understand the meaning.'

'My father knew that it is always better to keep your enemies close. He allowed the Romans to stay, partly because it allowed him to keep an eye on them, and to understand their intentions. He felt that it was possible to barter with the Romans without encouraging their further involvement in our affairs. In the end, he was proven wrong.'

'Did you approve of your father's decision? To allow the Romans to remain in Camulodunum?'

'To an extent. I accepted the need not to provoke Rome unnecessarily. But I also thought the presence of the merchants in our land was setting a dangerous precedent. That much was clear from the emperor's attempt to bribe the High Council.'

I couldn't help hitching my eyebrows at that. Here was an extraordinary statement. And just the sort of thing bound to grab the attention of the chattering classes who frequented the literary salons. 'You suspected imperial involvement in the plot?'

'The Druids were paid in Roman coin,' Caratacus said. 'A Roman merchant drafted the document transferring ownership to Moricanus. This was the work of imperial agents. I'm certain of it.'

Something puzzled me. 'Why would Rome bother to support the Atrebates in the first place? We had no treaty with Verica,' I reminded him, recalling the works I had consulted. 'There was no reason for Rome to back his claim.'

'I believe the emperor, or his associates, saw the vote as an opportunity to sow discord between the tribes.'

'Do you have evidence for this?'

'I do not need it. Why else would the Romans conspire to bribe the High Council? They knew it would be far easier to invade our lands if we were too busy fighting each other to unite against our common foe.'

'But this all happened many years before the invasion took place. Our emperor, Tiberius, had no interest in conquering your island at that time. He wasn't even in Rome. He'd retreated to Caprae by then.'

The smile inched across the Briton's lips. 'You're a historian, Felicitus. Don't you think that every emperor has secretly contemplated an invasion of our lands at one time or another?'

I had to admit, he had a point there. In the past our rulers had frequently (and publicly) contemplated military expeditions to Britannia, and the opportunity to burnish their reputations by completing the invasion Caesar himself had been forced to abort years before. The vital missing ingredient had always been the political will necessary to undertake such a risky (not to mention staggeringly expensive) campaign, but all that had changed when the Praetorian Guard had elevated that doddering old fool Claudius to the purple.

I decided to steer Caratacus back to the subject at hand. 'So Cunobelinus declared war on the Atrebates?' He nodded. 'Wasn't he worried that Verica would go running to our side for help?'

'My father did not consider it likely. The timing was fortuitous. Rome was preoccupied by an uprising of the Frisii, and if the Atrebates could be crushed swiftly enough it would be too late for Rome to intervene.'

'Your father was a shrewd man.'

There was a sudden flare of anger in the Briton's eyes. 'Does that surprise you?'

'Not at all. I was merely paying a compliment.'

'Our kings were as cunning as your own rulers,' Caratacus said with feeling. 'Do not make the mistake of thinking that we were guileless, simply because we lived in huts instead of palaces. Do you have any idea how difficult it is to command our tribes, to hold them together in spite of the jealousies and the blood feuds and the nobles who scheme to stab you in the back at the first sign of weakness?'

'I'm sorry.' I cleared my throat. 'I meant no offence.'

'That is why so many detest Rome, Felicitus. You are told you belong to the greatest civilisation the world has ever known, and you take your superiority over others for granted. Your generals made the same mistake in Britannia. They thought we were ignorant barbarians, and their legions paid for it in blood.'

I had no wish to be drawn into a tiresome debate with my client over the merits of the invasion of Britannia, so I decided to wait for his irritation to subside.

'What happened next?' I asked after a long pause. 'After your father had decided to go to war?'

'At first, not much. By then it was the early autumn. No fighting could be done until the next spring, for our men were needed to gather the harvest. But that gave me an idea. I saw an opportunity, you see. To whittle down the enemy's forces.'

I waited for him to continue. Across the room, shouts erupted as the two drunken chariot fans hurled insults at one another and threatened to come to blows. Caratacus stood up, signalling the end of the interview.

'Perhaps we can continue our discussion elsewhere?' I asked hopefully, eager to learn more about this tribal war. 'I know another tavern, a few streets from here. It's a little less . . . noisy. We can talk there?'

'Not tonight,' Caratacus replied. 'I'm tired. I wish to go home.'

I tried to mask my disappointment. 'When can we meet again?'

'Soon. A few days from now. I have some other business to deal with in the meantime. I will send one of my house slaves to your address with a message, when I'm ready to talk.'

I gave him my address. Then he put down some coins on the table, insisting that he settle the bill for both of our drinks. Say what you like about the Britons, and gods know they have their faults, but Caratacus showed remarkable generosity throughout our time together. More so than many of our city's wealthiest inhabitants, I might add.

Caratacus stood up and fixed me with a piercing stare. 'When we meet again, I will tell you of the pitiless war that was fought between my people and the Atrebates. We knew that the future of all that we held dear hung in the balance . . . A great power was watching our struggle with a growing appetite, tensing its sinews and bracing itself to spring across the sea to tear the tribes of Britannia to pieces and devour our lands. We did not fully grasp it at the time, but the war was a foretaste of the bitter horrors to come.'

PART FOUR

BROTHERS OF THE SWORD

CHAPTER TWENTY-THREE

Rome, AD 61

In the days before my next encounter with Caratacus the inns and bathhouses of Rome were full of feverish gossip about the murder of the city prefect, Lucius Pedianus Secundus, by one of his slaves. The Senate, in its finite wisdom, had ruled that all four hundred of Secundus's slaves should be put to death as punishment. When Nero decided to uphold the death sentence the mob had responded with predictable fury. There was rioting and plundering of shops and homes, until the emperor ordered soldiers onto the streets to restore order.

It was typical of Nero's reign as the emperor lurched from one crisis to another, constantly buying time through rash promises of free bread and more games to keep the mob distracted, while the worthy senators were too cowardly to stand up to him. I had seen it all before and was not unduly perturbed at the time.

Except, that is, for two rather curious events.

The first occurred at a lavish dinner party held by a friend of ours up on the Quirinal. Our host was a thrusting young senator who had recently paid for the publication of my history of his illustrious ancestors. One of my best projects, if I say so myself. I had skilfully traced the family of Appius Ovidius Calvus back to the days of the last Etruscan kings, conveniently omitting any whiff of plebeian blood from his lineage. In a burst of creative inspiration I had even placed one of his distant relatives alongside General Dentatus during his famous victory over Pyrrhus at the Battle of Beneventum, a detail which I am almost certain contributed to his successful election as one of the year's two censors. (Word of advice to any budding young hagiographer: always insert your subjects into battles which took place at least seventy years earlier. That way, there will be no surviving participants to dispute your version of events.)

Aelia and I had since become regular attendees at the senator's social gatherings, and although I often found them tedious affairs, full of the worst sort of political blowhards and idle aristocrats, they were a useful opportunity to court prospective commissions. They were also a lucrative source of palace gossip, since Calvus was on good terms with several of Nero's cronies. There is a ready market for information, like any other commodity, and every so often I supplemented my modest income by dishing the dirt on a corrupt senator. In the public interest, you understand. Don't ever accuse me of lacking morals, dear reader.

I had passed the first courses (stuffed larks, oysters from Baiae and roasted snails lathered in garum sauce) taking questions about the craft from one of my fellow diners, a frightfully dull lawyer of enormous girth whose name thankfully escapes me. The man explained that he had been contemplating a change in career, and he had convinced himself that earning a living as a writer would be much easier than his current profession. It's a claim I've heard more than once before, invariably made by those with no conception of the long hours one must spend toiling away into the small hours by the wan light of an oil lamp. Or, indeed, dealing with highborn imperial lackeys aspiring to be the next Virgil. As for the lawyer, I think I pleased him by pointing out that he was more than halfway to his goal thanks to the considerable practice he'd had creating fictions in court.

After the main courses had been taken away, the house slaves brought out silver platters of honeyed dates, cheese and nuts to graze on. While the musicians (Hispanians, hired at fantastic expense, Aelia had discreetly noted) performed one of their interminable laments, several of the guests retreated to a corner of the room to drink amongst themselves. To my immense relief the portly would-be writer excused himself from our conversation and went off in search of Calvus to petition him over some private affair. At which point my eye was drawn to a trio of fellows across the room, dressed in expensive tunics. They were broad-shouldered, with oiled ringlets, and their easy familiarity suggested that they were old friends. I hadn't seen them at any of Calvus's parties before, and for some

236

reason their informal little brotherhood piqued my natural curiosity. From the way they carried themselves and the snippets of conversation I overheard, I assumed they were military men. When I confidently pointed this out to the diner next to me, he replied with a curt assenting nod.

'They're retired officers,' he said. 'From the Twentieth. The brave and victorious.'

Now was that a trace of bitterness in his voice? I waved away the servant who stood over me, offering to refill my cup, and trained my full attention on the man. He was somewhat older than the three former officers. His face had been disfigured by a prominent scar on his left cheek, his eyes were bloodshot, and his neat beard was streaked with grey hair.

'Are they acquaintances of yours?' I asked.

'You could say that,' the man replied. He took another swig of mulsum and raised a fist to his lips, suppressing a belch. 'We were brother officers once. A lifetime ago.'

A memory stirred. 'The Twentieth Legion, you say? Didn't they take part in the invasion of Britannia?'

'That's right. We served under Legate Aculeo, the four of us. We were senior centurions at the time we crossed the Oceanus.'

'You must have seen plenty of action,' I said.

'Yes. We did.'

I waited for the fellow to elaborate, but instead he merely gazed past my shoulder. On the other side of the banqueting room, the three officers drunkenly began reciting the lines to a well-known marching song, their hoarse voices drowning out the warbling noise from the lyre-players. I couldn't decide which was worse.

'Your friends are clearly in high spirits,' I said to fill the silence.

The other man grunted. 'Why wouldn't they be? They're celebrating.'

'What's the occasion?'

'The Battle of Durocornovium,' the man replied. 'It's the anniversary today.'

I nodded, recalling the story from my research into the life of Caratacus. Durocornovium had been the site of a famous engagement between several cohorts from the Twentieth Legion and Caratacus and his band of warriors. For years after the invasion, the wily Briton and his followers had harassed Roman forces across southern Britannia, attacking supply lines and military outposts and slowing down the pace of the advance to a crawl. The exorbitant cost of maintaining the legions in that far-flung island had caused unrest in the imperial palace, and there had even been whispers at the time that Claudius might be compelled to order a tactical withdrawal from Britannia, much like Caesar had done generations before.

But then there had been news of a stunning victory over the Britons at a hill near a place called Durocornovium. Aculeo's men had destroyed Caratacus's army in a hard-fought battle, inflicting massive casualties on the enemy and forcing him to flee west with the shattered remnants of his war-band to the mountain tribes of the Silures and Ordovices. As a reward for his efforts, Legate Aculeo had later been made the governor of one of the eastern provinces. Several other senior officers had received decorations for playing their part. Victory had been generous indeed.

Which prompted the obvious question: 'If those gentlemen are friends of yours, why aren't you drinking with them? Surely you should all be celebrating such a splendid triumph?'

As a matter of fact, I couldn't remember this fellow saying a word to his comrades all evening, but I felt it would be imprudent to point that out to him.

The man shrugged. 'Just because we're comrades, doesn't mean we always see eye-to-eye on certain matters.'

'What do you mean by that?' I pressed.

He squinted at me. With his crinkled brow and puckered lips he looked like a man who had just trodden on a dog turd. 'You're that historian, aren't you?'

'Caius Placonius Felicitus, at your service.'

He nodded, as if this news disappointed him. 'You ask too many questions, Felicitus.'

I'm accustomed to such reactions from Roman aristocrats. After all, we live in a society where a loose tongue or a carelessly expressed thought can get you hauled out of bed in the middle of the night by the palace guards. But I'm not so easily dissuaded. 'I'm afraid I didn't catch your name, my good man.'

'Vulcatius Araricus.'

The name meant nothing to me then – this was years before the plot that ensured he would be remembered by posterity. At the time, Araricus held some minor role within the imperial administration. 'Have you been back long in our fair city?'

'Two years,' Araricus replied. 'I applied for a transfer back to Rome and saw out my service with the Praetorian Guard. Then I took my gratuity and chose retirement.'

'Any particular reason why you left the Twentieth? Did you grow tired of Britannia?'

Araricus laughed. When I asked him what was so amusing, he gave me a long, hard look and said, 'You haven't visited the province, have you?'

'No,' I replied. 'I'm afraid not.'

'Then consider yourself fortunate.'

People like to talk to me. I have found that if one affects a genuine interest in the other person, more often than not they'll want to engage with you. Particularly if the fellow in question is in their cups. So it was with Araricus.

'The place is a stinking pit,' he continued. 'The weather in Britannia is generally unpleasant, the food is barely edible and the land is made up of bogs, mountains and forests. As for the barbarians, the less said about them the better. If you ask me, we should have quit the island years ago and left them to fight amongst themselves. Saved ourselves the bother.'

The man's frankness surprised me. One rarely heard criticism of our strategy in Britannia, least of all from a senior military figure. Most officers who had served there continued to insist publicly that the newest addition to the Empire was fast becoming more civilised and would begin to repay the crippling costs of its administration any day now. Even if that position had been severely tested by the recent rebellion. I made some flippant remark about the descriptions of Britannia in the military memoirs I'd read, which suggested a bucolic landscape of abundant farms, exotic flame-haired women and noble but dull-witted native warriors who had grudgingly taken to the hypocaust, taxes and the many other benefits of Roman civilisation.

'You shouldn't believe everything you read in the memoirs,' Araricus grumbled. 'You of all people should know that, scribe.'

'But it can't have been all bad over there, surely?'

'It's a money-draining shithole. No other way of putting it. Years of fighting an enemy that fiercely contested us every step of the way. That's my experience of Britannia.'

'Still, it can't have done your career much harm. Just about everyone in the city has heard about Durocornovium. It's one of our finest victories over the natives.'

'If you say so.' Araricus gave a rueful smile. 'Personally, I wouldn't be so sure about that.'

'I'm not sure I follow.'

The ex-centurion was watching his old colleagues. Or perhaps he was simply staring into the darkness of the garden. From where I was sitting, it was impossible to tell. 'Things are not always as they seem. I thought it was bad in the legions, but here—'

Some momentary flash of sobriety overcame Araricus and he cut himself short.

'Yes?' I asked, intrigued.

'Forget it.' He set his wine cup down and abruptly rose to his feet before calling for his litter. 'I must be on my way.'

'You're leaving so soon?'

'I have duties to attend to at dawn. It was a pleasure to make your acquaintance.'

'Perhaps we might talk another time? About your experiences in Britannia. I'm always keen to know more about the invasion.'

Which was true. But selfishly, I also realised that a critical Roman counterpoint to the accepted narrative might prove useful. Araricus seemed to hold a refreshingly honest view of things in the province. If nothing else, he could help to fill in any gaps in Caratacus's memory.

'I've no wish to publish a memoir, if that's what you're implying. You might have better luck with my friends over there.' Araricus nodded at the brotherhood of officers. 'They seem to have a talent for self-promotion.'

He nodded a farewell as a slave indicated that his litter had arrived outside the entrance. I stared after him wondering what lay behind his dismissive attitude towards his former comrades.

The second incident occurred four days later, at a reading hosted at a bookshop in the Argiletum. The author, Marcus Cominius Largus, was an old friend, a modestly talented writer who had tried his hand at the theatre before turning to popular history of the worst sort. You know the type of thing: patriotic tales about heroic Roman officers standing firm against the barbaric hordes on some bleak frontier of the Empire. So far his work had been tremendously well received, as one might imagine, and the resultant commissions had enabled Largus to rent a large house on the upper slopes of the Caelian. I'm not ashamed to admit feeling a tinge of envy at his success. So does any writer when a colleague's fleet comes in.

That morning one of Caratacus's slaves had presented himself at my lodgings, informing me that his master would be ready to receive me at noon. With a few hours before our appointment, I had decided to attend Largus's reading – more out of boredom than any enthusiasm for the work itself. I stood with a small crowd in the dusty confines of the bookshop, listening to Largus read an excerpt from his pompous new history of the Samnite Wars. The work was up to Largus's usual standard, which is to say it had all the literary merit of the graffiti one occasionally finds scrawled on the wall of a Suburra latrine (and if you think I'm being unfair, then you haven't read his material). By the time Largus had finished, I would have preferred to perish in the Battle of Lautulae rather than listen to another word of his purple prose. I decided to leave while the rest of the crowd mingled, wanting to give myself plenty of time to head across Rome for my meeting with Caratacus. Before I could slip away, however, Largus moved swiftly across the room to intercept me.

'Felicitus! There you are!' he cried excitedly, clasping my forearm. 'So glad you could make it.'

'Of course. Anything for a brother scribe.'

'Tell me, what did you think?' He stabbed a thumb at the pile of scrolls on the table behind him. 'Be honest, now. The truth cannot wound me.'

'A first-rate work,' I replied with an admirably straight face. 'I almost felt as if I was campaigning alongside General Rullianus himself.'

'That means a great deal,' Largus said. 'Truly.'

'Not at all, dear fellow. Now, I'd love to stop and chat, but I really must get going.'

I started to make my excuses, but Largus interrupted, 'I wonder if I might have a word with you, actually.'

'All right, but it'll have to be quick.'

'In a bit of a rush, are we?'

'Something like that.'

Largus took me by the arm and led me over to a quiet corner of the room, away from the attendees devouring sweetmeats and cheap wine. For a dreadful moment I feared he was going to ask for an endorsement from one of my wealthy patrons, and I was already trying to think of a way to extricate myself when he said, 'Listen, Felicitus. I don't know how else to say this, but someone has been asking about you, and not in a good way,' he added with emphasis.

In Nero's Rome, there is one thing worse than not being being talked about and that is being talked about. His warning shook me, and it took a moment to recover my power of speech. 'Who?'

'One of Nero's coterie,' Largus said. 'He didn't give a name, and I didn't dare to ask. But I've seen him around the palace before.'

A hollow feeling spread through my chest. 'What did this man want, exactly?'

'Information. He said he knew you were working on a new project, something to do with the Britannia campaign, and since we were good friends, he wondered if I'd heard anything about it. The whole conversation was quite strange.'

'What did you tell him?' I asked.

'The truth. What else could I say? We haven't seen each other in weeks, and I know you don't like to talk about your commissions until you've finished writing them.' Largus peered at me with narrowed eyes. 'What *are* you up to, old friend?'

I ignored the question. 'Did he say anything else?'

Largus gave a shrug of his slender shoulders. 'He just told me that if I learned anything about your project, to let him know. There was a suggestion that there might be a reward in it, if I cooperated. I shan't relay the details of this conversation to him, naturally.'

'Thank you, Largus.'

He grinned and put an arm around me. 'Anything for a brother scribe. Now, why don't you buy me a jug of wine after I'm done here and tell me what's really going on, eh?'

I shook my head. 'I can't. I'm meeting someone across town.'

'A friend?'

'More of an acquaintance, actually.'

'Anyone I know?'

'Afraid not.'

'I see. Another time, then.' I nodded and turned on my heel to leave. 'And Felicitus?'

I stopped and looked back. 'Yes?'

'I didn't care much for the tone this fellow used with me. Whatever it is he wants to know about you, it does not bode well. Be careful.'

'Thanks,' I replied. 'I will.'

This troubling development plagued me as I left the Argiletum and navigated the streets running through the tenement blocks of the Suburra district, taking care to sidestep the heaps of discarded vegetables and rotting corpses of stray dogs that littered the streets of that fetid slum.

I crossed the Forum, weaving my way through the bustling mass of costermongers, perfume-sellers, and Phoenician street magicians looking to fleece unsuspecting tourists, occasionally glancing over my shoulder to see if I was being followed. Irrational, perhaps, and wholly futile: if the emperor's spies were indeed watching me, I was hardly going to spot them in such a heaving crowd.

As I passed the Circus Maximus and carried on towards the Aventine, my thoughts stayed with my conversation with Largus. I wondered how the imperial palace had learned about my project with Caratacus. My first thought was that Aelia had carelessly let it slip to one of her friends, but I swiftly dismissed the idea. I had sworn her to secrecy. Even my dear wife, with her insatiable appetite for gossip, knew better than to discuss the subject with others.

Perhaps Largus was overreacting, I told myself. It was always possible that there might be an innocent explanation for one of Nero's men enquiring about my work. But it seemed unlikely, and as

I reached the upper slopes of the Aventine, I felt a heavy burden of anxiety pressing down on my shoulders. At Caratacus's house I followed the doorman through to the study and found the grey-haired Briton standing in front of his shelving, scrutinising the text of a scroll. He looked up and gestured to the stool facing his desk.

'Have a seat,' he said. 'I was just re-reading some of Virgil's early poetry.'

The look on my face must have betrayed my reaction, because his expression shifted.

'You are surprised? One should always seek to learn about others. One's enemies, most of all. You need to understand how they think. Otherwise, you can never hope to defeat them.'

'Wise words.'

'I should think so. They were spoken by my father, many years ago.'

Caratacus replaced the scroll and ordered one of his kitchen slaves to fetch a jug of ale and cups, then levered himself down into the chair behind his imposing desk.

'Before we begin,' I said carefully, 'I think it might be wise if we agreed to meet somewhere else in the future. Somewhere a little more discreet.'

The Briton crinkled his worn features into a frown. 'Why? Is something wrong?'

'It's nothing like that,' I lied. 'But you live on a busy street.'

'Your powers of observation are remarkable, Felicitus.'

I leaned forward. 'What if your neighbours get curious about your new visitor? That might lead to some awkward questions, don't you see? Particularly if we are to keep this project secret for the foreseeable future.'

'My doorman, Davos, is more than capable of dealing with any inquisitive strangers.'

'I don't doubt it. But even so, wouldn't it be better to err on the side of caution?'

I had already decided that there was nothing to be gained by telling him about my conversation with Largus. It had taken all of my natural charm to persuade Caratacus to share his story in the first place, and I feared that any mention of imperial interest might cause him to clam up.

'Lugnus can help us with that,' he said. 'My friend. You met him the other day.'

'The Gaul? The one who owns the Drunken Boar down the hill?'

Caratacus nodded. 'He has some rooms above the tavern. I'd have to agree it with him first, but we could perhaps meet there instead.'

'I think that would be best,' I said.

'You are quite sure there is nothing else bothering you? Nothing at all?'

I shook my head. 'I just think it's good to be careful. In this city, one never knows who might be watching.'

He erupted into a booming laugh. 'Then, at least in one way, Rome is not so very different from the royal court at Camulodunum.'

The kitchen slave returned bearing a silver tray with a jug and a pair of cups. Caratacus performed the familiar ritual of pouring the drinks while I prepared to take notes.

'The last time we spoke, your father had declared war on the Atrebates,' I said.

'Yes.' Caratacus sipped his beer. Tiny buds of foam clung to his drooping moustache. 'This happened a while after the Battle of the Henge. Those were dark days for our tribe. So many of our nobles died in the fighting. Those of us who survived burned with humiliation. From that point on, we knew that it was going to be a hard fight against the Atrebates. That made many in our tribe anxious.

'Our kingdom had not been under threat for many years, not since the reign of my grandfather. Now we were faced with a life-and-death struggle against a powerful enemy. One with a force stronger than our own. Victory was far from assured. Many at the court feared that we might lose to Verica and his allies.'

'Did you share those fears?'

Caratacus rested his bunched fist under his chin. 'I felt that if we were going to win, then we would have to adapt our ways of waging war. But I did not wish for a bloody struggle between the tribes.'

'That is a curious thing to say, given that you spent most of your life fighting enemies.'

'A man does not have to enjoy war to be good at it, Roman. I would have been content never to raise my sword in battle, if I could have found a way to avoid conflict.'

'But war made you who you are today,' I pointed out. 'Without it, few in Rome would have ever heard of you. Now, you're the most famous Briton in the Empire.'

'I think there are a few who may argue otherwise, given the recent uprising. I dare say Queen Boudica's name will endure rather better than that of Caratacus in the ages to come.'

I sincerely doubted that Boudica's star would outlast that of Caratacus, particularly once my history landed on the shelves of Rome's bookshops.

'Did you know her?'

'In passing. Her husband, King Prasutagus, I knew well. An infuriating man, in some ways. Obstinate and proud to a fault, like all Iceni. He should have known better than to trust the Romans. But for all that he was a fine warrior.'

I sensed Caratacus was in danger of slipping into one of his meandering reminiscences about the less commercial aspects of his old life in Britannia, so I decided to gently guide him back to the thrust of our narrative.

'You said you had to adapt your fighting ways. What do you mean?'

'I knew we couldn't defeat Verica on the battlefield alone. Victory could only be achieved if we embraced less traditional methods of warfare.'

'I can't imagine that went down well with your tribespeople, given their pride in tradition.'

He gave a faint smile. 'It did not. Least of all with Adminius. He and many of his friends were opposed to my ideas. But I have never worried about telling people what they need to hear.'

'Is that so?'

'I only care for the truth, however painful. I would not be sitting here with you otherwise.'

There was no reason to disbelieve him, but I had the unnerving sense once more that the old king was cleverly manipulating me.

'Let's talk about the war with Verica,' I said. 'When did it begin?'

'In my nineteenth year.' Caratacus eased back, relaxing into his

246

chair. 'It was the last time I would know peace for many years. None of us knew back then that the campaign against the Atrebates would be so gruelling, or last for so long.'

CHAPTER TWENTY-FOUR

Camulodunum, AD 26

The Battle of the Henge was a disaster for our tribe. Dozens of our finest warriors and nobles were cut down, and it plunged us into a savage war that would have catastrophic consequences for much of what you Romans call Britannia. But it also taught me an important lesson. For the first time, I realised that Rome won its empire as much by stealth and guile as by courage and strength on the field of battle. The legions are but one weapon among many she deploys in the pursuit of power. And there were those among us who were willing to sell their souls in exchange for silver coin and promises of friendship. The plot to bribe the High Council of Druids was the first hint of what was to come later.

Few of us understood this at the time. Most of my fellow tribespeople failed to see the shadow Rome was casting across our island, even then. They cared nothing for foreign conspiracies or the slow creep of Roman influence. They were too busy preparing for the great conflict with the Atrebates.

We spent a few days after the fighting mourning lost friends and burying the dead. At my father's instruction Epaticcus and the rest of the wounded were given space in the guest quarters in the royal compound. Our womenfolk tended to them as best they could, making them comfortable and changing their dressings. Most did not survive, and each day a grim procession of mourners made their way through the gateway to consign their loved ones to the consecrated earth just beyond the capital. The warriors drank and vowed to take revenge against our hated foes, the wives wept in inconsolable grief, and the bards sang their songs, while the Druids performed the traditional funeral rites. Our faith in the Druids was shaken. They, who we believed had served the cult with integrity, had turned out to be no less venal than the basest thief. And yet, despite the evidence of their corruption, many of the tribespeople refused to abandon their respect for the corrupt Druids.

For a while, I feared Epaticcus might join the dead.

My father's personal healer took charge of his recovery. He was a scrawny man from one of the Belgic tribes who had some rudimentary medical knowledge, gleaned from the time he had spent as an assistant to a Greek medic in Lugdunum. After a close inspection of the wound Epaticcus had taken to his side, the healer cleaned it out with a mixture of honey and vinegar and drained it of pus. Then he closed the wound up with a suture made of fine thread before applying a fresh poultice to aid the healing.

'What are his chances?' I asked as the healer wiped his hands on a rag.

'He should survive, lord,' the healer replied guardedly. 'Your uncle has lost a significant amount of blood, but the sword edge struck below the ribs, thereby avoiding any fragmentation of the bone. Mercifully, it did not penetrate more than a few inches. You should be thankful that the favoured form of attack here is to cut.'

'Why does that matter?'

'In Gaul, many of the gladiators prefer to stab, which allows them to pierce several inches deep. If your uncle's opponent had stabbed him instead of slashing, he would have punctured his organs, and he would be dead by now. As it is, I expect him to make a full recovery. Assuming no poisons manifest themselves in the blood.'

'And if they do?'

'You'll know it if the wounds exude a foul odour. Then his fate is in the hands of the gods. The cure for such conditions is beyond the abilities of mere mortals, lord.'

I shot him a cold glare. 'You had better make sure it does not come to that.'

For two days my uncle remained unconscious, and there was nothing we could do for him except make the appropriate sacrifices to our gods. On the third day he woke up, and his condition began to slowly improve. The healer pronounced himself optimistic that my uncle would eventually make a full recovery. But he cautioned that he would not be able to return to combat for several months.

Later that afternoon, my father called his nobles and best warriors to the royal hall, and in the gathering dusk I made my way across the open ground towards the covered porch leading into the great seat of power of our tribe. Bladocus walked alongside me, for the king had summoned my Druid mentor to the meeting as well. Ahead of us I saw a loose throng of elderly men converging on the entrance.

'Why is the wise council here, Master?' I asked. 'Surely, there's no point in seeking their advice now?'

'Your father must obtain the consent of the council before war can be declared,' Bladocus explained. 'It is a wise move if he is to carry his people with him in the coming war.'

I stared at him. 'They cannot refuse him, surely? Not after Verica's cowardly actions at the grove.'

'That,' Bladocus said in a lowered tone, 'is the least of your father's problems, I fear.'

'How so, Master?'

The Druid gestured to the cluster of figures entering the hall. 'The council members are a fickle bunch.'

'What are you suggesting?'

'Many of these people were once ruled by the great Trinovantian kings, until your father's forces swept through their lands and put the king and his family to flight. At one time the Trinovantes ruled a mighty realm. Some may well hope for a return to those days if your tribe is humbled.'

'You think our kingdom is going to collapse?' Even as the words left my mouth, the notion seemed incredible, for our tribe was amongst the most powerful in Britannia at that time.

'All kingdoms must perish sooner or later. A dynasty is no more immortal than the oldest tree in the forest. Only a fool would think otherwise. A fool, or a Roman.' He shot me a stern look. 'Have you already forgotten your lessons from the sanctuary?'

'Even if that's true, Father won't be defeated easily. He's overcome his enemies in the past,' I reminded him.

'But not this time.' He paused before adding, 'Verica has the measure of your father, it seems. So far, at least.'

Something tightened in my stomach. 'Do you really think he's in trouble, Master?'

'A king cannot endure many defeats. Even one as powerful as your father. I fear his enemies in the wise council and the court will not tolerate another humiliation at the hands of the Atrebates. If that happens, they may start to look for a new ruler.'

I swallowed hard and looked away. Sometimes I hated the Druid for speaking the truth. 'They should be careful what they wish for. My father has conquered many lands and won them great spoils in the past.'

'That doesn't matter. No king can survive for long on past glories. Loyalty must be continually earned, either by heroic deeds or coin.'

The atmosphere in the hall was strained that day. The servants had cleared away the trestle tables and a small crowd of stony-faced nobles had gathered in front of the dais at the far end of the hall. Bladocus joined the other Druids, and I took up my place next to Togodumnus, Adminius and the other surviving members of our tribal aristocracy.

There was a respectful silence as my father, draped in a fur-trimmed cloak, emerged from his private quarters to the rear of the dais. One of his favourite hunting hounds padded along in his wake as he climbed the dais and took his seat upon the throne. He rested his hands in his lap and looked round the room as he prepared to speak.

'Brothers, the situation before us is clear,' he said. 'You have all heard of the act of treachery that took place at the sacred henge. At the behest of my advisers, I have tried my utmost to pursue a peaceful solution to the disagreement between ourselves and the Atrebates. Plainly, this approach has failed.' He paused to underscore the sad truth of his remark. 'Many of our finest young men now lie dead, and the Atrebatan faction under Moricanus remains in control of Lhandain. We have been betrayed by the corrupt amongst the Druid council, and their Roman conspirators. We are therefore left with no choice but to take Lhandain by force and crush our enemy.

'This will be a hard fight. The Atrebates have sworn to defend their allies at Lhandain. Make no mistake, our enemy is a formidable opponent, cunning and determined. He will not be easily defeated, and we must be prepared to pay a heavy price if we are to prevail. But

251

I see no other way. It is imperative that we seize control of Lhandain if we are to prevent the spread of any further Roman influence in our lands. The fate of this kingdom may depend on it. I challenge any man here to say different.'

The assembled nobles and tribal elders looked round at each other. Then one of them spoke up: a frail-looking man with a long, thin face and watery eyes.

'Sire, I believe I speak for all present when I say that we stand ready to support you. But how do you intend to defeat the Atrebates? We have all heard the reports from our spies in Calleva. Verica is assembling a vast host of warriors at his capital. Four thousand men, we are told.'

'Baloras speaks the truth,' a portly elder called Trenico said, above murmurs of agreement from his comrades. 'What is more, Verica's conquest of the Regni means that he now controls many of the richest lands in the south. With the grain and the iron ore for his bloomeries, the Atrebates will be able to fight a war of attrition, keeping their men fed and supplied for a long campaign.'

'The territory you speak of is an occupied kingdom,' my father replied. 'The chief of the Regni did not enter willingly into an alliance with the Atrebates.'

'That may be so, sire. But they will support Verica all the same. The Atrebatan warriors guarding the major settlements will guarantee that. We can hardly expect to defeat a force of such size.'

'Then we shall build up our forces over the winter months,' my father said. 'There will be no campaigning before the spring anyway. Verica's men, like ours, will be preoccupied with storing the grain and carrying out the numerous tasks that must be done before the first winter frost. By then, it will be too late in the season to mount an attack. We shall use this time to recruit men from the villages. As soon as the harvest has been gathered, we will summon every available man to take up arms. I'm sure there will be no shortage of warriors desperate to avenge their slain kinfolk.'

'Quite so, sire. But I fear that will not suffice. The villages have already provided many recruits in the past years. In some settlements, they have barely enough men to tend to their crops this year. I have heard stories of sick old men and small children working in the fields.'

'Which is why I have sent an emissary to our ally King Antedius. Our faithful allies, the Dobunnians, have vowed to provide men from their own tribe to fight alongside us. We can expect them in the spring.'

'How many men, sire?'

'I have asked Antedius for a thousand,' my father said. 'I expect he'll provide us with half that number.'

Baloras shook his head. 'Even with these new additions, sire, we will have no more than two thousand men in the war-bands. Verica has almost twice that number.'

'If we must take to the field with fewer men than the enemy, so be it,' Bellocatus interjected. The dark-haired warrior's face and arms were covered in scars and bruises sustained during the fighting at the henge.

'We are Catuvellaunians,' he went on proudly, thumping a fist against his chest. 'We do not tremble in the presence of our enemies. The fighting spirit of our warriors and the favour of the gods shall see us win through.'

'The bravery of our men is not in question,' Baloras replied carefully. 'But we will be fighting a more numerous enemy, with or without our Dobunnian allies . . . And that is assuming Verica does not succeed in bringing more tribes to his side over the coming months.'

My father gave a dry chuckle. 'Verica will not find it easy to win new friends. His actions at the henge will have seen to that. There are few tribes who will want to swear an oath of allegiance to a man who takes Roman coin. Our focus must be solely on building up our war-bands and making our preparations for the coming war.

'In the meantime, I have given the order for improvements to be made to the defences, both here and at Verlamion. Come the spring we will take to the field and fight with honour against our enemies. May the gods be with us,' my father said, concluding the gathering.

The nobles dipped their heads before the king and started shuffling towards the entrance, talking in muted voices. Many of them wore anxious expressions, and I sensed their ominous mood as they left the hall. Togodumnus stood at my side and puffed out his cheeks.

'Looks like you were right,' he muttered softly. 'This campaign is going to be harder than any we've fought in the past.'

'I thought you wanted to settle our quarrel with Verica in battle?'

'I do. But I'd rather meet our foes on equal terms.'

'Me too,' I replied softly. 'But what can we do? The Atrebates have more men than us. And they have the resources to feed and equip them. It is as Father says. We can only hope that Verica does not gain further allies before the spring.'

'Perhaps we should attack now,' Togodumnus said. 'Before the first of the winter snow. Strike Lhandain while Verica is least expecting it.'

'It wouldn't work. Our forces aren't strong enough to drive the enemy away.' I clenched my jaw in frustration. 'One thing's for sure.'

Togodumnus inclined his head. 'What's that, brother?'

'If those reports about Verica's forces are to be believed, then our war-bands are going to be badly outnumbered. Unless we can find some way of weakening the enemy, we're in serious danger of losing this war, before it's even begun.'

CHAPTER TWENTY-FIVE

Three days later, in the early afternoon, I returned to the hall to speak with my father. The royal compound was humming with activity ahead of the large feast he had arranged for that evening. All the chiefs of the surrounding settlements had been invited, along with their senior advisers. The feast would serve as an opportunity to announce the coming campaign against the Atrebates and to renew the blood oath each headman had sworn to the king. The men would vow to defend their ruler and their land, and the Druids would make many sacrifices to the gods in the hopes of bringing us great victories in the spring. The smell of pork roasting over embers hung thick in the air as kitchen slaves toiled over the cooking fires. Household servants were busy carrying in beer barrels, extra tables and other supplies from the royal stores.

Bladocus walked at my side as I approached my father's private quarters. The Druid had agreed to accompany me after I had briefly explained my plan to him earlier that day. I was aware that my proposal would encounter fierce resistance, and I felt that my mentor's presence might help to sway the argument in my favour.

The guard rapped his knuckles on the doorframe and admitted us with a wave of his hand. My father sat at the head of his council table, listening to a pair of elderly retainers as they discussed the planned entertainment for the evening feast. They both fell silent as soon as I entered, while my father lifted his gaze to me.

'Yes, my son?'

I bowed and explained that I wished to talk with him in private, on a most urgent matter. My father stared at me with a perplexed expression, then dismissed his advisers and gestured for us to sit.

'Well?' he asked impatiently once the nobles had left the room. 'What is it that you wish to tell me that cannot wait?'

I glanced at Bladocus and said, carefully, 'I have been thinking about the problem of how we might overcome Verica in battle in the spring.'

'That is a subject which presently occupies the imagination of every noble and warrior in Camulodunum,' my father said. 'I am weary of listening to the opinions of men who claim they alone know how to vanquish our enemies, Caratacus.'

'I am sure that is so,' I replied. 'But I believe you will want to hear what I have to say.'

My father sighed. 'Our war-bands have been weakened by years of continuous warfare. Our remaining forces are spread thinly across the lands of the Cantiaci to garrison the largest settlements and guard the grain stores, now that the Iceni have begun raiding our lands again. Furthermore, I am reliably informed that a number of Dobunnian nobles have protested against their king's decision to support our side and Antedius may not last much longer. Tonight I must stand before the gathered chiefs and promise to lead them in a war that will cost us the lives of many fine young men, with little hope of a decisive victory. What makes you think you have a better plan than my most experienced warriors and advisers?'

I took a deep breath. 'There is a way to beat the Atrebates, Father. One that does not involve waiting for the spring and requires only a small number of men.'

My father instinctively looked towards Bladocus, as if seeking his opinion. 'I have heard his thoughts on the matter, sire,' the Druid said. 'It is worth listening to the boy.'

The king stared at me with renewed interest. 'Go on, then. Speak, Caratacus.'

I swapped a brief look with Bladocus. The seed of my plan had been planted at my father's meeting with the wise council and had quickly taken shape in my mind, but I knew that much depended on how I presented my thoughts to my father. Our tribes were fiercely traditional, wedded to the ways of the past, and hostile to outside influences. We resisted new ideas, even when they held the possibility of saving us from destruction at the hands of our enemies.

'Father, we know that Verica is gathering a large number of warriors at Calleva. Four thousand men, according to the spies. With the bridge across the Tamesis, Verica will be able to reinforce the defences at Lhandain long before we can begin our attack. Against a force that size, in a well-defended position, we will have no chance of success, however hard our men fight.'

'What is your point?'

'If our war-bands are to stand any hope of victory, we must find a way to weaken Verica's forces ahead of the spring.'

'And how, pray tell, do you propose to achieve that?'

'Verica is widely despised by those he rules, especially amongst the tribes he has conquered. If we can foment trouble amongst them he will have to divert many warriors away from his army to guard his rear. Especially regions like the occupied lands of the Regni,' I explained. 'That is where we should strike.'

'We are not at war with the Regni,' my father replied warily.

'No,' I said. 'But the Regni farm the most fertile soil in the south. Verica depends on them to feed and equip his men. Unlike the larger settlements to the north, their villages are mostly unfortified. Which makes them more vulnerable to attack.

'Give me a small number of men, Father, and we will take the fight to Verica over the winter months. We shall live off the land and harass the enemy at every opportunity, burning their grain stores and attacking the mines. In this way, we'll deprive the Atrebates of the supplies they need for the war-bands and impede their ability to build up their forces. Moreover, the raids will compel Verica to divert some of his forces to the south. He will have no choice but to garrison every major settlement in the kingdom. At the very least, it will leave him with a smaller host to put into the field at Lhandain when the campaign season begins.'

My father steepled his fingers on the table and said, guardedly, 'It is certainly a bold strategy. But a raiding party is not an honourable way to fight a war, Caratacus.'

'Sometimes honour does not win wars,' I said. 'If we insist on fighting in the traditional way of our people, when our enemy is prepared to use treachery and knife us in the back with no sense of shame, then we are doomed to fail. Verica is responsible for this.

Though we may find it hard to stomach, we must meet his methods in kind if we are to survive. This is the only way to win. I wish there was another way, Father, but there is not. Either we do this, or we face the strong possibility of defeat in the spring.'

My father slid his gaze to Bladocus. 'What do you say? Surely you do not support this monstrous plan?'

The Druid bowed his head slightly. 'Sometimes, sire, necessity is more important than principle. We have seen how even the highest amongst the Druid brotherhood have broken with honour and tradition for the sake of Roman silver. These are dark times, and dark times require dark deeds if we are to see the light again.'

My father's eyebrows inched upwards in surprise. 'That is a sad thing for a Druid to say.'

'Nevertheless, sire, it is my belief that the boy's plan has merit.'

'You would encourage my son to fight in a manner that is disapproved of by the Druid High Council? You, an elected member?'

Bladocus said humbly, 'It is my belief, sire, that the High Council surrendered its moral authority the moment the other members shamed themselves by accepting Roman bribes. An act which brought shame on all of us in the brotherhood of Druids.'

'Breaking with the traditional way of war is a serious matter, Caratacus,' my father said. 'You cannot suggest otherwise.'

'Of course, sire. But I would argue that the Catuvellaunians are duty-bound to oppose the expansion of the Atrebates, given Verica's close relationship with Rome, by whatever means necessary. It is vital that we protect our cults against the evil corruption of foreign influence. Do you imagine for a moment that Rome respects our traditions? Our warrior code?'

'Even so, the High Council still holds sway over the tribes. If you or any of my men were taken prisoner and your identities were revealed, the Druids would be sure to damn our reputation throughout Britannia. Every tribe in the south would turn against us. Our alliances would crumble.'

Bladocus said, 'The boy has already thought of that, sire.'

'He has?' My father looked at me keenly. 'Well?'

'We shall disguise ourselves as Silurian brigands,' I explained. 'The deception will be easy enough to accomplish. I spent years living among the Silures in Merladion. I know their dialect and their tribal markings as well as anyone. In addition, we will make our approach from the west, across Dobunni territory. Anyone who spies our party will naturally assume that we are a band of raiders.'

'But the Silures share no border with the Regni. Their chiefs would be surprised to find the men of the mountains raiding among them, surely?'

'Not necessarily, sire,' Bladocus said. 'The tribes neighbouring the Silures have improved their defences recently, after years of raids. The Regnians will assume that they have been forced to roam further afield in search of easier loot.'

The king narrowed his eyes thoughtfully. 'That might work . . . in the short term, perhaps. But the Atrebates would be sure to see through your ruse before long.'

'We will only be raiding for the winter months,' I argued. 'The deception should fool the enemy for a short while. Long enough for us to deprive Verica of his supplies and divert his men.'

Bladocus glanced sidelong at me. 'Naturally, the fewer people who are aware of Caratacus's plan, the less chance there is of the enemy discovering the truth.'

My father nodded sagely. 'How do you intend to evade the Atrebates? Assuming your plan is as successful as you hope, Verica's men will be hunting for you.'

'We shall travel on horseback and keep on the move. Much of the Regnian kingdom is heavily forested, which makes it ideal for evading enemy patrols.'

'And you propose to survive in the open throughout the depths of winter? I think you underestimate the scale of your task, my son.'

I said evenly, 'I am ready for whatever trials the gods have planned for me.'

'Verica's men are unlikely to receive much support from the local population,' Bladocus interjected. 'It is well known that the Regni detest their occupiers. A grain shortage may even encourage them to rebel against their Atrebatan masters, sire.'

My father arched an eyebrow. 'I doubt the Regni will appreciate their villages being attacked, regardless of their sentiments towards the Atrebates.'

I was ready for this point. 'I disagree, Father. The Atrebates are responsible for the kingdom's security. Their ire will be directed towards Verica for failing to deter the attacks.'

'That, in turn, will require him to move further warriors to the south,' Bladocus put in. 'The last thing Verica will want is unrest to the south while the bulk of his forces are concentrated along the Tamesis.'

My father did not seem convinced.

'The plan is not without its risks,' I conceded. 'But this is the only way we can beat Verica. If he's forced to commit men to defend his possessions to the south, we will be able to meet him on equal terms at Lhandain. Either we take this path, or we lose many of our warriors in a one-sided struggle come the spring.'

My father canted his head to one side, deep in thought. 'If the Druid believes this is necessary, I am inclined to agree. But it is vital that this plan remains a closely guarded secret. Outside of this room, no one else must be aware of your purpose. Not a soul. We cannot take any chances.'

'As you wish, Father.'

'How many men will you need, for your raiding party?'

'Give me a hundred, and I'll show you what I can do.'

'You may have fifty.'

I started to argue but he cut me off. 'Fifty men or nothing. I can spare no more.'

'Fifty, then,' I agreed reluctantly.

'I shall give you my best men . . . the pick of my warriors.' My father leaned forward and looked me straight in the eye. 'If this endeavour is to succeed, it must be done properly. You will need men who can fight and endure prolonged hardship. Men who are unafraid of living in the wild forests, surrounded by our sworn enemies.'

I stared at him, grasping the implication of his words. 'That will mean taking some warriors from the ranks of Adminius's war-band,' I said. My father had recently promoted Adminius to leader of one of his most prestigious war-bands following our defeat at the Battle of the Henge. 'He will not be pleased.'

He said sharply, 'Leave Adminius to me. I will tell him that you are taking these men to buy horses from the northern tribes. You will need a guide, of course. Someone who knows the lands you propose to raid. This plan won't work unless you can gather information from the villages.'

'I understand that there are many Regni in Camulodunum,' I said. 'Those who fled their lands when the Atrebates invaded their kingdom. A few have even served in our war-bands. I'm sure we can find an appropriate scout from their number.'

'An excellent idea,' the king said, intertwining his hands. 'You'll also need a good subordinate . . . someone who knows the men. Eight years is a long time to be away from the war-bands.'

'I have someone in mind, Father.'

'Who?'

'Togodumnus,' I said. 'He has the makings of a fine warrior. He might be somewhat headstrong, but he's brave, and he has the respect of the men.'

My father stroked his chin and stared at me for a long moment. 'Yes,' he said at length. 'I see no reason why your brother cannot join you. He will savour the opportunity to stain his sword with the blood of our enemies. He is a Catuvellaunian prince, after all.'

'Thank you, Father.'

'You will need horses and supplies.' I nodded, and he said, 'Speak to my household steward. He will give you what you need.'

'Yes, Father.'

'Do you have any further questions? Either of you?' he asked, looking from me to Bladocus.

We did not.

'Then I suggest you begin your preparations at once. Meanwhile I shall speak with Adminius. I assume you will wish to leave as soon as possible?'

'Yes, Father. There's no time to lose if we are to succeed.'

'Very well.' The king rose from his stool and said gravely, 'Let us hope that the gods are with you, Caratacus. For all our sakes.'

CHAPTER TWENTY-SIX

The next few days passed swiftly, for there was much work to be done before we could begin our raids on the enemy. My first task was to inform Togodumnus of the plan and appoint him as my second in command; he received the news with a broad grin and wicked gleam in his eyes, as I knew he would.

'We will enjoy some fine hunting, brother,' he said, rubbing his hands expectantly. 'Verica won't be expecting trouble to the south. We'll catch that bastard by surprise and give him a bloody nose.'

'That is what I hope,' I replied. 'Father has agreed to provide us with his best men. You know them better than I do. Make sure that the warriors Adminius agrees to provide are of the best. Men we can trust.'

'You think our brother would try to undermine us?'

'When has that ever not been the case?'

'You are right, of course. Adminius won't want to lose his finest men, not to our party. He might even see it as an opportunity to get rid of some of his bad apples.'

'Then we must ensure that he does not succeed.'

I left Togodumnus to deal with Adminius, and to find a suitable guide from among the existing ranks of the war-bands. At the same time I turned my attention to the issue of equipment. Many of our men preferred to carry their individual weapons, armour and shields, but these could not be taken with us since their markings would identify their bearers as Catuvellaunian warriors. I therefore ordered the tribe's blacksmiths to fashion some plain swords to arm us, along with our spears, bows, arrows and some lead shot, giving them strict instructions not to mark their handiwork in any way. Provisions had to be obtained from the royal stores, sufficient to last our raiding party for several days until we could plunder further supplies. In addition we needed hunting equipment, beer and the thicker cloaks that could allow us to pass for Silurians.

By now it was the end of the harvest season, the time we call the first days of the darkening, when the nights close in and Lud opens the gates to the Otherworld so that the souls of our dead kin may join him. Our tribe lit massive fires and made sacrifices to ward off the dark spirits who escape Lud's domain and roam freely through our lands. The farmers slaughtered their livestock, and after the Druids had made the offerings to the gods the supplies of grain were stored in pits for the winter months. In the evening there was a great feast at the hall, with dog fights and roasted piglets distributed to the guests and much drinking. Places were laid at the trestle tables for our dead comrades. Bellocatus claimed the hero's portion after winning an entertaining contest against one of his cousins.

The next afternoon, the fifty men chosen for our raiding party were summoned by Togodumnus to one side of the royal compound. I explained that we would be departing the following morning to ride north for a few months to buy remounts from the Brigantes, so that they might pass this fabrication on to their families and friends and so misdirect any spies. Each warrior was instructed to present himself at first light at the main gate with his horse and saddlebags.

We made our farewells the next morning and rode away, heading north. After we had ridden for a few miles we halted at the edge of a clearing and the men were issued with their weapons, equipment and provisions: waterskins, drab tunics and black leggings in the style of the Silurian tribes, and haversacks filled with rations.

It was a fine autumn day with a clear blue sky and a brisk breeze that tugged at our woollen cloaks as I ordered the warriors to gather round. Togodumnus stood to my side, his muscular arms folded across his chest as I prepared to address the men.

'My brothers,' I began, intimating the kind of bond I wished to foster. 'I have called you here today for a mission of vital importance to our king and our people. Our journey will not take us to the Brigantes. Instead, we shall travel south, to the lands of our enemies. This service will require great sacrifice and hardship from each of you, but it is vital that we succeed. The fate of our tribe depends on it.'

They stared at me with a mixture of surprise and eager anticipation. These were powerfully built men in the prime of life. Many of them belonged to Adminius's war-band. Others came from the king's personal bodyguard. These were the toughest warriors in Camulodunum, highly trained swordsmen with many years of fighting experience between them.

Almost all of the warriors were older than me. That was a problem, I reflected: these veterans had spent years training in their war-bands, mastering the traditional fighting tactics of our tribespeople. Persuading them of the necessity of waging a dishonourable war against the Atrebates would not be easy. I would have to appeal to their sense of loyalty to their king, and the deep bond every true Celtic warrior feels to his tribe and the spirits of his ancestors.

'I will be blunt with you,' I said. 'The future of our people hangs by a thread. The war we must fight against the Atrebates is the great test of our age. If we are defeated then all the glory my father, our king, has won for the Catuvellaunian people will be scattered to the four winds. No longer will other tribes look to us for leadership and we will, instead, become the vassals of Verica and the Atrebates . . .'

I paused and looked round at the men. Several of them shook their heads and muttered foul curses under their breath.

'I can think of no greater humiliation than being subject to a ruler whose sense of honour is lower than the belly of a serpent,' I continued. 'I would fight to my dying breath to avoid such a fate. And I would fight with the deadliest tools that are available to me. Sometimes in war, the greatest sacrifice is overlooked by those who relate the sagas to the generations to come. But that does not diminish the role of great deeds.

'It may be that our part in the coming struggle never becomes the stuff of legend. So be it. The deeds of warriors do not need an audience for them to be judged great. Brothers, it is not for us to question the nature of the service we are about to undertake. Only to carry it out.' I let my words settle in the minds of my companions before I continued. 'There will be times when you will question the honour of our actions. Your heart will yearn for the glory of battle and our traditional ways of war. As will mine. But we must hold to our purpose and that is to win a victory over our greatest enemy. That is all that counts. It is a matter of mind over heart.

'We will be fighting from the shadows in the land of the Regni. That kingdom, as some of you may know, is vital to the Atrebates' war efforts . . . which makes it vulnerable to attack. That is where we shall hunt, raiding the enemy at every opportunity. We shall burn his grain, destroy his farms and deprive him of the iron he needs to make his weapons. Such actions, cruel as they are, will nevertheless be vital to the future survival of our tribe. We are going to spread chaos and fear, until that snake Verica and his lackeys are jumping at their own shadows. For those of you who might find our approach distasteful, remember your dead kinfolk, treacherously cut down at Senomagus. The Atrebates showed our brothers no mercy then – and now I intend to return the favour. Are you with me?'

The warriors exchanged glances as they digested my words. After a brief pause Togodumnus stepped forward. 'I am with you, brother. To the end. Come what may.'

'To the end,' I repeated deliberately. 'Come what may. That is the oath.'

One by one the others stepped forward and echoed their commitment. To my surprise, and relief, not one man among them asked to quit. When the last had spoken I gave them a small smile of gratitude.

'We will disguise ourselves as Silurians when we slip across the border. Some of you may object to this ruse, but it is vital that the enemy does not suspect our tribe's involvement, at least until the war is decided. When the winter is over we shall return across the border, ready to join our kin in the fight for Lhandain.

'That is the good news. The bad news is that we will have to spend the next few months sleeping in the cold without the prospect of a fire to warm our bodies. Worse, we will have to live as Silurian raiders. That means wearing our hair in unkempt locks, growing thick beards and talking like women.'

A chorus of laughter rippled through the ranks. It was a feeble jest, but it had the effect of easing some of the tension among them.

'I warn you, this will be unpleasant and dangerous work,' I went on. 'If we are successful, we will hamstring Verica's attempts to defend Lhandain, forcing him to divert men to the south. But if we are caught we can expect no mercy. I tell you this, because it is only right that you should appreciate the risks each of us must face.

'Our plan requires us to set aside the traditional fighting style of our tribe. But the situation confronting our tribe leaves us with no choice. Unless we succeed, given the strength of the enemy, it is almost certain that our kingdom will be defeated in battle. To succeed we must survive. We will have to fight as brigands, launching raids, evading enemy patrols and keep on the run. Wherever possible, we will avoid battle.

'Be under no illusions, brothers. The Atrebates are worthy adversaries. Some of you will not be returning home in the spring. But I promise you this: there will be spoils of war for you to share with your loved ones. Perhaps, if the gods are kind, our deeds will be remembered with honour. Then, when you are old men huddled round a winter fireplace, you can say you once rode with Caratacus. Others will fall silent and look to you, eager to hear your tale. All I ask of you then is not to bore the poor bastards to death.'

My words had the desired effect. The men erupted into lusty cheers and laughter, punching the air or grinning with excitement. I raised an arm, calling for quiet, and gestured to Togodumnus.

'You all know my brother, Togodumnus. He is my second in command. From now on, I expect you to obey any orders given by either of us without question.'

I searched the faces of the warriors, daring any of them to defy me. There was a silent pause before I went on.

'We shall ride west until we are deep into Dobunnian territory. Only then will we make our way south. Any who sight our party crossing the border will report seeing a group of Silurian raiders approaching from the direction of the mountains. Prepare your mounts.'

While the men trudged off towards their horses, I beckoned to Togodumnus. 'Where is our Regnian guide?' I asked. 'I wish to speak with him before we begin our journey.'

Togodumnus turned on his heel and marched over to the throng of warriors. He approached a slight and youthful-looking figure and led him over to me.

'This is Nemobnus,' Togodumnus said. 'One of the men from Adminius's war-band.'

Nemobnus bowed his head. 'My lord, it is a great honour to fight for the son of King Cunobelinus.'

His voice had a strong accent I had not heard before, thick and slow. Nemobnus had soft blue eyes and flawless teeth. His patterned cloak looked expensive, and his fair moustache drooped down either side of his delicate mouth. There was something animal-like in his movements, and his eyes were alert. Some of the markings on his face and cheeks did not belong to our tribe. They were the markings of the Regnian warrior-caste.

'How long did you serve with my brother, Nemobnus?' I asked.

'Two years, lord.'

'And what did you do before that?'

'I was a warrior, my lord. In the service of Tingetus, King of the Regni. I lived with my family in a village outside Noviomagus. At least, I did until the Atrebates invaded our lands.' I saw a flicker of hatred burning behind those gentle eyes.

'What happened?' I asked.

'Our forces were routed in battle,' Nemobnus said. He paused. 'We were badly outnumbered and didn't stand a chance. As soon as Tingetus fell, the others panicked and took flight. I managed to escape and made my way back to my family. I planned to bring them north, lord. But Verica's men had already attacked and burned the village to the ground. That's when I saw the bodies . . .'

Nemobnus looked away, apparently gripped by a silent fury.

'The Atrebates had slaughtered them,' he went on. 'Men, women, the aged . . . even the infants. None had been spared their fury. My wife and two sons had been thrown into the village well. I can never forget what I saw that day.' His voice drifted off. 'After that, I tried to reach my brother's family in Noviomagus, but by then the Atrebatan war-bands had seized the capital and there was nothing I could do for them. So I fled north to Camulodunum instead.'

'Why did you come here?' I asked.

'I had kin in these parts, lord. I live with them now.'

It was clear that Nemobnus had suffered appallingly at the hands of Verica's men, like so many of his fellow tribesmen. Verica was no respecter of the code of war that existed between our tribes – that much had been apparent from his actions at the Battle of the Henge. And his conquest of the Regnians had been similarly brutal: his warriors had slaughtered the flower of the Regnian nobility, instead of sparing their lives and holding them for ransom, as was customary. His crimes were abhorrent, and filled me with a cold rage. I told Nemobnus I was sorry for his loss and assured him that he would have the chance to avenge the deaths of his loved ones soon enough. He bowed his head before me again.

'Give me the opportunity, and I'll put that bastard Verica to the sword. Him and the rest of his cronies. I swear before Lud, they'll pay for what they did to my family . . .'

I said, 'You will have the most dangerous task of all, but also one of the most important. It will be necessary for you to enter the settlements from time to time and gather intelligence from the people.'

'I can do that, my lord,' he replied confidently.

'What story will you tell them?'

He thought quickly. 'I'll pose as a travelling bard, my lord.'

'Will that work?' asked Togodumnus.

Nemobnus smiled. 'My uncle was a bard. He taught me enough to get by. I know all the folk tales and the sagas. I won't have any problem passing myself off as a bard.'

'Are you likely to be recognised?' I asked. 'After all, you will be moving among your own people.'

'No, lord. Most of my kin were slain when the Atrebates seized our lands.'

'What of your brother's family? Are they alive?'

Nemobnus shrugged. 'I haven't seen them since I left the kingdom. They might have escaped.'

'Unless they were killed in Noviomagus,' Togodumnus muttered.

Nemobnus shot him a look but said nothing.

I said, 'We will also need to establish a hidden base camp. Somewhere isolated, near to our intended targets but close enough to the border that we can slip across freely if we are compromised.'

The warrior considered. 'I know of such a place, my lord. There's an old hunting lodge in the forest, half a day's ride from Noviomagus. The place has been abandoned for years.'

'Will the Atrebates know of it?'

'No, lord. The only people aware of the place are a few hunters.'

'Very well. That sounds very promising.'

A short while later we walked our horses out of the vale and started west along the mud-slicked track. We carried light oval shields bound in leather, and unmarked swords, daggers and thrusting spears produced by our tribe's most skilled craftsmen. We were dressed in the style of our own tribe, for I had decided that we would not change our appearance until we were close to the Regnian border. The sight of a horde of Silurian raiders would merely provoke alarm among the friendly villages and risked alerting the enemy to the true identity of our party.

Ahead of us lay a perilous journey into the lands of our sworn enemies. On our shoulders rested nothing less than the survival of my people and the vast kingdom we ruled. The burden was heavy for one so young, but I was determined to do everything possible to bring about the destruction of the Atrebates. I made a solemn vow to the gods that I would succeed in my plan, or die trying.

CHAPTER TWENTY-SEVEN

We rode west through a barren landscape of sodden fields and bare trees. On the second afternoon our party camped in a sprawl of woodland a few miles from Verlamion. The next day we swam our horses across the river demarcating the border between our tribe and the Dobunni. As we carried on through the kingdom of our allies, I gazed up at the leaden grey sky, shivering beneath my cloak, and felt a pang of dread at the thought of spending the next few months surviving in the forests and vales to the south.

At a small farmstead we bought ample supplies of biscuit, dried meat and ale to last us through the winter. The farmer was a wizened old man, with that mixture of gloominess and wit peculiar to his trade. He accepted in good faith our story that we were riding west to buy remounts and told us he would pray for our safety. When I asked him why, he grimaced and pointed to the surrounding landscape.

'It will be a hard winter this year,' he said in his guttural accent. 'The omens are bad. The geese have migrated already. Last month a foal was born with no front legs in Ledrid, and when the Druids made their harvest-offerings to Lud they say a black raven was seen flying to the east.'

Togodumnus laughed mockingly when I told him this later. 'Do you really believe those old wives' tales? Farmers are almost as bad as the seers when it comes to predicting doom.'

'I pray you are right, brother,' I said.

On the sixth evening we arrived at a secluded dell a few miles from the border with the neutral kingdom of the Belgae, whose lands we would have to pass through before we could reach enemy territory. Here we rested and fed our horses. While the others filled their aching bellies with hunks of bread and salted mutton, I called forward our two best riders.

Vassedo was a short, squat Trinovantian with unkempt hair, bushy eyebrows and a wicked glint in his eyes. He had been raised in a village outside Camulodunum, the son of a family of skilled hunters, and he had a huntsman's keen eye and instinctive feel for the land and everything that lived off it. He was a sturdy fellow, tough and capable of enduring any hardship.

The other man, Dubnocatus, was tall and sinewy and dark haired. He was only a few years older than me, but he had already earned a reputation as one of our tribe's most accomplished warriors. He was a quietly spoken fellow, brooding and temperamental. Like all the nobles in our tribe, he was an accomplished rider; he would have been a match for any Parthian cavalrymen. We Catuvellaunians were known as the finest horsemen in all of Britannia. We bred the best mounts, and started our riding lessons in early childhood, training relentlessly until it seemed as natural to us as breathing air. On a good mount, a Catuvellaunian warrior can ride for ten miles longer than the horsemen in any of the other tribes.

'From now on, we shall move cautiously,' I told the two warriors. 'You will ride ahead of us and scout the land for any sign of trouble. If you run into any patrols, do not engage. Return and make your report to me as quickly as possible.'

'Are we expecting trouble, my lord?' asked Vassedo.

'The Belgae are supposed to be neutral,' I replied. 'But their chief is sympathetic to the Atrebates, and we cannot risk alerting the enemy to our presence.'

Once I had finished briefing the scouts, I summoned Nemobnus. 'This abandoned hunting lodge of yours . . . how far is it from here?'

The Regnian squinted at the horizon and made a quick calculation. 'Three days, my lord, give or take. Assuming we maintain a good pace.'

I nodded. 'You will ride ahead with the scouts as soon as we cross the border. Once we arrive at the lodge, we'll need to make preparations for our first raid. We can't afford to waste any time if we are to damage Verica's supplies.'

Nemobnus grinned. 'There'll be plenty of targets, my lord, now that the harvest season is over. Mark my words. We'll catch them by surprise. They won't be expecting trouble.'

Early the next morning we changed into the plain tunics and leggings we had brought with us and braided our hair in the fashion of the Silures before continuing on our way east. Our beards would take longer to grow, but from a distance, to a casual observer, I felt sure that we would pass for a Silurian raiding party.

Our journey from Camulodunum had afforded me the opportunity to get to know the men, and I was beginning to develop a surer sense of their individual qualities. This was important, for the commanders of our war-bands do not have the luxury of instilling discipline at the end of a vine cane like your centurions, driving the men as if they were oxen in a field. In our tribes, one must lead by example.

Aside from our scouts, Vassedo and Dubnocatus, and our Regnian guide, Nemobnus, there was Maglocunus, a veteran Catuvellaunian from my father's royal bodyguard, a fierce-looking fighter with a thick red beard and a leather patch covering his left eye. The scars on the bodyguard's face and hands hinted at the many battles he had fought under my father's banner. Garmanus, another recruit from the royal bodyguard, was an enormous warrior with several missing teeth who had once been a wrestler before he had sworn an oath to defend our king. He was hot-headed and quick to take offence, and often got into fights with his comrades, but his courage in the heat of battle was without question.

We moved on quietly and camped that evening not far from the place we called Sorviodunum. Two days later, we crossed over into the territory of the Regni. This was a rich landscape of rolling green hills and vales, scattered with patches of woodland and brown fields stubbled with dead wheat stalks, and a handful of remote settlements, ideal for the type of raiding operations I had planned.

As the day wore on the air became colder and the wind quickly strengthened. We followed Nemobnus as he took us on a winding route through a great sprawl of dense forest, staying clear of the main droveways and settlements. I forbade any conversation, and for hours we heard nothing except for the snorting of the horses and the clatter of the bare branches in the biting wind. This was a time of acute tension, for I had privately feared that Verica might have discovered

272

my plans despite the many precautions we had taken, and the possibility of an enemy ambush constantly preyed on my mind. But to my relief the area remained free of threats.

Shortly before dusk encroached we came to a halt at the edge of a wide clearing hemmed in by dense clumps of skeletal oak and birch trees, prickly shrubs and patches of browned heather. A cluster of decaying wooden structures stood in a semicircle in the middle of this clearing, enclosed by a half-ruined low stockade. This was the site of the old Regnian hunting lodge. Here we would make our first temporary camp before commencing our attacks on the enemy.

The men were exhausted from the long march, but I immediately put them to work gathering bracken, ferns and twigs to fashion crude bedrolls. Once it was dark we lit a small fire in a fold in the woods close to the lodge, and took a meal of bread and mutton before we rested for the evening. The modest warmth of the flames did little to warm our bodies, and as darkness settled across the forest we lay huddled in our winter cloaks, shivering.

'By the gods, this is miserable,' Togodumnus muttered. He pulled his cloak tighter around him. 'Why the fuck did I agree to this plan of yours again?'

I chuckled. 'You've had it too easy, brother,' I said. 'All those years of living in luxury at home. Try sleeping on the bare floor in a hut in Siluria for years, living on scraps of meat and mouldy bread not fit for the wild beasts.'

'Sounds shit.'

'If you're too cold to sleep, we can sleep beside one another and share our body heat.'

'What?' Togodumnus shot me a disgusted look. 'Cuddling up together? Me and you? You must be joking. No offence, but I'd rather freeze my bollocks off.'

I shrugged. 'It worked for the Silurians. They used to do it to keep themselves warm during the winter in Merladion.'

Togodumnus pulled a face. 'Your Silurian friends have some odd ideas. Must be all that bloody mountain air.'

'Suit yourself.'

The next morning the weather turned colder still, hardening the muddied ground while the surrounding vegetation sparkled with a thin coating of frost. I was acutely aware of the need to begin attacking the enemy before our own supplies dwindled. Soon after dawn I sent Nemobnus and Vassedo south to gather information from the nearest settlements. While they were absent the men were kept busy with the numerous tasks needed to secure our camp. Sentries were posted around the clearing while a small party of men made repairs to the timber structures and erected a palisade around the perimeter.

Togodumnus arranged the rest of the men into foraging parties and I ordered that we would only light fires during the hours of darkness. In the daylight, the slightest trail of smoke would give away our presence. A small party of men went off in search of wild game; others were tasked with gathering roots and leaves to make the dyes we would need in order to pass for Silurian warriors.

Three days after our arrival, Nemobnus and Vassedo returned to the camp around noon. I listened closely as they made their report. Then I summoned the warriors to a meeting in front of the repaired huts.

'It is time, brothers,' I said. I grinned at Togodumnus. 'We shall go hunting tomorrow . . . but for a very different type of game.'

I caught the look of excitement on the men's faces. Togodumnus rubbed his hands expectantly, his eyes glowing in anticipation at the imminent prospect of action.

'What's the target, my lord?' asked Maglocunus.

'There is a village called Arundun, situated along the bank of the River Trisantonis. Half a day's ride from here.' I gestured to Nemobnus and continued. 'Nemobnus has been gathering information from the villages to the south. He has learned that there are substantial grain stores at Arundun, close to the chief's enclosure. Grain that is due to be sent north to feed Verica's forces.'

'How can you be sure of that, my lord?' asked Garmanus.

I turned to Nemobnus, who said, 'I overheard a pair of nobles in the tavern yesterday at Noviomagus. The Atrebatan harvest has been poor this year, and Verica's men have been seizing the grain from the local settlements. The local chief has agreed to hand over his surplus to Verica to help provision the war-bands. Once the remainder of the harvest has been gathered the grain will be sent on to Calleva.'

'Can't imagine the locals are too happy about that.'

'It's an outrage,' Nemobnus said. 'The farmers usually make a modest income from selling surplus grain to their neighbours in the east. Now they must hand over the fruits of their labours for nothing.' He spat on the ground. 'Many will go hungry this winter.'

'Why would the chief give his grain to the Atrebates?' Togodumnus asked.

'He's an ally of Verica,' Nemobnus explained. 'Every noble in the kingdom has been forced to swear their allegiance to him. If the chief refuses to support the Atrebates, they will remove him at the point of a sword and replace him with someone more biddable.'

'Arundun is poorly defended,' I said. 'It's far from the borders, and most of the warriors fled after the Atrebatan conquest. Which means the place is ripe for the plucking. We'll raid the settlement, taking the defenders by surprise and burning the grain stores. Then we'll take whatever supplies we need from the village before making our escape.'

Maglocunus knitted his craggy brow. 'How many defenders are we facing, my lord?'

'Verica has permitted the local chief to retain only a small number of bodyguards. Thirty at most, we think. Perhaps less.'

'And the rest of the villagers?'

'Farmers and craftsmen, mostly,' Nemobnus said. 'They'll be armed with nothing more dangerous than a few clubs and spears. They won't present much of a threat.'

'Our job is to frustrate Verica's ability to wage war,' I reminded the others. 'The grain surplus is vital if Verica is to feed his men. Without the extra supplies from the south, he'll be forced to choose between feeding his hungry warriors or his people. He cannot do both.'

I could see the unease in some of my warriors' expressions. 'I know this is dirty work, brothers. It sticks in my throat that we may inflict suffering on the blameless subjects of Verica, but if he is defeated and deposed then they can look forward to a better time. Besides, do you think he would treat our people any better if he is victorious? This is the burden of the war he forced on us. Never forget that.'

We made our preparations in the late afternoon, anticipation mingled with nerves, checking our weaponry and equipment, while others gathered the roots and plants taken from the forest and boiled the mixture in water to make the dye necessary to complete our disguise. The men watched closely as I painted Dubnocatus's arms and face with the intricate patterns I remembered from my time living among the Silurians. Then they were divided into pairs and began daubing each other in the same style. Once they had finished I had them form up in a long line so I could inspect their efforts. Most of their markings were good enough to carry off the ruse, but then my gaze landed on Togodumnus.

'Well?' he asked as I peered at the watery patterns decorating his face. 'What do you think?'

'Who painted you?' I asked.

'Maglocunus. Why?' Togodumnus drew his eyebrows together. 'What's wrong?'

As I looked on, the symbols above his brow began to run down his face in thin veins. I couldn't help chuckling at the ridiculous sight, further incensing my younger brother. Some of the others quickly joined in.

'What the hell are you lot laughing at?' Togodumnus snapped, a moment before the paint began dripping from his eyebrows. He frowned and touched his face, then held up his hand and glared at the thin dye smeared on his fingertips. 'Oh, for fuck's sake!'

'Sorry, my lord,' Maglocunus stammered, wringing his hands. 'I tried my best . . .'

'Bloody idiot.' Togodumnus glowered at him. 'I thought you said you knew what you were doing?'

'Wash it off,' I told my brother, before I turned to Maglocunus. 'Try again. Use a thicker mixture next time. We want to fool the enemy, Maglocunus,' I added with a slight grin. 'Not make them die of laughter.'

'Yes, my lord.' The warrior's scarred face flushed with embarrassment.

'The rest of you get some food and sleep,' I said. 'We'll make straight for Arundun at first light.'

CHAPTER TWENTY-EIGHT

We slipped out of the camp before sunrise. It was a dull winter's day, with grey cloud pressing down low in the sky. I left behind half a dozen men to guard the camp, under the command of Garmanus. He was bitterly disappointed by my decision, but he was a loyal servant and did not voice his protest. I told him that if we did not return by the following evening he was to assume that we had been captured or killed, abandon the camp and retreat to Camulodunum. The rest of us gathered our shields and weapons and began the journey south.

After several miles we emerged from the gloom of the forest and continued on through a patchwork of steep-sided vales and barren fields notched with muddied droveways and goat-tracks. Occasionally we saw evidence of the Atrebates' recent invasion of the kingdom: freshly-made burial mounds and the blackened frames of torched farmsteads. Further along we passed the ruins of a minor Regni village. The Atrebates had razed most of the huts and houses to the ground, leaving nothing behind but a few blackened timbers and piles of stone, and the skeletal remains of humans and animals.

'What happened here?' Togodumnus wondered aloud.

At my side I saw Nemobnus gazing across the destroyed village with his jaw clenched tight, and it occurred to me that we were not far from his own settlement.

He said, 'It is the same in many places in our land, my lord. Verica and his men showed our people no mercy when they invaded. They plundered this settlement, killed the chief and his warriors and made the others swear an oath of allegiance to their king. Those who refused were put to death or sold into the slave markets of Gaul.'

'How do you know this?' I asked.

Nemobnus shrugged. 'I had friends here once, lord. One of the elders escaped to Camulodunum and told me the story. The others were not so fortunate.'

I placed my hand on his shoulder. 'You will have your chance for revenge soon, Nemobnus. Gods willing.'

'Yes, my lord,' he replied sadly. 'But I wish it were not so.'

'You don't want to avenge the spirits of the dead?'

'I would rather drink in the company of my kinfolk, my lord. Revenge is a poor substitute for the smile of a friend.'

He spoke the truth. I tried to think of some words of comfort, but none came.

Later that afternoon we arrived at a narrow clearing and Nemobnus threw up his hand, signalling for our party to stop. I trotted forward and the Regnian guide pointed towards a low grassy hill to the south crowned with a patch of woodland.

'Arundun is the other side of that ridge, lord,' he said.

I beckoned to Dubnocatus. 'Stay here with the others,' I ordered. 'Make sure the men remain quiet. Not a sound, d'you hear?'

'Where are you going, my lord?'

'To reconnoitre the village.'

I swung down from my saddle and ordered Maglocunus to come with me, then we set off on foot, following Nemobnus as he picked his way along a narrow trail leading towards the top of the hill. At last we reached the ridgeline. We paused to catch our breath, then edged beyond the treeline and crawled on our bellies towards a shallow gully. From this position we had a clear view of the settlement in the vale below.

Arundun in the years before the invasion was a scattering of barns, animal pens and roundhouses set on raised ground near a bend in the Trisantonis river. Its position had allowed the locals to benefit from the burgeoning trades in hunting dogs, slaves and jewellery with Gaul, and the settlement had grown substantially over the years. A few small river boats were anchored beside the wharf, dark against the grey water. As with many of the minor Regnian settlements, no attempt had been made to establish a defensive rampart or ditch. Nearer to the quayside, a mile or so from our position, a pair of

Regnian warriors armed with spears stood guard outside a large rectangular structure.

'That's Arundun's grain store, my lord,' Nemobnus said. 'I've heard that their chief refuses to feed the poorest among his own kind, while his men protect grain bound for Atrebatan mouths. It's the only place being guarded in the village, other than the chief's quarters.'

Maglocunus smiled approvingly as he surveyed the village. 'This place is there for the taking. This shall be an easy victory for our side.'

'No fight is easy when men are defending their homes,' I cautioned.

We spent some time observing the village, noting the number of warriors and their movements, until at length dusk began to settle across the land. 'Come on,' I said. 'I've seen enough, brothers. Let's go.'

In the failing light we crept back through the treeline and moved stealthily down the far side of the hill until we emerged into the clearing. I gathered round the senior warriors and laid out my plan of attack.

We spent a few hours making our preparations for our night raid. We could not risk lighting cooking fires in such close proximity to the village and so the men grazed on rations of coarse bread and cheese from their haversacks, washed down with cups of beer. A short time later, in the dim light afforded by the crescent moon, I ordered the men to mount their horses.

'Remember, brothers,' I said, 'we are Silurians now. That means we must fight like them too. Act swiftly, steal whatever you can . . . and show no mercy to those who dare to resist us.'

Our band trotted out of the clearing, moving quietly as we followed a rough track that curved around the base of the hill, screened from view of the village by a dense sprawl of evergreen pine trees. As we continued down the path I heard the clod of hoofs against the rotted leaves, the whispered prayers of men and the faint clinking of horse bits.

We descended the gentle slope towards the valley floor, and then the woodland began to thin. Ahead of us, no more than a few hundred paces away, I descried the sprawling settlement at Arundun, the dark shapes of the roundhouses faintly visible against the night sky. At this late hour most of the inhabitants would be asleep, and the only signs of life were the faint lights of hearth-fires emanating from some of the roundhouses, and muted voices.

At my command we tugged on our reins and drew to a halt behind a clump of spindly silver birch trees. The men maintained silence as they dismounted and drove wooden pegs attached to the reins into the soft ground, fixing their horses in place. We crept across the open ground in the pitch black of the night, moving beyond the treeline until we reached a grassy hillock within missile range of the settlement. Torches were lit, and Togodumnus softly called forward a dozen warriors armed with incendiaries, the pick of our bowmen. The rest of our raiding party waited on the crest as the bowmen edged down the hill a short distance before coming to a halt. Then they plucked arrows from their quivers, holding the pitch-soaked tips to the torches gripped by their comrades. Togodumnus hissed an order, and the bowmen began loosing their fire arrows at the thatched roofs of the clustered roundhouses.

A ragged veil of glowing orange shafts arced through the night sky before they dipped down towards the settlement. Several of the missiles found their targets, embedding themselves in the roofs of the nearest huts and barns. Some struck the ground, others set ablaze haystacks or piles of timber. Within moments the fires had quickly spread, engulfing the roundhouses in writhing gouts of flame. Dozens of villagers spilled out of their homes, some snatching up buckets and racing over to try to put out fires, while others turned and ran for the hills, hurrying along with their screaming children.

Amid the carnage I caught sight of a man lying on the ground, pawing at an arrow shaft buried in his thigh. Another figure was struck through the neck as he tried to limp away. At the same time a stream of figures came rushing out of the chief's enclosure. Servants rushed over to the blazing roundhouses as they joined in the frantic effort to quench the fires, while the bodyguards snatched up spears and axes as they prepared to defend themselves.

Our bowmen released another fearsome barrage of incendiaries. A number of the shafts fell short of their intended targets and landed amid the animal pens, goring cattle. The beasts bellowed in terror, driven mad by the fires and the torrent of missiles raining down on them. Cries went up from the villagers as the frightened herd broke into a stampede and crashed through the flimsy fence. Several of the warriors were caught in the path of the onrushing beasts, and their terrified screams split the night air moments before they were trampled to death beneath the thundering hoofs. The animals charged through the main tracks in small droves, leaving behind a trail of shattered timber and broken bodies. The sight sickened me and I had to forcefully remind myself of its necessity as I silently cursed Verica for driving us to such extremes.

With the settlement in disarray I ordered my men forward. We raced down the hillock towards the burning village, our boots pounding against the frozen ground, the savage yells of our warriors intermingled with the panicked shouts of the villagers, the wild bawling of cattle and the crackling roar of the flames. I glanced across and saw Togodumnus and the other bowmen unsheathing their long swords as they raced to join the rest of our party. With our woad-painted bodies, braided hair and gleaming weapons, we struck a terrifying sight.

The man in front of me let out a shout of alarm as a stricken bull, its flank wreathed in flames, charged towards us. The beast slammed into the raider before he could leap out of its way, impaling the man on its horns. Instinctively I threw myself to the side of the track, narrowly avoiding the wounded beast as it charged past and on towards the black mass of the distant hills.

'Burn the stores!' I shouted at Togodumnus, pointing towards the storage sheds abutting the riverbank.

He nodded and called out to those men among us still gripping torches. At once they hurried down the main track, following my brother towards the grain sheds. While they destroyed the enemy's supplies, the bulk of our raiding force would deal with the chief and his retinue.

As we hastened towards the larger enclosure in the middle of the village the surviving bodyguards rushed forward to meet us, brandishing their spears and battleaxes. Our sides clashed in a flurry of flickering sword points reflecting the glow of the fires raging around us. I heard a shout and saw a broad-faced warrior with spiked hair charging at me, bellowing in the incomprehensible dialect of the Regni.

I hastily threw up my shield to meet the blow of his broadaxe. There was a splintering crack as the axe head bit deep into the surface, and I gritted my teeth as a burning pain shot up my forearm from the shuddering impact. The axeman roared in frustration and wrenched his weapon free before he came forward once more. I jerked back, narrowly evading the blow, then shifted to the side and slashed upwards, catching the bodyguard on his undefended flank before he could recover. The sword tore open a deep gash inches below the man's armpit, slicing through tendon and muscle. Before I could spring forward to make the kill another raider lunged at the axeman, slamming the tip of his spear into the warrior's chest with such force that the blow carried him off his feet.

Across the main track the bodyguards were putting up a determined fight. Among them I saw a man with lime-washed hair and a gold torc bellowing orders. His ornate armlets and the gleaming rings on his fingers clearly identified him as the local chief. His men were hopelessly outnumbered, their ranks denuded by the onslaught of missiles and the destructive force of the fires. Soon we had pushed the surviving warriors back towards their chief's enclosure. The ground was now a quagmire of mud, blood and viscera as more of the bodyguards were cut down beneath the relentless hacks and slashes of our men.

Amid the press of bodies I saw an older man with wild grey hair lunging at me with his thrusting spear. The leaf-shaped tip ripped through the loose fabric of my tunic, nicking flesh. I stumbled back, dimly aware of a searing pain on my flank, as the grey-haired Regnian came at me again. He launched a succession of thrusts and stabs, then swung his weapon round and caught me on the jaw with the base of the shaft. Something jarred in my skull. I saw a flash of white, and then I fell helplessly backwards and landed on the gore-soaked ground.

I saw the spear tip glinting above me and rolled desperately to my left a moment before the bodyguard drove his weapon down. The tip stabbed the dirt, and I struck out at the spearman before he could swing round to face me, slashing at his shin; my next attack caught him on the neck. There was a sharp hiss as the air escaped from the man's gashed throat; blood jetted out of the gash in a furious gush. He collapsed and died amid the shit and the pools of blood, his eyes bulging with shock as the lifeblood drained from him. It is strange how I can see every detail in my mind's eye even after so many years. But some deaths one never forgets. The poets and playwrights might claim otherwise, but there is no glory in war, only the appalling sights and sounds of men tearing at one another in a desperate struggle for survival.

How long the skirmish lasted I cannot say. Certainly not for long. Within a short time more than half of the chief's bodyguards had been cut down, many dead or dying. In the flickering light of the flames I saw Vassedo cleave open a warrior's head with his battleaxe, splitting it down to the man's jaw. Maglocunus roared in triumph as he rammed his long sword into another warrior's stomach. Further along the track I saw a Regnian warrior stumble out of a burning roundhouse, his body shrouded in flames, his agonised shrieks piercing the air. The man slashed blindly with his sword at two of my men before he was cut down.

Several of the bodyguards, sensing the imminent danger to their chief, turned and hastened away with their leader, making for the distant wooded slopes. I knew then that the fight was over. A handful of warriors stood their ground, determined to die a good death and give time for the chief to make his escape. Others threw down their weapons and raised their hands in surrender, but they were cut to pieces by men in the grip of fighting madness. In a matter of moments the last of the defenders had been slain.

As our men cheered their victory I glanced across my shoulder and felt a thrill of satisfaction at the sight of the burning grain stores. The buildings were fully ablaze now, the glimmer of the flames reflecting in the black waters of the river.

At once our men began plundering the settlement. I dispatched Vassedo with a force of men to search the huts that were not yet burning. He rounded up half a dozen exhausted warriors and they quickly set off towards the roundhouses, bringing out supplies of bread, hazelnuts, cheese and salted pork, along with a few plump chickens and several jars of beer. I tasked Nemobnus with taking mules from the chief's stables to transport our spoils back to our hideout.

'Take feed for the horses as well,' I added. 'As much as we can carry.'

The rest of our men helped themselves to valuables from the chief's quarters; others robbed the dead of their torcs and rings. This was necessary to add to our deceit, for no Silurian raiding force worthy of the name would leave such rich pickings behind.

A huddle of despairing villagers, those who had not been able to escape the settlement, looked on helplessly as my men carried out armfuls of booty from the chief's enclosure. Mothers sought to console their wailing babies. Older men watched us with hatred.

I did not wish for us to remain in Arundun a moment longer than necessary. The nearest major settlement was less than half a day's ride away, and it would not take long for the chief and his surviving men to reach it and raise the alarm.

A few moments later, Togodumnus marched over from the direction of the river to make his report.

'Well?' I asked.

'The stores have been destroyed,' Togodumnus said. 'Some of the supplies had already been loaded on the boats, but the lads boarded them before the crews could release the mooring ropes and set fire to the vessels. Verica won't be receiving a bushel of grain from this place. Not this year.'

I nodded in grim satisfaction. Togodumnus surveyed the ruined village in stony silence. A sickening odour hung thick in the black air. I can still smell it now. The appalling stench of charred flesh, mingling with the smell of burning wood.

'It has been a good raid,' I said.

My brother smiled ruefully. 'Still, I wish we did not have to do it. There is no honour in attacking farmers and old men.'

I shook my head. 'This is not about honour. Verica's actions have left us with no choice. This is the only way to save our people. If we fail we will end up under the yoke of the Atrebates, just like the Regni.'

'I know that,' he said miserably. 'But it would be better to fight Verica's war-bands on the battlefield, in the old ways of our tribe. There is glory in that, at least.'

I gave him a hard, uncompromising look. 'It will be a glorious defeat if we do not deprive Verica of his supplies before the first budding. If you do not have the stomach for this type of warfare, perhaps you should return to Camulodunum instead. I am sure Father would be glad to have you at his side.'

Togodumnus squared his shoulders. 'I swore an oath to you, brother. To the end, come what may. I intend to keep it. I would rather die than break my vow. You know that.'

'I draw no pleasure from this either. But it is necessary.' I slapped him on the back. 'Fear not. We will have an opportunity to fight on the battlefield in good time,' I reassured him. 'The odds will be in our favour, then. Come the spring, we shall destroy Verica and his war-bands.'

'We'd bloody better,' Togodumnus growled.

At that moment Nemobnus came over. 'Mules ready, my lord.'

I nodded and said to Togodumnus, 'Round up the men. We are to leave at once. We must put a good distance between ourselves and this village before first light.'

Togodumnus cupped a hand and shouted at the raiders, straining to make himself heard over the unrelenting roar of the fires. As we started towards the throng of mules waiting close to the wrecked cattle pen I heard a voice calling out. I glanced round and saw one of the villagers approaching Nemobnus. He was a frail-looking fellow, stooped and wrinkled and dressed in plain threadbare rags. The old man took another step towards Nemobnus, speaking in the harsh Regnian tongue and spreading his hands in a pleading gesture.

Nemobnus feigned incomprehension, playing the part of a Silurian raider, but the old villager continued to address him, gesturing towards a plump woman and a fair-haired boy standing beside one of the surviving roundhouses.

Nemobnus stood still, listening in silence as the man spoke. He shook his head and mumbled a few words, then turned on his heel to catch up with us as we continued towards the waiting mules.

'What was that all about?' I asked him.

'Some old goat accusing us of destroying his livelihood,' Nemobnus said. 'He wanted to know how he was supposed to feed his family over the winter months. I didn't know what to say.'

The old man's stinging words had clearly shaken him. 'It's too bad these people have to suffer,' I said.

'It is as you say, my lord,' Nemobnus said wearily. 'There is nothing else we can do. However hard it is, Verica has left us with no alternative.'

We hastened out of the settlement long before first light, our mules weighed down with provisions and sacks of silver coin, jewellery and other valuables. I led the raiders back up the hillock towards our tethered horses and gave the order for the men to mount. The loot we would bury in a cache on sacred ground not far from our hideout, ready to retrieve in case we needed to procure fresh supplies from across the border in the lands of the Belgae.

I climbed back into the saddle and spared a final glance at the devastated village behind us, pausing to admire our handiwork as flames swirled into the wintry sky.

Our shadow war against the Atrebates had begun.

CHAPTER TWENTY-NINE

Rome, AD 61

'Our raid on Arundun was only the first of many successes against the Regni,' Caratacus said in that faraway tone I had grown accustomed to over the past several weeks.

'Over the winter months we burned dozens of farmsteads and villages. Few dared to resist us. The sight of our woad-painted bodies swarming out of the darkness, gripping our swords and spears and bellowing the high-pitched battle cries of the Silures, was enough to drive most of the villagers from their homes. Those who tried to resist us paid with their lives. Their heads were parted from their shoulders and impaled on stakes, as a warning to all who dared to serve Verica, and we threw their corpses into the middens for the wild dogs to feast on. I deeply regretted the killing of civilians, but it was necessary given the importance of our mission. This was no longer a petty tribal squabble of the kind that had blighted our lands for so many years. Nothing less than the survival of our tribe was at stake. I foresaw that the age of warrior heroes was passing. It had become a time of survivors and lies, and in such a world there can be no mercy.'

I sat watching Caratacus in uncomfortable silence. It was hard to look at that old king, a man of surprising wit and intellect despite his enfeeblement, calmly describing the rampant pillage and murder of his fellow Britons.

Caratacus must have sensed my disquiet, because he tilted his head and gave me a quizzical look.

'You disagree with such tactics, Felicitus?' he asked in his lilting accent.

I shifted awkwardly. 'As I understand it, the Regnians were the victims of Atrebatan aggression, and yet your men slaughtered these villagers, destroyed their homes and livestock, robbed them of their possessions. Some might struggle to understand how you could justify such violence.'

Caratacus gave a wry smile. 'You have much to learn about your legions, Roman, and what they have done to my people.'

'I'm no fool, sir,' I retorted. 'I don't doubt a few of our soldiers committed the occasional atrocity in Britannia. War tends to bring out the wickedness in the hearts of men.'

The Briton's expression hardened, and he stared at me with a quiet fury in his eyes. 'You misunderstand me. I do not talk of an isolated massacre. What the Romans did was worse, far worse . . .'

He clenched his jaw tightly and looked away, struggling to hide his emotions. I squirmed in embarrassment and pretended to consult my tablet. The timeworn myth about the Britons being a hot-blooded lot was only half true, I realised. If Caratacus was any reflection of the general tribal character, they were also guided by an easy sentimentality. Even their nobles were given to frequent displays of emotion, in stark contrast to the austere manner of our own highborn aristocrats. (In public, at least. Catch them behind closed doors, in the privacy of their own homes, and it's an entirely different story. But that's for another day.)

He stared distractedly through the opening at the side of the study. After a few moments I judged that it was safe to nudge him along. 'What do you mean?' I asked him. 'About our soldiers in Britannia?'

Caratacus shook his head vigorously. 'We will talk about that later. There is much to discuss before we get to that point, and I must tell you my story as it happened.'

I had spent enough hours in Caratacus's company to know that it was futile to argue with him, so I made a mental note to return to the subject later. 'Fine,' I said. 'Let us return to the raids, then.'

'You wish to know how we justified our actions against the Regni?' I nodded. Caratacus took a long sip of beer, giving himself time to contemplate his answer. 'They were not our enemies, as you point out. But we were acting as Silurians, remember. We had to play the part, if we hoped to avoid detection. If we had shown any

288

mercy, the Atrebates would have quickly seen through our ruse. And the Regni were no innocent victims in our struggle. Many of their chiefs and headmen had willingly pledged their allegiance to Verica. As for the rest, they have only themselves to blame. They should not have allowed themselves to be subjugated by the enemy. If they had put up a stiffer fight, they would not have suffered at our hands.'

As he spoke I began to understand something about the nature of this once-powerful warlord. We Romans commonly assume that the Celtic tribes are little more than a bunch of uncultured boors, stubborn and brave, to be sure, but possessing no guile. Yet Caratacus was clearly much more than a proud warrior. Here was a man of cold calculation and tactical intelligence, willing to endure any hardship and determined to do whatever was necessary to defeat his enemies, even if it meant inflicting untold misery on his fellow islanders. In another lifetime, he would have made a brilliant Roman general. Some in our city had marvelled that a mob of hairy Britons had resisted our legions for so many years, but perhaps we have got this wrong, too. Given the incompetence of our own officers, many of whom are more interested in advancing their own careers than mastering the finer points of warfare, the real surprise is that Caratacus did not defy us for longer.

'What about your men?' I asked. 'Did any of them have doubts about your raids? You admit that many of your fellow tribespeople detested such ignoble tactics.'

'If they did, they never showed it. All our warriors, I think, grasped the importance of our task. Besides, they had sworn an oath to me before the gods. Where I come from, we do not break such things lightly. At any rate, the men were quick to appreciate the success of our raids. Victory is a powerful elixir. Soon we had deprived the enemy of much of his source of grain. My men destroyed his bloomeries, slaughtered his livestock and razed the workshops that made his chariots and bows. We killed any blacksmiths and craftsmen we captured, because such skills are not easy to replace. A while later we learned that there had been an uprising at Noviomagus. The townsfolk had turned on their king for failing to protect them from the raids.'

'Did they succeed?'

'No. The king's bodyguards crushed the rebellion, and many perished. But Nemobnus reported that there was growing discontent among the elders. This was good news, for I felt certain that we were disrupting the enemy, and it put the men in fine spirits. But I also knew that it was only a matter of time before the Atrebates responded.'

'So what happened then?' I asked. 'You and your men persisted in your raids throughout the winter?'

'For a while,' Caratacus said. 'After a month or so I judged that the men needed a rest, so we changed our appearances and crossed the border to the east, into the land of the Cantiaci, for a few days of drinking and feasting with the local friendly chief. He knew Dubnocatus and readily believed our story that we were patrolling the area to ward off cattle rustlers. Togodumnus complained about the break in our campaign and said that I was too soft on the men, but I have always felt that warriors fight best when they are properly fed and rested.'

'And the Atrebates? What of them?'

'At first, we heard nothing,' Caratacus replied. 'But when we returned to our camp, we learned disturbing news from our guide. Nemobnus had spoken with a Gaulish trader in a nearby village who had heard an announcement in Calleva several days earlier. Verica had let it be known that he would pay a generous amount in silver coin to anyone who came forward with information which led to our capture. Those suspected of providing assistance to us would be put to death, along with the rest of their families.

'It was a wise move. Verica's public notice made it much harder for us to glean information from the villagers. Many of the townsfolk became wary of talking to strangers. Before then, we had been able to purchase supplies from some of the more unscrupulous chiefs in the settlements along the border, but now they refused to sell anything. They were afraid of reprisals from the Atrebates.'

'I suppose one might say that you had become too successful for your own good.'

That teased a faint smile from the Briton. 'Yes. But I knew that our luck could not last. Verica was bound to react to the attacks on his supply lines eventually. Shortly after that, the Atrebates started sending mounted warriors into the forests to hunt for us. On a few occasions my scouts only narrowly evaded capture. At the same time, Verica sent men south to garrison many of the larger settlements. In some places, we found more than a hundred of them ready to defend the villagers. We achieved a few successes, but finding targets became increasingly difficult. Sometimes we would reconnoitre a village, only to find that the Atrebates had garrisoned it in strength when we returned to make our attack a few days later. Togodumnus suggested attacking one of the smaller garrisons, arguing that it would make an example of the defenders and compel Verica to send more men south to reinforce his positions, thereby depriving his war-bands of men for the coming campaign against our tribe. But I refused to commit my men. "We would inevitably suffer casualties," I explained to him. "It would be small reward for the loss of perhaps many men. We must be patient." There were some heated arguments between us at that time. But our troubles were only beginning. Worse, far worse, was yet to come. I should have foreseen the disaster that was about to befall us.'

'How do you mean?'

The old king put a fist to his mouth and coughed. I waited while he noisily cleared his throat and took a swig of beer. His face contorted as he struggled to get the words out.

'It was my fault,' he said, his voice reduced to a hoarse whisper. 'I should have known. Should have . . .'

He looked at me, then broke into a violent coughing fit that wracked his entire body and left him hunched over in his chair, groaning in agony. I shot up from my stool and called out for help while Caratacus sat wheezing and clutching his chest. A moment later the heavyset doorman rushed into the study, and I stood watching helplessly while he rushed over to his master and knelt down beside him.

'Is he all right?' I asked stupidly.

Before the slave could reply Mardicca came hurrying over from the direction of the courtyard.

'Take my husband to his room,' she ordered the slave in broken Latin. 'Now, Davos.'

'Yes, my lady.' The doorman slipped an arm around Caratacus's back and slowly helped him to his feet.

Mardicca gave me a look of disdain. 'You need to leave,' she said icily. 'My husband must rest.'

'I'm fine, my dear,' Caratacus said feebly. 'Inflammation of the lungs . . . that's all.' He turned to me and attempted a smile. 'We will talk again . . . a few days from now.' He winced with the effort. 'I will send Davos to call at your home. He will . . . let you know where to meet.'

I hastily gathered up my tablet and stylus and slipped out of the study. As I started down the hallway towards the main door, I heard Mardicca calling out after me, and I wheeled round to see her marching briskly over from the study. Behind her, Davos was supporting his master's weight as they made for another part of the house. Mardicca folded her arms and glowered at me, her eyes blazing with anger.

'Haven't you caused enough trouble already?' she snapped. 'How long do you plan on tormenting us?'

The shock of being addressed in such a fashion by a brutish Celtic woman left me momentarily speechless. I gathered my composure and replied, as calmly as possible, 'I'm sorry, my lady, but I have no idea what you are talking about.'

'Don't play games with me,' Mardicca said, her voice cracking with fury. She waved an arm at Caratacus's stooped figure. 'Can't you see? My husband is ill . . . very ill. All this talk of the old days is no good for his health. There's too much grief.'

'Your pardon, my lady. But your husband has mentioned nothing to me of an illness.'

She sneered. 'Of course he wouldn't. He's too bloody proud. Like all the warriors of our tribe. But this project of yours is the last thing he needs right now.'

'I'm just helping him tell his story,' I replied defensively. 'It's important, my lady.'

'For whom? My husband? Or you?'

I decided not to answer the question. 'One of my acquaintances knows an excellent Greek physician,' I said. 'I could ask him to pay your husband a visit, if you'd like. Perhaps he could be of some assistance.'

Mardicca laughed bitterly. 'We are Celts. We have no use for your godless Greek magic in this house. Besides, I know what you Romans are like. There's no such thing as free help with your kind, is there? Not without wanting something in return.'

Well, she had me there. Coarse-tongued termagant she might be, but the wife of Caratacus was obviously no fool. There was no profit in arguing with her further, so I muttered my excuses and hastened out of the front door while she watched me with a contemptuous gaze more becoming of a Suburran brothel owner than the spouse of a noble foreign king.

I crossed the neglected courtyard, slid back the rusted bolt on the door built into the perimeter wall and stepped outside. Dusk was already beginning to gather, bathing the city in a warm glow. A trio of drunkards were playing dice on a street corner. Beggars rooted through piles of rubbish for discarded scraps of food; a group of linkboys were preparing for their nightly trade. I calculated that I would have just enough time to return to my lodgings on the poorer side of the Esquiline before nightfall.

Our interview had gone well, but even so, a grim thought gnawed at me as I started back down the hill. What if Caratacus died before he had a chance to finish telling me his story? If Mardicca was to be believed, his condition was serious. The appalling prospect of an unfinished manuscript flashed before me, the greatest story of heroism of our age, and my own fortune, ruined by whatever ailment had infested his body. I would have to redouble our efforts to meet at every opportunity, and pray that he retained his health for a while longer. And that was not my only concern. I thought back to my earlier conversation with Largus: now I also had to worry about the interest in my project from Nero's cronies.

Writing Caratacus's story was clearly going to be more complicated and dangerous than I had bargained for. And yet I could not help myself wanting to know more. What had he meant when he'd said that worse was yet to come and that he should have foreseen the disaster that was about to befall him and his followers? I was desperate to meet him again and return to his story.

PART FIVE

LORD OF WAR

CHAPTER THIRTY

Britannia, early AD *27*

'Memory, I have lately discovered, is not always a reliable handmaid to the truth. The mind corrodes with age, as surely as our bones rust and our flesh shrivels. You don't believe me, Roman, but you are still young, and in time you will understand what I mean. Names and faces, once so familiar, now elude me, and I am no longer sure of the precise chronology of certain events; often my past seems fragmentary and confused, a jumble of images. But some details are seared so deep into my memory I will never forget them. Even if the gods permit me to live for another hundred years, I shall always remember that long and terrible winter we endured in the first year of the war between our tribe and our sworn enemies, the Atrebates.

We had been raiding the lands of their Regni allies for more than two months when the weather turned. The snow fell for several days, blanketing the landscape with thick white flakes. At night the air grew so cold it seemed to scrape against my throat every time I coughed. The men keeping watch stamped their feet on the snow in an effort to keep themselves warm, and my warriors cursed as they shivered beneath their woollen blankets.

Our camp was deep in the forest clearing, the land devoid of colour except for the poisonous red berries hanging from the branches of frosted trees, the sun wan and pale in the overcast sky. The veterans muttered about their discomfort and feared for their kinfolk at home who would grow hungry if the winter lasted longer than usual.

I believed then that our biggest problem would be continuing to harass the enemy in such abysmal conditions. But I was wrong.

Over the next few weeks we had sporadic successes, but with

Verica ordering his warriors to garrison the richer settlements it was a struggle to find worthwhile targets. The mounted patrols became more numerous, and every time my scouts left to reconnoitre a village, I worried that they might be captured and tortured into revealing our whereabouts. When one of my foraging parties reported that they had seen Atrebatan horsemen in the forest, only six miles from our position, I decided it was time to move to a new camp.

Togodumnus disagreed with my decision since we would be moving further from the border with the Belgae to the west. 'If we run into trouble, it will be much more difficult to escape,' he argued.

He was right, but we could not remain. It was only a matter of time before an enemy patrol discovered our camp. Besides, the enemy would not be expecting us to attack further east and I felt confident that we would find more promising targets in that direction.

We broke camp the next morning. The sky was smothered in folds of cloud, and the only sounds we could hear were the chirping of the robins, the snorting breath of the horses, and the soft crunch of the snow beneath their hoofs. We travelled for most of that day, passing through a landscape of bare forests and rolling fields stubbled with corn stalks, where clatterings of jackdaws pecked at the rotting husks. In the failing light, we reached a small wood at the end of a secluded valley. Nemobnus led us down an overgrown trail until we reached a patch of cleared land screened from view by the surrounding trees, half a day's ride from the nearest large village. This was to be our next camp.

The men erected crude pens for the animals we had looted from the farms, toiling with numbed hands and feet while thick swirls of snow gusted across the land. Sentries were posted to cover the main approaches while our scouts reconnoitred the surrounding territory. Each time they returned with the same disappointing news. The villages were heavily fortified and could not be attacked without significant loss of life. Many of the inhabitants of the smaller settlements had moved to the better-defended villages, taking their grain stores with them. We searched these places for provisions, but they had already been stripped by local brigands.

Our morale began to suffer. The men grew frustrated at the lack of action and took to quarrelling with one another. And then, a short time later, Nemobnus finally learned of a suitable target after speaking to a merchant in Malleva. There was a minor village a day's ride to the east, he said, in an area rich in iron ore deposits. The local chief had been supplying weaponry to the Atrebates, and during their drinking session the trader had let slip to our guide that the village was poorly defended.

I needed an experienced man to remain in charge at the camp. I chose Maglocunus: the veteran warrior was a man of few words, but he had the respect of the men and a sturdy demeanour. Then I set off with Nemobnus, Togodumnus, and my two best riders, Vassedo and Dubnocatus, to scout the place in detail. The weather had improved and a thaw had set in, turning the snow into a watery brown slush. We rode for fifteen miles through gloomy woodland until we reached a small dip in the shadow of a low hill. Then we dismounted and made our way on foot to the brow.

Below us, no more than half a mile away, I saw a large number of roundhouses set in the middle of a wide valley, with a separate area of workshops built to one side of the village. A brume of smoke drifted up from the furnaces and slag dumps; nearby, a throng of bare-chested warriors struck at a series of training posts with their long swords and axes. On the far side of the settlement, more men were busy constructing a sturdy-looking palisade above a ditch.

'By Lud, there's got to be at least a hundred warriors down there,' Togodumnus commented. 'I thought this place was supposed to be an easy target?'

Nemobnus shook his head. 'I don't understand,' the Regnian said. 'The trader said he was here less than a month ago. He told me the chief had no more than twenty warriors in his band.'

'Verica must have sent his men down to reinforce the settlement since then,' I said. 'I'll wager those men are Atrebatan warriors.'

Vassedo snorted. 'That bastard. He'll have his men guarding every village in the kingdom before long.'

'Look, my lord,' Dubnocatus said. 'Over there.'

The youthful warrior pointed towards a small group of noblemen gathered near the edge of the settlement. Among them stood a tall figure dressed quite differently to the others.

None of us had ever seen a Roman centurion before, but that is undoubtedly what he was. We had spent our childhoods listening to our elders talk of the red-crested devils who had invaded our lands generations ago, but this was the first legionary I had ever seen. Resplendent in his scarlet military cloak, the transverse crest of his helmet and the medallions on his harness gleaming dully, he appeared to be in charge of the village defences, issuing orders to the labourers and inspecting the section of the palisade they had erected.

Togodumnus said, 'It seems Verica has been making new friends.'

I clenched my jaw. I should not have been surprised. Verica had made no secret of his desire to seek ever closer ties with Rome. He was not the first tribal leader to prostrate himself at the feet of the emperor.

I wondered whether Rome had sent other men to assist the Atrebates. Perhaps even now there was a legionary detachment at Calleva, preparing for the campaign ahead. But I banished the thought. If large numbers of foreign soldiers had landed on our shores, we would have heard of it.

'We have seen enough,' I said to the others. 'Let's leave this place, before the breeze carries up the stink of the Roman.'

The next day, the weather became even more severe. It snowed all morning, and in the evening the temperature was so cold that it froze the surface of the water in the nearby brook. We lit fires each night and huddled in pairs around the flames in a forlorn effort to stay warm.

Two days later, I sent Nemobnus in search of extra provisions. Our guide claimed that the headman of one of the villages on the border with the Cantiaci was the son of an old friend. Nemobnus had once saved the father's life and felt certain that the younger man would not betray him. Togodumnus was not in favour of this venture, but many days had gone by without any notable success, and I decided that it was worth the risk. The people in that area were clannish and fiercely independent and cared nothing for the likes of Verica. Two days later Nemobnus returned with a bundle of meat, hard biscuit and a jar of beer: all that the impoverished villagers could spare. He also brought news of a promising target. A small but wealthy settlement to the west had been badly damaged during the late Atrebatan conquest, and the defences had not yet been repaired. I judged that it was worth taking a closer look, and the following morning I accompanied Nemobnus west with two dozen of my men. We would remain close by the village, ready to attack if the situation looked favourable.

The sun had risen as we reached a spinney of oak trees several miles from our camp. Nemobnus walked ahead to scout the village dressed as an itinerant bard, with a striped cloak over a pair of bright green leggings, while the rest of us sat wrapped in our cloaks, the icy wind howling around us.

'Lucky bastard,' Togodumnus muttered an hour or so later. 'He gets to enjoy a hearty meal and a good fire, entertaining the locals with song, while we sit here freezing our balls off.' He chewed on a chunk of biscuit. 'This had better not be another wasted expedition.'

'We shall find out soon enough,' I replied.

'Perhaps we should think about returning to Camulodunum soon.'

'We cannot. We must hold fast to our mission.'

'What for? What's the point of staying out here if Verica has garrisoned every village worth attacking? It's been weeks since we carried off a raid worthy of the name.' Togodumnus pulled his cloak tighter across his front.

I loved my younger brother dearly, but he lacked the ability to grasp the wider strategic picture. 'We must keep Verica's forces tied down here for as long as possible,' I explained. 'Every warrior he must commit to the defence of this kingdom further depletes his war-bands. That is the measure of our mission's success.'

'And what if we cannot find anywhere else to raid? What then?'

'Our luck will change. Verica cannot defend every inch of this land. In any case, we have no choice but to remain here until the beginning of the next campaign season, when the Dobunnian reinforcements start to arrive. Father cannot attack Lhandain until then.'

'As long as their king keeps his promise.'

'He will. I've met Antedius,' I said firmly, recalling the evening I had spent as the king's guest on my way back from the Druid sanctuary at Merladion. 'He is a man of honour. He will not let us down.'

'All the same, they are not Catuvellaunians. Personally, I don't trust the bastards.'

'There are those in our own tribe who I would trust less,' I said, thinking of our older brother. 'Come, it is not long until the spring. We must only continue our endeavours for a short while longer. Then we shall return home.'

'Maybe this fucking snow will have cleared by then.' Togodumnus spat on the ground. 'Perhaps the gods do not favour our tactics, to inflict such foul weather on us.'

The sun was beginning to set, painting the snow with a faint bluish hue, when Nemobnus finally returned. I rose stiffly to greet him as he dismounted, his face pale.

'I fear the target is too well defended, my lord,' he said anxiously. 'I counted at least eighty warriors.'

'And the defences?'

'The palisade and gateway been repaired, lord. It is impossible to attack without heavy loss.'

Togodumnus uttered a foul curse under his breath. 'Verica has thwarted us again.'

I barely heard him. I looked intently at Nemobnus, searching his milk-white face. 'What is wrong?' I demanded. 'You look like you have just seen Cruach himself.'

The guide shifted uneasily and looked away. 'It is nothing, my lord.'

'Come, now.' I placed a hand reassuringly on his shoulder. 'You are among brothers, Nemobnus. You may speak freely. What troubles you?'

Nemobnus closed his eyes for a moment, then drew in a deep breath and exhaled heavily. 'There has been an attack on a village to the west of here, my lord. I overheard some of the villagers discussing it among themselves. The Atrebates have vowed to take the lives of ten Regnians for every warrior lost to our raiding party. Every man in the settlement was put to death, and the women and children taken as slaves to Noviomagus, to be sold in the markets in Gaul.'

Togodumnus bristled with anger. 'That bastard Verica is desperate to capture us, it seems.'

'This is not the first time we have heard of such atrocities committed against your people,' I said steadily. 'Why do you grieve so now?'

Nemobnus hesitated. 'I do not wish to add to your burdens, my lord. I fear that we have troubles enough.'

'That is for me to decide. You will tell me the truth, Nemobnus. Or I will get it from you.'

'My brother was living in that village,' the Regnian replied, his voice cracking with despair. 'Him and his wife and two boys.'

He lowered his gaze. I said, 'But you told me that you had no kin here. You said that they had fled after the Atrebatan conquest.'

'I believed that was the case, my lord.'

'Then how is it possible that your brother and his family were still living in these parts?' I asked. 'Did you know this when we left Camulodunum?'

'No, my lord.' Nemobnus licked his lips. 'An old companion recognised me in Arundun, my lord. During our first raid. He told me that he had seen my brother in another village while he was visiting relatives there some months ago.'

I stared at him, my frown deepening as I recalled the grizzled villager I had seen exchanging words with the Regnian during our first raid months earlier. It seemed a lifetime ago now.

'Why would your brother stay in this area, instead of fleeing across the border to neutral territory?' I asked.

'His wife has family in the village, lord. Or at least, she did. They must have taken refuge on their farm. It is a small settlement, far from the bigger villages. Perhaps they assumed they would be safe there.' Nemobnus swallowed hard. 'Forgive me, my lord. I feared that if you knew that I had been recognised, you would order me to return to Camulodunum. I believed, or hoped, that my kin would come to no harm in the village. Now I see that I was wrong.'

He bit his lip and looked round anxiously at his comrades. For a moment no one said a word.

'Has anyone else recognised you since we have been raiding?' I asked. 'Answer me truthfully.'

'No, my lord. I swear it.'

I said, 'You understand, of course, that we cannot do anything for your brother's family. An attack on Noviomagus is out of the question. The place is a fortress.'

He nodded solemnly. 'I ask only that you permit me to stay here, my lord, so that I may help you fight the enemy. Then, if the gods favour us, I shall have my revenge come the spring, when the Tamesis will run red with the blood of those Atrebatan dogs.'

I considered sending Nemobnus back to Camulodunum as punishment, but then quickly dismissed the notion. The Regnian knew the local dialect and the landscape far better than any of my other men. Without his knowledge, our efforts to reconnoitre further targets would be severely constrained. I had to reluctantly concede that we had no choice but to let Nemobnus stay, but I made clear that if he deceived me again he would answer for it, and I discreetly instructed Togodumnus to keep a close eye on our comrade in the future.

We arrived back at our camp the next morning in a dejected mood. That evening the men were unusually quiet as they sat in small groups around the cooking fire. Our continued difficulty in locating a worthwhile target had added to their growing sense of despondency and even I had begun to despair of our carrying out any more raids. Unless our fortunes changed, we would struggle to maintain our campaign until the spring. Our supplies would soon run out. And that was assuming we could continue to evade Verica's patrols, and his Roman friends. These problems weighed heavily on my shoulders, and I decided that the next day we would make an offering to Lud, in the hope of a swift change in our fortunes. At last, my mind became fogged with exhaustion and I fell into a fitful sleep.

I awoke with a start. The sky was tinged with the faintest band of light, and dawn was not far off. Around me most of the men were still dozing under their blankets, close to the heat emanating from the cooking fire. Vassedo was kneeling beside me, speaking in a hushed whisper.

'We've got company, my lord,' the stocky hunter said anxiously.

I sat bolt upright and looked round in alarm. 'Where?'

Vassedo pointed towards the treeline beyond the clearing. 'In that direction. I heard the sound of men approaching.' He paused. 'Lots of them, lord.'

I looked towards the patch of forest Vassedo had indicated and pricked my ears, listening for the slightest sound, but I could hear nothing except the faint whisper of the cold breeze through the trees and the crack and pop of burning wood on the nearby fire.

'Are you sure?' I asked Vassedo quietly. 'I can't hear anything.'

Even as the words left my mouth, a chorus of distinctive whirrs split the air. In the next breath one of the warriors tending to the fire let out a cry of alarm. I swung round and saw the man tumbling to the ground, an arrow shaft protruding from his back. At the same time more missiles thwacked into the ground around our camp, interspersed with the cries of wounded men.

'To arms!' I roared.

CHAPTER THIRTY-ONE

I n those first moments of cold terror, as the arrows swept through the clearing, I understood what had happened. The Atrebates had learned of the whereabouts of our camp and had moved forward to surround us under cover of darkness. There was only a crescent moon that night, and we would not have seen them in the shadows of the trees. Once they had taken up their positions, they had waited for the first glimmer of dawn before launching their attack. Their bowmen would pin us down before the main force rushed forward to overwhelm us. Fine tactics.

Panic gripped my men. Several of our warriors had been struck by the initial flight of arrows, killed or injured as they slept huddled in their cloaks. I saw them in the lambent glow of the campfire, writhing figures with shafts protruding from torsos and limbs and faces. I snatched up my shield and bellowed at my men to form up around me; we had mere moments to organise ourselves. Those who had survived the furious initial barrage seized their weapons and scurried towards me, their shields raised above their heads to protect them from the arrows.

As the men hurried over to the middle of the clearing, I scanned the camp frantically for Nemobnus. He alone knew the best way through the sprawl of forest beyond the clearing; we would need his skills as a guide if we had to make a run for it. Then I noticed that his bedroll was empty. His blankets were missing, along with his haversack and his horse. I knew then that we had been betrayed. Nemobnus had given up our location to the enemy.

All around us there was confusion as another torrent of arrows whipped through the air. Garmanus spasmed as two shafts struck him

306

in the back. He staggered on for a couple of paces before tumbling to the snow. Another warrior screamed as an arrow punched through his right eye.

'Shields up!' I shouted.

More projectiles struck the horses; the wounded beasts whinnied in agony and fell heavily on their sides, while others tore free from the pegs tethering them to the ground and bolted for the woods. The enemy released two more flights of arrows, and then a war trumpet sounded its braying note, and a horde of wild-haired warriors charged out of the forest.

Hundreds of Atrebatans swarmed towards us, recognisable by their guttural war cries and woad markings. As they burst through the treeline, I realised we were hopelessly outnumbered.

Of the fifty men in our raiding party, at least a dozen had been killed or wounded in the opening moments of the attack. Some of the remaining warriors spun round to face the onrushing Atrebatans, but they swiftly disappeared beneath a flurry of sword and axe blows. As the enemy spread out across the camp, I knew the fight was lost. I filled my lungs and yelled at my men. 'Run, brothers! Flee!'

Our warriors needed no encouragement. I had told them many times that courage must sometimes be forfeited for survival, contrary to our warrior traditions. 'Better to live to fight another day,' I had said, 'than to die pointlessly so some bard may enrich himself by singing of your heroism at the feasting table.'

We had no time to grab our provisions or saddle our horses. We cast aside our arrow-pocked shields, since the weight of them would slow us down, and grabbed whatever weapons we could find. I momentarily considered taking my thrusting spear instead of my long sword but decided against it. The spear had the longer reach, but the shaft could easily get snarled in the undergrowth. In the close confines of the forest, the sword would be the better option. The others seized a variety of axes, slings and bows as we sprinted towards the far side of the clearing, racing away from the enemy and making for the dark mass of hills to the east, black as jet against the lightening band of the sky.

As we drew close to the treeline I glanced back at the camp and saw the enemy tearing into our stragglers. Several were quickly struck down; in panic, their companions turned and scattered in every direction. Some hurried down the slope towards the valley, but the Atrebatans chased after them, hunting them down singly or in pairs, and they were quickly cut to pieces. I saw one man screaming as his Atrebatan opponent cleaved his skull down the middle with his double-bitted axe. Others were run through with spears or swords or beaten to death. The snow was stained with the gore of many fine Catuvellaunian warriors that bloody dawn.

I ran on towards the trees. 'On me!' I roared. 'This way!'

We quickened our stride and plunged into the trees. Togodumnus was running alongside me, icy breath pluming in front of our mouths as we struggled on. Ahead of us loomed the thicker patch of forest, a mile or so further up the slope. We had scouted the area shortly after establishing our base; the dense woodland stretched for miles in that direction beyond the nearest crest. There we stood a chance of evading our pursuers. Some of the enemy warriors, grasping our intention, hurled their spears in an effort to prevent our flight. Most fell short or thwacked into tree trunks. One caught a burly warrior limping after us, piercing his thigh. He collapsed in the snow, shouting for help shortly before two Atrebatans fell upon him in a shimmer of furious cuts and stabs.

After a hundred paces the incline began to steepen, and I paused briefly to look back at the camp below. The Atrebates had killed most of the defenders. Those who were foolish enough to surrender were being killed on the spot. As I ran my gaze over the scene, I saw a group of mounted figures on the opposite side of the clearing. One of them I had seen before. The Roman centurion sat on a white horse, wearing his distinctive armour and crested helmet. Nemobnus was at his side, gripping the reins of a thick-coated pony. A black rage clenched around my heart at the sight of the traitor. Then I turned and pushed on up the hill with the survivors.

Eleven of us had escaped the ambush. Apart from myself and Togodumnus, our small group comprised our two scouts, Vassedo and Dubnocatus, plus Maglocunus and half a dozen other veterans. Almost forty of our tribe's best swordsmen had been killed in the fighting. The scale of the loss struck me like a fist in the stomach, but

I could not afford to show my grief. There would be time to mourn our fallen comrades later.

We struggled on through the forest. After a while the trees thinned out, and we carried on past clumps of gorse and heather. A short time later, as dawn spread across the sky, we paused at the crest of a hill and gazed back down the slope, watching to see if anyone had followed us. At first there was no sign of our pursuers, and Togodumnus eased out a sigh of relief.

'Looks like we've lost them, brother,' he said.

Before I could reply, Vassedo cried, 'There, lord!'

I looked down the slope and spied a loose group of horsemen working their way around the forest towards the ridge no more than a mile away. Moments later they disappeared behind a thicket of dense scrub and briar patches.

'We must keep moving,' I gasped.

We plunged down the slope towards the wooded vale below, wading through occasional snow drifts. A fierce easterly wind was blowing across the land and soon we were shivering beneath our winter cloaks. We stopped for nothing, moving as fast as our numbed bodies could carry us, but the snow impeded our pace, and when we ascended a hummock, I caught sight of the tiny dark figures on the brow of the hill behind us, and felt my heart sink.

'They're getting closer,' Dubnocatus said. 'We'll never lose them.'

'Keep going,' I urged the men. 'Into the trees.'

The horsemen kept up their pursuit all morning. Each time we emerged from openings in the forest growing along the vale we would stop briefly and look back, fervently hoping that we had lost them, but there were always riders in sight along the ridge. We had no food or water to replenish our tired bodies, and our pace began to slacken as we climbed out of the vale. I saw that the Atrebatans had gained on us again, and Togodumnus despaired of our chances of evading them.

We struggled on for another mile before the ground snaked through a narrow gorge cut into the landscape by a meandering stream. A pair of steeply wooded slopes flanked the sides of the track. As I scanned the trees an idea took shape in my mind. We carried on for another hundred paces or so. Then I called the men to a halt.

'Why have we stopped, lord?' Maglocunus demanded, his expression strained with exhaustion.

I drew a deep breath as my heart pounded. 'We cannot outrun those horsemen. They will close on us before long. We must turn and fight, if we are to avoid being hunted down like dogs.'

Togodumnus smiled in grim determination. 'What do you suggest?'

I said, 'Listen carefully. This is what we're going to do.'

The men watched me keenly as I explained my plan. There were no dissenting voices among them; all understood the desperate situation facing us. Once I had finished, we veered off the track to the right and climbed the sharp gradient, doubling back on ourselves until we reached a point fifty paces further down the trail, overlooking a bend in the stream. Then we moved slowly towards the edge of the treeline and dropped down to our stomachs, placing our swords flat in the snow while we settled down to wait.

We stayed very still in spite of the cold, watching for our pursuers. A twinge of doubt crept into my mind as I reviewed my plan, but I reassured myself that this was a good place for an ambush.

After what felt like a long while, Togodumnus touched my arm softly and indicated a patch of pine trees downstream from the bend. As I looked on, a mounted figure slowly emerged from the shadows wearing a wolfskin fur over his striped cloak and a sheepskin hat. I searched the trees for any sign of the other riders, but the man appeared to be alone.

'Their tracker,' Togodumnus whispered. 'Must be.'

We remained perfectly silent as the Atrebatan stopped a short distance from the bend. The man looked round, swung down from his saddle and stooped to examine the footprints we had left in the snow. After a pause he lifted his gaze to the slopes either side of the path, and I feared he had spotted us. Then he cupped his hands and called out towards the woods. The other riders slowly trotted into view and started up the path.

I tensed my fingers around the leather grip of my sword and concentrated my gaze on the rearmost rider, watching to see if any more men followed him out of the woods. I counted nine enemies in total, each armed with a long spear, sheathed sword and small round shield. Around us the dead silence of the snow-blanketed landscape was punctuated by the light jingle of iron bits and the snorting of the horses as they plodded further up the trail.

As the tracker drew level with the bend Togodumnus shifted forward, straining to catch a glimpse of the enemy and carelessly brushing against the low branches of a pine tree, dislodging the snow. The sudden movement caught the tracker's attention; he jerked on the reins and looked up the slope directly at me. Then he twisted round in his saddle, shouting at the riders behind him and waving an arm frantically at our position. The others halted their horses and swung their mounts round to face us.

'Now!' I bellowed.

At my command my men hurled the rocks they had gathered at the riders before they had a chance to raise their shields. We aimed for the Atrebatans instead of the horses beneath them: we would have need of the latter to make good our escape. One of our missiles struck a rider on the head and he fell out of his saddle; most of the rocks struck home and caused lesser injuries.

'Charge!' I bellowed. 'Kill them! Kill them all!'

We burst down the hillside with a collective roar, our lungs burning with the strain. Togodumnus and five others rushed towards the rear of the column. They had orders to attack the hindmost riders, while the rest of us would deal with the Atrebatans further forward. We closed quickly with the enemy, meeting them at the edge of the trail; the air was filled with the sharp crack of swords and axes slamming against shields, the grunts of fighting men and the shrill whinnies of terrified horses.

The riders put up a fierce resistance. One man to my right gasped in agony as a sword thrust caught him in the groin. Two others were thrown by the horses and trampled amid the swirling beasts and men. I parried the spear thrusts and hacked furiously at the horseman in front of me, a tall figure with a deerskin draped across his shoulders. The Atrebatan snapped his teeth and thrust his weapon at me at a downward angle; I threw my weight to the right; the leaf-shaped tip hissed past my torso; then I lunged forward, striking out at the man's neck. My sword blade slammed against his shield; the rider roared in battle madness and hammered his shield down towards me, forcing me to jerk backwards. I slashed at his exposed shield arm, opening up a deep wound in his flesh. The rider howled as blood gushed out of the wound, and I struck again before he could recover, plunging my sword deep into his guts. There was a sound like a knife slashing through a cloth sack, and then the man fell from his saddle, tumbling to the ground with a soft thud.

The fight was over very quickly. In the tight press of bodies and horses along the track the riders' long spears were an encumbrance. Our men swarmed like wild beasts over the last few riders, stabbing upwards at limbs and torsos. All nine Atrebatans were killed, at the cost of three warriors on our side. After finishing off the enemy wounded, we laid our dead to one side, with their arms folded across their weapons. Two men were wounded and while Togodumnus bounded their injuries with strips of cloth I checked the saddlebags for provisions. They contained a few meagre strips of salted meat, some barley biscuits and waterskins and feed nets for the horses – barely enough to sustain us for more than two days.

'What now, lord?' asked Maglocunus.

'We'll head east, towards the Mead Way river, until nightfall. Our pursuers will assume we're making for the lands of the Cantiaci, since that is the closest friendly territory from here. But we'll change direction when it's dark and go north instead, towards the Tamesis. They won't be expecting us to go that way, which should buy us time to cross the river.'

Togodumnus lifted his eyebrows. 'You forget, brother, that the Atrebatans control the only crossing point along the Tamesis. There is no other bridge near Lhandain.'

I said, 'We have the horses. We can find a patch of shallows and swim them over to the other bank without much difficulty. Many have crossed the Tamesis that way before.'

'But that route will take us through the heart of Atrebatan territory,' Maglocunus pointed out. 'If anyone sees us, we'll be fucked.'

'Not necessarily,' I replied calmly. 'The turn in the weather will have driven most of the locals indoors. We should be able to move relatively easily without being spotted.'

'Apart from the patrols,' Vassedo reminded me.

'That is so. But that would be the case in any direction we cared to ride.'

Maglocunus sucked the cold air between his teeth and said, 'All the same, it's dangerous. Perhaps it would be better if we carried on towards the border with the Cantiaci instead. They are our allies, and, as you say, it is closer.'

I gave the veteran warrior a sharp look. 'We cannot go east. The enemy will be expecting us to flee in that direction and will look to head us off. It's a two-day ride to the border, and they'll have the advantage of access to fresh mounts and an easy trail to follow. They would intercept us before we could reach friendly soil.'

'We could head west, lord,' Dubnocatus suggested. The smooth-faced youth looked round, as if seeking encouragement from the older men. None came, but he went on nonetheless. 'We could trick the Atrebates into thinking we're making for Siluria, then cut north towards the Dobunnians instead.'

Vassedo shook his head. 'That won't work. Verica and his men must know the truth by now. We have to assume that Nemobnus has told them about our mission.'

'That snake,' Togodumnus said. 'I'd like to tear his guts out.'

I had many questions about Nemobnus. Had he always intended to betray us? It was possible but I did not think it likely: Nemobnus had served our tribe for years, earning the trust of my father as one of his most loyal warriors. No. More likely, he had seized the opportunity to make a deal with the centurion after learning of the fate of his brother's family. It would have been a simple case of offering to lead the Atrebates and their Roman adviser to our camp in exchange for sparing his brother's wife and children from the horrors of slavery on a Gaulish farm.

I turned my thoughts back to our immediate situation. 'Travelling west would take us further away from our lands. No. We must make for the Tamesis if we are to stand any chance of evading the enemy. That is my decision.' I looked a challenge at the others: apart from Togodumnus and Dubnocatus, they were all several years older than me, and I knew I must nip any disobedience in the bud before it festered.

'I agree,' Togodumnus said after an uncomfortable silence. 'I am with you, brother. As are the rest of us.' He looked at the others in turn, daring them to defy me. 'As always.'

313

Maglocunus and Vassedo muttered their assent. The rest of the men agreed to my plan, though without any great enthusiasm. Perhaps they were unwilling to disobey their commander; or perhaps they simply understood our options were pitiful.

I straightened up and cleared my throat. 'We leave at once.'

We swung up onto our mounts, seating ourselves securely on the saddles. Then we jabbed our heels into the flanks of our horses. They whinnied and snorted in protest at having to move again so soon after their arduous journey through the snow, but they soon picked up the pace and we set off at a quick trot in a general easterly direction, making for the Mead Way and the border with the Cantiaci.

CHAPTER THIRTY-TWO

The weather worsened as we continued east that afternoon. The wind strengthened, lifting the snowflakes in great gusts, and the surrounding landscape was blotted out by an impenetrable sheet of white. Soon it was impossible to see more than two spear lengths in any direction, which helped to conceal us from the enemy. But it also meant that we did not know if we were being pursued, and there was the constant risk of running into an Atrebatan patrol, forcing us to slow our pace to a walk. Vassedo led the way: he had scouted in this direction before and knew the country. Every so often the squat hunter would throw up his hand, motioning for us to halt while he rode off to find some distinguishing local feature.

The cold was almost intolerable. The savage wind knifed across the hills, stabbing at hands and faces, and the agony in my bones was worse than anything I had ever known. At dusk, we took shelter in a hollow at the base of a rocky hill. The horses grazed on the feed from the nets attached to their harnesses, and we took a small meal of biscuits and salted pork. While the men gathered up withered fern fonds and cut reeds from a nearby stream to fashion crude bedrolls, I made a brief study of the night stars, remembering the lessons on navigation I had learned from the Druids at Merladion. I found the constellation our people know as Lud's Plough – I do not know your name for it – and orientated myself, laying down a spear pointing to the east, so we would know which way to set off the next day.

That night was a hard one. We covered ourselves with our cloaks and rested our tired heads against the saddlebags, but the wind howled constantly, and when we awoke at dawn, we were bitterly cold and exhausted, and I knew we could not hope to survive for much longer.

It snowed all the next day. We carried on east through a tapestry of ancient forests, heathland and rolling hills. Whenever we neared a village, we would put a dogleg around it, moving away from the settlement before we resumed our course east a few hundred paces further along. Togodumnus argued that such caution was unnecessary and only delayed our escape. But I did not want to take any risks. The Regnians of this part of the kingdom were known to be sympathetic to the Atrebates. I had no doubt they would alert the Atrebatans if they spotted us.

In the early afternoon we neared a place called Crulaigh, not far from where the Mead Way river flowed, marking the border between the Regni and the Cantiaci. Then we stopped and changed course, heading north for the Tamesis. The fresh snowfall helped to conceal our tracks from the enemy, but even so I kept a watchful eye on the horizon behind us. There was no sign of our pursuers, and as the hours passed, I started to believe that our ruse had worked. But any sense of relief was swiftly replaced by my concern for the worsening condition of my men. We must have cut a miserable sight: we were hungry and tired, and our clothes were damp. After a few hours, one of our injured men, Vellodnus, began shivering feverishly. An Atrebatan spear had torn into his flank during the fight at the gorge; despite our best attempts to clean and dress the wound his face soon took on a pallid complexion, his mind became confused, and I privately feared he would not last the night.

At dusk we rested in a shallow gully, shielding our broken bodies from the blizzard. I instructed Vassedo to make Vellodnus as comfortable as possible, but at daybreak we discovered his rigid corpse. We tried to bury him, but the ground was frozen solid and we were forced to abandon our efforts. This caused much bad feeling among the men, for they knew that without a ceremonial burial their comrade's spirit could not make the journey to the Otherworld.

The snow finally abated soon after first light. We set off north again under clear skies in a sombre mood, and along the way we passed a handful of scattered farmsteads. They looked quiet enough; the only signs of habitation were the thin wisps of woodsmoke eddying into the sky from the thatched roofs of the roundhouses.

'Seems most of the locals are staying bottled up indoors, lord,'

316

Dubnocatus remarked, a trace of envy in his voice. I knew what he was thinking: I, too, would have given anything to warm my hands in front of a hearth.

Togodumnus laughed bitterly. 'They are not fools. You'd have to be mad to venture out in this weather. Mad, or desperate.' He shook the snow from his hair.

'How long?' I asked Vassedo. 'Until we reach the Tamesis?'

The huntsman squinted at the horizon and made a quick calculation. 'Half a day's riding, my lord. No more than that. We should make the river soon after sundown. As long as this weather holds.'

'Surely it can't get much worse than this,' Maglocunus said, exasperated. 'The gods have punished us enough already.'

'It is not the gods that worry me,' I muttered in reply. I glanced back in the direction we had travelled.

Togodumnus said hesitantly, 'You think they might be following us still?'

'I don't know. But I'm sure of one thing.'

'What's that?'

'The Atrebates will be determined to stop us from escaping. The capture of two sons of Cunobelinus would present quite the prize for Verica.'

'If it comes to that, then let's make sure that we don't live to become prizes, brother,' Togodumnus resolved.

We carried on through a series of foothills and passed through a wooded vale, home to a herd of deer. Then, an hour or so later, I saw movement on the far side of the vale we had just crossed. In the distance, two miles or so from our position, I made out a line of riders trotting downhill, heading in our direction.

A frown notched Togodumnus's expression. 'No,' he said hoarsely. 'It can't be.'

Maglocunus stared at the figures in disbelief. 'I don't understand. How did they follow us here, lord? We left no trail, and the falling snow would have covered our tracks.'

'They must have a skilled tracker with them,' Vassedo answered. 'One of Verica's deer-stalkers, I'd wager. They're the only ones who would be able to hunt us in such conditions.'

'How do we get rid of them?'

'We don't. Those men have the instincts of a hound. Once they pick up a trail, they don't lose it.'

'Let's go,' I said urgently. 'We must keep moving.'

For the next few hours we rode hard. The flanks of our mounts were soon heaving with the burden we placed on them, but by the afternoon the enemy had steadily gained on us, and when I glanced back again they were less than a mile away. A while later, two of the horses collapsed from exhaustion. We had to abandon the mounts, and the riders climbed onto the two strongest remaining horses. The beasts protested at the extra weight they were being forced to carry, and soon they began to struggle to maintain a good pace.

'How in Lud's name have they drawn closer?' Togodumnus growled as the figures appeared on the brow of the hill behind us.

'They're in friendly territory,' I reminded him. 'They'll have access to fresh mounts from the villagers, and they'll know the fastest routes across the countryside.'

'Either way, they'll catch us soon enough,' Maglocunus said. He grimaced.

'What are we going to do?' asked Togodumnus.

I gripped my reins tightly. 'Keep riding. If we make it to the Tamesis we'll lose them on the other side.'

We carried on, but our pursuers were always in view on the horizon now, and I knew it would be a close-run thing if we were to reach the Tamesis before they could catch us.

Half an hour later we rounded the base of a low hill. After a hundred paces we reached a narrow trail running between pine trees where the boughs had shielded the ground from snow. I called our party to a halt and ordered the men to steer their horses through the forest, since the snowless trail would make it more difficult for our pursuers to follow us. At the same time we tied fallen branches to our mounts' tails, raking over the ground behind us to cover their hoof prints. We continued north for perhaps a mile, following the track as it ran parallel to a gently flowing stream before it emerged in a small valley leading towards a series of bare foothills.

'Do you think that will work?' Togodumnus asked as we paused to check the hills behind us half an hour later.

I shrugged. 'I don't know. It should gain us some time, at least. Even trackers cannot follow what is not there.'

'All the same, if they're as good as Vassedo claims, they'll pick up our scent again before long.'

'Let us hope that we are across the river by then,' I responded tersely.

We rode on for all we were worth, pushing the surviving mounts to the very edges of their physical endurance. They heaved with exertion, breathing hard through their nostrils, but our pace began to gradually slacken. Eventually, the horses were too weak to carry on, and we had to dismount and abandon the unfortunate beasts, leaving them to die by the trackside. Then we carried on towards the river on foot. In the gathering dusk we reached the marshes to the south of the Tamesis and followed an animal trail through an area of frozen waterways, stunted trees and dense masses of scrub and hawthorn. The dips and folds in the ground forced us to move at a slow pace, and we kept an anxious watch on the ground behind us, but we saw no sign of the riders through the mist hanging over the landscape.

Two miles further along, we reached a patch of firmer ground, barely higher than the surrounding marsh, crowned by a small copse. We followed Vassedo through a clump of gorse and made for a reedbed running along the southern shore of the Tamesis. We crept through the bulrushes, staying low to hide ourselves from any passers-by until we neared the edge of the riverbank. Then we settled down to observe the scene in front of us.

The Tamesis had frozen over in places. Drifts of snow had settled along the edges of the reeds and the frozen sections of the river were covered with a smooth sheet of snow over the ice. The landscape was perfectly still and silent.

Half a mile or so to the west a wooden bridge ran from the near bank to the sprawl of huts and timber-framed buildings that made up Lhandain. On the far bank, several hundred feet away, a row of warehouses lit up by torches fronted the quayside. A handful of fishing boats and small ships rode at anchor. Opposite our vantage point, a mile or so downriver, a stretch of dreary marshland was dimly visible behind a grey mist. Lhandain itself occupied a pair of low hills overlooking the Tamesis, bisected by a narrow brook. On the near side of the Tamesis, not far from the bridge, a campfire glowered.

'The gods mock us,' Vassedo said. 'We cannot cross this. The ice would not support our weight.'

Maglocunus clicked his tongue. 'Vassedo is right, lord. I have seen rivers in these parts freeze over before. This ice will be no more than two or three inches thick. I fear it will not be strong enough to bear the weight of a man.'

'It looks solid enough from here,' I commented.

'It is too risky, my lord,' Vassedo said. 'If the ice does not hold, we will drown.'

I hissed impatiently. 'But what choice do we have? We cannot stay here, and we cannot try our luck east or west. It will be the same story.'

'Why can't we use the bridge?' Togodumnus asked. 'That would be easier than taking our chances on the ice.'

I indicated the distant campfire. 'That's most likely to be Verica's men guarding the bridge. This is the only crossing point to Lhandain, and Verica will want to secure a line of retreat in case his forces are defeated.'

Maglocunus nodded grudgingly. 'Even if we could overpower the guards, someone would be sure to sound the alarm and we'd be trapped inside Lhandain with no way out.'

'We could swim across,' Vassedo suggested. 'It may be cold enough to freeze our balls off, but if we're taken on this side losing our bollocks will be the least of what the enemy will do to us.' He pointed to a deeper stretch of water along the quayside, downriver from our position. 'The river hasn't frozen there, lord.'

I had already considered that. 'It's too close to the bridge. The sentries would see us. We'd be cut down before we could reach the water.'

Togodumnus growled in frustration. 'There must be another way across. There bloody has to be.'

I turned my attention back to the river, searching in vain for another crossing point, or a place to hide. But the only dwelling in sight was a farm close to the bridge, faintly distinguishable in the light of the campfire. A pair of wagons rested in front of the roundhouse, beside the usual cluster of barns, storage sheds and animal pens. Taking cover there was out of the question.

We remained hidden in the reeds throughout the night, pondering our next move. Unless we could find a way across to the other side, the enemy would catch us eventually – they were bound to be patrolling this area in force. Verica would show us no mercy if we were captured. We would be put to death, I reflected soberly. Flayed and impaled, or burned alive in one of the wicker men favoured by the Druid cult of the Atrebates.

Shortly before dawn, I decided we could wait no longer. We would have to chance a crossing before the sun had fully risen, when we would be in full view of the sentries at the bridge. I was preparing to give the order when Maglocunus suddenly thrust out an arm.

'Lord! Over there. Look!' he whispered.

As I squinted in the gloom a lone figure emerged from the mist, picking his way across the ice. The man was gripping a hunting bow in his right hand and a quiver filled with arrows hung from his belt. The hunter appeared to be making for a point on the south bank, some fifty paces to the west, near to a willow tree leaning over the frozen river.

'What's he doing out in this weather?' Dubnocatus wondered quietly.

'Perhaps he's making for that vale we passed yesterday,' Vassedo said. 'Might be some game to be found there.'

'Who cares?' Togodumnus said. 'The river can be crossed. There's our proof! What are we waiting for?'

'Not yet,' I hissed sharply. 'For all we know, the ice may only be thick enough at certain points. Let's wait for our friend to make his way over to this side. Then we can question him.'

'What makes you think he'll cooperate, lord?' asked Maglocunus.

I smiled. 'We are eight desperate-looking fellows with weapons. He won't take much persuading.'

We edged back from the reeds and padded quietly along the bank, making for the willow tree to the west. Here we found a narrow gap leading between the rushes, partially concealed from view by a mass of brambles. From a distance, it would be easy enough to miss.

The men crouched either side of the opening amid the reeds,

while I peered between the spiky-tipped bulrushes, watching the stranger as he neared the southern bank. Although we had a clear line of sight to the hunter, we were concealed from view behind the thick growth of reeds, and in the half-light he would not see us. Not until it was too late.

Togodumnus pounced on him as soon as he stepped out of the reeds, knocking him to the ground. The man gasped as the impact drove the breath from his lungs, the hunting bow tumbled from his stunned grip, and before he could open his mouth and raise the alarm, I had my sword tip inches from his face.

'One word, and I swear before the gods it will be your last.'

The hunter saw the savage intent in my eyes and nodded quickly. I cocked my head at Vassedo. He moved off with Dubnocatus, keeping watch over the surrounding marsh, while the rest of us confronted the hunter. The fellow stared at our faces, blinking in confusion and terror as I took in his appearance. He was a lean fellow: his gaunt face and ruined teeth hinted at a life of toil and hardship.

'Do not be afraid,' I said. 'We do not want to hurt you, unless we have to. We have some questions we need you to answer.'

The hunter licked his lips. 'Who are you?' he asked nervously. 'Brigands?'

'Quiet!' Togodumnus cut in sharply. 'We are the ones asking the questions, not you.'

The hunter narrowed his eyes at my brother. 'I recognise that accent. You are Catuvellaunians . . .'

Before I could respond, Togodumnus struck the hunter on the jaw with his balled fist. The man's head snapped back, and he gave out a sharp cry of pain. I grabbed my brother by the shoulder and roughly pulled him away.

'What in Lud's name do you think you're doing?' I snapped.

'The wretch needs to be roughed up,' Togodumnus replied defensively. 'Quickest way to get him to spill his guts.'

I shot him a stony look and said, 'This man is not our enemy. We don't need to hurt him to make him cooperate with us.'

I turned back to the hunter. He eyed me warily, blood trickling down from a cut to his lower lip. 'What is your name?' I asked.

'Andoccus, of Lhandain,' came the hesitant reply. 'Please,' he said miserably, 'I am a poor man, with many mouths to feed at home. I seek no trouble.'

'Nor do we, Andoccus. Only answers to our questions.'

He stole a glance at my brother, then nodded. 'What is it you wish to know?'

'The river,' I said. 'We saw you crossing over. There is an ice ford, I presume?'

'That is so,' Andoccus replied anxiously. 'There is a stretch of shallows with a ford running across it. In the summer, you can cross the river on foot. In the winter, it freezes over, enough to support the weight of men. Though only just.'

'How do you know about it?'

'A few hunters use the ford. It is a secret between us. My uncle showed me the way across the ford when I was a boy. I have used it ever since.'

'Why do you not take the bridge?' Maglocunus demanded.

The hunter laughed derisively. 'If I did that, I would have to pay the toll. Life's hard enough already.'

'How do you mean?' I asked.

'There is not much grain to be had now that Verica's war-bands have arrived. They have seized most of the food.' He added despondently, 'Many of our people are already starving.'

I shared an alarmed look with Togodumnus. 'The Atrebatan forces are here?'

The hunter nodded. 'Verica and his warriors arrived several days ago. He had a Roman with him.' He spat with contempt. 'They say they are making their preparations for battle with the Catuvellaunians.'

'Where is the Catuvellaunian camp?' I asked.

The hunter stabbed a scrawny arm in the direction of Lhandain. 'That way. To the north, not far from the place where the old kings are buried.' He paused. 'They say Cunobelinus has assembled a vast host. All the chiefs of the Catuvellaunians and Trinovantes have joined forces with him. They say he will crush Verica's warriors when he offers battle.'

He spoke in a tone that suggested he hoped for such an outcome. 'If that is the case, why has Cunobelinus not yet offered battle?' Maglocunus asked.

Andoccus shrugged. 'Perhaps his Druids are waiting for favourable omens from the gods before they give their consent.'

'Makes sense,' Togodumnus said. 'He would not want to risk offending the gods by fighting without their blessing.'

'This ice ford,' I said, returning my gaze to the hunter. 'How do we get across, friend?'

'Friend?' The man looked at me suspiciously.

'It's clear you have no good will towards the Atrebates. We have the same enemy.'

Andoccus considered this for a moment, then nodded. He pointed to the other side of the river. 'You see those two timber posts on the mudflats, directly north of here?'

I squinted at the far bank. In the faint light I could just about see a pair of stout wooden posts, set at a distance one behind the other, backgrounded by the reeds and bushes. They were barely distinguishable from the surrounding growth.

'The posts were placed there to guide hunters across the ford. Keep them in line and you will make it safely across the ice to the other side.'

'That is all?'

He shrugged. 'It is easy enough. A child could do it. But do not veer off course,' he added gravely. 'The water is much deeper either side of the ford, and the ice will not be thick enough to hold your weight. Some have died because of such carelessness in the past.'

I said, 'We are in your debt. When our war-bands have triumphed, I will make sure our king rewards you.'

The hunter shook his head. 'I have no need of rewards. The sooner the Atrebates are banished from Lhandain, the better.'

'Then pray to Lud for our victory on the battlefield.' I regarded him for a moment, admiring his sturdiness and quiet dignity in the face of the grinding daily struggle for life. If only some of our chiefs had been as principled as this fellow, perhaps the invasion of our island might have turned out differently.

'Thank you, Andoccus.' I stepped back from him and barked an order at Maglocunus. The warrior fetched up the bow and handed it to the hunter. 'You are free to go,' I said.

'Wait,' Togodumnus intervened. 'What makes you think we can trust him?'

I still felt the humiliation of Nemobnus's betrayal, but I felt I had seen into the hunter's heart enough to believe in his hatred of the Atrebates. 'He's with us. You heard what he said.'

'But—'

'I've decided. He has helped us. I trust him.'

The hunter nodded his thanks. Then he promptly set off, moving across the ground with the ease of a born huntsman. He disappeared behind the dark boughs of the trees.

'Let's hope that he doesn't run into the Atrebatans on his way south,' Togodumnus remarked. 'Something tells me those horsemen won't go as easy on him as we did.'

'If the gods are just, they will protect him.'

'What is the plan, lord?' asked Maglocunus.

I glanced at the posts. 'We must cross the ice ford now, and make straight for my father's camp. If we maintain a good pace, we should get there before noontime.'

'Assuming that hunter was telling the truth about the route across the river,' Togodumnus muttered. 'Otherwise, we'll be walking straight to our fucking deaths.'

I had no desire to continue this argument. I turned to the others and said, 'Leave anything you do not need to carry with you. We'll stay here until there's enough light to see the posts clearly. Then we'll head across the ice.'

CHAPTER THIRTY-THREE

We stole through the reeds in the grey gloom before dawn. I led the way, with Togodumnus and the others following in single file. We had left behind the waterskins and haversacks we had taken from the scouts: anything that might reduce our weight on the ice. I had decided we would have to cross together, because dawn was coming up fast and it would take us too long to walk across the ice individually. As we approached the edge of the reedbed I looked across and thought that the other bank suddenly seemed very far away.

Behind me, Togodumnus said, 'Are you sure this is a good idea?'

'If you have a better one, now would be the time to share it.'

He made no reply.

The first hint of the coming dawn lined the eastern horizon and I forced my muscles to relax slightly as I took a tentative step beyond the reeds. Thick heaps of snow, blue in the pallid light, quilted the fringes of the river, and it was impossible to tell where the bank ended and the river began. Beyond was a mosaic of drift snow and patches of ice. In some places the ice was the colour of woodsmoke; in others, it looked as clear and smooth as glass.

I edged cautiously forward. The surface was slippery beneath the leather soles of my boots, and I had to take short steps to avoid losing my balance. Every few paces I paused to glance at the far bank, picking out the two wooden posts, jutting above the river like broken teeth, keeping them directly in line. Beneath me, the ice creaked softly from time to time, and I was certain that it would break apart beneath us; I imagined plunging into the icy waters, limbs flailing wildly as I sank to the bottom of the riverbed.

There was a panicked cry behind me, accompanied by a hard slap. I looked back and saw Togodumnus flat on the ice, shaking his head and cursing vilely. 'Are you hurt?' I whispered.

He climbed to his feet and snorted angrily, 'I thought that hunter said crossing this river would be easy.'

'Keep moving,' I said. 'And for Lud's sake watch your footing before you fall again and break the ice.'

We resumed our slow shuffle across the ice ford. Ahead of us a mist hung over the distant marshland, making it hard to see much further than the bulrushes piercing the edges, but it was growing ever lighter, increasing the risk of being spotted by the sentries at the bridge. Soon we would be dangerously exposed, I knew, and I had to fight a compulsive urge to quicken my stride and hurry across to the opposite bank.

We were perhaps halfway across the river when the ford crossed a patch of thinner ice. I took another step forward, and then a sharp splitting noise pierced the air. I looked down and felt the air trap in my throat as the ice fractured beneath me, hairline cracks spreading outwards, as if invisible hammers were striking it. I stopped dead in my tracks, threw up my hand and silently gestured for the others to stop. For a long moment, no one dared to move. The ice ceased rupturing. Then, very slowly, I inched forward, testing to make sure it could support my body weight. Only when I was certain that the surface would hold firm did we push on again.

It seemed to take for ever to reach the north bank, but at last we broke through the shoulder-high reeds, relieved to be back on solid ground. Then we stopped and crouched to orientate ourselves. To the east, half a mile or so downriver, I saw the dark mass of the defensive earthworks surrounding Lhandain. Ahead of us was a shallow valley with a stream running through it. Further west, a desolate sprawl of marshland stretched out towards a thicker bank of white mist.

'Which way now?' Togodumnus asked softly.

I said, 'We'll follow the stream. If we keep going in that direction, we should reach our camp eventually.'

We set off, staying close to the dense thickets of gorse and blackberry bushes that ran along the marshy ground at the edge of the stream. The strain of our escape from the south and the gnawing cold had taken their toll, and our pace slowed to a crawl as we made our way through the tangled undergrowth. Vassedo moved ahead, looking for any sign of enemy sentries, but always staying just within sight.

We had been walking for perhaps half an hour when we reached a sprawl of dense forest. A snow-dappled trail ran north of Lhandain, snaking through corridors of yew trees. Our small group continued in tense silence through the mist-threaded gloom, the bare boughs hanging overhead like interlaced fingers, the deathly silence broken only by the occasional caw of unseen crows, adding to the oppressive atmosphere.

Shortly after, I realised the trail seemed to be taking us in the wrong direction. The sun was rising on our right, which meant our camp ought to be somewhere ahead of us, but instead the track veered away to the west. A while later the mist began to lift, revealing a low mound off to one side of the trail. I decided to make for it in the hope that the elevation might give us a clearer view of our surroundings. As we neared the brow Vassedo froze and dropped to a crouch. I ordered the others to halt and crept forward, dropping to a knee beside the huntsman.

'What is it?' I asked.

'Listen, lord,' Vassedo replied urgently.

I tilted an ear and concentrated. At first, I could hear nothing. I wondered if Vassedo had begun to imagine things in his fatigued state. Then, very softly, a muffled sound drifted across the air.

'Voices, lord,' Vassedo said.

'How many, do you think?'

'More than a few, I'd say.'

'Ours? Or theirs?'

Vassedo listened, then shook his head. 'Too far away to tell.'

'I doubt our sentries would be this far from their camp,' I remarked.

'No, lord.'

'Wait here.' I padded back over to Togodumnus and instructed him to remain with the rest of the men beside a thicket of brambles while I stole silently forward with Vassedo, pricking my ears and straining my eyes as I searched for the unseen figures. They seemed to be directly ahead of us, somewhere beyond the mist, and as we drew closer to the voices, I could pick out the familiar harsh cadence of the Atrebatan dialect. Vassedo touched my arm and indicated an uprooted tree amid a growth of nettles and sedges, no more than a dozen paces away. We dropped to our hands and knees and crawled over to the moss-covered trunk, then scanned the ground ahead of us. A short distance beyond our vantage point the ground sloped down towards a wide clearing ringed with birch trees. On the near side of the clearing, no more than fifty paces away, several figures squatted around a cluster of tents, their solid forms just about visible through the thinning haze.

'War-band, lord,' Vassedo whispered. 'A small one, by the looks of it.'

'Verica's men?' I asked. But I already knew the answer.

'Must be. Who else would be out here?'

We silently observed the figures for a short while. Then, slowly, the mist began to lift, like a crew furling a mainsail, revealing a vast throng of tents and warriors scattered across the clearing.

'By Lud,' Vassedo said under his breath. 'There must be hundreds of the bastards down there.'

I scanned the scene and nodded.

'What are they doing in the woods, I wonder?'

'I don't know. But it can't be good news for our side.' I backed away from the tree trunk. 'Come on. Let's get back to the others. Before any of this lot catch sight of us.'

We moved cautiously back down the slope, taking care not to disturb the undergrowth or snap any twigs. I found Togodumnus and the rest of the men crouching beside the brambles and told them what we had seen in the clearing.

Togodumnus shook his head. 'I don't understand. Why would Verica move some of his warriors into the woods?'

'There's no time to worry about that. Right now, we've got to get clear of this place, before they realise we're here.'

I gestured towards a small track that twisted eastwards past a patch of gnarled oak trees. 'We'll head that way. It'll take us away from the camp. We should reach the edge of the forest sooner or later.'

Maglocunus said, 'If the Atrebates are out here, they'll have posted sentries, lord. The woods might be crawling with them.'

'Then we shall have to hope that the gods are on our side.'

We continued through the forest in what I hoped was an east-ward direction, picking our way through the dead bracken and fallen branches. Soon the mist thickened again: in places we could see no further than ten or fifteen paces in front of us, and we had to watch our footing to avoid stumbling on the exposed roots of ancient trees. In such conditions, making any kind of steady progress was almost impossible. The damp air and the proximity of the Atrebatan camp heightened the sense of unease among our small column, and every crack of a twig or rustle of a leaf had us reaching for our weapons.

We marched on silently through the forest until, some time later, we reached a flat area of scrubland bordered on all sides by thick forest. Forty paces further along, the track curved past a small pond of brackish water. As we neared the pond we heard the faint clomp of horse hoofs coming from somewhere beyond the whiteness. At once we threw ourselves to the ground, hiding in the scrub as we listened to the snorting sounds of the beasts. They were getting louder, but I could see nothing through the impenetrable mist.

'Shit. They're coming this way,' Togodumnus said. 'Whoever they are.'

'Quiet!' I hissed. 'Stay where you are! No one move.'

I rested my hand on the pommel of my sword and focused my attention on the noise ahead of us. The hoof beats were dangerously loud now. No more than twenty paces away, I spied the spectral form of a mounted warrior no armed with a thrusting spear. Behind him rode two more figures, barely visible against the mist mantling the forest. We watched silently as they dismounted near to the pond, and proceeded to water their horses. One of them said something to his two companions; from his accent, I realised he must be Atrebatan.

'A patrol,' Vassedo said, very softly. 'From that camp, I'd wager.'

'We should get out of here,' whispered Togodumnus.

'They'll spot us the moment we move,' I hissed. 'In any case, that track will take them right past us, and they're bound to see us then. We'll have to take them. As soon as I give the word.'

I steeled my muscles, gripping the handle of my sword tightly as I watched the Atrebatans. From somewhere up in the boughs of the trees, the loud call of a crow broke the silence. One of the Atrebatans spun round, looking in our direction, his hand reaching down to his sword. He stared for several moments, then looked away. As soon as he turned back to his companions I leapt up, drawing my sword and bellowing at the others to charge forward.

The Atrebatans simultaneously turned to face us. We were on them before they had time to defend themselves or scramble onto their mounts; I lunged bodily at the nearest man, deftly avoiding his ragged spear thrust; his face registered shock as I punched out with my sword, driving the blade into his guts. The man fell backwards, blood gurgling in his throat. Around me Vassedo, Togodumnus and the rest of my men threw themselves at the two other Atrebatans; one man tried to climb onto his mount, but the beast reared up in terror and he fell from the saddle. A few paces away his comrade threw aside his weapon and raised his hands above his head.

'Please, no!' he begged. He was a pale fellow, tall and wiry. 'Don't! I surrender.'

Togodumnus laughed and closed on the man, raising his sword to strike.

'No!' I snapped. 'Spare them.'

My brother reluctantly lowered his weapon while Maglocunus hauled the fallen rider to his feet with powerful hands. I wiped my blade on the slain figure's cloak, stretched to my full height and approached the two men. The pale-faced man looked to be in his middle years. His companion was much younger, no older than sixteen or seventeen, but thickly built, with freckled cheeks and flaxen hair.

'Don't kill us,' the older man said in a trembling voice. Sweat glistened on his brow; his eyes were wide with fear. 'Please.'

They both wore frayed tunics and threadbare leggings – unlike their dead comrade, I realised, whose fine gold torc and expensive cloak marked him out as a member of the Atrebatan nobility. Vassedo and Dubnocatus marched them over to a thicket of thorny bushes, while the others released their horses and dragged their dead companion off the trail.

'What are your names?' I demanded.

'Senetio,' the scrawny man answered.

'Caladocus,' the flaxen-haired youth quavered.

'Any of your friends close by?' I asked.

'None, lord,' Senetio replied. 'We are alone, I swear it before Lud himself.'

'Bollocks,' Togodumnus said. 'Why should we believe these stinking turds? For all we know they might be scouts for a much larger force. I say we gut the pair of them and get out of here, while we still have the chance.'

'Senetio speaks the truth, lord,' Caladocus insisted. 'It is just the three . . . I mean, two of us.' He stared at his lifeless companion a few paces away and dropped his head.

I regarded Senetio closely. He spoke with a strange accent and I did not recognise the markings on his cheeks. 'Where are you from? You do not look like an Atrebatan.'

'I was born in Leucomagus, lord,' Senetio replied. 'In the land of the Belgae.'

'I know of it. How did you come to serve an Atrebatan noble?'

'I married the daughter of a farmer, lord, in a small settlement outside Calleva. Been living there ever since, and happy enough. But then last month Verica's men showed up and recruited me and the lad here to serve in his war-bands, along with many others. Anyone fit enough to wield a spear was taken from the fields and forced to swear the oath of service to him.' He indicated the nobleman's body. 'We were marched straight up to Lhandain with the rest of Verica's forces.'

There was bitterness in his voice, and I sensed this man cared little for Verica and his cronies.

Maglocunus said under his breath, 'Verica must be desperate for men if he's taken to recruiting farmers, lord. It seems our raids have worked better than we could have hoped.'

'Yes,' I replied. I looked the two escorts in the eye. 'What are you doing out here, in the forest?'

The two Atrebatans glanced at each other.

'Speak true and speak fast. Otherwise my men will make you.'

Caladocus bit his lip, reluctant to betray his masters. Senetio, the older of the two, stared at me with suspicion and fear. Then he said,

'We were ordered to escort our master east to the camp of our allies, the Durotriges. That's where we were heading. He had a message for their king.'

I said, 'You lie. The Durotriges have no alliance with the Atrebates.'

'They do now, lord. I overheard my master discussing it with the other nobles. King Bogiodubnus took Verica's side after the fight at the henge near Lhandain, for fear of defying Verica.'

'Where are the Durotriges now?'

'A day's march upriver.' He gave the name of a village. 'King Bogiodubnus arrived there a few days ago, after Verica called on his allies to join the great battle against the Catuvellaunians.'

'But they have not moved east to join Verica? Why?'

'Bogiodubnus is waiting for the remainder of his forces to catch up with him. The terrain there is marshy and difficult to navigate, which has slowed his advance. Verica has ordered him to hurry east so they may join battle tomorrow. That's the message our master was carrying.'

'Cunobelinus is going to offer battle tomorrow?'

The prisoner nodded.

'How many men does Bogiodubnus have?'

'A thousand, I think, lord.'

Maglocunus puffed out his cheeks. 'That would certainly tilt the battle in their favour. With the reinforcements from his allies and the warriors camped out here, they'd outnumber our war-bands.'

Togodumnus said, 'Why did the Durotriges cross upriver, instead of joining their allies here, at Lhandain?'

'For the same reason Verica has hidden some of his warriors in this forest,' Maglocunus said. 'That bastard wants us to think we hold the advantage in numbers, so he can lure our side into a trap.'

'What is Verica's plan for the men in the forest?' I asked the prisoners.

'We do not know, lord.' Senetio shrugged helplessly.

'But you must have some idea as to their purpose. Answer me, if you value your lives.'

Senetio and Caladocus exchanged a look. Then Senetio said, 'All I know is that our master attended a meeting of Verica's war council last night. He said that tomorrow, when Cunobelinus offers battle and advances from the north, there will be a surprise waiting for him. He said the fields outside Lhandain will be littered with the enemy dead by the end of the day. The heads of the Catuvellaunian nobles will hang from the rafters of the great hall at Calleva, and the bards will sing of their feats for generations to come.'

'How many men are camped in the forest?'

Caladocus thought for a moment. 'At least four hundred. Under the command of Prince Moricanus.'

'Have any of our scouts been spotted nearby?'

'No.'

'You are certain?'

'As certain as I can be. If the enemy had been scouting these parts, they wouldn't have made it very far. Verica ordered Moricanus to double the number of sentries around his camp.'

I turned to my men. 'Verica's plan is clear, then.'

'It is?' Togodumnus said.

'He intends to launch a surprise attack on our forces,' I explained. 'Moricanus will wait until the battle lines are formed in front of Lhandain and both sides are committed. Our war-bands will not be aware of the ambushers waiting in the forest for the signal to attack. They'll charge out of the treeline and take our warriors in the flank.'

The realisation dawned on Togodumnus's face. 'That dog. He dishonours his ancestors with such base tactics.'

'No worse than us, then,' I pointed out. 'I fear, brother, that there will not be much honour to be had in this war. The stakes are too high for Verica. He will stop at nothing to extend his influence north of the Tamesis. Him and his Roman friends,' I added bitterly, recalling the centurion I had seen accompanying the Atrebates.

Something had been puzzling me during the exchange with the two Atrebatans. I turned back to face them. 'How does Verica know of our intention to attack tomorrow?'

Senetio glanced at his younger comrade, then said, 'Verica has a traitor in your camp, lord. I have heard our master speak of him with the other members of the war council. He has been passing information to our side for months.'

A hollow feeling spread through my stomach. 'Who?'

'That I do not know. His name was not mentioned . . . at least, not in our presence. His identity is known only to those members of Verica's inner circle.'

'Shit,' Togodumnus said through clenched teeth. 'A traitor. That's all we need.'

'Our father is in great peril,' I said. 'It's vital we find his camp as soon as possible and warn him of the danger, before he blunders into a trap.'

'What about these two, lord?' asked Dubnocatus, nodding at the escorts.

'Kill them, I say,' Vassedo hissed.

'Please, no!' Senetio cried. 'I beg you, my lord. We have done all that you asked. Let us go.'

'What? And let you betray our presence to the first enemy patrol you come across?' Maglocunus laughed cruelly. 'Why would we do that? It would be simpler to kill you both now.'

'We could take them prisoner,' Dubnocatus said. 'The king might wish to interrogate them.'

'Out of the question. We can't take them with us,' Maglocunus argued in a low voice. 'The men are tired enough as it is. Nursemaiding these fools is the last thing we need.'

I turned back to the prisoners. They stared at me in terror as I weighed up the risk of letting them live and flee back to their home on the far side of the river against the chance that they might betray us.

As I studied them I felt a pang of pity for these wretched souls. They had been dragged into a conflict they scarcely understood, to fight for their king's claim to a territory they had never previously visited, while their own lands were left to fall into ruin; it was hardly surprising that they resented having to take up arms in Verica's warbands.

Togodumnus took my arm gently. 'We can't take any chances, brother. Too much is at stake.'

I said, 'Our fight is not with the Atrebatan people. Only with their ruler and his cronies. There is no profit in killing a pair of men who have no wish to fight for their king.'

'And what if they run into their comrades on their journey to the marsh? If Verica learns that we have stumbled upon his hidden warband and learned of the arrival of his Durotrigan friends, he will send every man he can spare to hunt us down before we can warn our father.'

I was silent for a moment, reluctant to admit he was right. I have never liked the prospect of killing men in cold blood unless the situation demanded it, but my brother spoke the truth. There was too much at stake. My principles were just another casualty of the bitter conflict we were engaged in. I nodded at Togodumnus.

'You want me to deal with them?' he asked.

'No. The decision is mine.'

Togodumnus nodded at the dead Atrebatan noble.

'What should we do about him? And the others? We can't leave their bodies out here for the enemy to find.'

'We'll weigh them down with rocks and sink them in the pond. But keep the nobleman's head.'

'His head?' Togodumnus repeated. He pulled a face. 'This is hardly the time for taking trophies, brother.'

'No,' I said. 'But we may need it.'

The prisoners, who had overheard our conversation, watched in silent despair as Maglocunus unsheathed his sword, planted a boot on the messenger's chest and brought his blade down in three powerful blows, as if chopping wood. There was a sickening crunch as the sword edge sliced through the man's neck, hacking through cartilage, and then the sturdy warrior bent down and snatched up the severed head, wrapping it in a cloth bundle before he shoved it into a sidebag.

I faced the prisoners as my men formed a loose circle around them to forestall any attempt at escape. 'On your knees.'

CHAPTER THIRTY-FOUR

L ater that morning, as the winter sun emerged, our small party stumbled upon a trail winding up the side of a hillock. We trudged up the slope until we reached an area of gorse-choked ground. From here we had a clear line of sight across the rolling countryside beyond Lhandain. Directly north of the town was a wide plain, hemmed in on the western side by narrow rivers and streams, coppiced woods and minor hills, some topped with prominent burial mounds. A few miles to the east, the other side of the plain was bordered by a large tract of marshland cut through with another of the Tamesis's numerous tributaries. To the north of the floodplain, a pall of woodsmoke hung in the air above a large tented encampment set on an eminence, roughly two miles from Lhandain's northern gate. Beyond it, the ground rose up towards a series of foothills and low forested ridges.

Our mood improved with the knowledge that we were so close to our kinfolk, and we hurried down the reverse slope in good spirits, picking our way through the thinner patch of oak trees leading to the fringes of the plain. At the edge of the forest we stopped and observed the trackways criss-crossing the arable land in front of us, but the area seemed quiet enough, with most of the inhabitants either having fled north or taken refuge within Lhandain ahead of the anticipated battle between the tribes. We made our way towards the camp at a good pace, avoiding the main footpaths, constantly alert for enemy patrols.

Throughout this time, the fear of capture preyed on my mind. Unless we could alert my father to the threat lurking in the woods, our war-bands would advance into the trap set by Verica. Hidden amid the thickets and briars along the treeline, the enemy would not be seen by our forces until it was too late. The crushing victory of the Atrebates over our men at Lhandain would turn our allies against us. Camulodunum would fall, inevitably, and our family would be driven from the lands of our ancestors, fated to die in obscurity among the tribes of Gaul or Germania, like so many exiled Britannic noble families before us.

This gloomy train of thought persisted until we drew within a few hundred paces of our camp. We sheathed our weapons and moved cautiously forwards, acutely aware that we could be mistaken for the enemy. A jumpy sentry, spotting us from a distance, might easily sound the alarm and give the order to attack the strangers approaching the camp.

After fifty paces I ordered the men to halt and called out to the sentries I knew must be concealed amid the thick heather and gorse. A young warrior I did not recognise sprang up from the long grass no more than thirty paces away, his spear tip pointing in my direction. He took in the horde of wild-haired figures in front of him and issued his challenge to identify ourselves.

I kept my hands raised in the air as I made my reply. The warrior scoffed when I told him my name.

'Prince Caratacus, my arse! Make yourselves scarce. Go on, piss off, the lot of you.'

'I've had enough of this little turd,' Maglocunus snarled. 'No one gets to talk to Prince Caratacus like that.'

He stepped forward, reaching for his sword. 'No!' I shouted at him. I rounded on the sentry. 'Let us through at once. That's a fucking order. We've got vital news for the king.'

'No one gets to pass through the lines without permission. King's orders.'

Just then a heavily scarred veteran strode over to investigate the commotion. I recognised him at once. Parvilius had served on my father's bodyguard for many years and had accompanied us to that fateful assembly with the Druids the previous autumn. We exchanged warm greetings, the sentry stammered his apologies, and then Parvilius escorted us through the mass of leather tents, carts and tethered mounts towards my father's quarters at the centre of the encampment.

Four bodyguards stood in front of the tent opening, wielding their long spears. They eyed me with looks of frank astonishment when Parvilius explained who we were. I suppose I must have appeared more like a filthy vagabond than the son of the High King of the Catuvellaunians. They stepped aside, and I ducked through the goatskin flaps ahead of Togodumnus, while the rest of our bedraggled band waited outside in the mud and snow.

My father was sitting on a stool while several other men stood before him: all the members of my father's trusted war council. My Druid mentor, Bladocus, was at my father's side.

'Caratacus . . . Togodumnus,' my father blinked in surprise as he stood to greet us. 'My sons . . .'

'Father.' I bowed.

He did not embrace us. My father believed in upholding the old ways of our tribe, when kings taught their sons to be tough, fearless and respectful of rank. I admired my father for all that he had achieved for our people: his mastery of tribal politics, his fighting skill and his ability to identify weakness in others had allowed him to establish our tribe as the foremost power north of the Tamesis. But he was a hard man, harsh and aloof, and I never truly knew what he was thinking. That was what made him such a dangerous adversary, I suppose.

I clasped forearms with Epaticcus, relieved to see my uncle and pleased at the swift recovery he had made from the injuries he had sustained at the Battle of the Henge, and nodded a greeting at Adminius. A man I had not seen before stood at my brother's side. He had dark oily hair, a stubbly beard, olive skin, and his face bore no markings or tattoos indicating his tribal affiliation. His hands and cheeks were nicked with pinkish scars; his hairless torso rippled with honed muscle. If I had to guess at his profession, I would have said Roman soldier, or itinerant wrestler.

'A new friend of yours?' I asked.

Adminius flashed what I can only describe as a mocking sneer. 'This is my new bodyguard. Tejanus. A retired gladiator. Fought several times at the games at the Statilian amphitheatre.'

I had heard of the place: even we Britons knew of the Roman custom where men were obliged to fight each other to the death for the gratification of the Roman elite.

339

'Not sure I like the look of that one,' Togodumnus said to me in an undertone.

My father spoke again. 'This is a welcome sight, if most unexpected,' he commented as he took in our dishevelled appearances and torn clothes. 'But where are the rest of your men?'

'Outside, Father,' I replied. 'Five of them. The survivors.'

'I see.' There was a slight tightening around his eyes; a movement so small one could easily miss it, but enough to communicate his displeasure. 'And the others?'

'Dead,' Togodumnus said flatly. 'We were ambushed by the enemy a few days ago.'

'Enemy?' Bellocatus repeated. The dark-haired veteran looked puzzled. 'We had been told that you had travelled north to purchase remounts from the Brigantes over the winter.'

There was an uncomfortable pause while Togodumnus flushed bright red. I coughed and intervened, 'What my brother means to say is that we ran into some brigands on the way back here. They stole our mounts, took the money and killed most of our men before they made their escape.'

Out of the corner of my eye I saw Tejanus whispering something in Adminius's ear. I turned to my father and said, 'Perhaps we could talk in private, Father. I have urgent news for you.'

My father looked round at the nobles and said, 'Bladocus, Epaticcus. You may remain. The rest of you, return to your war-bands. We will resume this discussion later.'

Adminius looked at him with an affronted expression. 'And me, Father?'

'Leave us. We will talk again this afternoon.'

Adminius gave an incredulous laugh. 'I am the second in line to the throne. Whatever my dearest brother wishes to say, I should hear it as well.'

'Do not argue with me, Adminius.'

'But Father—'

'Leave. That is an order.'

Adminius started to protest further, then pressed his lips tightly shut and stared at me with cold fury. He snapped something at his bodyguard in Latin, and the two men followed the other nobles out

340

of the tent. Once they had departed, my father seated himself.

'What is this urgent news you speak of?'

I looked hesitatingly at Epaticcus. 'It is quite all right,' my father continued. 'Epaticcus knows the true purpose of your mission. You may speak freely.'

I told him of our discovery of Moricanus's force in the woods west of Lhandain. He sat bolt upright and drew his eyebrows together. 'The forest, you say?'

'Yes, Father. To the west of the plain. We stumbled upon the enemy camp on our way here. Moricanus and his men are waiting in a clearing. Four hundred of them.'

His frown lines deepened. 'But Adminius has scouted that area thoroughly. He has assured me that the forest is clear of enemies.'

'Then he is lying,' Togodumnus said.

'That is not all we discovered in the forest,' I said. 'There is a large force of Durotrigan warriors, led by Bogiodubnus, upriver from here no more than a day's march away. A thousand men. Verica has called on his allies to join him in battle tomorrow and complete the rout, once Moricanus has attacked our flank. At least, that is their plan.'

'How do you know all of this?'

I nodded at Togodumnus. 'Show him.'

He stepped outside the tent and beckoned to one of my men. A moment later he returned with Maglocunus. The latter reached into his sidebag and took out the severed head of the Atrebatan messenger, gripping it by a tuft of greasy hair. He bowed before the king, handed the head to me and swiftly departed the tent. I lobbed it to the ground; it rolled to a gentle stop at my father's feet.

'These are the markings of an Atrebatan warrior,' Epaticcus said as he stooped down to examine the tattoos on the cheeks.

'Where did you find him?' the king demanded.

'In the forest.' I described the encounter and the information we had extracted from the nobleman's escorts.

'And you believe this story? You don't suspect a ruse?'

'They had no reason to lie to us.'

My father's face darkened as the full enormity of Verica's trap was laid bare before him. At his side, Bladocus listened stony-faced.

'There is more,' I said.

'Yes?'

'The escorts claimed that there is a traitor in our ranks. Someone has been passing information to the Atrebates. Someone who is privy to their ambush plans and knows of your intention to give battle outside Lhandain tomorrow.'

Epaticcus's face darkened. 'That is impossible. Only those in the war council know the details of our campaign.'

'Nonetheless, I believe their claims are credible. How else could Verica know that you intend to fight him tomorrow?'

'He may have guessed as much.'

I shook my head. I had thought this through carefully since we had left the woods. 'Verica would not have ordered the Durotriges to rush to join him unless he was absolutely certain of your intentions. There is only one way he could know the truth. Someone is sharing your plans with him.'

My father looked at Bladocus, as if seeking advice. The latter said, in his thick Gaulish accent, 'I am inclined to agree, sire. We have our spies in the court at Calleva; it is hardly a stretch to imagine Verica might have his own man among us.'

'Then who is this traitor?' my father asked me. 'Did your prisoners reveal the name?'

'I am afraid not. And I have news of another traitor.' I told him how Nemobnus had betrayed us to the Atrebates, with devastating consequences.

'This business with Nemobnus. I assume, from what you two have told me, that Verica knows you are behind the raids against his allies?' my father said, eyes flitting between myself and Togodumnus.

'Yes. They will have learned the truth from Nemobnus. He would have told them everything.'

'That is most unfortunate. You should have been more careful, Caratacus. You have cost me forty of my best men. And the cost could be higher still if the Atrebates convince the other tribes that you, not the Silures, were responsible for the attacks on their farmers and their allies.'

'They have Nemobnus,' Epaticcus said. 'That will be proof enough.'

'The testimony of a traitor is hardly compelling evidence of our involvement in these attacks,' Bladocus intervened.

My father considered this. 'Is there anything else that might link the raids to us?' he asked, turning to me.

I thought hard and shook my head. 'No, Father. We were very careful to disguise ourselves at all times. The men carried nothing on their persons that might identify them as Catuvellaunians.'

'Then it seems we are in the clear, sire,' Bladocus said. 'I doubt Verica will insist on pressing the issue, given his involvement in the corruption of the ranks of the Druid High Council. If we were to raise that matter then it would outrage the other tribes of the island.'

Epaticcus laughed bitterly. 'I thought you Druids were supposed to be loyal to the other members of your cult.'

'This is a time of war,' Bladocus said. 'If the Catuvellaunians are defeated then who will lead the tribes when the Romans come to our lands, as they surely will? One must do what is necessary for the greater good in the long term. That is why the Catuvellaunians must triumph now. Whatever damage is done to the reputation of the Druids in the process.'

My father stared thoughtfully at the severed head. 'It seems Verica has set a cleverly worked trap for us, with the help of his spy. Of course, this means we will have to rethink our plan . . . even if there is not much time. And we'll deal with the traitor later, once we uncover his identity.'

'Do you still intend to offer battle tomorrow?' I asked.

'Yes. We shall fight on the northern plain, five hundred paces from Lhandain. Our bands will not advance until the afternoon, once the Dobunnians have joined us and had a chance to rest.'

Our allies, my father explained, were on their way to join us, having set off from their tribal capital some days ago. A short time earlier, Antedius, King of the Dobunnians, had sent a messenger to our camp; his advance guard had reached a small place called Brigandun, half a day's march to the west. The rest of his men were expected to reach Brigandun by dusk.

'How many men is Antedius bringing with him?' I asked.

'Four hundred. The pick of the Dobunnian warriors, I am told.'

'That is all?'

'We hoped for more,' Bladocus cut in. 'But the king's decision to offer his support has split his tribe. Many of the nobles refuse to lead

343

their warriors against the Atrebates out of fear of Verica's revenge should he win the day.'

'It is a pity,' said my father. 'But I am honoured that I can count on Antedius, and those that are with him will join us in battle. The question remains, gentlemen: how are we to counter Verica's plan?'

I spoke up. 'How many men does Verica have under his command at Lhandain?'

'A little under two thousand warriors, if our scouts' reports are correct.'

'Slightly less than our war-bands, then.'

'Yes. But with the men hidden in the forest, he will outnumber us.'

'And don't forget the Durotriges,' Togodumnus pointed out. 'There's a thousand of them camped upriver, if those men we captured were telling the truth. What are we to do about them?'

'The Durotriges are currently bogged down in the marshes, waiting for the remainder of their forces to catch up with them,' I pointed out. 'They will not move until they have received their orders from Verica, and it will be a day or so before the Atrebates realise their messenger has gone missing. Which gives us an opportunity to act now and defeat the Atrebates before their allies can join them.'

'Whatever we decide, we must fight tomorrow,' my father said. 'If we do not offer battle, Verica will have time to send for the Durotriges, and we shall lose the initiative.'

'Why should we fear the Atrebates?' Epaticcus asked. He beat a fist against his chest in defiance. 'We are Catuvellaunians. Our warriors are well trained. If the gods will it, we will sweep through the Atrebates, as we did at Durovernum against the forces of Eppillus.'

'It is not a question of the gods willing it,' said the king. 'Or a question of bravery. Caratacus is right. The men camped in the forest will tear into our upriver flank as soon as our forces are committed. We cannot simply walk into Verica's trap and blindly hope that our superior fighting skills will carry the day.' He shot a scathing look at Epaticcus. 'No, the issue before us is clear. We must find a way to turn Verica's plan against him, without revealing our knowledge of it to the traitor.'

Togodumnus said glumly, 'It's too bad we cannot set a trap of our own. I had been looking forward to seeing our enemies squirming on the end of our spears.'

Throughout this discussion I had been thinking feverishly. Then it occurred to me, in a moment of inspiration. I thought back to the ice ford across the Tamesis. The bridge guarded by the Atrebatan sentries. The Dobunnian force hastening towards our camp.

'Who knows that the Dobunnians are to join us tomorrow?'

The king thought quickly. 'Myself, Epaticcus, Bladocus, and my royal messengers.'

'No one else?'

'No,' he said. 'We decided to keep their arrival a secret, in case the enemy learned of our plans. Why?'

'Perhaps there *is* a way to defeat Verica,' I said.

My father's eyebrows hitched upwards. 'Another one of your plans, Caratacus? How many men will it cost me this time?' he asked icily.

Undaunted, I continued, 'It is not without risk, but if it works, it will give our men the opportunity to drive the Atrebatan forces from Lhandain . . . once and for all.'

'And why should I trust in you, given how you cost me nearly forty of my best men on your last mission?'

Bladocus intervened, 'We should at least listen to him, sire. His raids tied down many enemy warriors, after all, and he can hardly be blamed for one of his own men betraying them to the other side.'

My father drummed his fingers on his thigh and stared at me for several moments. Then he exhaled. 'Very well, Caratacus. Let us hear your plan.'

I breathed in deeply. 'If we are to have any chance of victory tomorrow, Father, we must turn the enemy's trap on its head. This is what must be done.'

CHAPTER THIRTY-FIVE

Exhausted by our escape from enemy territory, I slept like the dead that night. The next morning, the two thousand men of the Catuvellaunian, Trinovantes and Cantiaci war-bands prepared to meet the Atrebatan host on the open ground before Lhandain, in the great struggle to decide the fate of southern Britannia. At first light the war horns sounded their braying notes, rousing the warriors from their slumbers. On my father's orders each man had been permitted only one drinking horn of beer the previous evening, for he wanted them rested and clear-headed for the day's battle. Sheep had been seized from the surrounding farms, and soon the air was filled with the rich aroma of roasted meat as we took a morning meal of mutton, bread and cheese, our last before the moment came when we would have to charge the enemy.

The camp was alive with movement: men rushing back and forth, the shouting of orders, horses whinnying, servants fetching equipment from the carts stationed to the rear. At my father's tent, a continuous stream of messengers came and went, carrying orders intended for the Dobunnians hurrying towards us from Brigandun, our allies and our own war-bands. The players readied their carnyxes; our Druids cast their divination rods and chanted their incantations, inciting the wrath of the gods on the enemy. Bladocus announced that a crow had been seen perched on top of a yew tree before flying south, a sure sign that the omens were favourable; bondsmen helped their patrons into chainmail armour and polished the ornate helmets some chose to wear into battle, and charioteers greased the axles of their vehicles with animal fat. The Druids brought a white goat before my father; he slit its throat as an offering to the gods to seek their favour in the coming battle.

Men gathered around the standards of their respective war-bands, waiting for the order to advance on the enemy. Some offered prayers to the gods to save them crippling injury, or worse, the shame of cowardice; the less experienced warriors fiddled nervously with their equipment; others told crude jokes or talked eagerly of the feast they would enjoy in Lhandain that night, or any of the hundred things a warrior might do to remove from his mind the terrible knowledge that he must charge at the sword points of his foemen before the day is out. The older sweats, who knew better, contented themselves with saving their energy as they gazed quietly across the plain at the enemy host.

Several hundred paces away, across a patch of snow-carpeted ground, the forces of the Atrebates under Verica had formed up in front of Lhandain, spear tips and sword points twinkling in the blinding glare of the morning sun. They had filed out of the northern gate shortly before dawn, in readiness for the day's combat. Almost two thousand warriors faced us, strung out in a long line three ranks deep, the Atrebatan standards flickering in the light wind. Close by, I saw the chariots of the Callevan royal household, surrounded by a cluster of retainers and Druids, members of the cult followed by the Atrebates.

It was a fine clear morning, the sky as blue as the waters of your beloved Mediterranean. The pristine snow gleamed like marble, the warmth of the sun on our cheeks carried the first promise of the coming spring, and at my side, Epaticcus was saying it was a good day to fight.

'Think this plan of yours will work, lad?' he asked.

I glanced at my uncle. We were standing on a slope overlooking the plain. My father stood several paces away, surrounded by his entourage of bodyguards and subordinates, watching the enemy while our war-bands made their preparations. Among them I spotted Adminius, dressed in a vest of chainmail armour, a pair of leather bracers and a bronze helmet with a decorative raven perched on the crest. The handle of his coral-beaded sword gleamed in the sunlight. His bodyguard, Tejanus, remained dutifully close to his master, a meaty hand resting on the pommel of his sheathed sword.

Adminius met my gaze for a moment before he turned back to the other nobles.

'All plans can go wrong,' I said.

I looked away, hoping Epaticcus wouldn't notice the strain I felt must surely be showing on my face. The knowledge that we had a traitor close to the royal court had persuaded my father to withhold the details of the deception from the members of his war council. Aside from the king and myself, only Epaticcus, Bellocatus and Bladocus were privy to the plan; but if word somehow reached Verica despite our precautions, the outcome of the battle might yet go against us.

Defeat would be catastrophic for our tribe. At stake was far more than the right to claim Lhandain as our own: it would signify the end of Catuvellaunian domination. Verica would gain himself a toehold on the lands north of the Tamesis. With the Durotriges to support him, he would be free to launch attacks further north, threatening our tribal capital, and with it, my hopes of ever realising the future my Druid mentor had foreseen of one day claiming the throne of our people and uniting the tribes in readiness to face Rome.

'Let us pray the gods are with us today, then,' Epaticcus muttered. 'Something tells me we shall need their help.'

'You have doubts?'

He pursed his lips as he considered. 'It's not the way I would choose to fight. But I'm a warrior, not a thinker. Unlike your father. He's agreed to your stratagem, and that's good enough for me. As long as it ends up with us celebrating victory in Lhandain this evening.'

'Much depends on the Dobunnians,' I conceded. 'And Togodumnus. But this is our best hope. If everything goes to plan, we shall win the day.'

'Good. Because I don't plan on letting some ugly Atrebatan wretch parade my head through Calleva.'

I smiled grimly. 'Me neither.'

I fell silent and turned to survey the landscape before me. This is how things stood on the morning of the battle: to the south of our camp, five hundred paces to the rear of the Atrebatan forces, was the wealthy settlement of Lhandain. Further away, beyond the wharf, the timber bridge ran across the narrowest point of the Tamesis.

On the far bank, amid the reeds and rushes, I saw the farmhouse marking the spot where we had crossed the ford.

A mile or so to the west of the floodplain lay the forest where Prince Moricanus and his forces waited to spring their ambush on our war-bands. Three miles to the east of the plain the treacherous marshes stretched out towards the horizon. Should our plan fail, Verica's men would no doubt seek to scatter our forces into the marshland, where we would be easy prey for the enemy. To our right, several hundred paces from our camp, scouts occupied a high point on the low ridges facing the rolling landscape further west of Lhandain. They would keep watch throughout the day, ready to alert our commanders at the first sign of the approaching Dobunnian forces.

The plan I had outlined last night was relatively simple. Our forces would face each other across the plain and await the signal from the scouts that the Dobunnians were in sight. Then we would advance on the enemy host, with picked men from the royal war-band on our strengthened upriver flank in readiness for the ambush from the enemy troops in the woods. To add to the ruse the men wore plain tunics and woad paint to cover the striking tattoos identifying them as elite warriors. At the same time, Togodumnus and a small group of warriors were lying in wait among the reeds on the far side of the Tamesis. They had crept back across the ice ford in the dead of night, with orders to kill the small number of guards on the southern side of the bridge, barricade it with the wagons from the farmstead and set fire to the timbers.

Cut off from their only route of escape, the Atrebates would be forced to choose between standing to fight, fleeing into the marshes, or taking their chances on the frozen river. My plan would work, I reassured myself, as long as the Dobunnians were not delayed, and everyone followed their orders.

'Remember,' I had told Togodumnus during the briefing in my father's tent the previous afternoon. 'You must wait until Moricanus attacks from the forest, when Verica's forces will be fully engaged in the battle. If you go too early, the enemy will be wise to your plan, and they will attempt to stop you. We cannot help you then.'

'What if the Atrebates are holding back some of their forces in

349

reserve on the southern bank of the river? We won't stand a chance. It'll be a suicide mission.'

'It would be tactical madness for Verica to leave a body of men on the southern side. If he required reinforcements, then he would have to funnel them across the bridge during the fighting. No, Verica will have pushed his entire force north. That is the more logical move. Trust me, you won't have to deal with more than a few sentries guarding the bridge. When you get across the river, make sure you and your men rest. You are exhausted, brother. I need you fighting fit on the morrow.'

My brother had nodded his understanding, but even so I had seen him off that night with a pang of doubt. Few could match him for bravery in battle, but I was all too aware that his hot-headed nature could lead him into making rash judgements.

As the sun climbed above the treetops, the Atrebates whipped themselves up into a wild frenzy, beating their swords rhythmically against their shields, shouting their war cries and hurling invective at our warriors, denouncing our mothers in the vilest language while their bards loudly proclaimed the many glorious feats of their nobles. In response, our side retorted with a chorus of colourful abuse and taunts. 'Behold the dogs of the Atrebates!' one bard screamed furiously. 'See their wretched leader tremble before the glory of Cunobelinus! Your king, slayer of a thousand foes, the greatest hero of our age, implores you to destroy the enemy, and earn your place in the eternal glory of the Otherworld!'

The fellow kept up this interminable peroration until one wit shouted, 'Earn your own place, you bastard! Grab a spear and join us!' and we all laughed as he beat an embarrassed retreat to the safety of the rear rank.

The dull clatter of swords hitting shields echoed across the plain, rising to a deafening crescendo, accompanied by the cheers and yells of both sets of warriors, and I sensed the powerful determination of our men to close ranks with the enemy. Those in the front line of the Atrebatan ranks responded by giving their backs to us, dropping their leggings and baring their pale buttocks in our direction, prompting delirious cheers from their companions as they dared us to launch our attack.

'The bastards mock us.' Epaticcus spat and glowered at the enemy. 'We should be gutting these vermin, instead of letting them insult us.'

'We can't attack yet,' I said. 'We must wait here until the Dobunnians are in sight. Only then can Father safely give the order to advance.'

Epaticcus glanced anxiously past his shoulder at the scouts observing the low hills to the west. 'Let us hope they get here soon. If we have to listen to much more of this bollocks, I'll march over to Verica's mob and shut them up myself.'

A sudden movement on the bridge had caught my eye. A procession of mule-led wagons was making its way across the bridge towards the southern bank of the Tamesis, a handful of mounted Atrebatans in the van, one of them bearing the standard of the enemy's royal household.

'What's that?' I asked.

Epaticcus said, 'Verica's baggage train. He must be sending his possessions out of Lhandain while his warriors make ready. It's a good sign; he fears defeat, despite his plans.' He spat out a mouthful of phlegm on the snow. 'It's too bad about his wagons, though. The lads were looking forward to helping themselves to some prize booty once we've given them a good kicking.'

'There'll be plenty more spoils to be had,' I said.

We stood watching as the royal baggage train neared the far end of the bridge. The half a dozen warriors guarding the approach hastened aside to let the wagons pass. Then I saw a group of dark shapes emerging from the reedbed, directly below the dilapidated farmstead. A throng of tiny figures leapt up from the tall reeds and charged towards the crossing point a short distance downriver from the farm, armed with a mixture of spears and swords.

'That's Togodumnus and his men,' Epaticcus said as he shaded his eyes against the beating sun. 'What the fuck are they doing?'

I grasped their intentions at once and felt my stomach tense with dread. 'They're going to attack the baggage train.'

'Why would your brother do that? His orders are to wait for our signal.'

'He must think Verica is trying to make his escape,' I said, noticing

351

the royal standard flickering in the gentle breeze. 'He'll want the glory of capturing the king.'

'Shit.' Epaticcus hammered a clenched fist against his thigh. 'The fool. He's going to wreck the plan.'

I stood watching, helpless, and cursed my brother's recklessness. At the southern end of the bridge, the guards turned to face their attackers; even as I looked on the Catuvellaunians launched themselves at the horsemen; the rest swarmed round the wagons. The drivers to the rear of the column leapt down from their vehicles and sprinted back across the bridge towards Lhandain.

I made a quick assessment of the situation. My brother had twenty veterans under his command: sturdy warriors hand-picked by my father for the task of securing the bridge and torching it. They outnumbered the defenders on the bridge, but only narrowly, and it was a matter of moments before the drivers reached Lhandain and alerted their companions to the threat at their rear. I spun away and hurried over to my father. Bellocatus had already drawn his attention to the fighting on the far bank.

'Father,' I began, fighting to quell the tension in my voice. 'We must advance on the enemy at once. There's not a moment to lose.'

'Attack now?' Adminius said with an icy scowl. 'Have you lost your mind, dear brother? It's not yet time. Our scouts haven't had sight of the Dobunnians yet.'

I bit back on my anger and addressed my father directly. 'If we don't attack at once, Verica will be wise to the attack on the bridge. Togodumnus and his men will die.'

'Togodumnus?' Adminius stared at the skirmish coming to an end on the far side of the river. 'What is he doing over there?' He rounded on me. 'What is going on, you scheming bastard?'

I said nothing. Adminius glanced at my father, eyes widening with sudden realisation. 'The bridge! Togodumnus is going to burn it, isn't he? He's going to cut off the enemy's route of escape.' The king nodded. Adminius stared at him with an expression of burning rage. 'You lied to me. You told me Togodumnus was taking a message to the Dobunnians.'

'This is not the time, my son.'

Adminius snapped his gaze towards me. 'Why was I not told of

352

this? What else have you kept from me, brother? What foul poison have you planted in Father's heart?'

I ignored my brother and appealed to the king to save Togodumnus and attack at once.

'This is his own fault,' he responded angrily. 'We can hardly pull him from the fire, at the risk of the lives of our men, simply because he has had a rush of blood to the head.'

'This is not just about Togodumnus,' I said. 'If he fails, our plan is in ruins. If we are to have any chance of destroying Verica's forces in full, and preventing their escape, we must go in now.'

Adminius said with a sneer. 'Without the Dobunnians, we do not have the numbers to drive the enemy from the battlefield. If our reckless brother has attacked early that is his problem, not ours.'

'Our upriver flank is strong enough to hold off the enemy,' I said. 'We should be able to contain Moricanus's warriors, at least until the Dobunnians can reach us.'

Bellocatus said tersely, 'It is a risk, lord. If the Dobunnians have been delayed, or gods forbid, lost their way, we shall be cut to pieces.'

Our father had been quiet throughout this exchange, watching the enemy host across the plain with his tired gaze. Now he turned to Bellocatus and said, 'Give the order. We advance now.'

'But, sire. It is too early.'

'The Dobunnians, I am told, struck their camp before dawn. That means they cannot be far from here. We must attack now, and pray to the gods that they will reach us soon.'

Bellocatus began to protest further, but the king silenced him with a curt wave of his hand. 'I have made my decision. We are in the hands of the gods. Give the signal, or I shall relieve you of command.'

'Yes, sire.'

Bellocatus filled his lungs and yelled at his subordinates. They passed on the order, and the war horns blared their deep notes, a resonant din that drowned out the songs of the bards. Our warriors hastily snatched up their shields and weapons and closed ranks under the serpent-tail banners displaying the colours of our tribes: red for the Catuvellaunians, purple for the Trinovantes, and yellow for the men of Cantium. The servants and slaves remained to the rear of our lines of battle, waiting beside the empty wagons, ready to ferry the wounded from the field. Our chiefs took up their positions in the front ranks. My father climbed onto the bed of his chariot gripping a spear almost as tall as a man, the leather-panelled sides painted with images of hounds and stags. Several paces away, Adminius climbed onto the rear of an even more lavish chariot, decorated with gold and coral. The rest of our mounted force, some fifty chariots in all, were held back as a reserve, ready to charge forward and plug any gap in our line. I took up my place on foot on the extreme right flank, next to Epaticcus and Bellocatus. In keeping with our plan, this section of the line had been reinforced with elite swordsmen mixed in with some regular infantry, ready to meet the force hiding in the woods.

On the other side of the bridge, Togodumnus and his men had made short work of the guards around the baggage train. Most of the enemy had been cut down; the rest fled for the marshes. Some of our men were already shoving the abandoned wagons towards the bridge to block it. Further away, I glimpsed a number of Atrebatan warriors rushing over from the warehouses to confront them. They met my brother's force at the makeshift barricade at the far end of the bridge; from a distance they seemed evenly matched, and I sensed our prospects of victory, the future of our tribe, hanging in the balance.

As soon as my father was satisfied that our forces were ready to attack, he stabbed his spear at the Atrebatan host and bellowed the order to advance. There was no eloquent speech before the attack, such as those I have found in the fanciful works of your historians. Instead there was the blare of the horns, the commanders shouting at the bands to advance, the mounts snorting, the clomping of hoofs on the snow, the chinking of horse bits, the clatter of chariot wheels, the Druids screaming their imprecations, calling on Lud to smite down the Atrebatans, and the battle cries of two thousand men converging on our hated foe.

'Senomagus!' someone cried out, 'Remember our brothers who fell at Senomagus!'

Others took up the cry, and soon the warriors were shouting the name in unison as we swept down the slope and advanced steadily across the open ground towards the line of Atrebatans waiting to receive our attack. At a distance of twenty paces the call went up from the war-band commanders, and those warriors armed with throwing spears released them at the enemy. I saw a torrent of shafts dip down towards the wall of raised shields; from my position it was impossible to tell how many found their target. But it had the effect of spreading confusion and panic in the Atrebatan line, and the screams of wounded men were still piercing the air when our trumpets gave the signal, and we broke into a wild charge.

A moment later the enemy released a ragged volley of javelins at us. At such close range it was almost impossible for them to miss, and dozens of our men fell in that initial flurry of missiles. I heard a howl of agony to my right and saw a man keeling over, clutching at a spear shaft impaled in his guts. Others were struck down and crushed beneath the feet of their comrades. The ferocity of the enemy barrage momentarily stalled our advance, and then the enemy trumpets gave the signal to attack, and they charged towards us with a deafening cry.

Our tribes met in a thunderous crash of swords against shields as each man launched himself individually at his nearest opponent, and the struggle quickly deteriorated into a series of small fights and single combats along the line of the battle. I saw my father and Adminius hurling their javelins at point-blank range at the enemy before they leapt down to the snow, drawing their swords as they sprang forward to join the fighting; the charioteers skilfully manoeuvred their vehicles to the rear of the battle lines, where they would wait at a safe distance, ready to ride forward and rescue their riders if they were wounded or too exhausted to continue, or if the order was given to retreat.

'Get stuck in, lads!' Epaticcus shouted above the clamour of fighting and dying men around him. 'Kill the bastards! Kill every last one of them!'

I stumbled over a broken body sprawled on the snow, regained my balance and looked up to see an Atrebatan warrior charging towards me, naked from the waist up, his muscular torso daubed from head to toe in woad markings, his teeth bared in an expression of rage. A thin leather band ringed with human ears and wolf's teeth hung from his neck; the leather surface of his shield was decorated with the image of a wild boar, the sacred animal of the Atrebates. The warrior slashed downward, I threw up my shield, and there was a sharp ringing as his blade struck against the reinforced metal band. He cursed and swung again; I felt my shield arm burning with the strain

355

as I desperately blocked a succession of vicious blows.

As the warrior caught his breath, I realised his sword, no doubt of poor craftsmanship, had bent along its length from the force of the repeated impacts. My opponent, gripped with fighting madness, did not appear to have noticed the deformity. I waited for his next attack, the warped blade clattered feebly against the shield rim, and then I punched out, striking him in the face with the rounded iron boss. Before he had a chance to recover, I stepped forward and delivered a sweeping horizontal chop at his neck. The blow bit deep, severing flesh and tendon. Blood fountained out of the wide gash as he dropped to the snow, one hand clamped uselessly over his wound.

All around us, the warriors in our stiffened right flank were putting up a determined fight against the enemy, but it came at the price of weakening the centre of our line, and to my left I could see the other war-bands slowly edging backwards as they struggled against Verica's elite warriors. My father was in the thick of the fighting, slashing away at the enemy, flanked by his two best bodyguards: unlike your Roman generals, our leaders were expected to take their place alongside their warriors in the line of battle rather than viewing the struggle from afar. The ground became slippery with spilled blood and glistening entrails; the air grew thick with the vile odour of sweat and piss and shit, all the dreadful smells of battle. I looked round and saw Epaticcus cut down a naked warrior, yelling madly as he sought out his next enemy, his sword wet with Atrebatan blood. 'Who fucking wants it? Which one of you bastards wants to fight me next?'

Then came the strident note of a war-horn to our right. I looked over and saw the Atrebatans under Prince Moricanus bursting out of the woods in a triumphant din. Dozens of chariots raced ahead of the screaming wave of humanity, their drivers weaving around the patches of churned mud and melting snow with practised ease. Bellocatus roared a command at the top of his voice. Those veteran warriors who had been deliberately positioned to the rear of the line darted over to the right flank to join us. I dropped to a crouch, shrinking behind my shield as a chariot-bound noble in a check-patterned cloak braced his right knee against the wicker bands to steady himself and released his javelin at me. The iron tip punched through the wood with a splintering crack, missing my face by inches.

356

Even as I chucked aside my encumbered shield, I saw the noble jumping down from the chariot and lunging at me with his long sword. He had long, flowing dark hair, corded muscles and arms sleeved with tattoos; beneath his flowing cloak he wore a large pendant studded with coral. I dodged and parried his blows, my arm muscles burning with every attack: if you wish to know why we struggled against your legions, you should try fighting with a long sword. The weight of the blade makes it far more difficult to defend against your opponent's blows than the shorter weapon favoured by the legions, putting the Britannic infantryman at a disadvantage. But, of course, our rulers would never dare to admit such a thing.

I deflected another swingeing blow, the dark-haired noble followed up with a low slash, feinted, and caught me with a scything cut on my right bicep – I bear the scar to this day. I gasped in pain, the sword instinctively falling from my grip as I threw myself to the side, deftly evading his next attack, grateful that my Silurian trainers at Merladion had insisted on instructing me in feats of agility and speed as well as skill with a weapon. The Atrebatan gritted his teeth and hacked at me wildly. I dived to the ground, snatched up a short spear lying amid the wrecked equipment and mutilated bodies, and whipped round, thrusting upwards in the same movement and jamming the point into the soft flesh beneath my opponent's chin. The man spasmed, as if he had been struck by an invisible hammer, then coughed up blood; warm droplets of it spattered against my face. The noble fell and I quickly climbed to my feet as another thickset warrior stepped forward to take his place in the battle line. Him I sent to the Otherworld with an angled blow to the guts, skewering his vitals.

The battle now hinged on the extreme right of our line. To my left, near the centre of our line, the contest was going in the enemy's favour as they inched forward. The flanking attack, on which Verica had pinned his hopes of a crushing victory, had stalled in the teeth of the fierce opposition we had offered Moricanus and his men. No doubt they had been surprised to find themselves up against a band of battle-hardened warriors. But we lacked the numbers to drive the enemy back, or break them, and already I could sense our men beginning to flag from their efforts, for the style of fighting and the heavy weapons favoured by our tribes required a level of stamina that tested the physical limits of even the fittest warriors. Amid this carnage I saw Bellocatus several paces away, chest muscles heaving with exertion.

'Where are those fucking Dobunnians?' he rasped between snatched draws of breath. 'They should be here by now.'

Somewhere off to my right, my father was shouting at our warriors, urging them to keep up the fight, to give no ground to the accursed scum from the south. Men hurled themselves anew at the Atrebates, but whenever one of their warriors tired, another stepped forward to take his place, whereas we had no men left in reserve, as our charioteers were already engaged in supporting our centre. How long we fought, I cannot be sure. In the heat of battle, moments can feel like hours. At some point I gazed up to see thick grey plumes of smoke rising above the Tamesis. I knew then that Togodumnus had succeeded in setting fire to the bridge, but his accomplishment would count for nothing unless Antedius and his forces reached us in time. It all depended on the Dobunnians now.

Above the jarring thuds, grunts and piercing metallic rings of the battle, I heard one of the Atrebatans calling out excitedly to his comrades; another man cheered and stabbed his sword at the higher ground north of the woods, on the fringes of the floodplain. I looked up, and then I saw them: a line of armed figures, some riding on chariots, amassing on the brow of the nearest eminence. A moment later they charged down the slope towards us. They were too far away to pick out any details, but above the forest of spear shafts fluttered a black serpent's tail banner – a standard that instilled fear in the heart of every tribe in Britannia.

'Shit . . . it's the Durotriges!' Bellocatus yelled despairingly. 'We're fucking done for!'

CHAPTER THIRTY-SIX

Dismay spread through our exhausted ranks at the sight of the mass of fresh warriors sweeping towards us diagonally across the plain. Some of our men stood momentarily transfixed, as if unable to believe their eyes; others uttered foul curses and damned the Dobunnians for failing us in our hour of need. The Atrebatan warriors closest to the rear of the action turned to greet the onrushing force with hoarse cheers of excitement tempered with relief, certain that their imminent arrival would tip the contest in their favour. It was too much for Adminius: he turned away from the fight and hurried over to the king, his face pale with dread.

'We have to get out of here, Father,' he said in a quivering tone. 'Now, while we still have a chance.'

'Silence! Stay where you are,' I shouted at him.

'What, are you mad?' Adminius waved a hand in the direction of the advancing warriors. 'This is going to be a massacre, you fool. Come on,' he added, grabbing hold of my father by the bicep. But the king shook him off angrily.

'Unhand me, damn you!'

'But . . . the Durotriges,' Adminius cried, exasperated. 'They'll cut us to pieces. For Lud's sake, you must give the signal to retreat.'

'We stand and fight. That's my command.'

Adminius stared at us in open-mouthed incomprehension. Then he made a decision and cried out at his charioteer. The latter snapped his reins and the ponies broke forward, the wheels rattling across the battlefield. As soon as the chariot rumbled to a halt Adminius vaulted onto the platform, gripping the side panels to steady himself as he yelled at the driver to make for the camp. The chariot started back across the plain but made it no further than twenty paces before the wheels became mired in the churned-up snow and mud. The charioteer cracked his whip and urged the mounts forward, but the heavy wheels were stuck fast, to howls of frustration from my brother. He called out to his bodyguard; Tejanus hurried over, braced his feet and began pushing the vehicle, straining every sinew in an effort to dislodge it.

I swung back round to the fighting. The front ranks of the black-clad warriors were now only a few hundred paces away. We kept up our resistance, even as the Atrebatans tore into us with renewed purpose and enthusiasm. Above their voices I heard Moricanus spurring his men on, promising that their comrades would soon relieve them. Our king called on our brave warriors to stand firm, but we were in grave danger of being overrun. Out of the corner of my eye I saw Parvilius sinking to his knees, a sword buried in his chest. Others hacked desperately at the enemy despite their injuries, preferring a hero's death to the humiliation of surrender.

Then, at the last possible moment, the black serpent's tail carried by the approaching forces dipped down, and in its place the standard bearer raised the bright green standard of the Dobunnians.

The enemy's cheers swiftly turned to cries of alarm, as a wave of panic passed down their line. The Atrebatans had made no attempt to defend their western flank, and they had no time to organise themselves before our allies charged home. The warriors immediately in front of us were trapped in a tight press of bodies, caught between our fighters and the Dobunnians; they lacked the space to swing their long swords effectively, and many were cut down or crushed to death in the first moments of the attack, drawing hearty roars from our side. Those men further back tried to extricate themselves from the killing ground and fled south towards Lhandain.

Amid the carnage I saw Moricanus trying to escape on his chariot. I bellowed at my companions as the vehicle broke forwards, crushing wounded men beneath the wheels. A nearby Dobunnian heard my shout and speared one of the ponies through the flank before it could get away. The beast whinnied in agony and fell heavily, tipping the chariot onto its side. Moricanus gave a cry as he tumbled out; his injured driver ran away, ignoring his prince's pleas to help him. A trio of Dobunnians swarmed round Moricanus before he could climb to his feet, hacking mercilessly at the prince.

With the death of their leader the men lost their heart for the struggle and dozens of them retreated across the plain, streaming towards Lhandain. Our warriors met up with the Dobunnians in the middle. Then our combined force swept round to take the centre of the Atrebatan line in the rear, closing the trap. We outnumbered the enemy heavily; the arrival of the Dobunnians had given fresh impetus to our weary men, and against such a force the Atrebatans did not stand a chance. The wiser heads among Verica's war-bands, sensing all was lost, conducted a fighting withdrawal towards the settlement. Others were killed before they could surrender, hacked down by men in the grip of a killing frenzy. We took few prisoners that day; such was our hatred for the Atrebates. I doubt if our men would have obeyed had my father commanded otherwise.

The enemy line wavered a moment longer, then broke in disarray. Their tribal banners fell, trampled underfoot as the teeming mass of fighters ran pell-mell towards Lhandain, no doubt intending to rush across the bridge to their own lands, just as I had foreseen. In their shock and terror, their fighters had not noticed the coils of smoke rising above the warehouses. Or perhaps they had seen them but did not care, or assumed one of the timber structures along the wharf had caught fire. More probably, they knew what was happening but also understood that the bridge was their only means of escape from the slaughter behind them. It did not matter: our plan was working. The Atrebatans were being funnelled into a trap from which there was no escape. They would be caught in the settlement between the burning bridge and our war-bands.

'We've got them now!' Epaticcus roared. 'Kill every one of them! Spare no one!'

A routed army in full flight is at once a beautiful and terrible thing to behold for the victor, only too aware of how uncertain the outcome of a battle is. Our forces pursued the broken enemy through the settlement with a gleeful savagery, hunting them down singly or in small parties, fired by an unspeakable thirst for vengeance. I saw a few terrified Lhandainers sheltering in alleys or behind market stalls – one or two actually shouted their encouragement for our tribe – but most of them had taken refuge in their roundhouses, where they waited on the outcome of the violent struggle taking place along the rutted thoroughfares. Faces peered out from the open doorways, watching us with wary expressions. I did not blame them: we must have struck a terrifying appearance.

The main force of Atrebatans, or rather, what was left of it, bolted towards the river. By now fire had fully engulfed the far end of the bridge, swathing the timber planking and posts in smoke and flame. The scorching heat halted the Atrebatans in their tracks; in desperation, some scurried off to the right, making for the smaller gate on the western side of Lhandain. My father had anticipated this move, and a force of our men under Bellocatus circled round the edges of the settlement, cutting the enemy off before they could reach the gatehouse. The Atrebatans, most of whom had tossed aside their heavy shields, gave out sharp cries of surprise as they crashed into the waiting Catuvellaunians. Bellocatus's men rammed home their swords and spear points, cutting down their foes before they could defend themselves or flee in another direction. In a matter of moments, the ground was littered with enemy dead.

Across the settlement, more men were killed where they stood or shamefully pierced in the back with javelins as they tried to run away. Not even the dead were spared: groups of our warriors hacked at the bodies of dead nobles, taking their heads as trophies; fights broke out between some of our warriors as they argued over their competing claims to the severed heads. It was not uncommon for such disputes to turn violent, and I have even heard of men killing their companions in order to seize the trophy-head of a prized enemy.

I shoved aside a wounded Atrebatan clutching his blood-soaked chest, evaded the thrusting spear from a royal bodyguard and punched my sword into his groin, then dashed towards the struggle taking place at the quayside, where a loose throng of Atrebatans made their last stand against a heaving throng of Catuvellaunian warriors. My father was there, and Epaticcus, and perhaps two dozen others, battle-hardened men trading savage blows. Verica stood among his warriors, his fur-trimmed cloak spattered with blood, surrounded by a coterie of loyal bodyguards fighting furiously. His resonant voice sounded above the cacophony of battle, imploring his men to resist to their dying breath.

Behind them, bright orange gouts of flame consumed the bridge, rising into the morning sky, accompanied by the crack and roar of burning timber. The heat was appalling. Its fiery breath singed my hair, and the acrid smoke stung my eyes and throat. Around me men were coughing violently; the flames quickly spread from the bridge to one of the warehouses, adding to the blazing inferno along the northern bank.

The last of the Atrebatans put up a determined resistance, as I knew they would, for there are few more dangerous opponents than men who know there is no hope of escape or surrender. They fought with manic intensity, determined to protect their king at all costs, but against our much larger force they quickly grew exhausted. Those we did not cut down peeled away from the fighting and made for the ice, hoping to make their escape across the frozen stretches of the river.

A few of the Atrebatans had almost reached the tiny islets situated in the middle of the Tamesis upriver of the bridge where the ice was unbroken when a grinding crash split the air. The ice shattered; those figures furthest from the bank wailed in terror as they plunged into the freezing grey waters. The other men froze, stricken with fear and indecision as more areas of ice collapsed around them, and within a few moments most of the Atrebatans had slipped into the river, limbs flailing wildly, hands clawing in vain at the icy shards. Many of their warriors drowned that day in the Tamesis. The rest, those who could swim, were killed by our spearmen as they lined up on the near bank and speared the defenceless figures in the shallows At my shoulder, Epaticcus roared his approval and ordered our side not to stop until every Atrebatan had drawn his last breath. He had more reason than most to despise the southerners: they had very nearly claimed his life at Senomagus.

I had lost sight of Verica as I watched the carnage. 'Where's Verica?' I rasped, barely able to hear my own voice above the enemy's pleas for mercy. I swept my eyes across the river, but there was no sign of him or his bodyguards among the floating corpses, or the bodies lining the quayside.

'Sire!' Bellocatus called out to my father. 'There!'

I turned quickly and saw the small group of figures hurrying past the stone-built warehouses and workshops towards a moored cargo vessel further along the wharf, directly opposite the thinner patches of ice and water downriver from the bridge. Several paces ahead, a pair of wizened Atrebatan nobles were climbing awkwardly into the boat. A third man, dressed in the plain clothing of a servant, knelt down to cast off the moorings from a stout wooden post. Before he could release the rope a trio of bodyguards descended upon him, blades drawn, barking at the servant in their guttural dialect. I saw one of the warrior's blades flash in a horizontal arc, and then the man's headless corpse dropped to the quayside, blood spurting out of the ragged stump. The two nobles shouted and raised their hands in surrender; they were dragged from the boat while Verica and his retinue climbed aboard.

'Bastard's getting away,' Epaticcus shouted. 'Come on!'

I broke into a run beside my uncle, the fumes choking my lungs. Verica shouted at one of his men, the latter thrust the bow away from the shore and the bodyguards started pulling at the oars, and soon they were propelling the boat across the open water and sheets of thin ice on the surface of the Tamesis, the blades rising and dipping rhythmically below the metallic surface. They were already stealing clear by the time we reached the mooring point; Bellocatus seized a throwing spear from one of the dead warriors and hurled it after the vessel. The shaft arced in a low trajectory across the river before it splashed harmlessly into the water in the boat's wake.

Epaticcus gritted his teeth in frustration and uttered a string of foul curses at the escaping king. Bellocatus beat his thigh angrily. Out on the Tamesis, the bodyguards were rowing furiously towards the safety of the southern bank. They passed by two men thrashing about frantically in the water; one of them reached out to the passengers for help, rocking the boat on its side. Verica's guards clubbed the poor fellow with an oar and he disappeared beneath the water.

I looked round at the settlement. The last few Atrebatans trapped in Lhandain, realising their king had abandoned them, lost the will to continue the fight and threw down their weapons. Most were killed; a handful of noblemen were taken prisoner. Along the wharf, others had crammed into the fishing boats further downriver where the water was mostly open. The vessels sat dangerously low in the water, packed with desperate men, and they took many casualties as they struggled to pull clear of danger. Those enemies swimming or picking their way across the ice were easy prey for our bowmen. By some miracle, a small number managed to escape to the far bank, where Verica's boat ground against the reedbed.

We stood, exhausted, watching Verica stealing away into the gloomy marshes south of the river, closely followed by the surviving members of his entourage. The King of the Atrebates stopped briefly and glanced back at us, before he drew his sword and stabbed towards us in a defiant gesture. Then he turned and disappeared into the marshland.

'Bastard . . .' Bellocatus panted. 'We almost had him.'

'Who cares?' Epaticcus said. 'We won. That's all that matters. We beat the bastards.'

'Wait. Your brother,' Bellocatus said, turning to me in dawning horror. 'He's still over there. And the others.'

I shook my head. 'They'll be safe. Togodumnus had orders to retreat as soon as they had torched the bridge. They will make their way back across the ice as soon as it's safe.'

'With a pile of Verica's personal treasure, too, I expect,' my uncle added.

He turned to me and grinned broadly, his grizzled face smeared with blood and dirt.

'We did it.' He slapped me on the shoulder. 'We bloody did it, lad. Lhandain is ours!'

CHAPTER THIRTY-SEVEN

The Battle for Lhandain ended Verica's territorial ambitions north of the Tamesis. His losses were immense: more than half of his men had been killed or wounded in the day's fighting; most of the rest had perished in the flight across the Tamesis. In their frantic bid to escape, the Atrebatans had abandoned their supply wagons, horses, chariots and much of their weaponry and equipment. That was not all: shortly before their retreat, Togodumnus and his men had grabbed several large sacks of silver Roman coins from Verica's baggage train, along with numerous other treasures plundered from Lhandain's nobility, adding to the enemy's humiliation. The bards would later declare it the most glorious victory in the history of the Catuvellaunian tribe. But it was far from the end of the war. As long as Verica clung to power, we would not be able to rest.

Lhandain itself had not escaped the devastation. A strong northerly breeze had picked up, spreading the flames from the bridge, setting fire to several of the timber-framed buildings lining the quayside, including the grain stores. Epaticcus detailed a party of our weary men to tackle the blaze. They formed a chain along the bank, passing along buckets filled with water to douse the flames. Some of the local merchant community, realising that their livelihoods were at risk, rushed over to help, and within a short while the fires had been brought under control. The rest of Lhandain's inhabitants took the opportunity to loot the dead, stealing torcs, armlets, belts, shoes, cloaks and anything else of value. I saw one resourceful old man kneeling down beside a dying bodyguard and pulling the rings from the man's fingers even as he pleaded for water.

Teams of servants and royal slaves were tasked with gathering up the equipment littering the battlefield, while search parties were sent out to look for our missing. Some of my father's bodyguards were posted at the front of the great hall and the other royal sites within Lhandain, to prevent looting, while others were sent off to search for the council of Roman traders who resided in Lhandain. But they had made their escape during the frantic first moments of the assault, leaving behind their comfortably furnished homes. All the spoils of war were gathered up by groups of our warriors and taken to the royal hall, so that they might be shared among the nobles and their bondsmen, with each receiving a share according to his status. The most valuable items were handed to the Druids and cast into the Tamesis to dedicate the victory to our gods.

Across the thoroughfares, dozens of bodies littered the ground. The enemy dead were carried away to the midden beyond the defensive walls, for the wild dogs and birds to feast on. Our fallen would be buried in an area of ground near the battlefield, in accordance with our customs. Makeshift tents were erected in the marketplace abutting the quayside so that our healers could tend to the wounded, while the anguished groans of maimed and dying men filled the air.

Beyond the wharf, I glimpsed bloated corpses caught amongst the reeds in the shallows, amid a flotsam of debris from the destroyed bridge. Blackened stumps and a few smouldering fragments of burnt timber were all that remained. A group of prisoners sat on the dirt a short distance away, watched over by a handful of guards. The defeated men had been stripped of their finery and wore only their loincloths; their hair and beards were matted with blood, their wrists tightly bound with lengths of rope; they stared at us with expressions of sullen resentment. A number of these men would be handed over to the Druids for their ritual sacrifices. The rest would be sold on to the traders and sent across the sea, where they would fetch a healthy price in the slave markets of Gaul. The highborn nobles would be spared this terrible fate: they would be held hostage by our tribe until their kinfolk had paid the ransoms to free them.

'It has been a good victory, brother,' Togodumnus said. 'Those Atrebatan swine won't be troubling us again, not after the kicking we've given them today. That's for fucking sure.'

We were sitting on a bench at the edge of the devastated marketplace, sipping from our drinking horns. My father had ordered his servants to erect a crude shelter to provide refreshments for his weary warriors while he conferred with Antedius and the commanders of his war-bands in the great hall of Lhandain. The rest of us sat quietly, in small groups of two or three, drinking and mourning lost friends. I had found Togodumnus in the tent with the other surviving men from his party. Two of his warriors had fallen in battle. A third had been kicked in the head by an enemy horse and was not expected to survive. I listened to his account of how he and his men had retreated with the silver after setting fire to the bridge, only crossing the ice ford once they were certain the last Atrebatans had fled into the marshes. I could have berated my brother for attacking the bridge too early and endangering our plan, and the lives of our warriors, but I saw no profit in it. As Epaticcus had rightly pointed out, we had won. And that was all that mattered. For now.

Victory had come at a price. Our war-bands had suffered terrible casualties. More than three hundred had fallen in battle, and twice that number had been wounded. Many of them would not survive their injuries, despite the best efforts of our healers and the sacrifices their kin would make to the gods. The royal war-band had lost more than half its number, including some of our most experienced warriors.

I smiled grimly. 'We have won one battle, at a considerable loss of life on our side. There is still a war to be won, and Verica will not be so easily beaten. He'll be desperate for revenge after this.'

'He'll have to rebuild his army first,' Togodumnus said. 'If Verica manages to survive for that long. The Atrebatan elders won't stand for such a heavy defeat.'

'Maybe,' I said. But I wasn't so sure. Verica had shown himself to be a wily and resourceful ruler, buying the influence of numerous Druid cults, seeking out alliances with those tribes opposed to my father's dominance, and establishing ever closer ties with Rome. If anyone was capable of weathering the defeat at Lhandain, it would be the Atrebatan king.

'Where's Adminius?' Togodumnus asked as his gaze swept across the settlement. 'Haven't seen him anywhere.'

I nodded at the landward side of Lhandain. 'At the royal hall, I imagine. With the rest of Father's commanders.'

My father was a restless man. While his warriors celebrated the end of the battle with food, drink and rest, he had been busy making preparations for the defence of Lhandain. Scouts had been dispatched to watch the western approaches for the Durotriges, and the freshest war-bands had been posted around the earthworks, with supplies of lead shot, sheaves of arrows and throwing spears to deter any enemy assaults. But Epaticcus had reckoned the Durotriges were unlikely to attack our position, and I agreed with him. They were a fiercely independent and war-like tribe and had only joined forces with the Atrebates for the chance to plunder and kill. They would no doubt retreat back across the river, once they learned of their allies' crushing defeat.

Togodumnus said, 'Can't imagine Adminius will be happy about being kept in the dark about your ruse with the fake standard.'

'That was Father's decision, as much as mine. And it was the right call, regardless of what Adminius believes. We couldn't take the risk of word of our plan finding its way to the traitor.'

'Speaking of which. Any idea who that might be?'

'I have my suspicions,' I replied guardedly.

He glanced intently at me. 'Who?'

'I don't want to say. Not yet. Right now it's just an instinct, nothing more. I need to have something substantial before I can go to Father. In the meantime, we must guard against forewarning the enemy of our suspicions. Tell no one we suspect there is a traitor in our midst. Understood?'

Before he could reply, a familiar voice called out from across the tent, 'Caratacus! By the gods . . .'

I looked round and felt my heart swell with joy as I saw a powerfully built Dobunnian warrior striding towards me. 'Sediacus!' I cried.

We grasped forearms, while Togodumnus looked on curiously. 'Friend of yours?' he asked gruffly.

I introduced Sediacus to my younger brother, explaining how we had met years before at the Druids' sanctuary in Merladion. I thought back to the hardships we had jointly suffered, the gruelling training under the Silurians, the bullying at the hands of some of the older scholars. So much had happened since then, our time at Merladion often felt less like a memory and more like a dream.

'It is wonderful to see you, old friend,' he said, and smiled. 'And up to your old tricks again too. When your messenger arrived at our camp with the orders, I knew it must be your handiwork. No one else could have thought of such a thing.'

'It would not have worked if our men had not fought like devils,' I said. 'Ours . . . and yours.' I noticed the tattoos adorning his cheeks. 'I did not know you were one of the king's chosen men.'

'I am a leader of the king's bodyguard now,' Sediacus replied. 'We have both risen in the world.'

I offered my heartfelt congratulations, but he merely grimaced. 'It is not quite the achievement it seems.'

'How so?'

'The king only promoted me after the traitors in his court rebelled against his rule and fled to the south. Well, there is always opportunity to be found, even in the jaws of misfortune, if one is prepared to seek it out, as the Druids used to say.'

I told him that I had heard of the split among the nobles in the Dobunnian king's royal court. Sediacus said, 'It is better that the king came to know who amongst his people were loyal, and who were traitors. I doubt the rebels will attract much support to their side . . . not after today. Now that the Atrebates have been crushed in battle, the king's position will be more secure than ever, and his enemies will be wary of making any moves against him. For a while, anyway.' He slapped me on the back, the relief evident on his face. 'It is a good thing we won, my friend. For both our tribes.'

'Yes,' I said, and felt the tension lifting from my shoulders for the first time in months. 'Yes, it is.'

He looked at us both in silence, lips pursed, and his brow crinkled in thought. 'It's strange. I heard some rumours about a band of wild brigands causing trouble around Noviomagus, burning villages and the like.' He eyed us both closely. 'You wouldn't happen to know anything about that, would you?'

I said coolly, 'I heard they were Silurians.'

'So did I. But now I'm not so sure. Noviomagus is a long way from Siluria, and their raiding parties tend to limit their attacks to their immediate neighbours. Why would they travel all the way to the lands of the Regni?'

'Perhaps they were looking for easy targets.'

'Perhaps. Still, you must admit, it is quite the coincidence. A party of brigands attacks Verica's southern allies, burning his supplies and tying down a large number of his warriors when your tribes are on the cusp of war. And you trained under the Silurians for many years.'

'As you say. It is a coincidence.'

Sediacus stared at me for a moment. Then he shrugged and looked away, gazing out across the smouldering wreckage of the bridge, the broken bodies carpeting the settlement, the corpses lying still on the sheeted ice, their torsos pierced with spears and arrows.

He said, very softly, 'It is quite the sight, is it not? I do not have the words for it, but it is something I shall never forget.'

I said I felt the same way, but I fervently hoped that we did not have to witness too many similar scenes in the future.

'Why do you say that?' Sediacus asked. 'Surely you desire to see the Atrebates crushed, especially after all the trouble Verica has caused your people?'

'There are other threats,' I replied. 'Ones that our tribes will have to face together, as one, if we wish to stand any chance of success. We cannot afford to keep quarrelling with one another like this.'

'You speak of Rome, I assume?'

I nodded, thinking of my Druid mentor, Bladocus, and his fervent desire that our tribes would one day set aside their differences and unite under a common banner to fight against the Romans when they returned en masse to our shores. As they inevitably would.

Togodumnus said, 'Even if that's true, we've got to knock Verica on the head first. The odds are with us now. Verica is finished . . . it is only a matter of time before he's forced from his throne.'

I said, 'Not if he seeks help from his friends across the sea.'

Sediacus pulled a face. 'You think Verica will go to the Romans for help?'

'I don't know. It's possible. Verica has already sought their help in the past. It does not take a great leap of the imagination to think that he might ask for their direct intervention in our affairs. Especially if he is desperate.'

'Do you really think he'd stoop so low?'

'I fear Verica is capable of anything, if it serves his political interests.'

We stood in sombre silence for a short time, until Epaticcus marched over from the royal hall. He nodded a greeting at Sediacus, whom he had met once before, then turned to me and said seriously, 'Come with me, lad.'

'What for?'

'Your father wants a word.'

'Right now?' I was tired, every muscle ached abominably, my face and clothes were smeared in dirt and the dried blood of the enemies I had slain on the battlefield, and my mouth was parched. I craved nothing more than a warm meal and a few hours of rest on a comfortable bedroll.

'Just come with me.'

I stood up, handed my drinking horn to Sediacus and followed my uncle through Lhandain to the royal hall. A large crowd of our warriors and nobles had gathered either side of the central aisle, their battle scars illuminated by the flickering glow of hearth-fires. I saw faces still caked in blood; tunics and leggings torn; men with wounds wrapped in strips of light cloth, and bruised faces.

At the end of the avenue stood my father, King Cunobelinus, flanked by his royal bodyguards. Adminius stood at his side with a face like thunder. Bladocus was there too, I noticed. My father beckoned to me; I approached, no wiser as to the purpose of this summons, feeling the eyes of the warriors watching keenly. As I neared the stone dais my father stepped towards me and motioned to a slightly built man in a fine tunic. The servant approached my father and handed him a golden-spiralled torc with a pair of hounds' heads at the terminals. My father turned to me, a smile teasing the corner of his mouth, and then I knew.

'My son,' he began, his stentorian voice echoing around the hall from where Lhandain's princes had once ruled. 'Our kingdom has won itself a great battle today, one that will be remembered for generations to come. Our descendants will speak in reverence of the Battle of Lhandain, and the heroic deeds of our men, as certainly as our bards sing of the brave feats of Tasciovanus and Cassivellaunus. To you, Caratacus, we owe a great debt, for you have played your part in the destruction of the Atrebatan force. Your actions on the battlefield have demonstrated beyond doubt your fighting ability, and your talent for outwitting your enemy. Those are rare qualities in one so young, and we shall need them in abundance, in the long struggle against the Atrebates, and all those who would seek to deny us our rightful place as the most powerful kingdom in Britannia. We displease the gods when such achievements go unrecognised. Therefore, I now appoint you warlord of the Catuvellaunian kingdom, and overall commander of our war-bands.'

My father placed the torc around my neck. I welcomed the weight of the gold trophy with a surge of pride. Bellocatus handed him an ornate sword with a jewel-encrusted hilt. I dropped to a knee before my father; Bladocus approached, and as I knelt before him, I recited the sacred oath committing myself to defending my tribe and king from all perils, even at the cost of my life. Then my father tapped me lightly on the shoulder with the flat of the blade, and my uncle yelled at the top of his voice, 'All hail Caratacus!'

At once the assembled warriors stabbed their swords into the air, cheering loudly as they roared my name: 'Caratacus! Caratacus! Caratacus!'

And that, Roman, is how I became warlord of our people, and was later to become the scourge of your legions.

CHAPTER THIRTY-EIGHT

Rome, AD 61

Caratacus fell silent. We were sitting at a table in a sparsely furnished room above the Drunken Boar, on the lower slope of the Aventine. A cheap straw-filled bedroll occupied one corner of the gloomy space, next to a pair of slop buckets; the wooden shutters had been flung open to admit some light, which had the unpleasant consequence of revealing the movements of the cockroaches shimmering across the floorboards. A stench of shit and grilled meat drifted up from the street below, mingling with the acrid tang of woodsmoke that seemed to hang permanently over the city.

Hours had passed since Caratacus had begun talking; I had been so engrossed in his tale I had almost forgotten the grim surroundings of our latest interview.

'That is quite the story,' I said, reluctant to return to the present.

I glanced down at my hastily scribbled notes. I had many questions. What became of King Verica after his forces had suffered their stunning defeat at Lhandain? How did Adminius react to his brother's battlefield promotion to warlord? How long did the war rage between the Catuvellaunians and the Atrebates, and how did it end? What of their preparations for the Roman invasion? And who did Caratacus suspect of being the traitor in his father's war council?

Before I could question him further, Caratacus started to rise from his stool, signalling an end to our session. 'I have given you only the beginning of my tale, Felicitus. There is much more to tell – but that is for another day.' He gave a tired smile. 'Twenty years ago I would have sat here and talked all night, reliving the old days, but my strength is not what it once was. We can resume my story another time.'

'When?'

'Tomorrow. The sixth hour. Then I will tell you of an even greater adventure, Roman. We shall talk of the final battle against Verica, the terrible betrayal that split apart our tribespeople, pitting father against son, brother against brother, and the day the legions of Rome returned to our islands – as we always knew they would.'

Caratacus drew himself fully upright. Something fiery gleamed behind those deep-set eyes; his scarred features and impressive frame dominated the room. In his bearing I caught a glimpse of the once-powerful warrior who had waged a pitiless war against us for so long. This was a side to him I had not seen before – a striking contrast to the sinewy fellow I had laid eyes on for the first time at Nero's banquet. Here, indeed, was Caratacus, warlord of Britannia. The man who had defied the greatest empire the world had ever seen.

'Your emperor Claudius and his generals thought they would easily conquer us. Such is the nature of Roman arrogance. They looked upon our small war-bands with contempt and planned for a swift victory. But they neglected one simple truth.'

'What was that?'

'We were fighting for our land. Our beliefs. Our entire way of life. For we were the last of the unconquered Celts. Some of us were prepared to surrender without a fight; but many more of us were ready to die to defend our soil. And when the Roman legions came, we made sure they were in for a far tougher challenge than they had ever imagined . . .'

AFTERWORD

Some years ago, during the time of the consulship of Turpilianus and Caesennius, I began the task of writing the history of the late High King of the Britons known as Caratacus. For reasons beyond the control of the author, compelled to safeguard the scrolls at his own considerable risk and expense, the work could not be published until now. It is my fervent hope that this history will help restore the reputation of a great warrior, one of Rome's most notorious adversaries.

I had the great pleasure of getting to know Caratacus during his final years in Rome. Contrary to the well-worn image of the Britons as ignorant savages, I found him to be an eloquent witness to the events he narrated. His account was always clear-eyed and meticulous. Where possible, I have attempted to preserve the strength and spirit of his voice; elsewhere, a light editorial hand has sufficed.

To avoid confusion for my Roman readers, I have retained the Roman units of miles and hours throughout the text. Additionally, I have employed the Roman versions of Britannic place names and personal names, except in cases where the Celtic version is familiar, or where no Latin equivalent exists. Some may quibble with this approach, but my aim has been to make the story accessible to the general public, not to appease obscure scholars of the Celtic tongue.

Observant readers will note that several episodes related by Caratacus contradict the established version of events documented by various Roman historians and memoirists of the Britannia campaign. I have attempted, where possible, to verify Caratacus's account. In all other instances, I have remained faithful to his recollections, since he has sworn that his version of events is the truth, untainted by the colouring of any political agenda.

The violent rebellion of Queen Boudica is no more than a distant memory now. Since that final flame of revolt, the world of the Britons has changed irrevocably. Villas, arenas, temples and bathhouses have taken the place of their sacred groves and the timber-framed halls where the kings and their retinues once feasted.

It is time the truth was told about those often represented by Roman propagandists as little more than uncouth barbarians. Perhaps now, with this story of the greatest of all Britons, we can restore Caratacus and his people to their rightful place as worthy foes, and the last defenders of a forgotten way of life.

Caius Placonius Felicitus
In the Year of the Consulship of Bassus and Crassus, eight hundred and seventeen years after the Founding of Rome

HISTORICAL NOTE

The tribes of Iron Age Britain existed on the mist-wreathed fringes of the Roman world. The Britons (although they would not have thought of themselves as such) were largely illiterate and left no written accounts of their laws, customs or culture. The historian must rely on archaeological records, coin distribution and classical sources, but the picture that emerges is often frustratingly incomplete.

Within these limitations, it is possible to conjure a sense of life in Britain in the early first century AD. At this time, parts of the island were experiencing rapid social and cultural change. The southern tribes had developed extensive trading links with Gaul: grain surpluses allowed the tribal elites to exchange corn, cattle and slaves for olive oil, wine and other luxuries. The richest and most powerful kings – men such as Cunobelinus – had even begun to mint their own coins. But increased prosperity did not lead to peace. Celtic society placed great emphasis on individual heroism and martial prowess. The major tribes were locked in a near-constant state of conflict, competing for prestige, land and wealth. In the longer term, these deep tribal divisions were to prove fatal to their survival.

Only the Druid cult had the ability to unite the various tribal factions. Contrary to being the white-robed figures of popular imagination, it is likely that the Druids were far more than mystics or priests: they were held in high regard as wise men and experts in divination; they adjudicated in tribal disputes; and they educated the sons of the nobility.

More controversially, they participated in rituals of human sacrifice. The Romans wrote lurid accounts of victims burned alive in giant wicker men, in sinister sacred groves and on blood-soaked altars. How much of this is accurate is impossible to say with any degree of confidence. But such tales certainly helped to justify Rome's argument that the Britons were backward 'barbarians' in need of the Empire's civilising hand. The Romans were quick to recognise the Druids as a threat to peace in the new province, hence their efforts to wipe out the cult during the conquests of Gaul and, later on, Britannia.

One can imagine the Druids in Britain listening in horror to the latest news from across the Channel: the destruction of sacred groves, the massacre of cult members and the imperial edicts outlawing their ritual practices. Those not blinded by greed or self-interest would surely have understood the grave threat to Britannia posed by the Romans. It is quite easy to imagine some of the more far-sighted Druids advancing the political fortunes of those who stood the best chance of resisting the legions. As the largest and most powerful tribe at the time, the Catuvellauni represented the best hope for victory over Rome.

As *Warrior* concludes, Verica is on the defensive. Catuvellaunian power is in the ascendancy. But the struggle for supremacy among the most powerful Britannic tribes is far from over. In the coming campaign, Cunobelinus and his sons will find their loyalties severely tested, as they confront enemies both on the field of battle and in the murky world of the royal court. Caratacus will need all his wits about him if he is to see off the threats to his father's empire and prepare for the day when Rome will return to Britannia's shores – in a war that will determine the fate of the island.

Simon Scarrow
T. J. Andrews
January 2023

BIBLIOGRAPHY

Adkins, Lesley, and Adkins, Roy A., *Handbook to Life in Ancient Rome* Oxford University Press (1994)

Allen, Stephen, *Lords of Battle* Osprey Publishing (2007)

Angela, Alberto, *A Day in the Life of Ancient Rome* Europa Editions (2009)

Berresford Ellis, Peter, *The Druids* William B Eerdmans Publishing Company (1994)

Chadwick, Nora, *The Celts* **2nd Ed.** Penguin (1997)

Cottrell, Leonard, *The Great Invasion* Readers Union (1958)

Cunliffe, Barry, *The Ancient Celts. Second Edition* OUP Oxford (2018)

Cunliffe, Barry, *Iron Age Communities in Britain* Book Club Associates (1975)

de la Bédoyère, Guy, *Defying Rome* The History Press (2003)

de la Bédoyère, Guy, *The Real Lives of Roman Britain* Yale University Press (2015)

de la Bédoyère, Guy, *Roman Britain* Thames and Hudson Ltd (2010)

Frere, Sheppard, *Britannia* Cardinal Books (1974)

Green, Miranda J., *Celtic Myths* British Museum Press (1993)

Green, Miranda J., ed., *The Celtic World* Routledge (1995)

Green, Miranda & Howell, Ray, *Celtic Wales* University of Wales Press (2000)

Haywood, John, *The Historical Atlas of the Celtic World* Thames and Hudson Ltd (2009)

Henig, Martin, *The Heirs of King Verica* Amberley Publishing (2010)

Hutton, Ronald, *Blood and Mistletoe* Yale University Press (2011)

Mattingly, David, *An Imperial Possession* Penguin (2007)

Matyszak, Philip, *Ancient Rome on Five Denarii a Day* Thames and Hudson Ltd (2007)

Piggott, Stuart, *The Druids* **2nd Ed.** Penguin (1975)

Pryor, Francis, *Britain BC* **New Ed.** HarperCollins (2004)

Richmond, I. A., *Roman Britain* **Reprint Ed.** Penguin (1967)

Roberts, Alice, *The Celts* Heron Books (2015)

Ross, Ann, *Everyday Life of the Pagan Celts* **New Ed.** Corgi Childrens (1972)

Russell, Miles & Laycock, Stuart, *UnRoman Britain* The History Press Ltd (2010)

Salway, Peter, *A History of Roman Britain* Oxford University Press (1997)

Webster, Graham, *Rome Against Caratacus* Routledge (1993)

Webster, Graham, *The Roman Invasion of Britain* **2nd Ed.** Routledge (1993)

Wheeler, R. E. M., *Prehistoric & Roman Wales* Oxford Clarendon Press (1925)

Wilcox, Peter, *Rome's Enemies (2): Gallic & British Celts* Osprey Publishing (1988)

If you enjoyed *Warrior*, discover another epic military adventure novel from Simon Scarrow

AD 60. Britannia is in turmoil. The rebel leader Boudica has tasted victory, against a force of tough veterans in Camulodunum.

Alerted to the rapidly spreading uprising, Governor Suetonius leads his army towards endangered Londinium with a mounted escort, led by Prefect Cato. Soon it's terrifyingly clear that Britannia is slipping into chaos and panic, with ever more tribal warriors swelling Boudica's ranks. And Cato and Suetonius are grimly aware that little preparation has been made to withstand a full-scale rebellion.

In Londinium there is devastating news. Centurion Macro is amongst those unaccounted for after the massacre at Camulodunum. Has Cato's comrade and friend made his last stand?

Facing disaster, Cato prepares his next move. Dare he hope that Macro – battle-scarred and fearless – has escaped the bloodthirsty rebels? For there is only one man Cato trusts by his side as he faces the military campaign of his life. And the future of the Empire in Britannia hangs in the balance.

Available now

HEADLINE

For more Roman military adventures, discover Simon Scarrow's unmissable . . .

AD 60. Britannia. The Boudica Revolt begins . . .

Macro and Cato – heroes of the Roman Empire – face a ruthless enemy set on revenge

The Roman Empire's hold on the province of Britannia is fragile. The tribes implacably opposed to Rome have grown cunning in their attacks on the legions. Even amongst those who have sworn loyalty, dissent simmers. In distant Rome, Nero is blind to the danger.

As hostilities create mayhem in the west, Governor Gaius Suetonius Paulinus gathers a vast army, with Prefect Cato in command. A hero of countless battles, Cato wants his loyal comrade Centurion Macro by his side. But the Governor leaves Macro behind, in charge of the veteran reserves in Camulodunum. Suetonius dismisses concerns that the poorly fortified colony will be vulnerable to attack when only a skeleton force remains.

With the military distracted, slow-burning anger amongst the tribespeople bursts into flames. The king of the Iceni is dead and a proud kingdom is set for plundering and annexation. But the widow is Queen Boudica, a woman with a warrior's heart. If Boudica calls for death to the emperor, a bloodbath will follow.

Available now

HEADLINE

And if you can't get enough of Macro and Cato, read Simon Scarrow's

AD 59. BRITANNIA.

Fifteen years after Rome's invasion of Britannia, centurion Macro is back. The island is settled now, bustling with commerce. Macro's goal is to help run his mother's Londinium inn, and exploit his land grant. He's prepared for the dismal weather and the barbaric ways of the people. But far worse dangers threaten all his plans.

A gang led by an ex-legionary rules the city, demanding protection money and terrorising those who won't pay up. The Roman official in charge has turned a blind eye. Macro has to act. He needs the back-up of the finest soldier he knows: Prefect Cato. But Cato is in distant Rome. Or is he?

As the streets run red with blood, the army's heroes face an enemy as merciless and cunning as any barbarian tribe. The honour of Rome is in their hands . . .

Available now

HEADLINE

Discover Simon Scarrow's first thrilling
CI Schenke novel

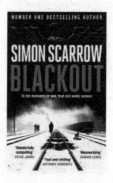

BERLIN, DECEMBER 1939.

As Germany goes to war, the Nazis tighten their terrifying grip. Paranoia in the capital is intensified by a rigidly enforced blackout that plunges the city into oppressive darkness every night, as the bleak winter sun sets.

When a young woman is murdered, Criminal Inspector Horst Schenke is under pressure to solve the case, swiftly. Distrusted by his superiors for his failure to join the Nazi Party, Schenke walks a perilous line – for disloyalty is a death sentence.

The discovery of a second victim confirms Schenke's worst fears. He must uncover the truth before evil strikes again.

As the investigation takes him closer to the sinister heart of the regime, Schenke realises there is danger everywhere – and the warring factions of the Reich can be as deadly as a killer stalking the streets . . .

Available now

HEADLINE

**Join CI Schenke in another exhilarating read
from Simon Scarrow . . .**

BERLIN. JANUARY 1940.

**After Germany's invasion of Poland, the world is holding
its breath and hoping for peace. At home, the Nazi Party's
hold on power is absolute.**

One freezing night, an SS doctor and his wife return from an evening
mingling with their fellow Nazis at the concert hall. By the time the sun
rises, the doctor will be lying lifeless in a pool of blood.

Was it murder or suicide? Criminal Inspector Horst Schenke is told
that under no circumstances should he investigate. The doctor's
widow, however, is convinced her husband was the target of a hit.
But why would anyone murder an apparently obscure doctor?
Compelled to dig deeper, Schenke learns of the mysterious death
of a child. The cases seem unconnected, but soon chilling links
begin to emerge that point to a terrifying secret.

Even in times of war, under a ruthless regime, there are places no man
should ever enter. And Schenke fears he may not return alive . . .

Available now

HEADLINE